GUARDIANS OF THE THRESHOLD

THE EARTHBOND SAGA, BOOK 2

Written by Diane Kann

Brought to you by Volans Galaxy Press

Published by Kannceptual Creations LLC

An imprint of Volans Galaxy Press

ISBN: 978-1-969569-32-6

Printed in the United States of America

First Edition, December 2025

TABLE OF CONTENTS

Dedication 1

Chapter 1: The Whispering Gate 2

Chapter 2: Verdant Echoes 31

Chapter 3: The Silent Song of Flora 63

Chapter 4: The Corporate Shadow 92

Chapter 5: The Resonant Divide 121

Chapter 6: Mending the Threads 151

Chapter 7: Whispers of Sentience 187

Chapter 8: Echoes of Home 224

Chapter 9: The Shifting Thresholds 256

Chapter 10: The Navigator's Heart 284

Chapter 11: Verdian Diplomacy 317

Chapter 12: The Unseen Scars 344

Chapter 13: The Ethics of Advancement 374

Chapter 14: Convergence 403

Chapter 15: Thresholds of Tomorrow 433

Glossary 461

DEDICATION

To my steadfast companions, whose boundless loyalty and extraordinary senses bridged the gap between worlds, making the impossible not only navigable but profoundly beautiful. Your intuition was the compass, your unwavering trust the anchor, and your quiet presence the truest echo of home, no matter how far from Earth we roamed. This story is as much yours as it is mine, a testament to the silent, powerful language spoken between a human heart and a canine soul. May we always walk the paths of understanding together, guided by the resonance of mutual respect and the gentle hum of hope. To the myriad creatures who share our planet and countless others, seen and unseen, whose existence enriches the tapestry of life and deserves our deepest reverence and protection. To the quiet strength of ecosystems, the intricate dance of nature, and the enduring power of connection that binds us all, from the smallest microbe to the grandest star. And to the persistent belief that even in the face of overwhelming odds, humanity can choose empathy, stewardship, and a future woven with threads of kindness and responsibility across all dimensions.

May this tale inspire a deeper appreciation for the world around us and the incredible potential that lies within us all to be guardians of the threshold, protectors of the fragile and the wondrous.

CHAPTER ONE

THE WHISPERING GATE

The air thrummed with a low, resonant hum, a sound that was both deeply familiar to Niko Thorne and utterly alien. It emanated from the shimmering, opalescent curtain that pulsed gently at the edge of his research outpost's perimeter. This was the Whispering Gate, a recently stabilized nexus point, a tear in the fabric of reality that offered glimpses into other Earths, other possibilities. Standing beside him, her intelligent amber eyes fixed on the ethereal display, was Kira, his Border Collie. More than a pet, she was his partner, his confidante, and, in many ways, the true sensor of this strange new frontier.

Niko, a man whose brilliance in xenobotany was matched only by his reticence, knelt and gently scratched Kira behind the ears. Her fur, a dense coat of black and white, felt warm and solid beneath his fingers, a grounding anchor in the face of the impossible. Kira responded with a soft thump of her tail against the reclaimed wood flooring of their open-air observation platform. The hum of the gate seemed to intensify slightly, a subtle shift that only Kira's finely tuned senses could detect. She let out a low, almost imperceptible whine, her ears swiveling towards the pulsing light.

"What is it, girl?" Niko murmured, his voice a low rumble. He understood her cues. That particular whine, laced with a hint of curiosity rather than alarm, meant the gateway was stable, its dimensional resonance harmonic, a sign that whatever lay beyond was not immediately hostile or chaotic. It was a language they had developed over years of partnership, a silent dialogue that transcended spoken words. Kira's innate sensitivity, honed by years of close companionship and, unbeknownst to most, subtle bio-enhancements that amplified her natural canine senses, allowed her to perceive frequencies far beyond human comprehension. These 'resonances' were the key to understanding the nature of the gateways, their stability, and the potential dangers or wonders they concealed.

The outpost itself was a testament to Niko's philosophy: a fusion of cutting-edge technology and a deep respect for the natural world. Solar panels, woven into living trellises of climbing vines, provided power. Reclaimed lumber and recycled composites formed the structures, integrated seamlessly into the surrounding environment rather than imposed upon it. Even the air filtration systems mimicked the natural processes of plant photosynthesis. This was the home base of the Resonant Pack, a clandestine organization dedicated not to conquest or exploitation of the multiverse, but to understanding, preservation, and cautious exploration. Their mandate was clear: to tread lightly, observe deeply, and protect fragile nascent ecosystems from the rapacious greed that some other factions, like the notoriously aggressive OmniCorp, were all too eager to unleash.

Niko watched Kira as she continued her silent vigil, her body language a complex tapestry of subtle cues. A low growl, a sharp bark, a contented sigh – each held meaning. Today, it was a soft, expectant posture, her gaze unwavering. The gateway was broadcasting a calm, steady signal, a melodic hum that spoke of balance and harmony. It was the kind of resonance that promised discovery, a world brimming with potential, perhaps even life forms that existed in perfect symbiosis with their environment. The very air around the gate seemed to shimmer with latent energy, a promise of the unknown.

He rose, stretching his long limbs. The late afternoon sun, filtered through the dense canopy of Earth's own familiar forests, cast dappled shadows across the platform. It was a stark contrast to the ethereal glow of the gateway, a vibrant reminder of the world they were sworn to protect, and the myriad other worlds that existed just beyond their reach. This quiet moment of training, of honing Kira's already remarkable abilities, was crucial. Every expedition, every step through the shimmering veil, carried inherent risks. The multiverse was a vast, untamed expanse, and while many gateways offered stable passages, others were volatile, unpredictable, even dangerous.

Kira's senses were their most vital tool, an early warning system that could detect subtle shifts in the dimensional fabric, atmospheric anomalies, or the presence of unseen life long before human instruments could register them. The bio-enhancements were minimal, designed to amplify her natural capacities, not to fundamentally alter them. It was about partnership, not subjugation. Niko trusted Kira's instincts implicitly, a trust forged in countless shared experiences, some mundane, some profoundly extraordinary. She was not merely an animal; she was an integral part of his consciousness, an extension of his own senses.

He remembered the early days, the tentative steps into understanding Kira's unique abilities. It had been a journey of mutual discovery, of patience and observation. He had learned to read the almost imperceptible flickers of her ears, the subtle tension in her stance, the varied pitches of her whines and barks. In return, Kira had learned to trust Niko's judgment, to understand his commands not just through rote training, but through a deep-seated bond of affection and shared purpose. The resonance of the gateway, a complex symphony of dimensional frequencies, was something she perceived as a physical sensation, a vibration that ran through her very being. She could tell when a gateway was stable, when it was fluctuating, or when it was about to collapse.

As Niko watched Kira, a flicker of something new registered in her posture. Her head tilted, her ears perked, and a soft, inquisitive rumble emanated from her chest. It wasn't the low growl of warning, nor the anxious whine of unease. This was different. It was a sound of dawning recognition, of a subtle but significant shift in the gateway's 'tune.' He reached for his portable scanner, a device that interfaced directly with Kira's internal sensors, translating her perceptions into comprehensible data streams. The readings flickered, then coalesced.

"Interesting," Niko murmured, tapping his chin. The resonance patterns were... complex. Not unstable, not chaotic, but layered. It suggested a world with a rich, intricate biosphere, possibly one where life had evolved in ways that were deeply intertwined with the very fabric of its reality. There was a richness to the energy signature, a vibrant hum that spoke of immense ecological potential. Yet, beneath that promise, there was also a faint tremor, a subtle dissonance that hinted at an underlying fragility. It was a world that beckuoned with beauty, but warned of inherent instability.

He looked at Kira, her tail now giving a slow, deliberate wag. She seemed to feel it too, this potent mix of wonder and caution. It was a perfect reflection of their mission. They were explorers, yes, but more importantly, they were guardians. Their role was not to exploit these new worlds, but to understand them, to protect them from those who would see them only as resources to be plundered. The Whispering Gate was more than just a doorway; it was a threshold, a point of no return, a promise of both unparalleled discovery and profound responsibility. And as the hum of the gate continued, a subtle yet insistent melody in the twilight air, Niko knew that their quiet vigil was about to be interrupted. A new symphony was about to begin, and he and Kira would be its first, most attentive listeners. The weight of that knowledge settled upon him, not as a burden, but as a sacred trust. This was what they were made for.

The sun dipped lower, painting the sky in hues of orange and purple, a terrestrial prelude to the alien spectrums they might soon encounter. The gateway pulsed, a gentle invitation and a silent challenge. Kira, sensing Niko's renewed focus, sat beside him, her body a warm, solid presence against his leg. Their bond, forged in years of shared purpose and quiet understanding, was a beacon in the encroaching dusk, a testament to a connection that transcended species and, perhaps, even dimensions. The unknown awaited, and they, the Resonant Pack, were ready to listen to its whispers.

Niko's gaze drifted from the pulsating gateway to the familiar trees surrounding their outpost, their leaves rustling gently in the evening breeze. It was a moment of quiet contemplation, a brief pause before stepping into the extraordinary. He recalled the countless hours spent in classrooms, poring over textbooks, and the even more countless hours spent in the field, learning from the intricate, often overlooked, languages of Earth's own ecosystems. But Veridia, as they would soon come to know it, promised a fluency in a dialect far more ancient and profound.

Kira, ever attuned to his emotional state, let out a soft sigh, a sound of contentment that eased the tension in his shoulders. Her empathy was a constant, gentle current, a reminder that even amidst the profound complexities of interdimensional travel, the simplest connections often held the greatest power. He looked down at her, meeting her steady gaze. There was an unwavering trust there, a silent question: "Are we ready?"

He offered her a small, reassuring smile. "Always, girl. Always."

The gate's hum deepened, a subtle crescendo that filled the air with a palpable energy. It was a sound that spoke of immense forces at play, of realities brushing against each other, of opportunities and dangers intertwined. Niko's scanner, still cradled in his hand, registered a slight increase in ambient chroniton particles, a tell-tale sign of active dimensional flux. It wasn't alarming, not yet, but it was a sign that the gateway was not merely a static portal, but a dynamic entity, responsive to unseen currents in the multiverse.

He thought of the data he had already collected. The initial spectral analysis of the atmosphere beyond the gate indicated a unique composition, rich in exotic gases that refracted light in peculiar ways. This explained the faint, amethystine tinge he'd observed earlier, a preview of a world potentially bathed in hues unknown to Earth's natural spectrum. The gravitational field seemed to be within acceptable parameters, a relief given the unpredictable nature of some newly stabilized gateways. But it was the resonance readings, Kira's domain, that truly held his attention. They spoke of a complex, interconnected biosphere, a network of life far more integrated than anything documented on Earth.

He imagined colossal fungi, bioluminescent and towering, replacing the familiar trees. He envisioned carpets of moss that pulsed with soft, internal light, creating a living tapestry on the forest floor. These were not idle fantasies, but educated guesses, informed by the faint echoes of energy that radiated from the gateway. It was a world painted in shades of violet and emerald, a symphony of light and life waiting to be understood.

Kira, as if sensing his thoughts, nudged his hand with her wet nose. She was a creature of instinct and keen observation, her world interpreted through scent, sound, and the subtle vibrations of energy. Yet, she possessed a remarkable capacity for abstract understanding, a testament to the deep bond they shared. She could sense the implications of these readings, the potential for wonder, and the inherent risks.

"It feels different, doesn't it?" Niko whispered, his voice barely audible above the gate's hum. "Like a song we haven't heard before, but one that feels... familiar. Like a deep echo of something ancient."

Kira responded with a soft whine, her tail giving a tentative thump. It was a confirmation, a shared understanding that transcended logic. The resonance she perceived wasn't just a scientific measurement; it was an emotional landscape, a complex interplay of energies that spoke of life, balance, and the delicate dance of existence. She was not just sensing the gateway; she was sensing the world it led to, its very essence.

The thought of this world, so different and yet so full of life, filled Niko with a quiet excitement. His passion for xenobotany had always been driven by a desire to guardstand the myriad ways life could manifest, the infinite possibilities of evolution. Veridia promised a breathtaking canvas for that exploration. But with that excitement came the ever-present undercurrent of responsibility. Their mission was not to catalog and collect, but to observe and protect. The delicate balance of Veridia, hinted at in Kira's subtle resonance readings, was precious and vulnerable.

He recalled the protocols of the Resonant Pack, etched into his mind and deeply ingrained in Kira's training. Non-interference was paramount. They were guests, observers, not arbiters of destiny. Any interaction, any intervention, had to be a last resort, a carefully calculated measure taken only when the fundamental integrity of an ecosystem was threatened. This was a stark contrast to the methods of OmniCorp, whose operatives saw the multiverse as a frontier to be exploited, a resource to be extracted with little regard for the consequences.

The image of OmniCorp's scarred landscapes and polluting technologies flashed in Niko's mind. Their presence was a blight, a testament to a philosophy of dominance rather than stewardship. It was this contrast that fueled Niko's dedication, that transformed his reserved nature into a quiet but unyielding resolve. He wouldn't allow the wonders of worlds like Veridia to be despoiled by such greed.

Kira sensed the shift in his demeanor, the hardening of his resolve. She pressed closer, offering a silent reassurance. Her presence was a constant reminder of the profound connection they shared, a partnership that was as much about emotional support as it was about scientific collaboration. She was not just a tool, but a companion, a fellow traveler on this extraordinary journey.

The hum of the gateway seemed to deepen, a resonant thrum that vibrated through the very soles of Niko's boots. It was a sound that spoke of immense power, of worlds waiting to be discovered, and of the delicate balance that governed them all. The sun had now fully set, and the gateway's opalescent glow seemed to intensify, casting an ethereal light on the familiar landscape. It was a beacon, a promise, and a challenge.

Niko took a deep breath, the cool evening air filling his lungs. He looked at Kira, her silhouette sharp against the shimmering portal. Her senses were finely tuned, her instincts honed, her loyalty unwavering. Together, they were ready. The whispers from the unknown were growing louder, and they were prepared to listen. The journey of understanding, of protection, of discovery, was about to begin anew. The threshold beckoned, and the quiet anticipation that had settled over them was now tinged with the electrifying certainty of adventure. The first steps into Veridia would be cautious, observational, guided by Kira's keen senses and Niko's profound respect for life in all its forms. The stage was set for a new chapter in their shared odyssey, a chapter that would undoubtedly be filled with the silent songs of alien flora and the echoes of unseen life.

Kira's Sixth Sense

The opalescent curtain of the Whispering Gate pulsed with a rhythm that was not merely visual, but visceral. To Niko Thorne, it was a symphony of complex energy readings, a vibrant tapestry of data visualized on his portable scanner. But for Kira, his Border Collie and invaluable partner, it was a world of sensation far more immediate and profound. Her amber eyes, pools of liquid intelligence, were fixed on the shimmering anomaly, her body language a meticulously nuanced communication of her perceptions. The subtle bio-enhancements Niko had painstakingly integrated into her physiology over the years hadn't fundamentally altered her canine nature; rather, they had amplified her innate sensitivities, turning her into a living, breathing sensor array capable of interpreting the multiverse in ways humans could only dream of.

Her reactions to the gateway were a language unto themselves, a dialect Niko had spent years deciphering. A low, guttural growl, almost a vibration in her chest, was an unequivocal signal of instability. It spoke of chaotic energy, of frequencies that clashed and snarled, threatening to tear the fabric of the dimensional passage. Such a sound would immediately prompt Niko to retract, to assess the risk, and perhaps even initiate a shutdown sequence. Conversely, a soft, melodic whine, devoid of alarm, indicated a resonant harmony, a stable passage where the dimensional frequencies aligned in a pleasing, almost musical, accord. This was the kind of sound Kira was emitting now, a gentle exhalation of breath, her tail giving a slow, rhythmic thump against the reclaimed wood of the observation platform. It was a sound of welcome, of curiosity mixed with reassurance, a confirmation that the path ahead was clear, at least for the moment.

But today, there was something more. Beyond the usual indicators of stability, Kira's posture was subtly different. Her ears, usually swiveling with hyper-vigilance, were held in a position of rapt attention, angled slightly forward, as if straining to capture a distant melody. A low, almost imperceptible rumble, deeper than a whine but softer than a growl, emanated from her throat. It wasn't a sound of fear or of immediate danger, but of something akin to dawning comprehension, a mental 'click' as disparate threads of perception wove together into a more complex understanding. Niko watched her, his own scientific curiosity piqued. He'd learned long ago that Kira's intuition, amplified by her enhanced senses, often preceded his own analytical conclusions.

He knelt beside her, his hand resting gently on her broad, muscular back. The warmth of her fur was a comforting anchor, a tangible connection to the familiar as they stood on the precipice of the utterly alien. "What do you sense, girl?" he murmured, his voice low and soothing. He didn't need her to bark or whimper a complex explanation. He read her subtle shifts in muscle tension, the almost imperceptible flick of her ear, the dilation of her pupils. Her response was a slow blink, a sign of trust and comfort, followed by a soft press of her head against his knee. It was an acknowledgment of his presence, but her gaze remained fixed on the gate, her internal world clearly occupied by something far more intricate than the immediate physical environment.

Niko brought up his scanner, its sleek, bio-integrated casing fitting comfortably in his palm. He activated the neural interface, a delicate process that allowed the device to tap into the subtler bio-electric fields generated by Kira's enhanced sensory organs. The readings that flooded his screen were immediately intriguing. The primary resonance frequencies were indeed stable, aligning with Kira's soft whine. The atmospheric composition data, already flagged as unusual, now showed a more dynamic interaction with the gateway's energy field. But it was the secondary and tertiary resonance patterns that commanded his attention. They were complex, layered, and incredibly nuanced. It wasn't a single note, but a rich chord, a symphony of interconnected frequencies that spoke of an ecosystem of profound complexity.

Kira's rumble deepened, and she let out a soft huff, her breath misting in the cool evening air. It was a sound of contemplation, of processing. Niko interpreted it as Kira sensing not just the physical presence of another world, but its inherent 'feeling,' its emotional or spiritual resonance. Her bio-enhancements allowed her to perceive the subtle energetic signatures that living organisms emitted, and on a world with such an intricate biosphere, those signatures would undoubtedly be potent and interconnected. It was as if the planet itself was singing, and Kira was picking up the melody.

He recalled the theoretical models of interdimensional resonance. While most gateways acted as relatively simple portals, allowing passage between similar dimensional planes, some, like this one, seemed to tap into deeper, more complex matrices. These were the gateways that led to worlds where life had evolved in ways that were deeply intertwined with the fundamental forces of their reality, where the boundaries between the physical and the energetic were blurred. Kira's ability to 'feel' these resonances was invaluable. She could detect the subtle ebb and flow of life force, the energetic hum of a thriving ecosystem, or the discordant static of an ailing one.

A particularly strong pulse emanated from the gateway, and Kira's tail gave a sharp, decisive thump. This wasn't a sound of joy or pure harmony, but one of focused interest, a subtle shift towards what Niko recognized as 'engaged observation.' Her body language now indicated an active attempt to decipher, to categorize the nuances she was perceiving. She was not just hearing the song of the world beyond; she was beginning to understand its lyrics.

"You're picking up on the biological signatures, aren't you?" Niko mused, his gaze sweeping over the data on his scanner. "The interwoven energy fields of the flora and fauna. It's stronger than anything we've encountered before." He pointed to a particularly complex waveform on the screen. "This cluster here... it's almost like a shared consciousness, a distributed network of... something. It's not individual thoughts, not like us, but a collective awareness."

Kira whined softly, her head cocked. It was a sound of agreement, of confirmation. She was indeed sensing this network, this intricate web of life. It wasn't just the individual presences of plants and animals; it was the sum of their interconnectedness, a planetary-scale biological network humming with life. This explained the subtle dissonance Niko had detected earlier in the resonance readings – not a flaw, but an inherent characteristic of such a complex, interconnected system. It was the sound of a world that breathed as one.

The research outpost itself, a marvel of sustainable engineering, provided a stark, grounding contrast to the ethereal wonders of the gateway. Solar panels, disguised as broad, iridescent leaves on genetically engineered vines, climbed the weathered, reclaimed timber walls. Water was purified through a series of bio-filters that mimicked natural wetlands, and the air itself was kept fresh by an array of carefully selected mosses and hardy, low-growing ferns integrated into the very structure. This was the Resonant Pack's sanctuary, a testament to their core philosophy: to work *with* nature, not against it, to harness technology as a tool for understanding and preservation, not for dominion. OmniCorp, with their sterile, sprawling complexes and disregard for environmental impact, represented the antithesis of everything they stood for.

Niko glanced at a small, intricately carved wooden bird perched on a nearby railing. It was a gift from a child on a long-ago scouting mission, a world where the dominant species resembled highly intelligent avian creatures. The memory brought a faint smile to his lips. Every interaction, every observation, enriched their understanding of life's boundless potential. And

Kira, with her enhanced senses and innate empathy, was their bridge to that understanding.

He watched as Kira's tail began to wag again, a little more vigorously this time. The rumble in her chest subsided, replaced by a series of soft, inquisitive yips. This was her 'curiosity mode,' a precursor to focused investigation. She was no longer just perceiving the general hum of the world beyond; she was beginning to isolate specific signals, to draw the gateway's attention, as if a gentle nudge for clearer transmission. It was an extraordinary display of instinct and learned behavior, a partnership that had evolved beyond simple commands and responses.

"You want to get a closer look, don't you?" Niko said, a hint of amusement in his voice. He knew that look, that bright-eyed eagerness. Kira was as eager for discovery as he was, perhaps even more so, driven by a purer, less analytical form of wonder. "Alright, alright. But we go slow. And you lead the way, as always."

He rose, stretching his long frame. The twilight was deepening, the last vestiges of sunlight painting the sky in bruised purples and fiery oranges. The gateway seemed to absorb the dying light, its opalescent glow intensifying, casting long, dancing shadows across the platform. The hum, once a gentle whisper, had become a more insistent, melodic thrum, a siren song from another reality.

Kira, sensing his readiness, trotted to the edge of the platform, her body taut with anticipation. She looked back at Niko, her tail giving a short, excited wag. It was a silent question: "Are we going?"

Niko met her gaze, a profound sense of trust settling over him. He didn't doubt her senses, her instincts. She was the early warning system, the compass, the interpreter of the unspoken. Her ability to perceive the subtle energetic flows, the emotional undertones of alien ecosystems, was a gift. It allowed them to tread with a respect born of true understanding, to approach new worlds not as conquerors, but as humble students. The bio-enhancements were designed to augment her natural abilities, to allow her to process and communicate these complex perceptions more effectively. It was about enhancing the partnership, not replacing it.

He joined her at the edge, his hand resting on her flank. The air crackled with latent energy. The gateway was not just a hole in space; it was a living, breathing entity, a conduit that responded to the universe's subtle vibrations. Kira's sixth sense, as he'd come to think of it, was the key to navigating its unpredictable currents. It allowed her to discern the smooth, clear currents from the treacherous eddies, to feel the 'texture' of dimensional space.

A soft, happy sigh escaped Kira as she pressed closer to Niko. It was a sound of profound contentment, a reassurance that, no matter how strange or daunting the unknown might be, they faced it together. The subtle energetic vibrations she perceived were not just data points; they were a testament to the vibrant, interconnected tapestry of life that existed beyond the veil. And she, with her heightened senses, was uniquely equipped to appreciate its delicate beauty.

The gateway pulsed again, a wave of soft, amethyst light washing over them. Kira's tail began to wag with renewed vigor, a pure expression of her excitement. She was not just sensing a new world; she was sensing its potential, its life-affirming energy. Niko felt a surge of adrenaline, a quiet thrill that never diminished, no matter how many gateways they explored. The data was one thing, but Kira's direct, intuitive understanding was another, providing a depth of insight that no instrument could replicate. Her 'sixth sense' was not just about detecting danger or stability; it was about feeling the very pulse of existence, a connection to the universal symphony of life that resonated within her, and through her, within him. The threshold awaited, and with Kira by his side, Niko felt not trepidation, but an exhilarating sense of purpose. They were ready to listen to the whispers, and to understand the songs, of Veridia.

The hum of the gateway wasn't just a scientific anomaly to Niko; it was the prelude to their work. The Resonant Pack, a name that echoed their operational philosophy, was built on a foundation of profound respect for the unknown. Their mandate was etched into the very core of their being, a guiding principle that set them apart from the rapacious entities that also bartered with the ephemeral fabric of dimensional gates. OmniCorp, with its sterile ambition and insatiable hunger for resources, viewed these passages as mere highways to exploitation. For the Pack, they were sacred thresholds, leading to worlds that deserved to be understood, not plundered.

Niko often reflected on the inherent danger of their profession. Each gateway, a potential Pandora's Box, could unleash forces beyond human comprehension, or worse, lead to the irreversible degradation of delicate, nascent ecosystems. This was where Kira, his remarkable Border Collie, truly shone. Her bio-enhancements were not about brute force or artificial intelligence; they were about amplifying her innate canine instincts, her ability to sense imbalance, fear, and the subtle energetic whispers of life. She was their early warning system, their empathic translator, capable of discerning the health and harmony of an alien biosphere long before any sensor could provide definitive data. Her soft whines and guttural rumbles, once enigmatic signals, were now a language Niko understood as intimately as his own heartbeat.

The Resonant Pack was a carefully curated tapestry of individuals, each possessing unique skills and a shared ethical compass. Anya Sharma, their xenobotanist, was a quiet force, her hands as adept at coaxing life from alien soil as they were at manipulating intricate genetic sequencers. Her knowledge of planetary flora was encyclopedic, her ability to predict ecological collapse almost prophetic. Then there was Jax, a grizzled ex-military operative whose pragmatism was tempered by a deep-seated awe for the natural world. Jax's role was security and logistics, ensuring their operations were conducted safely and efficiently, but beneath the hardened exterior lay a heart that beat in rhythm with the Pack's conservationist creed. He was particularly fond of the genetically enhanced canines that served as their trackers and guardians, each breed selected for specific environmental adaptations and sensory capabilities.

Among these dedicated companions was Kaelen, a robust German Shepherd whose lineage had been subtly augmented for enhanced thermal and olfactory perception. Kaelen possessed an uncanny ability to track not just physical trails, but energetic disturbances, a trait that made him invaluable in sensing subtle shifts in the atmospheric composition of new worlds. His presence was a constant, reassuring anchor for the human members of the Pack, his deep bark a signal of vigilance, his gentle nuzzle a gesture of unwavering loyalty. He worked in tandem with Zephyr, a sleek, agile Saluki, whose enhanced low-light vision and incredible speed made her the perfect scout for navigating dimly lit alien landscapes. Zephyr's movements were a silent ballet, her keen eyes missing nothing, her presence a testament to the Pack's commitment to utilizing augmented, but fundamentally natural, abilities.

Their ethical guidelines were not mere rules; they were the bedrock of their existence. The prime directive, as they informally called it, was non-interference unless absolutely necessary for preservation. This meant meticulously studying an ecosystem before any interaction, understanding its intricate web of life, and ensuring that their presence left no lasting negative impact. They operated under the assumption that every world, no matter how seemingly primitive, possessed an inherent right to exist undisturbed. This starkly contrasted with OmniCorp's modus operandi. Niko had seen the holographic projections, the leaked reports detailing their destructive mining operations, their ruthless terraforming projects that obliterated indigenous life in pursuit of mineral wealth and exploitable resources. OmniCorp saw life as a commodity, a stepping stone to ever-greater corporate power. The Pack saw it as a miracle, a precious, interconnected web that demanded reverence and protection.

"The resonance is... complex," Anya murmured, her gaze fixed on a holographic display that shimmered with intricate biological data. The readings from Kira's neural interface, relayed to Anya's console, were a symphony of bio-signatures, a testament to the vibrant, interconnected life on Veridia. "It's not just individual species," she continued, a note of awe in her voice. "It's like... a planetary network. Everything is communicating, sharing information on an energetic level."

Niko nodded, his hand stroking Kira's flank as she leaned against his leg, her amber eyes still fixed on the pulsing gateway. "Kira's picking that up too. She's sensing more than just atmospheric composition or thermal signatures. She's feeling the 'mood' of the world, the collective consciousness, if you can call it that." He gestured towards a particularly vibrant cluster of waveforms on his own scanner. "This is what she's reacting to. It's... beautiful, in a way. But also incredibly fragile."

Jax, who had been checking their perimeter for any signs of OmniCorp activity, approached the observation platform, his brow furrowed. "Fragile how? Anything we need to worry about in terms of direct threat?"

"Not a direct threat from the environment itself, Jax," Anya explained, her voice calm. "More like... the risk of inadvertently disrupting it. Imagine a finely tuned instrument. One wrong note, one careless touch, and the entire symphony goes out of tune. This world's biological network is so interconnected, so deeply integrated, that even a small perturbation could have cascading effects. We have to be surgical."

Kaelen let out a low, contented rumble from his spot at Jax's feet, his tail giving a slow, steady thump against the reclaimed wood. He seemed to understand the gravity of the situation, his instincts attuned to the subtle energies of their surroundings. Zephyr, perched regally on a nearby railing, twitched an ear, her gaze sharp and observant, taking in every nuance of the conversation.

"OmniCorp wouldn't even register this level of complexity," Niko said, a hint of bitterness in his tone. "They'd see potential resources, nothing more. They'd blast their way in, extract what they want, and leave behind a barren wasteland. They're the antithesis of everything we stand for."

"Which is why we're here," Anya said, meeting Niko's gaze. "To be the counter-balance. To ensure that worlds like this have a chance. To understand them, protect them, and hopefully, learn from them. The universe is too vast, too wondrous, to be treated as mere real estate for corporate expansion."

The opalescent curtain of the Whispering Gate seemed to throb in response to their conversation, its light intensifying, casting an ethereal glow on their faces. Kira whined softly, a sound of anticipation, her tail giving a hopeful wag. She felt it too, the pull of the unknown, the promise of discovery. But for Kira, it was also a feeling of profound responsibility. Her enhanced senses were not just tools; they were a burden of awareness, a constant reminder of the delicate balance of life. She felt the interconnectedness of Veridia, the vibrant hum of its biosphere, and with that awareness came an instinctual desire to protect it.

"She's eager," Niko observed, a faint smile touching his lips. "She feels the harmony, but she also senses the potential dissonance that our presence could introduce. It's a finely honed instinct, honed by years of observation and augmentation." He knelt beside her, scratching her behind the ears. "Easy, girl. We'll be careful. We always are."

The concept of the 'Resonant Pack Protocol' was more than just a set of rules; it was a living document, constantly evolving with each new discovery. It emphasized patience, meticulous observation, and a deep ethical consideration for any life form encountered. It was about understanding the intricate dance of evolution, the delicate dependencies that formed the fabric of an ecosystem. When they encountered nascent life, as they suspected Veridia harbored, the protocol dictated extreme caution. They would deploy passive observation drones, gather data from a distance, and only, *only*, interact if there was a clear and present danger of extinction that they could mitigate without causing further disruption.

"The data suggests that Veridia is in a crucial phase of its biological development," Anya reported, her eyes still glued to the readings. "The interconnectedness of its flora and fauna is at a peak. It's a period of incredible biodiversity and energetic exchange, but also extreme vulnerability. Any significant external biological introduction, or even a drastic alteration of their energy balance, could be catastrophic."

Niko's gaze drifted from the gateway to the small, intricately carved wooden sparrow perched on a nearby railing. It was a memento from a scouting mission to a world where the dominant species resembled intelligent, feathered beings, a world they had managed to protect from OmniCorp's avarice. That sparrow, a simple carving, represented a profound success, a testament to the Pack's mission.

"We need to establish a secure perimeter," Jax stated, his voice firm. "No unauthorized incursions. We'll establish automated drone surveillance, passive energy scanners, and Kaelen and Zephyr will be on constant patrol. If there's even a hint of OmniCorp interference, we alert Command immediately."

"And Kira will be our primary sensor," Niko added, his hand finding Kira's soft fur. "She'll be our early warning, our guide. Her ability to perceive the energetic signatures of life is more sensitive than any technology we possess. She can feel the pulse of the planet. She can tell us when we are truly welcome, and when our presence is an intrusion."

The pack members moved with a practiced efficiency, a silent understanding that spoke of years of shared experiences and unwavering trust. Jax began coordinating with the remote drone deployment team, his voice a low, steady murmur over the comms. Anya meticulously cross-referenced her findings with existing data on planetary development, her fingers flying across the holographic interface. Kaelen and Zephyr took up their positions, their keen senses already scanning the surrounding environment with an almost supernatural focus.

Niko knelt beside Kira, offering a quiet reassurance. "You're doing good, girl. You're sensing the song of this world. Just keep listening. We'll do our best to understand it, and to protect it." Kira responded with a soft sigh, pressing her head against his hand. It was a gesture of trust, a silent acknowledgment of their shared purpose. She understood the responsibility that rested on their shoulders, the profound importance of their mission.

The Whispering Gate continued its ethereal dance, its opalescent light a beacon of the unknown. But within the Resonant Pack, there was no trepidation, only a quiet determination. They were not conquerors, not exploiters. They were guardians, observers, a pack united by a shared vision of a universe where life, in all its myriad forms, was cherished and protected. And with Kira, their canine compass, leading the way, they were ready to embrace the symphony of Veridia, to listen to its whispers, and to ensure its melody continued to play for eons to come. The Resonant Pack Protocol was not just a framework for exploration; it was a promise, a commitment to the sanctity of life itself, a promise they were ready to uphold on this vibrant, nascent world.

The soft glow of the command console, usually a comforting beacon in Niko's dimly lit quarters, suddenly flared with an insistent crimson pulse. A priority alert. His heart gave a familiar, almost unwelcome lurch. He glanced at Kira, who had been resting her head on his knee, her amber eyes mirroring the console's urgent rhythm. A low whine rumbled in her chest, a sound that spoke of immediate awareness, of the shifting energies that signaled a new directive.

"Looks like we're not going to get to finish that atmospheric survey of Xylos after all," Niko murmured, his fingers already dancing across the holographic interface. The alert's origin point was starkly displayed: Central Command. Not just any directive, but one that bypassed the usual protocols, demanding immediate attention. The message itself was terse, encrypted, but the keywords jumped out: "Unusual Resonance," "Ecological Potential," "Critical Instability," "Immediate Deployment."

Kira nudged his hand with her nose, her gaze fixed on the blinking alert, a silent affirmation of her readiness. She could sense it too, the subtle tremor in the fabric of reality that preceded the opening of a new gateway. This wasn't just a tremor; it was a shriek, a siren song of both immense promise and profound peril.

He accessed the brief data stream. A new gateway had stabilized. Not just stabilized, but exhibited resonance patterns unlike anything they had cataloged before. Anya's preliminary analysis, still fragmented, spoke of a world teeming with life, a biosphere in a state of rapid, interconnected flux. The implications were staggering. Such rapid evolution often occurred in isolation, shielded from external influences, creating unique, often delicate, ecosystems. But the "critical instability" warning was a stark counterpoint, a red flag that amplified the urgency. It suggested that this gateway, while offering a glimpse into a world of unparalleled biological wonder, also presented a significant threat, not only to the nascent world itself but potentially to their own.

The source of the alert, Central Command, was a marvel of bio-integrated design. Nestled within a vast, reclaimed forest ecosystem, its structures were grown rather than built, its energy needs met by geothermal vents and solar arrays woven seamlessly into the forest canopy. It was the antithesis of OmniCorp's sprawling, scar-like industrial complexes that poisoned the very ground they occupied. Central Command represented humanity's best hope for coexisting with the universe, a beacon of sustainable exploration and a testament to the Resonant Pack's core philosophy. For a priority alert to originate from its deepest, most secure channels meant the situation was far beyond routine.

"Central Command... a critical alert... that means it's big, Kira," Niko said, his voice tight with a mixture of apprehension and a familiar thrill of purpose. He ran a hand over her sleek fur, the familiar feel a grounding force. "They wouldn't pull us from active survey for anything less than something that could redefine our understanding of life... or threaten it on a massive scale."

He initiated the preliminary packing sequence. Specialized environmental suits that could adapt to a wide range of atmospheric conditions, ranging from cryogenic to searing heat, were automatically loaded into their deployment module. Bio-scanners, designed to detect even the subtlest energetic signatures, were meticulously calibrated. Anya's contribution would be vital; her xenobotanical kits, filled with a diverse array of nutrient pastes, microbial cultures, and soil analysis tools, were packed with her characteristic precision. Jax's role would be to ensure their tactical gear was ready – sonic deterrents, non-lethal containment units, and advanced sensor arrays that could detect OmniCorp's insidious signatures from miles away.

Kira watched, her tail giving a slow, deliberate sweep of the floor. She knew the drill. The focused energy in Niko's movements, the quiet intensity in his eyes, all signaled an imminent departure. She felt the subtle shift in the ambient energy of their quarters, a prelude to the gateway's activation, a low hum that resonated in her very bones. Her enhanced senses were already reaching out, tasting the air, searching for the faint traces of the unknown world that awaited them.

The weight of responsibility settled onto Niko's shoulders, a familiar, heavy cloak. Each new gateway was a gamble, a leap of faith into the unknown. But this felt different. The urgency, the unusual resonance patterns... it hinted at a delicate balance, a fragile nascent world that could be easily tipped into oblivion. Their mission, as always, was to observe, to understand, and above all, to protect. But the inherent instability suggested that mere observation might not be enough. They might be called upon to intervene, to make impossible choices, to play the role of a guardian angel on a world that might not even understand the concept of an angel, let alone a threat.

"Get ready, girl," Niko said, his voice a low rumble. He clipped the secure comms device to his belt, its surface cool against his skin. "We're going to need to move fast. Whatever is on the other side of that gate, it's important. And it's calling for help."

Kira responded with a soft, affirmative bark, her gaze unwavering. She understood. Her role was not just to sense danger, but to perceive the subtle currents of life, to act as a conduit between the complex bio-energies of alien worlds and the understanding of her human pack. She was their compass, their early warning system, their empathic translator. And on this new, unstable world, her instincts would be more critical than ever.

The deployment module, a sleek, utilitarian craft designed for swift atmospheric entry and minimal environmental impact, was already being prepared for launch. Its interior was a testament to the Pack's commitment to efficiency and preparedness. Modular compartments held everything from advanced medical supplies to terraforming stabilizers, should the need arise for extreme intervention. But the first step, always, was reconnaissance, a gentle probing of the unknown.

Niko ran a final diagnostic on Kira's neural interface, a discreet implant behind her ear that allowed for a seamless, though still filtered, exchange of sensory data. It wasn't about turning her into a machine, but about amplifying her natural abilities, allowing him to perceive the world as she did, at least in part. He felt a surge of gratitude for her, for the unique bond they shared, a bond forged in shared purpose and unwavering trust. She was more than a partner; she was family, a vital organ of their collective consciousness.

The hum of the gateway, now projected on a large screen in the preparation bay, intensified. It was a swirling vortex of opalescent light, a mesmerizing dance of energy that promised passage to another reality. The readings emanating from it were chaotic, a symphony of discordant notes interspersed with breathtaking harmonies. Anya's preliminary notes flashed across a secondary display, detailing potential atmospheric hazards, unique microbial signatures, and fluctuating gravitational anomalies.

"The primary resonance signature is unlike anything in the database, Niko," Anya's voice crackled over the comms, a hint of professional excitement cutting through the urgency. "It suggests a biosphere that is actively, almost aggressively, self-regulating. Think of it as a planetary immune system on overdrive. The potential for rapid adaptation is immense, but so is the risk of complete systemic collapse if that regulation is disrupted."

"Aggressively self-regulating," Niko repeated, a shiver tracing its way down his spine. "That doesn't sound friendly."

"Not necessarily unfriendly," Anya corrected, her tone still measured. "Just... fiercely protective. It's like a nascent organism fighting to define its own boundaries. The instability could be a natural part of its growth cycle, or it could be a symptom of an impending crisis. We won't know until we get closer."

Jax's voice cut in, gruff and to the point. "Module is prepped. Engines are hot. We're on your command, Niko."

"Understood, Jax. Kira, you ready?" Niko asked, looking down at his canine companion.

Kira met his gaze, her tail giving a decisive thump. Her posture was alert, her senses attuned to the very air around them, which seemed to crackle with anticipation. She felt the pull of the gateway, a magnetic force drawing her toward the unknown. But more than that, she felt the immense, complex energy signature of the world on the other side. It was a tapestry woven with threads of vibrant life, interwoven with strands of anxiety, of a desperate struggle for equilibrium. It was a world crying out, not necessarily for rescue, but for understanding.

"Let's go," Niko said, the word a quiet command that resonated with the weight of their mission. He offered Kira a reassuring scratch behind the ears, then turned towards the ramp of the deployment module. The red alert on the console faded, replaced by the cool, steady glow of the operational status indicator. The Whispering Gate, once a distant theoretical possibility, was now a tangible threshold, and the Resonant Pack, with Kira at its forefront, was about to step across. The call had been answered. The journey into the heart of instability had begun.

The air within the deployment module thrummed with a low, resonant vibration that mirrored the thrumming in Niko's own chest. Kira, pressed close against his side, emitted a soft, continuous rumble, her amber eyes wide and fixed on the swirling nexus of light that now filled the forward viewport. It was no longer a distant projection on a screen, but a tangible, almost solid phenomenon, a shimmering tapestry of iridescent hues that pulsed with an unseen energy. The "Whispering Gate," as Anya had cryptically termed it, was no longer a concept, but a threshold. The mission parameters, stark and absolute, played on repeat in Niko's mind: observe, assess, do not interfere unless absolutely necessary. But the "critical instability" warning gnawed at him, a persistent whisper of dread against the thrill of discovery.

"Ready, girl?" Niko murmured, his hand finding the familiar warmth of Kira's flank. Her response was immediate – a sharp, decisive nod of her head, her gaze never leaving the vortex. She could sense it too, the profound alienness of the energies coalescing on the other side, a symphony of biological processes so complex and rapid they bordered on chaotic. It was a symphony that spoke of immense vitality, but also of a precarious balance, like a mountain stream rushing over a precipice.

Jax, ever stoic, gave a curt nod from the pilot's seat. "Stable transit window projected for thirty seconds. Initiating."

The module lurched forward, a smooth, almost imperceptible accceleration that propelled them into the heart of the opalescent maelstrom. For a fleeting moment, reality seemed to fragment. Colors bled into one another, sound distorted into a cacophony of ethereal whispers and deep, guttural groans. Niko felt a disorienting pressure, as if being squeezed through an impossibly small aperture, and then, with a sudden release, they were through.

The transition was jarring, not in its violence, but in its abruptness. The swirling colors vanished, replaced by an entirely new spectrum of light, a deep, resonant violet that seemed to emanate from the very atmosphere. It painted the alien landscape in shades of amethyst and indigo, casting long, distorted shadows from flora that defied any terrestrial classification. The air, when it filtered through the module's external sensors, was a riot of unfamiliar scents – earthy, sweet, and tinged with a metallic tang that prickled the back of Niko's throat.

Kira was already reacting. Her ears swiveled, catching sounds that were imperceptible to Niko's human hearing, and her nostrils flared, processing the complex olfactory tapestry. A low whine escaped her, a sound of pure, unadulterated wonder mixed with a primal caution. She nudged Niko's hand insistently, her body tensed, her senses on high alert. This world was alive, profoundly alive, and its life sang a song of an entirely different melody.

"Atmospheric composition nominal, though with unusually high levels of airborne particulate matter, likely biological in origin," Anya's voice, tinged with scientific awe, crackled through the comms. "Temperature is a stable 22 degrees Celsius, humidity at 70 percent. Gravitational pull is approximately 0.9 G. And the light... the primary light source appears to be a diffuse, atmospheric luminescence rather than a localized star. Fascinating."

Niko surveyed the scene unfolding before them. They had emerged into a vast, undulating plain carpeted with what appeared to be a low-lying, phosphorescent moss that glowed with a soft, internal light. Towering above this verdant carpet were colossal, crystalline structures that resembled trees, their translucent branches reaching upwards, refracting the violet light into a dazzling array of spectral patterns. Some of these "trees" pulsed with a slow, rhythmic luminescence, as if their very sap was composed of light. Smaller, more mobile flora dotted the landscape – bulbous, spherical plants that floated a few feet above the ground, tethered by thin, fibrous tendrils, their surfaces rippling with unseen currents. And the sounds... a constant symphony of clicks, whistles, and deep, resonating hums, a language of the biosphere that Kira was already beginning to translate.

"Kira, what are you sensing?" Niko asked, his voice a low murmur, allowing her to focus.

She whined softly, then nudged his leg, her gaze sweeping across the landscape. Niko felt a faint impression in his mind, a rush of sensory data filtered through Kira's unique perception. It wasn't words, but feelings, impressions: *vibrant, alive, a thousand whispers, a frantic pulse, caution, wonder, the ground breathes, the air sings.* The most potent impression was one of overwhelming interconnectedness. This world wasn't just teeming with life; it was a single, massive, interwoven organism, its every component contributing to a collective, dynamic equilibrium.

"She's sensing a high degree of interconnectedness, Anya," Niko relayed. "A planetary-scale biological network. And she's picking up on... instability. A sense of a frantic pulse, like something is struggling to maintain balance."

"That aligns with the resonance patterns we detected," Anya replied, her voice sharper now, the scientific curiosity now laced with a pragmatic concern. "The rapid shifts, the energy spikes... it suggests a biosphere in a state of extreme flux. The question is, is this a natural phase of rapid evolution, or is something fundamentally wrong?"

The deployment module settled gently onto a patch of firmer ground, the landing gear sinking slightly into the bioluminescent moss. The ramp lowered with a soft hiss, and for a moment, no one moved. It was the unspoken protocol for any new world: a moment of absolute stillness, a respectful pause before stepping into the unknown. Niko took a deep breath, the alien air filling his lungs, strangely invigorating.

"Jax, stay with the module. Maintain comms link with Central Command and monitor for any OmniCorp signatures," Niko ordered, his voice calm and steady. "Anya, you'll be monitoring our sensor readings from here. Kira and I will take the initial reconnaissance."

Kira, as if understanding her cue, trotted to the edge of the ramp, her body alert, her tail held high. She scanned the immediate vicinity, her keen senses absorbing every detail. Niko followed, his environmental suit humming softly as it adapted to the local conditions. The moss beneath his boots felt surprisingly springy, emitting a faint, pleasant warmth. He activated his personal scanner, its holographic display flickering to life, projecting a detailed analysis of his immediate surroundings.

The "crystalline trees" were not geological formations but incredibly complex, silica-based organisms. Their internal structures pulsed with a slow, bioluminescent flow, a circulatory system of light. The floating spherical plants, Anya's preliminary scans suggested, were a form of aerial flora, drawing nutrients from the atmosphere itself, their surfaces rippling with captured solar energy. The ground beneath the moss was a dense, intricate network of mycelial threads, the dominant connective tissue of this world's vast biological network.

"The instability is emanating from the north-east quadrant," Niko reported, pointing his scanner in that direction. The display showed a subtle but distinct ripple in the ambient energy field, a point of greater agitation within the otherwise vibrant hum of the ecosystem. "It's like a localized tremor in the planetary pulse."

Kira let out a soft huff, her gaze fixed on the distant north-east. She seemed to understand the urgency, the need to investigate this anomaly. She nudged Niko's hand, a silent invitation to move forward.

"Alright, girl," Niko said, a surge of purpose overriding the lingering apprehension. "Let's see what's whispering from over there."

They moved out, their footsteps rustling softly on the luminous moss. The violet light cast an otherworldly glow, making familiar shapes seem alien and strange. The air was alive with subtle vibrations, a constant hum that resonated through Niko's suit and into his very bones. It was a symphony of life, a testament to the universe's boundless creativity, but somewhere within that symphony, a discordant note was being played, a note of struggle, of impending crisis.

As they ventured further, the flora began to change. The crystalline trees became more gnarled, their luminescence flickering erratically. The floating spheres appeared more agitated, their internal rippling more frantic. The air grew heavier, charged with an almost palpable tension. Kira's low rumble intensified, a constant thrum of awareness that vibrated through their shared neural link. She was picking up on more than just energy signatures; she was sensing the subtle emotional currents of the world around them, a tapestry of biological stress and desperate resilience.

"The energy readings are spiking, Niko," Anya's voice, tight with concern, cut through the ambient hum. "The instability is increasing. I'm also detecting unusual localized atmospheric distortions. Nothing hostile, but definitely anomalous."

Niko surveyed the terrain. The ground ahead seemed to shimmer, as if the very fabric of reality was undulating. In the distance, a cluster of the crystalline trees seemed to be convulsing, their branches shedding shards of light like tears. A low, mournful keening sound began to emerge from that direction, a sound that spoke of profound distress.

"We're getting closer," Niko said, his voice tight. He checked his equipment, ensuring his non-lethal deterrents were readily accessible. The res_onant pack's primary directive was to protect, and while they were not equipped for combat, they were prepared to de-escalate and defend. But the nature of this instability was still a mystery. Was it a geological event? A biological plague? Or was it something... sentient, something struggling against an unseen oppressor?

Kira suddenly stopped, planting her paws firmly on the moss. She let out a low growl, a sound of pure warning. Her gaze was fixed on a point just beyond a cluster of writhing crystalline trees. Niko followed her gaze, his own senses straining. At first, he saw nothing but the agitated flora. Then, a subtle shift in the violet light, a flicker of movement that was not part of the natural luminescence. It was a disturbance, a rent in the otherwise coherent energy field of this world.

"What is it, girl?" Niko whispered, his hand resting on Kira's powerful shoulder.

She whined, a sound of apprehension. The impression that flooded Niko's mind was one of profound wrongness, of an alien presence that felt...

parasitic. It was a discordant note that was actively trying to unravel the planetary symphony.

"I see it," Niko said, his voice grim. "Amniotic bubble... or something like it. Wavering, unstable. It's... bleeding something into the atmosphere. Something that's disrupting the local energy field."

Anya's voice, now laced with alarm, crackled over the comms. "The readings are off the charts, Niko! That disturbance... it's radiating a chaotic energy signature unlike anything we've ever encountered. It's not part of this world's biosphere. It's an intrusion."

The implications slammed into Niko with the force of a physical blow. This wasn't just an unstable ecosystem; it was a world under attack, a nascent biosphere being threatened by an invasive force. The "critical instability" was not a natural phase of growth, but a symptom of an external assault. Their mission had just shifted, from observation to potential intervention. The Whispering Gate had led them not just to a new world, but to a battle for its very existence. He looked at Kira, her body tensed, her gaze unwavering, a silent testament to their shared purpose. The unknown was no longer just an abstract concept; it was a tangible threat, and they were standing at its very precipice.

CHAPTER TWO
VERDANT ECHOES

The deployment module had settled with an almost imperceptible grace, its landing struts sinking into a carpet of emerald and sapphire mosses that pulsed with a gentle, inner luminescence. The ramp hissed open, revealing a panorama that stole the breath from Niko's lungs. Gone were the stark, utilitarian greys of the transit module. Before them lay a world painted in hues of amethyst and indigo, a symphony of color orchestrated by an atmosphere thick with gases that captured and refracted light in ways that defied terrestrial physics. This was Veridia, a name that already felt profoundly right, resonating with the vibrant, verdant life that now unfolded before their eyes.

Niko, a botanist by training and a naturalist by heart, felt an immediate and visceral connection to this alien biome. His eyes, accustomed to the subtle greens and browns of Earth's flora, widened in sheer, unadulterated wonder. Dominating the landscape were not trees in the conventional sense, but colossal, bioluminescent fungi. Their stalks, thick as ancient redwoods, rose hundreds of feet into the violet sky, crowned with expansive caps that glowed with a soft, pulsing light. These caps weren't static; they seemed to breathe, their luminescence ebbing and flowing in slow, rhythmic cycles, casting shifting patterns of light and shadow across the undulating terrain. Some of these fungal giants were a deep, velvety purple, others a vibrant, almost electric blue, their sheer scale dwarfing anything Niko had ever cataloged. The air, filtered through his suit's sensors, carried a complex olfactory profile: earthy, with an undercurrent of sweet, decaying organic matter, and a peculiar, almost metallic tang that spoke of novel biochemical processes.

"Incredible," Niko breathed, the word barely audible above the gentle hum of his suit's life support. He stepped onto the mossy ground, his boots sinking slightly into its yielding surface. The moss itself was a marvel, a dense, interwoven tapestry of fine filaments that shimmered with embedded microorganisms, each one contributing to the overall soft glow. It felt alive beneath his feet, a living, breathing substrate. He activated his scanner, its holographic projection blooming in front of him, already filling with data that was both exhilarating and overwhelming. The dominant light source, Anya had noted, wasn't a star in the typical sense, but an atmospheric phenomenon, a diffuse, ambient luminescence that bathed the entire planet in its ethereal glow. This light, filtered through the unique atmospheric composition, was what created the pervasive amethyst hue that defined Veridia's skies and painted its landscapes.

Kira, usually so keenly attuned to any hint of threat or strangeness, seemed to find a peculiar solace in this new environment. The initial tension that had gripped her during the transit had begun to dissipate. Her ears, which had been swiveling with extreme caution, now relaxed, her posture softening. She nudged Niko's hand with her nose, then tentatively explored the immediate vicinity of the deployment module, her tail giving a slow, almost hesitant wag. It wasn't the unbridled joy of a familiar park, but a gentle acknowledgment of the profound, resonant peace that seemed to emanate from this world. Niko felt it too, a subtle vibration that seemed to harmonize with his own bio-rhythms, a sense of deep, primal calm that settled his nerves. He reached down and scratched behind her ears. "It's alright, girl," he murmured. "This place... it's different. But it's not hostile. Not yet, anyway."

His scanner displayed a dizzying array of data. The fungal structures, he confirmed, were indeed biological, their internal vascular systems filled with a viscous, bioluminescent fluid. Their caps were intricate structures, designed not just for spore dispersal, but also, it seemed, for light absorption and energy conversion. Interspersed between these giants were smaller, more varied flora. Bulbous, sac-like plants pulsed rhythmically, their translucent membranes rippling with internal currents, suggesting they might be drawing nutrients directly from the humid air. Delicate, vine-like growths, adorned with crystalline nodes that glittered like jewels, snaked their way up the stalks of the larger fungi, creating intricate aerial gardens. The ground cover was not uniform; patches of the glowing moss gave way to areas of what appeared to be a low-lying, velvety lichen, and in some spots, clusters of small, intricate polyps that unfurled petal-like structures when Niko's shadow passed over them, only to retract again with a silent, swift motion.

"Anya, can you get a preliminary spectral analysis of the atmospheric composition and the light source?" Niko requested, his voice filled with an almost childlike enthusiasm. "I'm seeing incredibly complex light interactions here. The refractions and diffractions are unlike anything I've encountered."

Anya's voice, though tinged with her usual scientific detachment, carried an undeniable note of wonder. "Working on it, Niko. The primary light source appears to be a form of atmospheric chemiluminescence, amplified by exotic atmospheric particulates. The gases... they're a complex mixture. High concentrations of noble gases, several complex organic aerosols, and something that's... unusual. It's not on any known element or compound list. It's reacting with the ambient energy fields in a way that's generating these intense, coherent light patterns. It's why everything is bathed in this deep violet-amethyst spectrum. It's... quite beautiful, actually."

Beautiful was an understatement. It was breathtaking. Niko moved slowly, his scanner documenting everything. He focused on a cluster of what looked like enormous, iridescent mushrooms, their caps swirling with patterns that shifted and changed like living nebulae. They emitted a low, resonant hum, a sound that Kira seemed to respond to with a slight perking of her ears. He carefully extended a sampling probe, collecting a small section of the moss. The scanner immediately began its analysis, identifying complex cellulose structures interwoven with intricate mycelial networks. This wasn't just a collection of individual plants; it was a deeply integrated ecosystem, each component interconnected and reliant on the others.

"The ambient resonance Kira is picking up on seems to be generated by these larger fungal structures," Niko reported. "It's a complex energy field, but it's incredibly stable, almost... soothing. It's as if the entire biosphere is humming a lullaby." He paused, observing a small, quadrupedal creature, roughly the size of a terrestrial fox, dart out from behind a fungal stalk. It was covered in short, shimmering fur that shifted color from deep blue to emerald green as it moved, its large, dark eyes blinking slowly. It paused, regarding them with an expression that seemed more curious than fearful, before disappearing back into the vibrant undergrowth. Niko made a mental note to initiate wider fauna scans.

He knelt down, gently touching one of the pulsating sac-like plants. It felt cool and slightly rubbery to the touch. His scanner indicated it was actively absorbing atmospheric moisture and trace nutrients. "These aerial flora are fascinating," he mused. "They seem to be independent of the ground-based mycelial network, at least partially. They're like... living balloons, feeding directly from the air."

Kira, meanwhile, had ventured a little further, drawn by an unseen stimulus. She was sniffing intently at the base of one of the colossal fungal stalks. Niko watched her, his hand instinctively reaching for his sidearm, though he knew it was unlikely to be necessary. Kira's internal bio-monitors would alert him to any immediate danger long before he would perceive it. She let out a soft whine, then looked back at him, her amber eyes conveying a mixture of intrigue and a slight unease. It wasn't fear, but a recognition of something... different.

"What is it, girl?" Niko asked, walking over to join her. He scanned the area she was focusing on. The base of the fungal stalk was intricately textured, covered in a velvety, dark red growth that seemed to absorb the ambient light rather than reflect it. It was here that the subtle hum seemed to intensify, becoming a more distinct thrum. "Something down here?"

Kira nudged the red growth with her nose, then began to paw at it gently. Niko activated his scanner's micro-analysis function. The results flashed up: a highly specialized symbiotic organism, not a parasite, but a complex mutualistic partner to the giant fungus. It appeared to be responsible for processing certain atmospheric compounds and converting them into a form the fungus could readily absorb, and in return, it received... nourishment, and a stable environment.

"It's another organism," Niko relayed to Anya. "A symbiont. It's... intricate. They seem to be exchanging something directly. This is a level of biological integration I've only theorized about." He watched as Kira nudged a small, almost invisible opening in the red growth. A faint mist, smelling faintly of ozone, wafted out. Kira inhaled deeply, then gave a satisfied huff.

"The resonance is strongest here, Niko," Anya reported. "It's not just passive energy; it's a modulated field. I'm detecting complex waveforms. It's almost as if... the fungi are communicating. Or perhaps, more accurately, sharing information across the entire planetary network."

"Communicating?" Niko repeated, a thrill coursing through him. The idea of a sentient, or at least a deeply communicative, global biosphere was both exhilarating and daunting. He thought of Earth's own complex ecosystems, the intricate web of life that scientists were only just beginning to understand. Veridia seemed to have taken that complexity to an entirely new level.

He spent the next several hours meticulously documenting the immediate surroundings of the deployment module. He cataloged over a dozen distinct species of fungi, each with its unique luminescence and structural variations. He documented the various forms of ground cover, from the shimmering mosses to the dark, light-absorbing lichens. He even managed to observe several species of aerial fauna, small, winged creatures with translucent wings that flitted between the fungal caps, their flight patterns intricate and purposeful. Kira, for her part, seemed to be finding her own rhythm. She explored the area with a growing confidence, her initial caution replaced by a calm curiosity. She would occasionally lie down in a patch of particularly vibrant moss, her body thrumming with the same gentle resonance that filled the air, her amber eyes half-closed in what looked like deep contentment.

"Niko, I'm picking up a localized increase in atmospheric particulate density about two kilometers north-east of your position," Anya's voice cut through the ambient hum. "The spectral signature is consistent with airborne spores, but they're... unusual. Highly complex organic structures. Not within the expected dispersal patterns of the dominant flora we've cataloged so far."

Niko consulted his scanner's topographical map. North-east. The area where he'd sensed that initial subtle ripple of instability. "I'm seeing it too, Anya. There's a slight... distortion in the energy readings from that direction. Nothing alarming, but definitely a deviation from the baseline resonance." He looked at Kira. She had lifted her head, her ears now pricked forward, a low, steady rumble emanating from her chest. It wasn't the rumble of aggression, but of focused awareness, of sensing something significant.

"I'll head that way," Niko decided. "Kira seems to be sensing something of interest. Jax, maintain situational awareness at the module."

"Understood, Niko," Jax's clipped voice responded from the module. "Comms are clear. No anomalies detected from this end."

As Niko and Kira moved away from the relative safety of the deployment module, the landscape began to subtly shift. The colossal fungi still dominated, but their luminescence seemed less uniform, flickering more erratically in places. The ground cover changed too, with larger, more bulbous growths appearing, their surfaces rippling with a more pronounced internal activity. The air itself felt heavier, the scent of ozone more pronounced. Kira's rumble deepened, a constant, reassuring vibration that grounded Niko. She walked with a more deliberate pace now, her gaze fixed on the north-eastern horizon.

"The energy readings are increasing, Niko," Anya said, her voice tightening with a scientific concern that echoed Niko's own unspoken apprehension. "And those airborne particulates... they're aggregating. It's like a fog, but it's made of spores. Very dense."

Niko activated his suit's advanced atmospheric sensors. The fog Anya mentioned was indeed approaching, a shimmering, almost iridescent mist that seemed to catch the ambient violet light and refract it into a kaleidoscope of colors. It was beautiful, in a terrifying sort of way. And as it drew closer, Niko could see that it wasn't uniform. Within the swirling mist, there were pockets of intense darkness, areas where the light seemed to be actively absorbed.

"I see it, Anya," Niko said, his voice low and steady. "It's not just a spore cloud. There's something... generating it. And those dark patches... they're not just shadows." He pointed his scanner towards one of the darker pockets. The readings were alarming. A localized energy drain, a disruption of the natural bio-electric field that permeated Veridia. This wasn't a natural phenomenon. It was an intrusion. The amethyst world, so full of life and wonder, was showing signs of distress, a subtle but undeniable wound appearing in its vibrant tapestry. Kira let out a low growl, a sound that spoke of primal instincts recognizing a discordant note in the planet's otherwise harmonious symphony. The mission had just taken a sharp turn, from exploration to investigation of a potential threat.

The air, if one could call the thick, breathable atmosphere of Veridia 'air' in the terrestrial sense, vibrated with an unseen presence. Niko's sensors, while adept at cataloging the macro-level flora and atmospheric composition, were blind to the subtler nuances of movement and scent that Kira's evolved senses could readily perceive. She, the quadrupedal member of their small exploratory unit, was the true barometer of the immediate, untamed wilderness. Her ears, sensitive enough to detect the faintest whisper of displaced molecules, twitched incessantly, tracking unseen trails that wove through the colossal fungal forests and across the bioluminescent moss beds. Her nose, a finely tuned instrument of olfactory detection, would occasionally flare, drawing in the complex aromas of Veridia, sifting through the earthy, sweet, and metallic undertones for any anomaly, any hint of an indigenous creature.

"She's picking up something," Niko murmured, his gaze sweeping across the vibrant, yet seemingly empty, landscape. Kira's posture had shifted; the relaxed curiosity that had settled upon her earlier had been replaced by a focused alertness. She was no longer merely exploring, but actively tracking. A low, almost imperceptible rumble vibrated in her chest, a sound that wasn't a growl of aggression, but rather a deep, resonant hum of heightened awareness, a sonic confirmation of her internal bio-monitors registering subtle shifts in the environment. It was a sound Niko had come to trust implicitly, a primal signal that transcended the sterile readouts of his suit's HUD.

Anya's voice, usually a calm stream of data, carried a slight edge of anticipation. "My long-range passive sensors are detecting minimal thermal signatures in your immediate vicinity, Niko. Nothing indicative of large fauna within fifty meters. However, there are localized micro-variations in atmospheric density, consistent with small-scale movement, but too diffuse to pinpoint."

"That's where Kira comes in," Niko replied, his eyes following the slight, almost imperceptible shift of her head as she navigated a particularly dense cluster of the crystalline-nodded vines. "She's our early warning system for the truly indigenous. We're still operating under strict non-interference protocols. Unless there's an immediate threat to ourselves or the module, we observe. We document. We don't engage unless it's unavoidable." He reiterated the primary directive, a mantra for their mission on this alien world. The sanctity of Veridia's native life was paramount. They were not conquerors, nor even colonizers, but transient observers, privileged guests in a world that had evolved for millennia without their interference.

Kira paused, her body held in a low crouch, tail giving a slow, deliberate sweep. Her gaze was fixed on a dense thicket of the pulsating, sac-like plants, their translucent membranes rippling with what seemed to be internal currents. Niko's scanner registered them as complex photo-synthetic and atmospheric moisture collectors, but Kira's attention suggested something more. She nudged a patch of the dark, velvety lichen that carpeted the ground in that area, then looked back at Niko, a soft whine escaping her. It was a sound of subtle persuasion, of a discovery that warranted closer inspection.

He approached cautiously, his boots sinking slightly into the yielding ground cover. The lichen itself felt surprisingly resilient, its texture akin to a dense, damp velvet. The air around it carried a faint, distinct aroma, different from the general exhalations of the larger fungal structures – a musky, earthy scent, overlaid with a subtle sweetness that reminded him of decaying fruit, yet somehow cleaner, more vibrant. He activated his micro-scanner, directing its beam towards the area Kira indicated. The readings were subtle, almost imperceptible at first. Tiny, ephemeral heat signatures, flitting in and out of detection range within the dense foliage. Not single organisms, but a multitude, moving in concert.

"There's something here," Niko confirmed, his voice a low rumble. "Small... numerous. They're either incredibly adept at thermal cloaking, or they're generating minimal heat. Kira's picking up scent trails, but my sensors are struggling to get a definitive lock." He gestured for Anya to focus her broader sensor arrays in their direction. "Anya, can you try to amplify passive thermal detection in sector Gamma-7, focused on ground-level and low-lying vegetation?"

"Acknowledged, Niko," Anya replied. A moment later, her voice returned, a note of surprise coloring her usual professional demeanor. "The amplification is revealing clusters of incredibly faint thermal signatures. They are moving erratically, almost... skittishly. And the scent you're detecting? My spectrographic analysis indicates it's a byproduct of a unique metabolic process involving the breakdown of complex organic compounds found in this particular lichen species. It's a complex pheromonal signature, possibly for intra-species communication or marking territory."

Kira, meanwhile, had begun to inch forward, her body low to the ground. She moved with a preternatural grace, her paws barely disturbing the lichen. Niko followed, his own movements deliberately slow and measured. He could feel the subtle thrum of the planet beneath his feet, the omnipresent bio-energetic resonance that seemed to emanate from the very soil. It was a feeling that permeated everything on Veridia, a gentle, constant hum that soothed the mind and quieted the anxieties of interstellar travel. Kira seemed particularly attuned to it, her body often aligning with the subtle shifts in the planetary resonance, as if drawing strength or information from it.

As they approached the epicenter of Kira's interest, the pulsating sacs began to emit a softer, more diffused luminescence. The rhythmic rippling within them became more pronounced, almost as if they were reacting to the unseen activity in the lichen. And then, Niko saw them. Not individually, at first, but as a collective movement. A ripple in the lichen, a subtle shift in the shadows. Tiny, insectoid creatures, each no larger than a human thumbnail, began to emerge. Their exoskeletons were a mottled, earthy brown, perfectly camouflaged against the lichen, and their forms were delicate, almost ethereal. They possessed multiple, spindly legs that moved with astonishing speed and precision, and their heads were dominated by two large, multifaceted eyes that reflected the ambient violet light like tiny jewels.

They weren't overtly alarming, but their sheer number and their coordinated movements were captivating. They moved in intricate patterns, spiraling around the base of the pulsating plants, occasionally pausing to nibble at the lichen or to probe the luminescent sacs with what looked like delicate, prehensile antennae. Niko activated his detailed scanner, focusing on one of the creatures that had ventured a little too close to his boot.

"Fascinating," he breathed, as the data flooded his HUD. "Small, arthropod-like organisms. Highly specialized. They appear to be feeding on the lichen, and also interacting with the pulsating flora. The energy readings from their interaction are... unusual. It's not just consumption; they seem to be facilitating a transfer of energy or nutrients between the lichen and the plants." He paused, observing the intricate ballet of their movements. "It's a symbiotic relationship, but more complex than typical. They're acting as intermediaries, perhaps even cultivators."

Kira let out a soft chuff, a sound of acknowledgment, not alarm. She lowered her head, sniffing gently in the direction of one of the pulsating sacs. The small creatures didn't scatter; instead, they seemed to partition around her, maintaining a respectful distance, their tiny antennae twitching with what Niko interpreted as a cautious curiosity rather than fear. This was not the panicked flight of prey; it was a nuanced interaction, a recognition of a larger, potentially dominant life form that posed no immediate threat.

"They're not afraid," Niko noted aloud, a sense of wonder growing within him. "They're aware of us, but they're not exhibiting typical fear responses. They're integrating our presence into their environment without disruption. It speaks to a long evolutionary history of co-existence, or at least, a profound lack of predatory interaction with larger beings." He carefully extended a gloved finger towards the pulsating sac, not to touch, but to observe. As he drew closer, the sac's luminescence intensified, and the small creatures around it seemed to momentarily freeze, their antennae pointed towards his hand.

Anya's voice crackled through his comms. "Niko, I'm detecting a subtle increase in the planet's ambient resonance originating from your position. It's not significant enough to be a cause for alarm, but it's directly correlated with the increased activity of these micro-fauna and the pulsating flora. It's as if the entire localized ecosystem is responding to the interaction."

"It's like a biological orchestra," Niko mused. "The fungi are the bass notes, the resonance of the planet is the underlying rhythm, and these little creatures and the pulsating flora are the intricate melody, weaving in and out of the larger composition." He watched as one of the creatures delicately extended a pair of fine, brush-like appendages to the surface of the pulsating sac, and a faint shimmer of energy seemed to pass between them. "They're actively managing the sac's luminescence and nutrient intake. It's a form of bio-engineering on a micro-scale, facilitated by these seemingly simple organisms."

He recalled the directive: observation, not interaction. He was already pushing the boundaries, his mere presence influencing the behavior of these native life forms. He retracted his hand slowly, allowing the small creatures to resume their intricate dance. Kira, sensing his intent, nudged him gently, then began to lead him away from the cluster, her steps guided by her finely tuned senses. She wasn't just following scent trails; she was navigating by an instinctual understanding of the environment, a connection to Veridia's subtle energies that he could only glimpse through his technology.

As they moved deeper into the fungal forest, the character of the undergrowth began to change again. The glowing moss became less prevalent, giving way to patches of a deeper, almost black, spongy material that seemed to absorb light. Interspersed within this dark substrate were clusters of what appeared to be crystalline growths, sharp and angular, catching the ambient light and scattering it into brilliant, fleeting prismatic displays. Kira's attention was drawn to these crystalline formations. She approached one cluster cautiously, her nose twitching.

"These crystals," Niko said, activating his scanner. "They're not mineral in origin. They're biological secretions. Extremely complex molecular structures, storing and releasing energy. Anya, can you analyze the spectral signature of these crystals? I'm detecting residual energy signatures that don't align with the ambient planetary field."

Anya's response was immediate. "Analyzing, Niko. The crystalline structure is composed of intricate carbon lattices, laced with trace elements not previously identified. The energy signature is indeed anomalous. It appears to be a form of stored bio-electricity, released in short, high-intensity bursts. The patterns are... almost like a coded message."

Kira let out a soft whine, her ears swiveling towards a patch of the dark, spongy material near the base of the crystals. Niko knelt down, his scanner focusing on the spot. He detected faint, almost imperceptible vibrations emanating from within the spongy mass. "There's something moving under here too," he reported. "Even smaller than the insectoids, and incredibly well hidden. They seem to be symbiotic with the crystals, or perhaps utilizing them for some purpose."

He watched as Kira gently nudged the spongy material aside with her nose. Beneath it, nestled in a shallow depression, was a cluster of tiny, luminescent orbs, no bigger than marbles. They pulsed with a soft, internal light, a spectrum of blues and greens that shifted and swirled. And from these orbs, a delicate, almost melodic series of chimes could be heard, a sound so faint that without Kira's keen senses, it would have been entirely lost. The chimes seemed to resonate with the energy bursts from the crystals.

"The orbs," Niko murmured, awestruck. "They're emitting sonic frequencies that are directly interacting with the crystalline energy release. And the crystals, in turn, seem to be influencing the orbs' luminescence and frequency output. It's another layer of interconnectedness, a complex interplay of light, sound, and energy." He observed the small, almost invisible tendrils connecting the orbs to the spongy material. "These orbs are drawing sustenance from this substrata, and in return, they're... harmonizing the environment. They're like living tuning forks, orchestrating the release of energy from the crystals."

"The sonic frequencies are incredibly complex, Niko," Anya confirmed, her voice filled with academic fascination. "They're not random. There are discernible patterns, repeating sequences. And they are interacting with the stored energy in the crystals in a way that suggests... information transfer. It's highly probable these organisms are communicating, and using the crystals as a form of data storage or amplification."

The concept was staggering. Veridia wasn't just a planet teeming with life; it was a world where life itself had evolved sophisticated methods of communication and energy management, far beyond anything humans had conceived. The giant fungi, the glowing mosses, the pulsating flora, the micro-fauna, the crystalline energy conduits, and now these sonic orbs – each component was a vital part of a planetary-scale biological network, a symphony of life playing out in the violet light.

Kira, having seemingly absorbed all the relevant information from the vicinity, nudged Niko once more, her gaze directed further into the dense, dimly lit forest. The rumble in her chest had subsided, replaced by a quiet confidence. She was not just a scanner; she was a participant in this intricate web of life, her own bio-rhythms harmonizing with Veridia's gentle thrum.

"She wants to keep moving," Niko observed, standing up. "And I have a feeling there's more to discover. This is just the fringe, isn't it? The edge of something far more profound." He scanned the path ahead, the towering fungal stalks creating a canopy that filtered the ambient light into an ethereal twilight. The air here felt thicker, richer with the complex aromas of alien life. There was a palpable sense of ancientness, of processes unfolding over eons, unseen and unheard by any but the native inhabitants of this world.

As they ventured deeper, the hum of Veridia seemed to intensify, a gentle pulse that resonated not just in the air and soil, but within Niko's very bones. It was a profound, almost spiritual experience, a connection to a living, breathing planet that transcended mere scientific observation. He felt the weight of his responsibility, the importance of their non-interference. To disturb this delicate balance, this ancient symphony, would be an act of unimaginable desecration. Veridia was a testament to the boundless creativity of life, a living library of biological marvels, and they were merely privileged to turn its pages, to listen to its whispers, and to learn from its verdant echoes. Kira, trotting ahead with an unhurried grace, was not just leading him to new discoveries; she was guiding him deeper into the heart of Veridia, into the very essence of its native soul.

Niko's fingers danced across the holographic interface projected from his wrist-mounted comm unit, his movements precise and economical.

The glowing lines and nodes coalesced, forming a three-dimensional representation of the immediate surroundings, not as a visual likeness, but as a symphony of energy. This was the nascent Resonance Map, a conceptual tool forged from a blend of cutting-edge atmospheric analysis and Kira's remarkably attuned bio-feedback. He wasn't just mapping terrain; he was charting the subtle, pervasive vibratory field that characterized Veridia, a field that resonated with the very life force of the planet.

"Anya, can you feed Kira's proximate sensory data into the energy flux equation?" Niko requested, his voice a low murmur, lost in the ambient hum of the Veridian forest. He watched as the map flickered, new layers of information overlaying the initial energy readings. Kira, sensing his focus, had settled beside him, her head cocked, her large, intelligent eyes tracking the subtle shifts in the holographic projection as if she, too, understood its significance. A soft, rhythmic purr emanated from her chest, a steady frequency that Niko had learned to interpret as a state of deep communion with Veridia's ambient energies. This resonance was more than just a passive byproduct of life; it was an active, dynamic force, and Kira's ability to sense and interpret it was invaluable.

"Processing, Niko," Anya's synthesized voice replied. "Integrating Kira's neural impulses related to atmospheric pressure gradients, localized humidity variations, and subtle electromagnetic field fluctuations. Her sensitivity to these micro-changes is registering a significantly higher resolution than my passive sensors can achieve independently. The data is highly complex, but I am establishing correlative markers."

The map began to shift, swirling patterns of violet and emerald green depicting areas of high energy concentration, while cooler blues and silvers marked zones of relative stillness. These weren't static landmarks; they were currents and eddies in Veridia's energetic flow. Niko pointed to a particularly vibrant emerald cluster on the map, a locus of intense activity. "This area, where Kira detected the micro-fauna and the crystalline energy conduits, shows a distinct spike in the planetary resonance. It's as if the interaction itself is amplifying the ambient field. Anya, can you quantify the delta?"

"Calculating," Anya responded after a brief pause. "The resonance intensity in sector Gamma-7, specifically around the observed symbiotic cluster, is approximately 18.7% higher than the average ambient reading for this zone. Furthermore, the spectral analysis indicates a highly organized, non-chaotic emission pattern, consistent with a structured energy exchange rather than random dissipation."

Niko nodded, a thoughtful frown creasing his brow. "The small, chittering organisms and the sonic orbs were essentially acting as conductors, weren't they? They were channeling and perhaps even modulating the energy released by the crystals. This resonance map isn't just showing us where the energy is; it's showing us *how* it's being used, *how* it's flowing between different life forms." He traced a shimmering blue line that snaked away from the emerald cluster. "This suggests a pathway, a conduit for this modulated energy, perhaps feeding into the larger fungal network. Kira, are you sensing anything along this line?"

Kira rose fluidly, her body fluid and instinctive. She nudged Niko's hand with her nose, then turned and began to trot purposefully in the direction indicated by the blue line on the map. Her movements were no longer exploratory but directed, guided by an internal compass attuned to the planetary resonance. Niko followed, the holographic map now a dynamic extension of his own perception, seamlessly integrated with Kira's primal awareness. This was the fusion they had envisioned: technology augmenting, not replacing, the profound biological intelligence that Veridia possessed.

"Her purr frequency is stabilizing," Anya reported, her voice reflecting a growing intrigue. "This indicates a state of focused tracking, a harmonious alignment with the observed energy flow. The map is showing a gradual decrease in resonance intensity along her current trajectory, but the pattern remains coherent. It suggests a directional flow, a consistent pathway rather than an amorphous diffusion."

The Resonance Map was more than just a scientific instrument; it was a testament to the interconnectedness of all life on Veridia. The very act of charting these energy flows was revealing the planet's intricate biological infrastructure, a vast, living network that facilitated communication, nutrient exchange, and energy distribution. It was a symphony of life, and they were beginning to decipher its score.

"The crystals we observed earlier," Niko mused, his eyes fixed on the map, "they weren't just storing energy; they were acting as distributed nodes in a planetary data network. And the sonic orbs, the 'tuning forks,' were the transceivers, modulating that data into frequencies that could be understood and utilized by other organisms." He tapped a point on the map where the blue line seemed to dissipate into a wider network of fainter lines. "This looks like a nexus, a central hub where multiple energy conduits converge. Anya, can you correlate this convergence with any known atmospheric or geological formations?"

"Cross-referencing with orbital scans and subsurface geological surveys," Anya replied. "The nexus point you've indicated aligns with a significant concentration of geothermic activity and a unique atmospheric layering phenomenon. There are localized pockets of unusual gas compositions and highly stable atmospheric pressures. My sensors are also detecting a subtle, cyclical fluctuation in the local gravitational field at that nexus, consistent with the presence of a concentrated bio-energetic field."

Niko's breath hitched. A concentrated bio-energetic field. This was precisely what they were here to understand. The gateway, the very reason for their mission, was believed to be a manifestation of such a field, a point where Veridia's potent life force intersected with dimensional energies. The Resonance Map was becoming a crucial tool, not just for understanding the local ecosystem, but for identifying potential gateways, for predicting shifts in Veridia's energetic equilibrium that could impact their mission and the stability of the gateway itself.

Kira stopped abruptly, her ears perked forward. A low, resonant hum vibrated in her chest, deeper than before, a sound that seemed to echo the very pulse of the planet. The Resonance Map flared, a brilliant burst of emerald light blooming at the nexus point. "She's found it," Niko breathed, awe coloring his voice. "The nexus. And it's active."

The hum intensified, a palpable wave of energy washing over them. It wasn't a physical force, but a sensation, a deep thrum that resonated within their very beings. Niko felt a strange sense of calm, of belonging, as if the planet itself was welcoming them, acknowledging their presence not as intruders, but as observers who respected its intricate workings. The holographic map pulsed in sync with the planetary hum, its lines and nodes glowing with an almost sentient vibrancy.

"The resonance is increasing exponentially," Anya announced, her synthesized voice tinged with an undeniable sense of wonder. "The energy signatures are no longer just localized; they are expanding outwards, creating a localized distortion in the dimensional field. The readings are unprecedented, Niko. This is unlike anything we've encountered."

Niko looked at Kira. Her fur was rippling with a subtle luminescence, her eyes wide and luminous, reflecting the swirling energies of the map and the forest around them. She was not merely sensing the resonance; she was a part of it, an embodiment of Veridia's harmonious existence. This was the kind of deep, intuitive understanding that his advanced sensors could only approximate. The Resonance Map, in conjunction with Kira's innate abilities, was revealing the true nature of Veridia: a living, breathing entity, its lifeblood flowing through energy conduits, its consciousness expressed through resonant frequencies.

"This nexus," Niko said, his voice barely a whisper, "it's more than just a concentration of energy. It's a focal point, a nexus of Veridia's consciousness. The gateway... it must be connected to this. Or perhaps, this *is* the gateway, in its most primal, natural form." He continued to trace the pathways on the map, the complex interplay of light, sound, and energy unfolding before him. Each organism, from the smallest micro-fauna to the colossal fungal forests, played a role in maintaining this planetary symphony.

He zoomed in on the nexus on the map, the intricate latticework of energy lines converging there. "Anya, can you isolate the dominant frequency patterns at the nexus? I want to see if there's a harmonic convergence that suggests communication, or even intent."

"Analyzing dominant harmonic frequencies," Anya replied. The map flickered, and distinct melodic patterns began to emerge within the emerald bloom, like a complex chord being struck. "The patterns are intricate, cyclical, and highly structured. There are recurring motifs that suggest information encoding. It's not just energy transfer, Niko. It's a deliberate exchange of information, a planetary dialogue."

Niko felt a profound sense of humility. They had come to Veridia to study its unique biology, its potential for terraforming, but they were discovering something far more profound: a world that had evolved its own form of intelligence, expressed not through spoken language or advanced technology, but through the very fabric of its energetic being. The Resonance Map was evolving beyond a simple charting tool; it was becoming a Rosetta Stone, helping them to decipher the language of Veridia.

He looked at Kira again, her presence a grounding force amidst the overwhelming sensory input. She nudged him gently, a silent affirmation. She understood. She was connected. Her intuition, honed by millennia of evolution on this vibrant world, was a key component in unlocking its secrets. This was not just a scientific endeavor; it was a dialogue, a bridge between two vastly different forms of intelligence, facilitated by technology and guided by the ancient wisdom of the natural world.

"We need to document this nexus," Niko stated, his voice firm with purpose. "Its stability, its energetic output, the nature of the information being exchanged. This is critical for understanding the gateway and for ensuring we don't inadvertently disrupt this delicate balance. The Resonance Map is our primary tool for this. We need to create a baseline, a detailed record of its current state."

He spent the next several hours meticulously refining the Resonance Map, Anya feeding him constant streams of data, Kira providing real-time confirmations through subtle shifts in her posture and purr. They charted the ebb and flow of energy, the precise frequencies of the sonic orbs, the energy signatures of the crystalline conduits, and the intricate web of connections that pulsed with life. The map expanded, becoming a living document, a testament to the intricate dance of energy and information that defined Veridia. It was a map not of land, but of life itself, a testament to a world that sang with the power of its own existence. The implications were staggering: Veridia was not just a planet with advanced ecosystems, but a planet with an emergent, distributed consciousness, expressed through an intricate, interconnected web of resonant energies. This map, born from the fusion of cutting-edge science and the innate wisdom of an alien creature, was their key to understanding not just this world, but the very nature of life itself.

The air grew thick, heavy with the scent of damp earth and decaying organic matter, as Niko, Anya, and Kira pressed deeper into the heart of the fungal forest. Colossal fungi, their caps spanning dozens of meters, formed a living canopy, filtering the diffused sunlight into an ethereal twilight. Bioluminescent mosses clung to their colossal stalks, casting shifting patterns of emerald and sapphire across the spongy, yielding ground. The symphony of Veridia's ambient hum, so recently a source of wonder, now seemed to carry an undertone of hushed expectation, a latent tension that settled upon the small expedition.

Kira, who had been trotting ahead with her usual fluid grace, suddenly froze. Her ears, usually twitching with curiosity, swiveled forward, catching subtle sounds beyond the range of human perception. Her body tensed, a low, guttural growl vibrating deep within her chest, a sound that was primal and unnerving, a stark contrast to the comforting purr she had exhibited earlier. Niko, whose senses had become keenly attuned to Kira's every nuance, immediately brought the team to a halt. He instinctively raised a hand, signaling for Anya to cease her environmental scans, her usual torrent of data momentarily silenced.

"What is it, Kira?" Niko murmured, his voice barely disturbing the heavy silence. He watched her, his eyes scanning the dense undergrowth, the gnarled roots, the towering fungal stalks. Kira's large, intelligent eyes, usually reflecting a serene curiosity, now held a sharp, focused intensity. She wasn't looking at anything obvious – no hulking beast, no immediate physical threat. Her gaze was fixed on a particular cluster of iridescent, pulsating pods that were nestled amongst a tangle of root systems, about twenty meters ahead. These were unlike the passive, crystalline structures they had encountered earlier. These pods seemed to possess an almost organic vitality, their surfaces rippling with a soft, internal light that pulsed in a slow, rhythmic beat.

The growl deepened, a rumbling warning that resonated not just in the air, but in Niko's very bones. It wasn't a sound of aggression, but of profound caution, a primal alarm bell ringing through the alien landscape. This was Kira's expertise: a finely tuned sensitivity to subtle shifts, to imbalances in the natural order that his advanced sensors might overlook. Her intuition, forged over eons of existence on this vibrant, often unpredictable world, was their most reliable early warning system.

"Her bio-readings are fluctuating," Anya reported, her synthesized voice devoid of emotion, yet carrying an undeniable weight of concern. "Elevated heart rate, heightened neural activity consistent with heightened alert states. She's detecting something, Niko, something that registers as a significant threat. Her focus is locked on those pulsating pods."

Niko's mind raced, cross-referencing Kira's reaction with the data he had gathered on Veridian life forms. He had studied reports of territorial creatures, of bio-luminescent flora that could emit disorienting sonic pulses or release soporific spores. But Kira's growl felt different. It was a more fundamental unease, a sense of deep-seated wrongness. It wasn't just a warning of a predatory animal; it hinted at something more profound, something that stirred the very energetic currents of the planet that Kira was so attuned to.

He activated his personal scanner, directing its beam towards the cluster of pods. The readings flickered, then stabilized, presenting a confusing array of data. The pods were emitting a faint, fluctuating electromagnetic field, not unlike the energy conduits they had previously mapped, but with an erratic, unpredictable pattern. There was also a low-level sonic emission, a sub-audible frequency that was causing a slight distortion in Anya's sensory input. And most alarmingly, the ambient resonance map, which Niko had projected onto his wrist-mounted comm unit, showed a localized pocket of extreme instability emanating from the pods. The vibrant, harmonious flow of Veridia's energetic signature was fractured around that specific area, like a ripple distorting a perfectly still pond.

"The energy field is highly unstable," Niko reported, his voice low and steady, betraying none of the tension coiling in his gut. "And the resonance... it's not just fluctuating; it's chaotic. It's like a knot in the planet's energetic fabric. Kira, what do you sense beyond the instability?" He addressed her directly, knowing that even without verbal communication, she would understand his intent.

Kira shifted her weight, her paws sinking slightly into the mossy ground. She let out a soft chuff, a sound of frustration mixed with a lingering wariness. She lowered her head, her nose twitching, sampling the air. Then, she let out another low growl, this time accompanied by a slight, almost imperceptible tremor that ran through her body. Her gaze flickered from the pods to the surrounding fungal stalks, then back again. She was sensing something more complex than mere instability; she was sensing a *presence*.

"She's not just detecting energy," Anya observed, her voice picking up a faint hint of awe. "Her neural patterns indicate she's processing a complex sensory input that correlates with an active, biological entity. But my sensors are not picking up any definitive life signs in the immediate vicinity beyond the fungal flora and the micro-fauna we've already cataloged. The energy signature from the pods is anomalous; it's not consistent with any known Veridian organism in our database. It's... *active.*"

Niko understood. Kira's senses were picking up on something that transcended the physical. She was detecting the subtle echoes of intent, the faint psychic residue that even the most alien of life forms might leave behind. The pods, he theorized, were not just simple energy storage devices or conduits. They were something else entirely. Perhaps they were part of a larger organism, a symbiotic network that was currently dormant or in a defensive state. Or, more disturbingly, they could be a manifestation of something far more alien, something that tapped into the very dimensional energies that had brought them to Veridia.

"The resonance distortion," Niko mused aloud, "it's not just random. It's following a pattern. A cyclical pattern. Almost as if the pods are... breathing energy." He zoomed in on the holographic projection, highlighting the chaotic flux. The emerald and violet hues, usually so vibrant and clear, were now muddy and swirling, interspersed with sharp, jagged lines of crimson that indicated extreme energetic discharge.

Kira nudged his hand with her nose, then turned and began to move slowly, deliberately, around the perimeter of the pulsating pods. Her growl softened, becoming a low rumble of intense focus. She wasn't retreating; she was investigating, assessing. She kept a respectful distance, her body coiled and ready, but her movements were guided by an undeniable curiosity, albeit a cautious one. She would periodically stop, sniff the air, and then flick her ears, as if processing new information.

"Her trajectory suggests she is attempting to map the extent of the anomaly," Anya noted. "She is not moving directly towards the source of the disruption, but rather circling it. This indicates a strategic approach, a desire to understand the boundaries of the potential threat before committing further. Her physiological responses remain elevated, but the acute panic signals have subsided, replaced by a sustained state of vigilance."

Niko watched Kira, a profound sense of gratitude washing over him. Her innate understanding of Veridia was invaluable. She was navigating this alien world with a grace and intelligence that no amount of technological advancement could replicate. He thought of the theoretical dangers they had been warned about, the unknown elements that made Veridia such a high-risk, high-reward mission. Kira was their living, breathing safeguard. Her warnings, her instincts, were the first line of defense against threats they could not even comprehend.

He recalled the initial briefings about the potential for pocket dimensions, for localized spacetime anomalies that could manifest as volatile energy fields. Could these pods be a nexus point for such phenomena? Were they attracting or perhaps even generating these distortions? The idea was both terrifying and exhilarating. If these pods were linked to dimensional instability, they could be crucial to understanding the gateway itself.

"Anya, can you isolate the specific harmonic frequencies being emitted by the pods?" Niko asked, his gaze still fixed on Kira. "I want to know if there's any correlation between these frequencies and the resonance distortions. Is it possible these pods are actively manipulating the ambient energy field, or are they merely reacting to an external influence?"

"Analyzing harmonic frequencies," Anya replied. A moment of silence passed, filled only by the distant chirping of unseen Veridian life and the low rumble from Kira's chest. "The primary emission is a complex, multi-layered waveform. It exhibits characteristics of both bio-electrical signals and a modulated quantum fluctuation. The patterns are cyclical, with a distinct period of approximately 4.7 seconds. During the peak of each cycle, there is a measurable increase in localized gravitational distortion and a spike in the chaotic resonance readings."

Niko frowned. Gravitational distortion was a significant indicator. It suggested forces at play that were beyond simple electromagnetic manipulation. This was deep, fundamental physics, possibly linked to the very fabric of spacetime. And the fact that it was tied to these seemingly organic pods was mind-boggling. It implied a level of biological sophistication that defied their current understanding of life.

Kira suddenly stopped, her head cocked, her gaze fixed on a point just beyond the cluster of pods. A new sound emerged from her, a soft, almost mournful whine. She took a tentative step forward, then hesitated. Her tail, which had been held low, now twitched with a subtle, almost nervous energy.

"What is it, Kira?" Niko whispered, his own sense of unease intensifying. He adjusted his scanner, trying to pinpoint what she was reacting to. The energy readings remained focused on the pods, but Kira's attention was elsewhere. She was sensing something in the space *between* the pods, something invisible to his instruments.

"She's picking up a residual trace," Anya stated, her voice a whisper. "A faint echo of bio-signature. It's degrading rapidly, but it's distinct from the pod's emissions. It suggests that something, or someone, was recently in close proximity to these pods. Something that has since departed, or... been absorbed."

The implication hung heavy in the air. Kira's warning growl, her focus on the unstable pods, her sense of a presence – it was all starting to coalesce into a disturbing picture. The pods weren't just a source of energetic chaos; they were a focal point, a trap, or perhaps a gateway for something far more dangerous. And whatever had been here recently had either been consumed by this phenomenon or had intentionally interacted with it, leaving behind a ghostly imprint that only Kira could detect.

Niko knelt beside Kira, placing a calming hand on her warm flank. "Easy, girl," he murmured, his fingers tracing the subtle vibrations coursing through her fur. He looked at the pulsating pods, their iridescent surfaces now seeming less alluring and more menacing. They were beautiful, yes, but their beauty was the allure of a venus flytrap, a deadly deception. Kira's warning was not just about physical danger; it was a deep, guttural plea to avoid something that was fundamentally inimical to life as they understood it, something that disturbed the very essence of Veridia's harmonious existence.

"We need to understand what these pods are," Niko said, his voice firm, a decision made. "But we also need to respect Kira's warning. We proceed with extreme caution. Anya, maintain a constant scan of the surrounding area, focusing on any subtle shifts in atmospheric pressure or localized energy fields that might indicate a larger, unseen entity. Kira, you lead, but stay alert. If you sense any immediate danger, we retreat."

Kira met his gaze, her eyes holding a depth of understanding that transcended language. She gave a soft, affirmative huff, and then, with a renewed sense of purpose, began to move forward, her body a sleek silhouette against the eerie glow of the fungal forest. The low growl had subsided, replaced by a steady, determined gait, but the underlying tension remained, a silent testament to the unseen forces that governed this enigmatic world. They were treading on the precipice of the unknown, guided by the primal wisdom of a creature that was more attuned to Veridia's heartbeat than any human technology could ever hope to be. The warning had been issued, a stark reminder that Veridia, for all its breathtaking beauty, held secrets that could unravel their very existence. And as they advanced, the pulsating pods seemed to watch them, their internal light flickering with an ominous rhythm, as if acknowledging the trespassers, and the powerful instinct that had momentarily drawn them into their unsettling embrace.

The air, which had been thick with the scent of damp earth and decaying organic matter, now carried a new, subtler note – a faintly acrid aroma, like ozone after a distant lightning strike, mingling with a damp, musky scent that was undeniably animal. Kira, who had been moving with a slow, deliberate grace, her body a coiled spring of watchful energy, paused once more. Her ears, swiveling with an almost imperceptible motion, were no longer focused on the pulsating pods themselves, but on the space *between* them and the dense, moss-laden roots that snaked across the ground. She let out a soft, almost inaudible whine, a sound that spoke not of fear, but of profound awareness, a deep recognition of something that existed just beyond the veil of their immediate perception.

Niko followed her gaze, his eyes scanning the immediate vicinity of the pods. The bioluminescent flora cast an ethereal glow, painting the gnarled fungal stalks and spongy ground in shifting patterns of emerald and sapphire. His advanced sensors, calibrated to detect even the faintest energy fluctuations, still registered the chaotic resonance emanating from the pulsating pods, but they offered no insight into what had captured Kira's attention. It was a blind spot, a void in their technological understanding that Kira, with her innate Veridian senses, was beginning to fill.

Anya's synthesized voice, usually a steady stream of data, was now tinged with a hint of surprise. "Niko, Kira's neural activity is showing a significant shift. She's not reacting to the energy signature of the pods anymore. Her focus has shifted to a localized area approximately three meters ahead of her current position. There's a faint bio-signature detected... it's intermittent, almost like a ghost signal. My atmospheric sensors are detecting a minute thermal anomaly, and a subtle displacement of airborne particulates that suggests movement."

Niko crouched, mirroring Kira's posture. He felt the subtle vibrations of her muscles tensing beneath his hand, a silent communication that conveyed a mixture of caution and profound curiosity. Kira was not sensing aggression, not yet. She was sensing a presence, an awareness that was intricately woven into the very fabric of this environment. He instructed Anya to widen her scan parameters, to search for any unusual patterns in the light refraction, any minute distortions in the fungal structures that might indicate concealment.

Slowly, deliberately, Kira began to move. She didn't advance directly towards the anomaly but skirted its periphery, her movements fluid and unhurried. She was not hunting, but observing, mapping the boundaries of this unseen entity. As she moved, the very air around a particular section of gnarled roots and thick moss seemed to shimmer. It wasn't a trick of the light; it was a visual manifestation of something actively camouflaging itself. The moss seemed to deepen its hue, the shadows beneath the roots coalesced, and the very texture of the ground appeared to subtly shift, blending seamlessly with its surroundings.

Then, a section of the gnarled roots near the ground seemed to unfurl. It wasn't a violent movement, but a deliberate, unfolding, like a petal opening to the sun. From this newly revealed opening emerged a creature, roughly the size of a large dog, but with a form that defied easy categorization. Its body was elongated and serpentine, covered in a mosaic of scales that, at first glance, appeared to be the same earthy tones as the surrounding soil and roots. However, as the creature moved into the faint bioluminescent glow, the scales began to pulse with a soft, internal light, shifting through shades of emerald, sapphire, and amethyst, mirroring the dominant colors of the fungal forest. Its head was wedge-shaped, with large, dark eyes that seemed to absorb the light rather than reflect it. A pair of slender, prehensile limbs, tipped with sharp, dark claws, were held close to its body, not in aggression, but in a posture of wary readiness.

The creature's bioluminescent scales pulsed rhythmically, a gentle ebb and flow of light that seemed to synchronize with the faint, rhythmic beat of the nearby pods. It was a living embodiment of its environment, a master of camouflage and subtle illumination. Niko recognized it, vaguely, from the initial ecological surveys of Veridia's less-explored regions. It was a *Chroma-serpentis*, a species known for its incredible adaptive camouflage and its symbiotic relationship with certain bioluminescent flora, though never had any been documented in such close proximity to phenomena as anomalous as the pulsating pods.

The Chroma-serpentis did not charge or hiss. Instead, it adopted a low, defensive stance, its head raised, its dark eyes fixed on the intruders. A soft, guttural hiss emanated from its throat, a sound that was more of a warning than a threat. Its scales pulsed with a slightly brighter intensity, a visual declaration of its territorial claim.

Kira, seeing the creature, responded not with aggression, but with a soft chuff, a sound of acknowledgment. She lowered herself further, her body language radiating calm and respect. She understood that this creature was not a monstrous predator, but a guardian, an integral part of the intricate tapestry of Veridia's ecosystem. Her own luminous markings, usually a soft azure, began to shimmer with a subtle, reassuring glow, a visual dialogue of non-aggression.

Niko, observing the interaction, felt a profound sense of awe settle over him. He raised his hands slowly, palms open, a universal gesture of peace. "Easy, girl," he murmured, his voice low and steady, addressing both Kira and, he hoped, the Chroma-serpentis. "We mean no harm." He turned to Anya. "Any readings on its intent? Is it exhibiting any signs of predatory behavior?"

"Negative, Niko," Anya reported. "Its bio-signature indicates a heightened state of alertness, consistent with territorial defense. However, there are no elevated adrenaline levels or muscle tension indicative of imminent attack. Its primary focus appears to be on deterring intrusion, not on engaging in combat. The pulsing of its scales is synchronized with the ambient energy field, suggesting a deep connection to the surrounding environment, and specifically, to the pods."

Niko's gaze was drawn back to the pulsating pods. The Chroma-serpentis, the guardian, was positioned directly between them and the team. He began to hypothesize, piecing together Kira's intuitive understanding with Anya's data and his own scientific knowledge. The pods were clearly not inert. Their energetic fluctuations, their interaction with the Chroma-serpentis, and the faint bio-signature detected nearby all pointed to a complex biological or perhaps even quasi-biological function.

"The pods," Niko mused aloud, "they're not just generating energy. They're regulating something. Something vital to this ecosystem. And this creature... it's a sentinel. It's not just guarding the pods from predators; it's guarding them from disturbance, from anything that might disrupt their function." He zoomed in on his wrist-mounted comm unit, projecting a holographic overlay of the energy readings from the pods. The chaotic patterns were still present, but now, when he overlaid the Chroma-serpentis's bio-rhythmic pulses, a correlation began to emerge. The creature's luminescence seemed to exert a subtle, stabilizing influence on the pods' energetic emissions.

"It's a feedback loop," Niko realized, a spark of excitement igniting within him. "The pods provide... something. Perhaps a localized energy source, or a nutrient-rich medium, and in return, the creature ensures their integrity. It's part of a larger reproductive or developmental cycle. The pods might be releasing gametes, or a generative energy, and the creature's presence, its very bio-energy, might be crucial for fertilization, or for guiding the nascent life forms towards dispersal."

The Chroma-serpentis shifted, its head tilting as if it could sense the shift in Niko's understanding. It took a slow, deliberate step away from the pods, its scales dimming slightly. It was not retreating out of fear, but rather making a calculated assessment. It seemed to recognize that the team, and particularly Kira, posed no immediate threat. Kira's calm, non-confrontational posture, her own subtle display of bioluminescence, had communicated a message of mutual respect.

"It's acknowledging Kira," Anya observed, her voice tinged with a rare note of wonder. "Her bio-signature is being interpreted as non-hostile, and by extension, the entire group is being assessed as such. The creature's territorial display is de-escalating. It's still vigilant, but the immediate defensive posture is subsiding."

The Chroma-serpentis moved a few more steps away from the pods, still keeping a watchful eye on the team, but its body language had softened. It began to weave its way back towards the dense root system from which it had emerged, its form gradually re-dissolving into the shadows and textures of the undergrowth. Its bioluminescent scales faded, blending seamlessly with the dappled light, until it was once again indistinguishable from its surroundings. The acrid, musky scent dissipated, leaving only the familiar aroma of damp earth and decaying organic matter.

As the creature disappeared, the intense, chaotic resonance from the pods seemed to mellow slightly. The jagged crimson lines on Niko's resonance map softened, replaced by a more muted, though still irregular, pattern of energetic flux. The local ecosystem had reasserted its delicate balance, the guardian having fulfilled its role.

Niko let out a slow breath, a mixture of relief and exhilaration coursing through him. He looked at Kira, who was now nudging his hand, her luminous markings glowing with a soft, contented light. Her tail gave a gentle wag, a clear indication that the perceived threat had passed.

"You did good, Kira," Niko murmured, scratching her behind the ears. "You understood. You bridged the gap."

Anya's voice broke the moment of quiet contemplation. "Niko, the ecological significance of this interaction is profound. The Chroma-serpentis's role as a guardian of these reproductive pods suggests a complex interdependence. It confirms that even seemingly passive elements of Veridia's biosphere are actively managed and protected. This reinforces our mission parameters regarding non-interference. We observed, we learned, and we did not disrupt."

Niko nodded, his mind already racing with the implications. They had come seeking answers about the gateway, about Veridia's enigmatic nature, and they had stumbled upon a microcosm of its intricate, interconnected life. The pulsating pods, the Chroma-serpentis – they were not anomalies, but vital components of a living, breathing world. Their purpose, though alien, was clear: the perpetuation of life.

"It's a reminder," Niko said, his voice carrying a newfound respect for the alien world around them, "that every creature, no matter how seemingly insignificant, has a role to play. And sometimes, those roles are carried out by guardians we can barely perceive. The Chroma-serpentis, like Kira, is an extension of Veridia itself, an unseen guardian ensuring the cycle continues."

He stood, stretching his limbs. The brief encounter had been a powerful lesson. It reinforced their commitment to observing and understanding, rather than intervening. They were guests in this vibrant, unpredictable biosphere, and their presence, however well-intentioned, carried the potential for disruption. The encounter with the Chroma-serpentis had been a potent reminder of that responsibility.

"Let's move on," Niko said, his gaze sweeping over the now-peaceful scene. "We have a lot more to learn. Anya, continue monitoring the energy signatures of the pods. I want to understand their full cycle, and the Chroma-serpentis's role within it, even if we can't observe it directly."

Kira, sensing his intent, trotted ahead once more, her steps lighter now, her curiosity reignited. The fungal forest, with its hushed whispers and hidden guardians, continued to unfold before them, a testament to the resilience and ingenuity of life, a symphony of Verdant Echoes playing out in the twilight of an alien world. The unseen guardian had receded, its duty fulfilled, leaving the team with a deeper appreciation for the quiet, persistent forces that shaped this extraordinary planet. The lesson was clear: to truly understand Veridia, they had to look beyond the obvious, to listen to the silent warnings, and to respect the intricate dance of life that played out in every corner of this vibrant ecosystem.

CHAPTER THREE

THE SILENT SONG OF FLORA

Niko's fingers, accustomed to the delicate touch required for manipulating delicate alien flora, now traced the intricate patterns on his holographic display. The data streamed from the myriad sensors embedded in his suit, the probes scattered across the landscape, and Kira's own enhanced senses painted a picture of a world far more complex than their initial scans had suggested. His current focus was on the bioluminescent fungi, their ethereal glow a constant, guiding presence in the dim light of Veridia. But his research had led him deeper, far beneath the surface, to a realm of interconnectedness that hummed with a quiet vitality.

He had initially theorized that the fungi operated as individual colonies, perhaps communicating through chemical signals released into the substrate. That assumption, however, proved to be a gross oversimplification. What his instruments were now revealing was a vast, subterranean network, an intricate mycelial web that spanned kilometers, linking not just individual fungal fruiting bodies but also the roots of the towering, alien trees and the sprawling carpets of phosphorescent mosses. It was a biological superhighway, invisible to the naked eye, yet teeming with activity.

"Anya, cross-reference the nutrient flux readings with the bio-electrical impulse data from the moss beds," Niko instructed, his voice a low murmur, almost lost in the ambient hum of the forest. "I want to map the primary nutrient transfer routes. And overlay that with the fungal spore dispersal patterns. I suspect a direct correlation."

Anya's synthesized voice responded, devoid of emotion but rich with the precision of her analysis. "Processing, Niko. Initial correlation indicates a 78.4% overlap between identified nutrient pathways and the primary fungal hyphal networks. Bio-electrical signals from the mosses appear to be propagating along these same pathways, exhibiting a pulse frequency consistent with information transfer. Spore dispersal is indeed concentrated around major nexus points within the hyphal network."

Niko leaned closer to the display, his breath misting slightly on the cool surface. The implications were staggering. This wasn't just a passive sharing of resources; it was an active, dynamic system of exchange. The fungi, through their extensive mycelial networks, acted as conduits, drawing up vital minerals and water from the deeper soil layers, processing them, and then distributing them to the mosses and the vascular plants that depended on them. In return, the mosses, with their vast surface area and photosynthetic capabilities, provided sugars and other organic compounds, fueling the growth and maintenance of the fungal network. It was a perfectly balanced, self-sustaining system.

But the most profound discovery lay not just in the transfer of physical sustenance, but in the transmission of something far more subtle: information. The bio-electrical signals that Anya had detected were not random discharges; they were patterned, rhythmic, and appeared to carry specific data. Niko theorized that these signals were akin to a biological internet, a vast communication system that allowed the flora of Veridia to share information about their environment, their needs, and even potential threats.

He watched as a section of the fungal network on his display flared with a sudden burst of energy. Simultaneously, the mosses in a nearby area shifted their luminescence, a wave of emerald light rippling through the carpet. Kira, who had been sniffing at a particularly vibrant cluster of fungi, suddenly tilted her head, her large, intelligent eyes gazing into the distance as if listening to an unheard melody. She let out a soft, inquisitive whine, her ears swiveling.

"She feels it," Niko murmured, a sense of wonder washing over him. "She's sensing the network. The 'silent song,' as I've started calling it in my logs."

The 'silent song' was his own descriptive term for the pervasive, almost imperceptible energetic hum that resonated through the flora. It wasn't a sound in the conventional sense, but a complex interplay of bio-electrical signals, nutrient fluctuations, and subtle energetic exchanges that seemed to bind the entire plant ecosystem into a single, cohesive entity. Kira, with her Veridian heritage, seemed uniquely attuned to this subtle communication, her own bio-luminescent markings sometimes pulsing in sync with the shifting patterns on his display, a testament to her deep connection with the living world around her.

"The network appears to be facilitating a form of collective consciousness within the flora," Niko explained to Anya, though he knew she was already processing the data far more efficiently than he could articulate. "It's not individual plants acting in isolation; they are nodes in a larger system. They can share resources, warnings, perhaps even 'memories' of environmental conditions. Imagine a single tree detecting a blight; it could potentially signal its neighbors, and even the fungi supporting them, initiating a preemptive defense or resource reallocation."

The pack's advanced scanners, designed to penetrate dense foliage and analyze complex bio-signatures, were proving invaluable. They mapped the intricate web of hyphae, the pulsing bio-electrical currents, the flow of nutrients like an underground circulatory system. It was a level of ecological integration that defied conventional biological understanding, suggesting a form of hyper-evolutionary cooperation that had taken root on Veridia over millennia.

"The scale of this network is unprecedented, Niko," Anya reported. "Our current projections indicate that the primary subterranean network extends across at least 80% of the continental landmass. Smaller, localized networks connect to it, forming a truly planet-wide biological infrastructure."

Niko allowed himself a small smile. It was breathtaking. He had always been fascinated by the hidden lives of plants, the quiet resilience and intricate adaptations they displayed. But Veridia had taken that fascination to an entirely new level. Here, the plants weren't just living; they were communicating, collaborating, and forming a unified consciousness that governed the very pulse of the planet.

He brought up another data stream, this one focusing on the atmospheric composition and the subtle energy fields. He noticed that certain areas within the fungal network exhibited higher concentrations of specific trace gases and a more pronounced energetic resonance. These areas often coincided with dense clusters of the bioluminescent fungi and the thickest moss carpets.

"Anya, focus on those high-resonance zones," Niko commanded. "Are they acting as information hubs? Data processing centers, perhaps? Or are they energy accumulators, reservoirs for the network?"

"Analysis in progress," Anya replied. "The higher resonance appears to be linked to a more rapid and complex exchange of bio-electrical signals. It suggests that these zones function as central processing nodes, coordinating communication and resource allocation across wider regions of the network. There is also a minor, but consistent, emission of low-frequency electromagnetic waves originating from these hubs. The function of these emissions is currently unknown, but they appear to be integral to the network's operational stability."

Niko nodded, his mind racing with possibilities. These 'hubs' could be the nexus points of the Veridian flora's collective consciousness. They might be where decisions were made, where the 'silent song' was composed and broadcasted. He imagined the ancient trees, their roots intertwined with the fungal network, sharing their millennia of wisdom, their stored experiences of drought, fire, and rebirth. The mosses, constantly bathed in the ambient light, absorbing and processing its energy, could be the network's primary sensory organs, relaying information about light intensity, atmospheric changes, and the presence of external stimuli.

He looked at Kira, who was now resting beside him, her breathing slow and even. Her luminous markings glowed with a soft, steady azure, a stark contrast to the pulsing emerald and sapphire of the fungi around them. Yet, he felt an undeniable connection between them, a shared understanding that transcended words. Kira was not just a companion; she was a bridge, an interpreter of Veridia's subtle languages.

"It's not just about survival, is it?" Niko mused aloud, his gaze sweeping over the alien landscape. "It's about existence. About a shared experience of life. They are all connected, a vast, living tapestry, woven from roots, hyphae, and bio-electrical impulses. Each part contributes to the whole, and the whole sustains each part."

He thought about the Chroma-serpentis they had encountered earlier, the creature that had guarded the pulsating pods. Its symbiotic relationship with the flora, its ability to synchronize its own bioluminescence with the surrounding environment, was further evidence of this profound interconnectedness. It was not an outlier, but a perfectly integrated component of Veridia's complex ecosystem, a guardian acting in concert with the silent song of the plants.

"The entire biosphere operates as a single, interconnected organism," Niko concluded, his voice filled with awe. "The flora, the fauna – they are all part of this grand, symbiotic network. The fungi and mosses are the nervous system, the trees and other plants are the vital organs, and the animals, like the

Chroma-serpentis, are the immune system, the protectors, the facilitators. And we, with our technology, are merely observers, trying to decipher the ancient, silent symphony."

His research on Veridia was no longer just about cataloging species or analyzing atmospheric compositions. It had become a deep dive into the very nature of life itself, a philosophical exploration of consciousness and interconnectedness. The 'silent song' was not just a biological phenomenon; it was a testament to the power of cooperation, a whispered promise that even in the vastness of the cosmos, life found ways to connect, to share, and to thrive, not as isolated individuals, but as a unified, resonating whole. He knew that understanding this network was crucial to understanding Veridia's true nature, and perhaps, in doing so, they might even glean insights that could help their own struggling world. The quiet hum of the planet was, he realized, a song of hope, waiting to be heard.

The ethereal glow that permeated the Veridian landscape, initially dismissed as mere biological byproducts or passive atmospheric interactions, had revealed itself to be far more profound. Niko, hunched over his holographic interface, his fingers dancing across the projected controls, now understood that the bioluminescence of Veridia's flora was not an incidental feature but a deliberate, nuanced language. It was a silent song, sung in photons, an intricate symphony of light that conveyed an astonishing spectrum of information. He had spent weeks meticulously cataloging these luminous displays, his instruments capturing the subtle variations in hue, intensity, and rhythm that pulsed through the fungal networks, the moss beds, and even the bark of the towering arboreal giants.

"Anya," Niko murmured, his voice a hushed reverence, "isolate the sequences correlating with the nutrient upwellings near the Crimson Falls. I want to see if there's a discernible light pattern associated with high-phosphorus zones."

Anya's synthesized voice, a calm counterpoint to the visual cacophony of data, responded promptly. "Processing, Niko. Cross-referencing nutrient flux data with bio-luminescent spectral analysis in Sector Gamma-7.

Identified a recurring pattern of rapid sapphire pulses, interspersed with slow emerald oscillations, emanating from the primary fungal conduits in that region. The intensity of the sapphire pulses directly correlates with the concentration of available phosphorus."

Niko's eyes widened, a thrill of discovery coursing through him. Phosphorus. A vital nutrient, and here it was, being signaled by a specific sequence of light. It wasn't just a passive indicator; it was a broadcast. He imagined the subterranean network, a vast, silent nervous system, chattering about its resources, directing traffic, and optimizing distribution through these visual cues. The emerald oscillations, he theorized, might indicate a slower, more stable flow, perhaps signifying reserves or areas with less immediate demand.

His research had shifted from merely observing the bioluminescence to actively attempting to decipher its syntax. He had compiled libraries of light sequences, each painstakingly linked to specific environmental triggers: the subtle seismic tremors that preceded a subsurface water shift, the minute atmospheric pressure changes that heralded an approaching storm, the arrival of specific pollinator species, even the subtle chemical signatures left by grazing fauna.

"And the moss beds, Anya?" Niko pressed on, zooming in on a particularly dense region of phosphorescent growth. "Any correlation between the moss luminescence and the presence of the 'Glimmerwing' insectoids?"

"Affirmative, Niko. When Glimmerwing swarms are detected within a 50-meter radius, the moss beds exhibit a distinct synchronized pulsing of iridescent green light. The frequency of this pulsing increases with the density of the swarm. Furthermore, spectral analysis indicates a slight shift towards the yellow spectrum when the Glimmerwings are in close proximity, suggesting a reactive or perhaps a signal amplification mechanism within the moss itself."

Niko leaned back, a slow smile spreading across his face. Reactive. Signal amplification. The mosses weren't just passive beacons; they were active participants in this luminous dialogue. They amplified messages, perhaps even translated them, acting as intermediaries between the fungi, the trees, and the mobile fauna. The landscape was alive with conversation, a constant, vibrant exchange that had been unfolding for millennia, entirely unseen and unheard by those who didn't possess the means to perceive it.

Kira, who had been lounging nearby, her own subtle markings pulsing with a soft, contented azure, suddenly perked up. Her head tilted, her large, intelligent eyes fixed on a patch of fungi a few meters away. A low, inquisitive whine rumbled in her chest. Niko followed her gaze. The fungi, which had been emitting a steady, gentle blue, suddenly flared with an intense, rapid series of violet bursts, unlike anything he had logged before.

"What is it, girl?" Niko whispered, reaching out to gently stroke her sleek, dark fur. He brought up his wrist-mounted scanner, its sensors whirring as they focused on the illuminated patch. "Anya, analysis of Kira's interest zone. What are we seeing?"

"Bio-luminescent signature is anomalous, Niko," Anya replied, her synthesized tone gaining a fractional hint of surprise. "The violet emission is of an unprecedented spectral purity and intensity. Furthermore, it is accompanied by a localized increase in ambient bio-electrical field strength. Preliminary readings suggest a novel chemical compound being released, or perhaps a rapid phase transition within existing compounds. The pattern of the violet bursts is highly complex, exhibiting fractal properties. It is not consistent with any previously cataloged communication sequence."

Niko felt a prickle of apprehension mingled with his excitement. This was new. Something outside their established understanding of Veridia's luminous lexicon. He activated his suit's environmental analyzer, his breath held tight. Kira, sensing his tension, pressed closer, her body a warm, reassuring weight against his leg.

"Atmospheric analysis complete," Anya announced. "No airborne toxins detected. No significant atmospheric pressure or composition changes. The anomaly appears to be entirely contained within the fungal substrate and its immediate emanations."

The violet light continued to pulse, a frantic heartbeat in the dim undergrowth. Niko's mind raced. Was it a warning? A distress signal? Or something else entirely, a communication so complex it bordered on abstract expression? He remembered the Chroma-serpentis, the guardian creature they had encountered near the pulsating pods. Its ability to mimic and synchronize with the bioluminescent flora had been uncanny. Was this a similar, perhaps more primitive, form of interaction?

"Can you isolate the frequency of those fractal patterns, Anya?" Niko asked, his gaze locked on the pulsing light. "Try to map them against known communication protocols, even our own encrypted frequencies, for any kind of structural resonance."

"Attempting to isolate and analyze fractal patterns. This is computationally intensive, Niko. The complexity is... significant. Initial analysis suggests a non-linear informational structure. It is not a simple code, but rather a dynamic, evolving data stream. If I were to draw an analogy, it would be less like a binary signal and more akin to a highly complex musical composition, where each note and its timing carries profound meaning."

Niko nodded, the analogy resonating deeply. Music. He had often thought of Veridia's interconnectedness as a symphony, a grand, silent song. But this... this was different. This was a solo, a sudden, urgent improvisation, or perhaps a revelation. He watched as the violet pulses began to ebb, softening into a gentle, pulsating amethyst. Kira, sensing the shift, let out a soft sigh and relaxed against him.

"The intensity is decreasing, Niko," Anya reported. "The spectral signature is stabilizing. The fractal complexity is reducing, becoming more linear. It appears to be transitioning back to a recognizable, albeit still unfamiliar, pattern of slow amethyst pulses."

Niko exhaled slowly, the tension easing from his shoulders. He meticulously logged the entire sequence, tagging it as "Anomaly Violet-Amethyst 7-G." He made a note to revisit the genetic sequencing of the fungi in that specific location, wondering if a new mutation or a unique interaction with the substrate was responsible for this outburst.

He then turned his attention back to the broader patterns, the everyday conversations of Veridia's flora. He studied the way the bioluminescent mosses would brighten their glow in unison as a passing cloud momentarily obscured the dim, alien sun. It was a collective acknowledgement, a shared experience of changing light. He noted how certain areas of the fungal network would flare with a warm, golden light when resources were abundant, a silent invitation to neighboring colonies, or perhaps a signal to the fauna that food was plentiful. Conversely, when resources were scarce, a muted, flickering blue would emanate, a subtle indication of caution, of conserved energy.

"Kira," Niko said softly, kneeling beside her and meeting her intelligent gaze. "You feel it, don't you? You understand pieces of it."

Kira responded with a soft chirp, her own luminous markings mirroring the gentle glow of the surrounding flora. Niko believed that her native Veridian biology, unlike his own human physiology, allowed her to perceive these light signals not just as visual input, but as a more integrated sensory experience, perhaps even with a tactile or energetic component. Her own bioluminescence, he suspected, wasn't just decorative; it was likely a form of personal expression within this grand, planetary conversation, a way for her to contribute her own unique 'voice' to the symphony.

He recalled his initial theories about chemical signaling. While chemical communication certainly played a role in the Veridian ecosystem, the sheer speed and complexity of the bioluminescent displays pointed towards a far more advanced and rapid form of information transfer. It was akin to the difference between a snail mail letter and an instantaneous data burst. The mycelial networks acted as the conduits, the information highways, but the bioluminescence was the carrier wave, the visible manifestation of thought and intent.

"It's not just about resource allocation or environmental alerts," Niko mused, more to himself than to Anya or Kira. "I believe it goes deeper. Think about the reproductive cycles. The flowering periods. The dispersal of seeds. Imagine a tree signaling its readiness to reproduce through a specific chromatic display, attracting specific pollinators or even triggering synchronized budding in neighboring trees. The entire forest, the entire ecosystem, could be orchestrating its life cycles through this luminous ballet."

He projected an image of a massive, ancient-looking tree, its bark etched with intricate patterns. The roots of this tree, as revealed by deep-penetrating scans, were deeply intertwined with a dense, pulsating network of bioluminescent fungi. "The older trees, Anya, do they show more complex luminescent patterns? Are they repositories of information, their light sequences carrying historical data, imprinted over centuries of existence?"

"Processing historical luminescent data for ancient arboreal specimens," Anya responded. "Preliminary analysis indicates that older specimens exhibit a broader spectral range in their bioluminescence, and their light patterns are indeed more intricate and layered. There is also a discernible overlap in certain spectral frequencies and pulse rhythms with the ancient fungal networks, suggesting a long-standing symbiotic relationship and a potential for knowledge transfer across generations, both within individual species and across the ecosystem."

Niko felt a profound sense of awe. It was a living library, a testament to evolutionary resilience and cooperation, encoded in light. The very landscape was a testament to this interconnected consciousness, each flicker, each pulse, a word in a sentence, a note in a melody, all contributing to the grand, silent song of Veridia. He understood now that his initial focus on the fungi and mosses had been a vital starting point, but the luminescence was a planetary phenomenon, a shared language that permeated every level of the Veridian biosphere. The flora wasn't just living; it was communicating, collaborating, and evolving in real-time, a continuous, luminous conversation that held the secrets to its survival and its extraordinary vitality. And he, with Kira by his side, was slowly, painstakingly, beginning to learn its language. The intensity of the light, the subtle shifts in color, the intricate rhythms – they were no longer just phenomena to be measured, but messages to be understood, fragments of a cosmic dialogue waiting to be deciphered, a testament to the boundless ingenuity of life.

The intricate tapestry of Veridia's bioluminescent communication, Niko was discovering, was more than just a language of resources and environmental cues. It was, in essence, a barometer of the planet's very stability. Kira, with her innate connection to the ebb and flow of the Veridian biosystem, served as an astonishingly sensitive instrument in this regard. Niko had observed, with growing fascination, that her own subtle luminous markings, which shifted in hue and intensity with her emotional state, often mirrored the ambient bio-electrical fields and light patterns of the flora around her. When the flora pulsed with a strong, harmonious rhythm, a steady, resonant hum of life, Kira's markings would glow with a clear, steady azure, and a low, contented purr would emanate from her chest. In these moments, Niko's scanners would register a robust bio-electrical flow, indicating a stable dimensional threshold, a healthy interpenetration of Veridia's unique energetic signature.

It was in these moments of pristine balance that the planet seemed to breathe with a quiet, confident regularity. The light, pulsing from the vast fungal networks beneath the soil to the canopy of towering flora above, was a testament to interconnectedness. Each flicker, each subtle shift in color, contributed to a larger, overarching harmonic. Niko had begun to correlate these harmonious light emissions with specific bio-electrical readings, noting that when the planetary network pulsed in unison, the ambient energy field held a consistent, predictable resonance. This resonance, he theorized, was indicative of a stable dimensional threshold, meaning Veridia was securely anchored within its own reality, its energetic boundaries intact. Kira's own internal luminescence would intensify, reflecting the external harmony, a visual confirmation of the planet's well-being. Her curiosity would be piqued, her movements graceful and exploratory, as if sensing the unhindered flow of life energy around her.

However, the narrative of Veridia's light and energy was not always one of serene uniformity. There were instances, Niko had documented with growing concern, where the luminous displays became erratic. Rapid, disjointed flickers, a draining of light that left entire sections of the landscape dim and muted, or a discordant cacophony of colors that seemed to clash rather than harmonize—these were signals of distress. It was during these times that Kira's demeanor would change dramatically. Her azure markings would become agitated, flashing with nervous amber or a dull, fearful grey. A low whine would escape her, her posture tense, her large eyes wide with an apprehension that mirrored Niko's own growing unease. Simultaneously, Niko's instruments would detect a significant disruption in the bio-electrical flow. The steady hum would devolve into a chaotic stutter, and the spectral analysis of the flora's light would reveal disturbing anomalies. The resonance readings would plummet, indicating a weakening of Veridia's dimensional integrity.

Niko meticulously logged these occurrences, his scientific mind grappling with the implications. He began to hypothesize that these moments of instability might be linked to external dimensional bleed-through, a phenomenon where energies or even fragments of other realities might be intruding upon Veridia's own. The erratic light pulses and the draining of energy could be the flora's struggle to either repel these intrusions or adapt to the alien energetic signatures. Alternatively, these disruptions could stem from internal ecological stress. Perhaps a disease affecting a critical species, a depletion of a vital nutrient in a key region, or even a shift in the planet's geological activity could ripple through the interconnected network, manifesting as visual and energetic chaos.

He recalled an incident near the shimmering crystalline caves, where the flora had displayed an unnerving, flickering scarlet for several hours. Kira had been visibly distressed, her fur bristling, and she had refused to venture closer than fifty meters from the area. Niko's scanners had confirmed a significant drain on the local bio-electrical field, and the spectral analysis had shown an unusual absorption of specific light frequencies, as if the very energy was being siphoned away. He had later discovered, through deep soil scans, a localized anomaly in the crystalline structure of the cave walls, a subtle warping of their usual geometric patterns, which he suspected was the root cause of the energy drain. The flora, in its attempt to maintain equilibrium, had responded with the distress signal of flickering scarlet, while Kira, sensitive to the energetic imbalance, had reacted with fear and avoidance. The correlation was undeniable: Kira's emotional state was a direct echo of Veridia's bio-network health, and the network's health was intrinsically tied to its dimensional stability.

Niko began to see Kira not just as a companion, but as a living, breathing embodiment of Veridia's vital signs. Her curiosity, when the planet was calm and its light flowed harmoniously, was a sign of robust ecological health. Her anxiety, when the light flickered erratically or dimmed, was a warning of impending instability. He started to develop a dual-spectrum analysis, cross-referencing his scientific readings with Kira's observable reactions. He would note, for instance, that when the fungal networks pulsed with a steady, emerald glow, indicative of optimal nutrient distribution, Kira would be engaged in playful bouts of chasing iridescent beetles. Her internal luminescence would be a vibrant, unbroken cyan. Conversely, a patch of fungi emitting a weak, flickering violet, coupled with a noticeable dip in Kira's energy levels and a dulling of her markings, would signal a region under stress.

This symbiotic relationship between Niko's technology and Kira's intuition provided him with a more holistic understanding of Veridia's intricate systems. His instruments could quantify the bio-electrical field strength and the spectral composition of the light, providing objective data. Kira, on the other hand, offered a qualitative assessment, an intuitive grasp of the planet's energetic state that often preceded or amplified the measurable signals. When Kira would whimper softly and press against his leg, her markings pulsing with a muted indigo, Niko knew to scrutinize his readings for subtle anomalies, for early signs of disruption that his instruments might not yet flag as significant. Her instinctive aversion to certain areas, her preference for others, became invaluable data points, guiding his investigations and confirming his hypotheses.

He started to develop a predictive model, integrating Kira's responses into his algorithms. If Kira exhibited signs of distress in a particular sector, Niko would prioritize scanning that area for energetic imbalances or unusual luminous patterns. If her markings glowed with an unusual intensity and purity of color, he would focus his analytical efforts on understanding the positive environmental factors at play, such as areas of exceptional biodiversity or abundant resources. This approach not only deepened his scientific understanding but also fostered a profound sense of partnership with Kira. He was no longer just an observer; he was a collaborator, working in concert with one of Veridia's own to decipher its deepest secrets.

The concept of a "stable dimensional threshold" began to take on a more tangible meaning. It wasn't just an abstract scientific term; it was the palpable sense of well-being that permeated the planet when its flora sang its silent song in harmony. It was the feeling of unhindered life, of interconnectedness, of a reality firmly grounded. When that harmony faltered, when the light grew erratic, it was as if Veridia itself was being stretched, thinned, or even threatened by something from beyond its own existential boundaries. Kira's sensitivity to these shifts was a testament to the deep, almost spiritual, connection she had with her homeworld. Her very essence seemed to be woven into the luminous fabric of Veridia, her well-being directly proportional to the planet's.

Niko mused on the implications for potential colonization or long-term habitation. A planet whose very stability was intrinsically linked to the energetic resonance of its biosphere presented unique challenges and opportunities. Understanding and maintaining these harmonics would be paramount. Any external influence that disrupted this delicate balance, be it from natural planetary cycles or from the unintentional introduction of foreign energies, could have catastrophic consequences. The luminous flora, acting as a planet-wide nervous system, would be the first to signal distress, and creatures like Kira, with their innate sensitivity, would be the living embodiments of that distress.

He remembered the vibrant, almost electric, pulse of light that emanated from a vast forest of luminescent trees after a period of intense solar activity from Veridia's distant, twin suns. The light had been a brilliant, cascading spectrum of gold and rose, and Kira had bounded through the undergrowth with unparalleled energy, her own markings flashing a dazzling, effervescent green. His readings had shown a surge in the bio-electrical field, a heightened energetic resonance that indicated Veridia had not only absorbed the solar influx but had integrated it, transforming it into a surge of vitality. It was a testament to the planet's resilience, its capacity to not only withstand external forces but to thrive from them.

However, there were also darker manifestations. During a period of unusual seismic activity, a tremor so deep that it shook the very foundations of the land, the bioluminescence in the affected region had been a sickly, pulsing crimson, punctuated by moments of complete darkness. Kira had refused to leave Niko's side, her body trembling, her markings a dull, flickering charcoal. The bio-electrical readings had been dangerously low, chaotic, and Niko had worried that the dimensional threshold had been severely compromised. He had spent days analyzing the seismic data and the luminous responses, attempting to understand the precise mechanism by which the geological upheaval had disrupted the planet's energetic equilibrium. He theorized that the sheer force of the tremors had momentarily fractured the subterranean mycelial networks, severing crucial communication pathways and causing a cascade of energetic collapse.

These experiences solidified Niko's understanding: the silent song of Veridia's flora was not merely a language of information, but a symphony of stability. The harmony of its light, the steady flow of its bio-electrical energy, the vibrant resonance of its dimensional threshold – these were all interconnected facets of a living, breathing planet. And in Kira, Niko had found an invaluable interpreter, a creature whose very being resonated with the health and stability of Veridia, bridging the gap between cold, hard science and the intuitive wisdom of the natural world. Her emotional landscape was a mirror to the planet's energetic state, her luminous markings a visible manifestation of the invisible currents that sustained Veridia. Together, they were learning to read the intricate harmonics of stability, to understand when Veridia sang its song of vibrant life, and when its melody faltered into discord.

The air in the Whispering Woods had been thick with a subtle tension all morning. Niko, his instruments humming softly, had noticed it almost immediately: a faint, discordant shimmer in the usual symphony of bioluminescence, a barely perceptible dissonance that prickled at the edges of his perception. Kira, ever attuned to the planet's energetic pulse, had mirrored this unease. Her usually vibrant azure markings had softened to a pale, almost anxious cyan, and she'd kept a watchful, low-to-the-ground posture, her sensitive ears swiveling to catch sounds that weren't there. It was a distant anomaly, a ripple far beyond the immediate grove, but enough to cast a shadow over the normally serene forest. Niko had been about to reroute their exploration when a faint, persistent glow caught his eye.

Nestled amongst the moss-covered roots of an ancient, towering flora, was a seed pod unlike any he had cataloged. It was roughly the size of his palm, its outer husk a pearlescent, opalescent shell that seemed to hold a captured twilight within. From within this shell, a gentle, unwavering luminescence pulsed, a soft, warm amber that seemed to push back against the encroaching unease in the air. It wasn't the sharp, vivid bursts of warning signals or the diffuse glow of nutrient-rich soil. This was something different entirely—a steady, unwavering beacon of light. Intrigued, Niko extended a gloved hand, his bio-scanner whirring to life. The readings that flickered across his display were... extraordinary.

The seed pod emitted a subtle, harmonic resonance, a low hum that was almost inaudible but deeply felt. It was a frequency that seemed to bypass the auditory canals and resonate directly within the listener's very bones. Niko watched, fascinated, as Kira, who had been pacing nervously a few meters away, visibly relaxed. Her posture softened, her ears relaxed their vigilant perking, and her cyan markings deepened, returning to a more confident azure. A soft, contented rumble, a sound Niko had come to associate with Kira's deep contentment, began to emanate from her chest. The seed pod's light, he realized, wasn't just visually appealing; it was actively soothing, a balm to the subtle energetic disturbances that had been unsettling them.

He carefully adjusted the parameters of his scanner, focusing on the unique energetic signature. It was unlike anything he'd encountered in his studies of Veridia's flora. The pod seemed to generate a field of pure, unadulterated calm, a pocket of stability in the otherwise dynamic and sometimes volatile energetic landscape of the planet. His initial hypotheses began to form, wild yet grounded in the data his instruments were meticulously collecting. Could this seed, with its steady, calming resonance, hold the key to stabilizing the very dimensional thresholds he had been observing? Could its unique luminescence be capable of not just soothing Kira, but of actively mending the energetic tears that sometimes appeared in Veridia's fabric? The thought sent a thrill of scientific anticipation through him. This wasn't just a new specimen; it was a potential paradigm shift.

The pack's protocols for collecting specimens were stringent, born from a hard-learned respect for the delicate interconnectedness of Veridia's ecosystems. Before even considering extraction, Niko initiated a comprehensive scan of the immediate vicinity. He needed to ensure the seed pod wasn't integral to the health of the surrounding flora, or worse, a sentinel guarding something vital. He traced the faint tendrils of energy connecting the pod to the ancient tree, his sensors searching for any signs of dependency. The readings were reassuring. While the pod drew a minuscule amount of ambient energy, it didn't appear to be a keystone species, nor did it exhibit any defensive energetic signature. It seemed to exist in a state of gentle self-sufficiency, radiating its calming influence outward without demanding much in return.

Niko engaged the specialized extraction tool, a non-invasive device designed to gently levitate and contain specimens. The amber light of the seed pod seemed to pulse brighter as the tool approached, not with alarm, but perhaps with a gentle acknowledgment. The process was slow and deliberate, each micro-adjustment calibrated to avoid any disruption. Kira watched, her tail giving a slow, curious sweep against the mossy ground, her initial apprehension replaced by a focused, quiet interest. The pod detached from its roots with a soft, almost sighing sound, and was carefully enclosed within the tool's containment field. As it floated into the sterile enclosure, its warm amber light filled the small chamber, and Niko felt a wave of profound tranquility wash over him, a direct echo of the resonance he had detected.

He knew, with a certainty that transcended mere scientific deduction, that this was more than just a botanical discovery. This seed pod, this "Seed of Hope" as he had already begun to mentally dub it, represented a profound potential. Its ability to emit a calming resonance and stabilize energetic fields, even on this small scale, suggested possibilities that were both staggering and deeply desirable. Imagine, he mused, a galaxy struggling with fractured dimensions, with worlds teetering on the brink of energetic collapse. A species like this, a natural conduit for stability and harmony, could be a lynchpin in the galactic endeavor to heal and protect. It was a testament to the sheer ingenuity of evolution, a quiet whisper from Veridia suggesting that even in the face of immense cosmic challenges, life found a way to create balance, to generate hope, to sing its own silent, stabilizing song.

Niko carefully secured the containment unit, its soft amber glow a constant reassurance. He glanced at Kira, who was now nudging his hand with her head, her eyes bright with curiosity. The distant anomaly that had unsettled her was still present, a faint smudge on the planet's energetic canvas, but its influence seemed diminished, less potent. The Seed of Hope, even contained, continued to project its calming aura, a miniature sanctuary of peace. He felt a surge of responsibility, not just as a scientist, but as a custodian of this nascent potential. He had to understand this seed, to unravel the secrets of its remarkable properties, not for personal gain or scientific acclaim, but for the hope it represented – a hope that could ripple outwards, touching not just Veridia, but perhaps countless other worlds in need. The silent song of flora, he was realizing, was far more complex and profound than he had ever imagined, and this tiny seed was its most eloquent testament yet.

The journey back to their research outpost was a different experience. The usual subtle fluctuations in the forest's bioluminescence, which Niko had grown accustomed to interpreting as minor environmental shifts, now seemed less like noise and more like individual voices in a vast, planetary choir. His attention, however, kept drifting back to the Seed of Hope, safely secured within its containment unit. The amber light pulsed steadily, a miniature sun of tranquility. He found himself running simulations in his mind, projecting the seed's unique resonance onto larger scales. Could these pods, if cultivated, form a network? A natural, living grid of energetic stability that could counteract the creeping instability he had been observing in Veridia's dimensional thresholds?

He recalled his early hypotheses about dimensional bleed-through, the idea that Veridia's reality could be thinning, allowing intrusions from... elsewhere. The erratic lights, the energy drains, Kira's palpable distress – these were all symptoms of a system under strain. But what if this seed offered a solution? What if its inherent ability to generate and broadcast a calming, stabilizing frequency could actively mend those tears, reinforcing Veridia's dimensional integrity? It was a tantalizing prospect, a scientific hypothesis that felt more like a profound revelation. It suggested that nature itself held the keys to its own resilience, that the solutions to even the most complex existential threats might be found not in advanced technology alone, but in understanding and harnessing the inherent wisdom of life.

Kira, sensing his contemplative mood, nudged his hand again. She then looked towards the containment unit, her gaze steady. There was no fear in her eyes, only a profound, almost knowing calm. It was as if she, too, understood the significance of their discovery. Her own luminous markings, which had been a muted azure since they'd encountered the distant anomaly, now held a deeper, richer hue, tinged with the very amber of the seed pod. It was a subtle but undeniable shift, a testament to the seed's pervasive influence. Niko felt a surge of gratitude for his companion; she was not merely an observer in his scientific endeavors, but an integral part of the process, a living barometer of Veridia's energetic state, and a testament to the profound interconnectedness he was striving to understand.

He initiated a more detailed spectral analysis of the seed pod's light, pushing his scanners to their limits. He was looking for the underlying energetic frequencies, the specific wavelengths and amplitudes that contributed to its unique calming effect. The data that streamed back was complex, a beautiful, intricate dance of harmonic resonance. It wasn't just a single frequency; it was a symphony of overlapping waves, each contributing to the overall effect. There were low-frequency oscillations that seemed to resonate with planetary magnetic fields, mid-frequency pulses that mirrored the natural rhythms of biological processes, and even high-frequency harmonics that hinted at interactions with subatomic particles. It was, in essence, a perfectly balanced energetic signature, a masterclass in natural stability.

Niko's mind raced with the implications. If he could replicate this signature, even partially, could he create artificial devices that mimicked its effect? Could he develop localized stabilizers for areas experiencing dimensional flux? Or, even more ambitiously, could he engineer a way to encourage the growth of these seed pods, to reintroduce this stabilizing influence on a larger scale throughout Veridia? The latter, of course, would require a deep understanding of their reproductive cycle, their ecological needs, and the delicate balance of the environments they inhabited. It was a long road, fraught with scientific challenges, but the potential reward – a Veridia more resilient, more stable, and more vibrantly alive – made the endeavor profoundly worthwhile.

He found himself sketching diagrams on his datapad, rough schematics of potential cultivation chambers and resonance amplifiers, all inspired by the simple, elegant design of the seed pod. He cross-referenced the pod's energy output with the readings he had taken of areas exhibiting signs of dimensional stress. The contrast was stark. Where distressed areas showed chaotic, fluctuating energy signatures, the seed pod radiated a consistent, unwavering harmony. It was like comparing a storm to a perfectly still lake. The seed was not merely emitting energy; it was *imposing* order, gently guiding the chaotic energies around it towards equilibrium.

The pack's guidelines on ethical collection were absolute: observe, analyze, and only collect if no harm is caused and the specimen is not essential to its immediate environment. Niko had meticulously followed every step. The area around the ancient flora was still vibrant, undisturbed. The seed pod, while emitting a beneficial influence, had not shown any signs of being a critical component of the local ecosystem's structure or energy flow. It was, in essence, a gift offered freely by Veridia, a chance discovery that held immense promise. He felt a sense of profound respect for the pack's foresight, for the wisdom embedded in their protocols. It was this very reverence for life, for the delicate tapestry of existence, that had allowed him to make such a potentially transformative discovery.

As they neared the outpost, the distant anomaly, though still detectable, seemed to recede further into the background, its dissonant hum less insistent. The steady, comforting amber glow from the containment unit served as a constant reminder of the solution that had been found. It was a beacon of hope, a tangible symbol of Veridia's capacity for healing, for renewal, for maintaining its own serene existence against the encroaching chaos of the universe. Niko knew this was just the beginning. The study of this Seed of Hope would be his primary focus, a journey into the heart of

Veridia's resilience, a quest to understand the silent song of flora that held the promise of stability, and perhaps, even salvation.

The spectral analysis of the seed pod's energetic signature, a task Niko had begun with fervent scientific curiosity, continued to yield astonishing data. He had expected to find complex wave patterns, perhaps an amplification of ambient planetary energies, but the reality was far more nuanced. The seed didn't merely resonate with existing frequencies; it actively generated a harmonized field, a carefully calibrated symphony of energetic vibrations that seemed to possess an inherent ability to smooth out discord. His instruments, usually adept at deciphering the subtle language of Veridia's flora, struggled to fully categorize the sheer elegance of the pod's output. It was as if evolution, in its boundless creativity, had engineered a living Rosetta Stone for energetic harmony.

He began to correlate these findings with the faint, unsettling readings that had initially drawn their attention. The subtle flicker in the forest's bioluminescence, the almost imperceptible dissonance that Kira had felt as a prickle of unease – these anomalies were minuscule, almost statistical noise in the grand scheme of Veridia's vibrant energy scape. Yet, they were undeniably present. Niko's equipment, tuned to detect even the most minute energetic fluctuations, registered them as transient dips and swells, brief moments where the planet's natural resonance seemed to falter. He had initially attributed them to atmospheric anomalies or perhaps the passing of an unusually energetic celestial body. But now, with the Seed of Hope's unique properties laid bare, a new, more profound explanation began to coalesce.

"It's like a tiny tremor, Kira," Niko explained, pointing to a fluctuating graph on his datapad. "Not a geological one, but an energetic one. These little spikes... they're brief moments where the fabric of our reality here feels... thinner." He gestured to the screen, where a series of rapid, erratic waveforms depicted the anomaly. "My instruments can pick them up, and you, with your heightened sensitivity, can feel them as a general unease. It's a disturbance, a subtle bleed-through."

Kira's response was a soft chuff, her luminous markings shifting through shades of amber and azure, reflecting her contemplative state. She nudged the containment unit holding the seed pod, her posture one of calm assurance. The amber light emanating from within the pod seemed to absorb the visual representation of the anomaly, its steady glow a stark contrast to the jagged lines on Niko's screen.

"You're saying these are like... cracks?" Kira's voice was soft, her understanding of abstract concepts always profound. "Tiny fissures opening up?"

"Precisely," Niko confirmed, his gaze fixed on the seed. "And what's fascinating is that they're not random. They seem to occur in patterns, almost as if something is... testing the boundaries. And the Seed of Hope," he tapped the containment unit gently, "its resonance seems to push back against those very fluctuations. It's like it's reinforcing the integrity of our dimensional space, moment by moment."

The concept of 'dimensional leaks' had been a theoretical footnote in xenobotanical studies for decades, a fringe hypothesis explored by a few daring minds who dared to consider the possibility of realities brushing against each other. Most dismissed it as pure speculation, a fantastical extension of quantum physics. But here, on Veridia, it was becoming a tangible, observable phenomenon. The leaks were subtle, so subtle that most life forms, even many sapient species, would likely never perceive them. But for Niko, equipped with advanced sensory technology, and Kira, with her innate connection to Veridia's energetic currents, they were undeniable.

These weren't the catastrophic breaches that tore worlds apart, the kind that led to interdimensional wars or swallowed planets whole. These were more akin to microscopic tears in a vast tapestry, barely visible but indicative of a fundamental stress on the fabric of existence. The flora of Veridia, with its complex bio-energetic systems, was particularly susceptible. The bioluminescence, a product of intricate biochemical reactions, was like an early warning system, flickering erratically when the underlying energetic stability wavered. Kira's sensitivity was a more direct, visceral response, a primal awareness of the planet's energetic health.

Niko zoomed in on another section of his data, highlighting a series of energy readings taken over the past solar cycle. "See here," he said, pointing to a period of increased anomalous activity. "This corresponds to a slight dimming of the western bio-luminescent plains and a noticeable drop in the ambient energy field. It's subtle, but it's there. The ecosystem registers the disturbance." He looked at Kira, his brow furrowed. "And you felt it too, didn't you? That lingering sense of unease?"

Kira nodded, her gaze fixed on the Seed of Hope. "It was like a faint whisper from beyond the veil," she murmured. "Not menacing, not yet. But... *other*. A subtle wrongness in the usual song of the forest. It made my fur prickle, even when there was no physical threat."

The pack's protocols had always emphasized vigilance. They were not merely catalogers of exotic life; they were custodians of Veridia's delicate equilibrium. Their mission extended beyond identifying new species to understanding the complex interplay of forces that sustained the planet. The presence of these minor dimensional leaks, while not an immediate crisis, served as a stark reminder of the constant, unseen threats that Veridia faced. It underscored the importance of their work, the necessity of understanding every facet of this vibrant world, from the macro-scale dynamics of its magnetosphere to the micro-scale energetic signatures of its flora.

"These aren't just random glitches, are they?" Kira asked, her voice laced with concern. "If they're happening now, what does that mean for the future?"

Niko sighed, running a hand through his short, dark hair. "That's the million-credit question, isn't it? Theoretically, these leaks could widen over time. Increased dimensional bleed-through could destabilize local energy fields, disrupt biological processes, and eventually... well, the worst-case scenarios are pretty grim. Imagine environments where the laws of physics become fluid, where different realities overlap unpredictably. It would be catastrophic for any life adapted to a stable framework."

He paused, his gaze returning to the pulsing amber light of the seed pod. "But that's why this discovery is so vital. If this seed can generate a field that reinforces dimensional integrity, then perhaps we can understand how to cultivate it, how to spread its influence. It could be a natural defense mechanism, a way for Veridia to heal itself from these subtle incursions." He looked at Kira, his eyes alight with a mixture of scientific ambition and a deep-seated hope. "Think about it, Kira. If we can harness this, we're not just studying Veridia; we're helping to safeguard it. We're using its own inherent wisdom to protect it from external pressures."

The implications of these dimensional leaks extended beyond the immediate planetary system. Veridia was not an isolated world; it existed within a complex galactic ecosystem, a network of stars and planets where dimensional stability was a constant, unspoken concern. Many worlds had fallen victim to more severe forms of interdimensional intrusion, their ecosystems shattered, their populations decimated. The subtle leaks on Veridia were a low-level symptom of a much larger, more pervasive phenomenon that affected the galaxy as a whole. Understanding and potentially mitigating these leaks could have far-reaching consequences, offering a path towards greater interdimensional harmony across countless star systems.

Niko continued his analysis, cross-referencing the detected leak patterns with data from other planets in their sector. While direct evidence of similar leaks was scarce, there were anecdotal reports from deep-space exploration vessels and interstellar archeological teams of 'anomalous zones' where natural laws seemed to behave erratically, where strange energetic phenomena were observed, and where lifeforms exhibited peculiar adaptations. These reports, often dismissed as sensor malfunctions or misinterpretations, now seemed to fit a disturbing pattern. The subtle whispers Kira had felt, the fleeting flickers Niko had detected – these might be the universal precursors to much larger, more destructive dimensional instabilities.

"It's a reminder," Niko mused aloud, his voice softer now, filled with a profound sense of responsibility. "A reminder that the universe is far more complex and interconnected than we often perceive. That the boundaries we take for granted are, in fact, quite fragile. Our role here, Kira, is to understand that fragility, to listen to the silent songs of this world, and to find ways to strengthen its voice against the cacophony of the unknown."

He activated a long-range sensor sweep, extending their detection radius to encompass the wider Veridian system. He was searching for any correlation between the leaks and celestial phenomena, for any environmental factors that might exacerbate or mitigate these dimensional incursions. The data began to trickle in, a stream of numbers and spectral analyses that painted a picture of a dynamic, energetic system. He noted subtle fluctuations in the planet's magnetosphere, minute shifts in solar radiation patterns, and even faint gravitational anomalies from distant celestial bodies. Each piece of data was a potential clue, a breadcrumb leading towards a deeper understanding of the forces at play.

"It's not just about this seed, is it?" Kira said, looking out into the lush greenery of the Whispering Woods. "It's about understanding the whole system. How the light, the resonance, the very air we breathe, all contribute to keeping Veridia stable. The leaks are a symptom, but the cause... the cause is likely something far more intricate."

"Exactly," Niko agreed, his fingers flying across his datapad. "The seed is a powerful tool, a potential solution. But to truly combat this threat, we need to understand its origins. Why are these leaks occurring now? Is it a natural cycle, or is something external influencing Veridia's dimensional integrity? Are there other worlds experiencing similar phenomena, and if so, what are they doing about it?"

He initiated a cross-reference with the galactic database, searching for patterns of interdimensional activity and reports of similar ecological disturbances. The results were a sobering reminder of the vastness of the cosmos and the myriad challenges faced by its inhabitants. There were records of entire star systems rendered uninhabitable by dimensional rifts, of civilizations forced to abandon their homeworlds due to encroaching pocket realities. Veridia's current predicament, while worrying, was a relatively mild manifestation of a much larger, more insidious universal trend.

The seed's resonance, however, offered a glimmer of hope. Niko began to hypothesize about the mechanics of its influence. Was it actively repelling encroaching energies? Was it subtly altering the vibrational frequency of Veridia's space-time continuum to make it less permeable? Or was it something even more complex, a form of natural entrainment that gently guided unstable energies back into equilibrium? He ran simulations, extrapolating the seed's localized effect to a planetary scale. The results were promising, suggesting that a sufficiently dense network of these pods, or even cultivated flora exhibiting similar properties, could create a robust energetic shield.

"Imagine a planetary immune system," Niko mused, sketching a complex network of energy conduits on his datapad. "A natural defense mechanism that doesn't rely on aggressive countermeasures, but on harmonizing the environment. The seed doesn't fight the anomalies; it neutralizes them by bringing them into alignment with Veridia's fundamental frequency. It's elegant, it's sustainable, and it's entirely biological."

Kira watched his work with quiet intensity, her own understanding of energetic flows providing a complementary perspective. "It's like the planet is singing a song of stability," she offered, her voice barely above a whisper. "And the leaks are dissonant notes. The seed... it helps the planet find its true pitch again."

The immediate task, however, remained focused on understanding the nature and origin of these leaks. Niko initiated a series of localized, high-resolution energy scans, focusing on areas where the anomalies had been most pronounced. He deployed miniature sensor drones, equipped with advanced chronometers and spectral analyzers, to map the precise temporal and spatial distribution of the dimensional flickers. The data they collected would be crucial in identifying any patterns or triggers.

"We need to track these incursions," Niko stated, his voice firm. "Understand their frequency, their intensity, and any correlating environmental factors. If we can predict when and where they're most likely to occur, we can deploy the seed's influence preemptively. It's about proactive stabilization, not just reactive repair."

He knew that the implications of this research extended far beyond the confines of their current mission. If Veridia's flora held the key to interdimensional stability, then understanding and preserving it became paramount, not just for the planet itself, but for the wider galactic community. The silent song of flora, he was beginning to understand, was not merely a biological phenomenon; it was a cosmic language, a fundamental principle of universal harmony that had been largely overlooked in the relentless pursuit of technological advancement. And for the first time, Niko felt a profound sense of purpose, a realization that his life's work was not just about cataloging the wonders of Veridia, but about unlocking its secrets to potentially safeguard existence itself. The subtle threats from beyond the veil were a stark warning, but the Seed of Hope, pulsing with its steady amber glow, was a promise of resilience, a testament to the enduring power of life to find balance, even in the face of the unimaginable.

Chapter Four

THE CORPORATE SHADOW

The hum of Niko's instruments, a familiar lullaby in the heart of the Whispering Woods, abruptly shifted. It was a subtle change, almost imperceptible to an untrained ear, but to Niko, it was like a sudden discord in a perfectly tuned symphony. The steady, organic resonance he had become so attuned to, the gentle pulse of Veridia's lifeblood, was being overlaid by something alien, something sharp and jarring. His multi-spectral scanner, usually a tool of serene discovery, flickered with an unfamiliar, harsh signature. It was metallic, devoid of the complex bio-energetic waveforms he'd been meticulously cataloging. This wasn't the subtle tremor of dimensional leaks; this was an intrusion, a deliberate, forceful presence.

"Kira," Niko's voice was a low growl, the scientific curiosity in his tone instantly replaced by a sharp edge of concern. He gestured to his datapad, the screen now displaying a series of jagged, angular readings. "We have company. And it's not native."

Kira's head snapped up, her luminous markings, which had been softly pulsing with the ambient light of the forest, now flared a fierce, warning crimson. Her ears, finely tuned to the subtlest shifts in her environment, twitched, then flattened against her skull. A low, guttural sound rumbled in her chest, a sound that spoke of ancient instincts awakened, of primal territoriality. The air, moments before alive with the chirps of unseen insects and the gentle rustle of leaves, seemed to grow heavy, charged with a nascent tension. She could *feel* it too, an invasive resonance that grated against her very being, a cold, sterile vibration that had no place in the vibrant, interconnected web of Veridia.

"What is it?" Kira's voice was a low hiss, her gaze sweeping the dense foliage, her powerful limbs tensing as if ready to spring. Her senses, far more acute than Niko's technological array, were already picking up the alien presence. It was a scent, faint but distinct, of ozone and processed metals, a smell that spoke of machines and artificial environments, a stark contrast to the rich, earthy perfumes of the jungle. And beneath it, a chilling emptiness, a void where natural energy should have flowed.

Niko's fingers danced across the datapad, his brow furrowed in concentration. "The signatures... they're technological, but not in any way I recognize as indigenous to Veridia. They're broadcasting across multiple spectra, aggressively probing. And the energy profiles... they're incredibly precise, almost surgical. No biological overlap, no organic integration." He paused, a grim realization dawning on him. "These are not accidental encounters. This is an exploration, but a very deliberate, potentially invasive one."

He tapped a specific set of readings, highlighting a particularly aggressive spike. "This pattern, Kira. It matches some of the data we intercepted from the outer systems, from unregistered deep-space vessels. The energy signatures are too... *clean*. Too manufactured. They lack the chaotic, organic hum of natural life." He looked up at Kira, his eyes wide with a dawning, unwelcome certainty. "These are unauthorized. And given the nature of their probing, I suspect they're looking for something specific. Something they can exploit."

Kira's growl intensified, her muscles coiling. The peace of their research, the quiet unfolding of Veridia's secrets, had been shattered by this sudden, discordant intrusion. Her role as a guardian of this ecosystem, a duty ingrained in her very being, surged to the forefront. These were not fellow explorers; they were potential predators, their presence a direct threat to the delicate balance they were sworn to protect. The very thought of these outsiders, with their harsh, sterile energies, disrupting the intricate web of life sent a wave of primal anger through her.

"Exploit?" Kira echoed, the word tasting like ash in her mouth. Her enhanced vision scanned the canopy, her sharp ears straining to pinpoint the source of the unwelcome emissions. She could feel the subtle distress emanating from the flora around them, a faint ripple of unease spreading through the otherwise harmonious energetic field. The bioluminescent fungi, usually a steady beacon, flickered erratically, as if mirroring her own rising alarm. "What could they possibly be looking for that requires such a crude, invasive approach?"

"That's what worries me," Niko admitted, his gaze sweeping across the wider system readings. "These energy signatures are highly focused. They're not just scanning for general biological data; they're sweeping for specific energetic signatures. Remember the Seed of Hope? The dimensional anomalies we've been tracking? I'm starting to suspect they're not here for the usual xenobotanical survey. They're here for the anomalies, or for anything that can influence or interact with them."

He brought up a comparative analysis of the detected signatures against a known database of interstellar organizations. His fingers hovered over a specific entry, a name synonymous with ruthless exploitation and unchecked ambition. "This is... this is precisely the kind of energy signature OmniCorp uses. Their exploration vessels are designed for deep-space extraction, for 'resource acquisition' with little regard for ecological impact. Their technology is designed to cut through, to analyze, and to extract, without any consideration for the natural world."

The name hung in the air, heavy with unspoken threat. OmniCorp. A name whispered in hushed tones throughout the galaxy, a byword for corporate avarice and environmental devastation. Their history was a tapestry of ruined ecosystems, of exploited worlds stripped bare, of indigenous species driven to extinction in the relentless pursuit of profit. Kira felt a cold dread wash over her. If OmniCorp was on Veridia, then their peaceful research was over. The planet itself was now in danger.

Kira let out a low growl, a sound that promised retribution. Her tail lashed back and forth, her fur bristling. "OmniCorp," she spat, the name anathema to her very nature. "They have no respect for life. They see only resources to be plundered." Her mind flashed to images from her training, of worlds scarred and broken by OmniCorp's insatiable hunger. It was a bleak and terrifying prospect.

"Their approach is often to bypass consent, to simply take what they deem valuable," Niko confirmed, his voice tight with frustration. "And given the nature of the dimensional leaks we've been observing, and the unique properties of the Seed of Hope... it's highly probable they've detected something of immense interest. Something that could give them an edge in their ongoing interdimensional resource wars, or perhaps a way to control or exploit dimensional rifts for their own gain."

He zoomed in on the directional vectors of the energy signatures. "They're not just in orbit; they're deploying ground probes. Small, highly mobile units. They're actively scanning the immediate area, zeroing in on the high-energy zones we've been monitoring. They're heading this way, Kira. Directly towards our position." The urgency in his voice was palpable. Their sanctuary, their carefully guarded observation post, was about to be breached.

Kira's instincts screamed danger. She could feel the encroaching presence like a physical weight, a suffocating pressure that sought to crush the vibrant life of Veridia. The sharp, metallic tang of their technology was starting to overpower the natural scent of the forest. It was an assault on her senses, an affront to the very essence of the planet. She looked at Niko, her amber eyes blazing with a fierce protectiveness.

"We can't let them reach the Seed," she stated, her voice a low, determined growl. "If OmniCorp gets their hands on it, they'll twist its purpose. They'll weaponize its harmonizing properties, or worse, use it to destabilize other worlds for their own gain. Veridia's hope will become their tool of destruction." She lowered her head, her body coiled in a predatory stance. "We need to divert them. Or, if necessary, stop them."

Niko nodded, his mind already racing through potential strategies. The sheer arrogance of OmniCorp's intrusion, the casual disregard for Veridian sovereignty, ignited a righteous anger within him. His scientific detachment was being overshadowed by a fierce determination to protect this world and its incredible discoveries. "I agree. Their methods are abhorrent. We need to make them understand that Veridia is not theirs for the taking." He began accessing the local sensor net, rerouting power to defensive countermeasures and advanced cloaking systems, rudimentary though they were. "They might have superior technology, but we have the advantage of this planet. We know its rhythms, its secrets. We can use that."

The serene hum of the forest was now a discordant symphony of alien signals and Kira's rising unease. The air grew thick with an unseen tension, the once welcoming environment now felt like a battlefield where nature's subtle harmonies were about to clash with the brutal, unyielding force of corporate ambition. Niko's scanners painted a grim picture: multiple incoming probes, closing fast, their metallic energies like a physical blight upon the vibrant landscape. Kira's senses were on high alert, the scent of ozone and processed metal growing stronger, an olfactory warning of the approaching threat. The peaceful exploration had just taken a dangerous turn, and the future of Veridia, and perhaps the Seed of Hope itself, hung precariously in the balance. The intruders were on the horizon, and their intentions were far from benevolent. The quiet sanctity of their research was shattered, replaced by the chilling certainty of conflict.

The once vibrant, emerald tapestry of the Veridian undergrowth now bore the jagged scars of haste and carelessness. What had been a thriving ecosystem, pulsating with the gentle, harmonious energies Kira and Niko had meticulously documented, was now marred by the invasive intrusion of OmniCorp. They moved through the desecrated terrain, the acrid scent of ozone and processed fuels clinging to the air like a shroud. Niko's instruments, which had once hummed with the symphony of Veridia's life, now registered a cacophony of disruptions – erratic energy fluctuations, localized atmospheric contamination, and the chilling silence where complex bio-signatures should have been.

"Look at this," Niko's voice was a low, guttural sound of pure disgust, barely audible above the unsettling quiet. He gestured with a trembling hand towards a section of the forest floor. Where the bioluminescent flora had once painted the twilight with ethereal, soft glows, there were now patches of blackened, withered growth. The delicate, light-emitting fungi, so crucial to the local fauna's nocturnal navigation and communication, had been trampled, their radiant pulse extinguished. "They didn't even bother to circumnavigate. They simply bulldozed through." He knelt, his gloved fingers hovering over the ruined vegetation, a wave of anger washing over him. His research, painstakingly conducted with the utmost respect for Veridia's intricate web of life, was being systematically dismantled by the crude, brutish methodology of a corporation driven by profit. "The bio-luminescence cycles are completely disrupted. These organisms are adapted to precise energy frequencies, to specific nutrient flows. What they've done here isn't just destruction; it's an ecological lobotomy." He pointed his scanner at a particularly desolate patch. "The soil itself is depleted, the microbial communities likely annihilated. They've injected trace amounts of heavy metals and synthetic compounds. It's... it's an affront to everything Veridia is."

Kira moved with a fluid grace that was starkly at odds with the devastation surrounding them. Her normally inquisitive, gentle demeanor was replaced by a taut vigilance, her sleek, obsidian fur bristling with an emotion that was a complex blend of disgust and anxiety. She lowered her head, her sensitive nostrils flaring as she inhaled deeply, sifting through the layered olfactory assault. The metallic tang was pungent, overlaid with the faint, sickly sweet scent of discarded nutrient pastes and chemical solvents. Beneath it all, she could sense the residual echoes of the OmniCorp team's passage – a discordant vibration, a residue of their hurried, anxious emotions, their focus solely on extraction rather than coexistence. It was a psychic imprint of their lack of empathy, their utter disconnect from the living world they were tramping through. She nudged a piece of twisted, oxidized metal with her snout, the material cool and alien against her sensitive whiskers. It was a fragment of some discarded probe, its once functional components now corroded, leaking a faint, iridescent sheen into the soil.

"This metal," she murmured, her voice a low rumble, her body language radiating a profound sense of unease. "It feels... cold. Empty. There's no resonance within it, no connection to the planet's energy. It's just dead matter, left to poison the earth." She shook her head, a shiver running through her. "They were careless. So incredibly careless. They left their waste, their polluting technology, scattered like seeds of decay. It's not just the physical damage; it's the lingering dissonance. The disruption to the natural flow of energy, to the collective consciousness of this place." She could feel the faint tremors of distress rippling through the surrounding flora, a subtle plea for balance that was being drowned out by the invasive frequencies of this abandoned debris.

Niko's gaze swept over the scene, his scientific mind struggling to process the sheer magnitude of the environmental vandalism. He had seen orbital scans of worlds stripped bare by OmniCorp's relentless resource extraction, but witnessing the direct impact, the localized devastation, was a far more visceral experience. These weren't simply abstract data points; these were the broken threads of a vibrant, interconnected ecosystem. "Their operational protocols are built around efficiency, not sustainability," he explained, his voice tight with controlled fury. "They deploy, extract, and depart, leaving behind a wasteland. They have no concept of stewardship, no understanding of the long-term consequences of their actions. They see Veridia as a mere inventory of usable assets, not a living, breathing entity with its own inherent value." He activated a different sensor array, the readouts painting a grim picture of localized chemical imbalances. "Their probes are designed for rapid deployment and data acquisition. They're not built for subtle observation or minimal impact. They're designed to cut, to scan, to analyze, and to transmit, with little to no consideration for the biosphere they're operating within. The sheer volume of waste they've already generated, even in this short transit, is appalling."

Kira circled a larger piece of debris, a segment of what looked like a solar array, its surface cracked and scarred. She could feel a faint, residual energy signature emanating from it, a ghost of the power it once channeled, now corrupted and unstable. "They are like a blight," she stated, her gaze hardening as she looked towards the direction the probes had likely entered and exited the forest. "They spread, they consume, and they leave behind only emptiness. Their presence is a violation of the natural order. It's a discord that doesn't belong in Veridia's symphony." She recalled ancient tales from her people, stories of beings who consumed without giving back, who took without replenishing, leaving entire lands barren. OmniCorp, in her mind, embodied that destructive archetype. The contrast between their methods and the Resonant Pack's approach was stark, a chasm that defined the core conflict of their existence on this planet.

Niko stooped to pick up a small, metallic disc, its surface etched with an unfamiliar corporate logo – a stylized O entwined with a sharp, upward-pointing arrow, a symbol of relentless ambition. He turned it over in his hand, his thumb brushing against the cold, smooth metal. "This insignia," he mused, his mind already cross-referencing it with his databanks. "It's OmniCorp. Their mark is everywhere in the galaxy, always associated with the same pattern: rapid industrialization, ecological collapse, and eventual abandonment." He tossed the disc aside with a grimace. "They're not explorers, Kira. They're locusts. They descend upon worlds, strip them bare of any perceived value, and move on, leaving the indigenous life to adapt or perish." He looked around at the damaged landscape, his earlier scientific curiosity replaced by a profound sense of outrage. "My instruments are detecting residual thermal signatures from their propulsion systems, indicating a rapid, high-energy descent and ascent. They likely landed within this sector, conducted their scans and extraction, and then retreated, leaving their detritus behind without a second thought. This isn't exploration; it's vandalism on a cosmic scale."

Kira lowered herself to a crouch, her eyes scanning the undergrowth for any further signs of their passage. She found more discarded components, fragments of synthetic material that felt unnaturally smooth and brittle. One piece, a convoluted network of wires encased in a dull grey polymer, had been snapped in half, its severed ends sparking faintly with residual energy. She recoiled, a low growl escaping her throat. "The energy residual is unstable," she warned. "It's polluting the ambient field. It's like a fever in the forest, and they are the disease." Her gaze swept across the immediate area, her keen senses picking up the subtle signs of distress from the surrounding plant life. The leaves of a nearby sapling were curled inwards, its bioluminescent veins pulsing erratically, a silent scream against the invasive forces. "They have no respect for the natural cycles, for the slow, deliberate rhythm of life. They impose their own frantic pace, their own destructive logic, and expect the world to bend to their will."

Niko agreed, his voice heavy with the weight of his observations. "Their technology is designed for brute force. They bypass natural defenses, override ecological balances, and prioritize speed and efficiency above all else. It's a philosophy of domination, not integration. They don't seek to understand Veridia; they seek to conquer it, to bend it to their extractive agenda. Even their discarded equipment is a testament to this disregard. It's not designed for recyclability or minimal environmental impact; it's simply disposable, designed to be replaced rather than repaired, and certainly not to be reintegrated into a natural system." He activated a trace analysis on his scanner, the results confirming his suspicions. "The polymer composition is highly resistant to natural biodegradation, meaning these fragments will persist for centuries, leaching micro-plastics and trace toxins into the soil and water. It's a permanent scar, a reminder of their passage. And the energy signatures... they're indicative of rapid, localized energy dissipation, suggesting their equipment was designed for single-use operational bursts, then discarded. This is not the work of responsible explorers; it's the hallmark of corporate predators."

Kira nudged a discarded nutrient paste packet with her paw. The wrapper, a dull, metallic sheen, was torn open, its contents spilled and partially decomposed, but still emitting a faint, artificial odor. "They consume, they discard, they move on," she stated, her voice laced with a deep sadness. "They do not witness the beauty they destroy. They do not feel the pain they inflict. They are blind to the interconnectedness of all things, deaf to the silent whispers of the planet." She looked at Niko, her luminous markings dimming slightly, reflecting her own growing concern for the world they had come to cherish. "Our methods are slow, deliberate, and respectful. We learn, we observe, and we integrate. Theirs is a swift, violent invasion, a brutal imposition of will. This difference, Niko, is the heart of our struggle. It is the fundamental clash between the old ways and the new, between life and the relentless drive for consumption."

"And their footprint is as vast as their ambition," Niko added, his gaze fixed on the environmental data his scanner was providing. "The localized atmospheric contamination, while not immediately catastrophic on a planetary scale, is significant in this micro-environment. It will impact the delicate respiration cycles of the smaller fauna, potentially affecting their migration patterns and breeding cycles. And the soil contamination... that will take decades, perhaps centuries, of dedicated ecological restoration to rectify, assuming it can be rectified at all. OmniCorp doesn't concern itself with such long-term consequences. Their investors demand quarterly returns, not ecological legacies. They operate on a scale of galactic exploitation, treating entire planets as mere resource depots to be plundered until depleted, then abandoned for the next unsuspecting world. Their technology is designed for this rapid exploitation, for maximum extraction with minimum expenditure on environmental remediation. It is a model of profound irresponsibility, a dark reflection of unchecked industrial ambition."

Kira let out a soft sigh, a sound laden with the weight of her observations. She could feel the subtle vibrations of the forest attempting to reassert themselves, the faint hum of life striving to overcome the lingering dissonance, but the scars were undeniable. "They are a shadow, Niko," she concluded, her voice barely above a whisper. "A corporate shadow cast across Veridia's light. And we are here to ensure that shadow does not consume the dawn." Her resolve hardened, her focus shifting from the immediate evidence of their desecration to the greater threat they represented. The contrast between their methods wasn't just a matter of scientific curiosity or aesthetic preference; it was a fundamental philosophical divide that would dictate the fate of Veridia.

The air, still thick with the lingering scent of ozone and alien decay, did little to quell the growing storm in Niko Thorne's mind. Kira's words about the corporate shadow echoed in his thoughts, a stark reminder of the very forces he had dedicated his life to opposing. This wasn't a new adversary; it was an old, insidious enemy, a specter from his past that had haunted his every waking moment since he'd walked away from the gilded cage of OmniCorp. The fractured forest floor, the blackened flora, the discarded, polluting detritus – it was all a visceral, sickening replay of the nightmares he'd tried to outrun.

He remembered the sterile gleam of OmniCorp's research facilities, the hushed reverence with which his colleagues spoke of the company's boundless ambition, their unwavering pursuit of progress. Progress. The word had once resonated with him, a siren song of discovery and innovation. He'd genuinely believed, in those early days, that he was contributing to something meaningful, something that would elevate not just humanity, but all sentient life. He'd been young, eager, and desperately seeking validation, and OmniCorp had offered it in spades, along with a salary that could secure a comfortable future for generations.

His initial assignment had been ostensibly benign: charting the bio-signatures of newly discovered worlds, cataloging their flora and fauna for potential symbiotic integration. He'd been thrilled, armed with cutting-edge technology, eager to apply his ecological principles on an interstellar scale. But the gloss of discovery soon began to chip away, revealing the rot beneath. He'd noticed the subtle pressures, the nudges towards prioritizing species with quantifiable economic value, the dismissiveness towards indigenous life forms that didn't fit neatly into OmniCorp's profit-driven matrices.

There was the incident on Xylos Prime, a world teeming with crystalline flora that pulsed with a gentle, harmonic energy. Niko had spent months documenting its intricate symbiosis, its unique method of energy transfer. His findings suggested a slow, deliberate ecosystem, one that could be studied for centuries without disruption. But OmniCorp's geological survey teams had identified rare mineral deposits beneath the surface, deposits that could be extracted with their proprietary seismic fracturing technology. Niko had presented his data, pleading for a more nuanced approach, suggesting a phased extraction that minimized ecological impact. He'd been met with polite condescension. His concerns were "sentimentality," his ecological models "inefficient." The seismic fracturing had begun, and the crystalline forests, with their delicate energy webs, had shattered, their light extinguished within weeks. He'd watched, helpless, as entire biomes dissolved into dust, the very air thick with the metallic tang of pulverized minerals.

Then came the whispers, the hushed conversations about 'resource optimization protocols,' 'bio-asset liquidation,' and 'terraforming for utility.' These weren't the terms of scientific exploration; they were the language of conquest. He'd started seeing the direct correlation between OmniCorp's presence and widespread ecological devastation. Worlds that had once been vibrant hubs of biodiversity were reduced to barren industrial landscapes, their unique life forms either eradicated or, in the crueler cases, subjected to genetic manipulation for the creation of bio-engineered commodities.

His breaking point had come during an expedition to the Kepler-186f system. The planet, a verdant paradise he'd nicknamed 'Emerald Haven,' was home to a species of sentient, arboreal creatures that communicated through complex scent-based pheromones and bioluminescent displays. Niko had established a tentative rapport with them, learning their simple, peaceful ways, observing their deep reverence for their planetary home. OmniCorp, however, had seen them as a source of potent, naturally occurring neurotoxins, highly sought after in the interstellar black market. The 'harvesting,' as it was euphemistically called, was brutal. The creatures, unable to flee the planet, were rounded up, their toxins extracted through excruciating methods, leaving them weakened and dying. Niko had witnessed the sterile efficiency of it all, the way the OmniCorp operatives treated the creatures as mere biological specimens, their sentience an inconvenient anomaly. He'd tried to intervene, to shield a group of younglings, but his efforts were swiftly curtailed by corporate security. He'd been threatened, his career jeopardized, his ethical objections dismissed as insubordination.

The memory of those frightened, luminescent eyes, dimmed by pain and betrayal, was a constant ache in his chest. He had walked away from OmniCorp that day, not with a badge of honor, but with the weight of his complicity pressing down on him. He'd resigned, forfeiting his lucrative position, his access to advanced technology, and the promise of a comfortable life. He'd left the corporate world behind, but the corporate shadow, he now realized, had followed him.

He looked at Kira, her obsidian fur a stark contrast against the ravaged earth. He saw in her eyes a reflection of his own quiet fury, his own deep-seated anger. She, too, was a guardian of the natural world, a protector of its inherent worth. Their mission with the Resonant Pack, this endeavor to understand and coexist with alien ecosystems, was not just a scientific pursuit; it was a deeply personal crusade, a penance for the sins he had witnessed, and in some small way, participated in.

"They operate with a fundamentally flawed premise," Niko began, his voice rough with emotion, directing his words not just at Kira, but at the memory of his former employers. "They see life as a resource, a commodity to be exploited. They lack the most basic understanding of interconnectedness, of the delicate balance that sustains all living systems. My time with them... it opened my eyes to the sheer, unadulterated greed that drives some factions of our species. They are driven by a hunger that can never be sated, a desire to consume and control that leaves nothing but emptiness in its wake."

He ran a gloved hand over a jagged piece of discarded OmniCorp plating, its surface strangely smooth, almost unnaturally so. "This material," he murmured, his scanner still passively analyzing it, "it's designed for rapid deployment and eventual disposal. There's no thought given to biodegradability, to its impact on the local biosphere. It's a temporary solution for a temporary problem, as far as they're concerned. They don't build things to last, to be integrated, to become part of the earth. They build things to be used and thrown away, leaving behind a trail of pollution that can persist for millennia."

He remembered the internal memos he'd seen, the casual discussions about 'environmental externalities' as mere accounting line items. The cost of cleanup, of ecological restoration, was always deemed too high, an unnecessary expense when compared to the profit margins of rapid resource extraction. It was a cold, calculated indifference that chilled him to the bone.

"I remember arguing for years about the ethical implications of their bio-harvesting protocols," Niko continued, his gaze distant, lost in the echoes of past debates. "They would justify it by saying they were 'optimizing' natural resources, that they were bringing efficiency to a chaotic, inefficient universe. But it was never about optimization; it was about exploitation. They would strip a planet bare of its unique biological components, turning living creatures into mere ingredients for their alchemical concoctions, their wonder drugs, their potent weapons. And the sentient beings who called those worlds home? They were either collateral damage or, worse, simply another resource to be harvested."

He recalled the holographic simulations he'd been privy to, showing the projected trajectories of OmniCorp's operations. They would identify a promising world, deploy automated probes for resource assessment, then send in the extraction teams. The process was designed for maximum speed, minimal oversight, and absolutely no long-term ecological considerations. The goal was always to extract the most value in the shortest amount of time, then move on to the next unsuspecting planet. Abandonment was not a failure; it was the endgame.

"I tried to push for a more ethical approach, a method of research that prioritized understanding over exploitation," Niko confessed, his voice barely a whisper, as if confessing a crime. "I proposed interspecies dialogue, collaborative research, a model of mutual benefit. But my ideas were consistently dismissed. They saw me as an idealist, a naive dreamer who didn't understand the realities of interstellar commerce. They wanted replicable, scalable results, not the slow, messy process of true ecological understanding."

He clenched his jaw, the memory of one particularly heated exchange replaying in his mind. He had presented a detailed proposal for a sustainable bio-harvesting method on a fungal planet, one that would allow the fungi to regenerate and continue to produce their valuable spores. His supervisor, a man named Valerius Thorne (no relation, a fact Niko had often been grateful for), had sneered, "Thorne, your sentimentality is a liability. We don't nurture our livestock, we process them. These fungi are no different. Maximum yield, minimal effort. That's the OmniCorp way."

The casual cruelty of that statement, the dehumanization of a complex biological system, had been the final straw. He'd walked out of Valerius's office that day, his career in ruins, but his conscience, for the first time in a long time, clear.

"They taught me the worst kind of science," Niko said, his voice gaining a steely edge. "The science of reduction, of dissection, of stripping away all context and meaning. They taught me how to break down a complex ecosystem into its constituent parts, not to understand its entirety, but to identify its exploitable elements. They honed my skills, yes, but they also corrupted my purpose. They turned my passion for understanding life into a tool for its domination."

He looked down at his hands, now stained with the alien soil. These were the hands that had once operated OmniCorp's most advanced scanners, that had charted paths for their resource extraction fleets. Now, they were the hands of a protector, of a researcher committed to a different path.

"That's why this is so personal," Niko admitted, meeting Kira's steady gaze. "I know their methods. I know the insidious way they erode ecosystems, the justifications they use, the cold, hard logic they employ to mask their rapacious hunger. I've seen worlds die because of them. And I will not stand by and watch them do it to Veridia." He took a deep breath, the scent of the damaged forest a bitter reminder of his past and a stark motivator for his future. "This isn't just about protecting a planet, Kira. It's about fighting back against the very philosophy that threatens to consume everything that is wild, and beautiful, and inherently valuable in this universe. It's about proving that there's another way, a better way, to interact with the wonders we discover."

He extended a hand, his fingers brushing against a patch of soil still blackened by OmniCorp's passage. "They are a shadow, yes," he echoed Kira's earlier sentiment, his voice firm with renewed resolve. "But shadows can be dispelled. And I, for one, have had enough of living in their darkness."

Kira's ears twitched, her obsidian fur rippling as if caught by an unseen breeze. She tilted her head, a low growl rumbling in her chest, a sound that resonated with a primal awareness Niko had learned to trust implicitly. It wasn't just the visual evidence of OmniCorp's destructive presence that spoke of their transgressions; it was something far more subtle, something that eluded his more conventional sensors. Kira was perceiving the energetic residue of deception, the lingering psychic static left behind by the corporate shadow.

"There's a dissonance here, Niko," she vocalized, her voice a blend of soft purrs and sharp, worried undertones that he could now translate with remarkable clarity. "Where they touched, the world... it feels *dishonest*. The metal, the discarded plastics, even the soil where they trampled – it all hums with a discordant frequency. It's like a badly tuned instrument, jarring against the natural harmony of Veridia."

Niko knelt beside her, his own senses straining to grasp what Kira so readily perceived. He could detect the faint traces of residual radiation from the energy cells, the microscopic particulate matter left by their machinery, but Kira was sensing something deeper, something akin to a spiritual stain. OmniCorp, in their relentless pursuit of profit, had always been masters of misdirection, of burying their true intentions beneath layers of corporate jargon and carefully crafted public relations. They dealt in half-truths and outright lies, and it seemed their very presence left an energetic imprint of that duplicity.

"Dishonest how?" Niko prompted, his gaze sweeping over a shattered piece of what looked like a sensor array, its once-gleaming surface now dulled and cracked. He ran a diagnostic sweep with his gauntlet, but the readings were inconclusive, showing only standard material degradation and faint power signatures. Yet, Kira was clearly picking up on more.

"It's the echoes of their intentions," she explained, her tail giving an agitated flick. "When they were here, they weren't just extracting or building. They were *hiding*. They were masking their true actions, broadcasting false signals, setting up systems designed to mislead. The equipment itself... it holds a memory of that deception. It's not just inert material; it's imbued with the intent behind its creation and deployment."

Niko remembered the elaborate subterfuges OmniCorp had employed during his tenure. They would deploy 'environmental monitoring stations' that were, in reality, sophisticated surveillance hubs, gathering data on local life forms for later exploitation. They would initiate 'terraforming projects' that were, in fact, prelude to massive mining operations, their seismic surveys disguised as atmospheric studies. Their entire operational paradigm was built on a foundation of obfuscation.

"So, you're sensing residual surveillance technology?" Niko mused, his mind racing through the possibilities. OmniCorp would undoubtedly have deployed automated sentinels, passive listening devices, or even bio-integrated sensors to monitor the area long after their initial departure.

Kira shook her head, her whiskers quivering. "It's more than just the technology, Niko. The technology is a symptom, not the disease. The *lie* is the disease. It's in the way they positioned things, the energy signatures they intentionally masked, the false trails they left. Imagine a predator trying to lure prey. They don't just set a trap; they radiate an aura of safety, of normalcy. OmniCorp does that, but in reverse. They leave behind an energetic signature of... *untruth*. It's a low-frequency hum of falsity, designed to lull any natural sensitivity into a false sense of security. They don't want anything to *sense* them, not truly."

He looked at the scattered debris again, now seeing it through Kira's unique perception. The shattered sensor array wasn't just broken; it was a monument to a specific act of concealment. The discarded power conduits weren't just scrap; they were pathways for deliberately misleading energy signals. The very ground, churned and disturbed by their passage, held the energetic imprint of their clandestine activities.

"They are masters of misdirection," Niko said, his voice low and tinged with his old resentment. "Even when I was inside, I saw it. They could build a perfectly functional ecosystem simulation for their researchers, but beneath it, there were always hidden subroutines designed to skew the results, to favor certain outcomes that benefited their bottom line. They treated truth as a variable to be manipulated, not a constant to be respected."

Kira nudged his hand with her head, a gesture of comfort and solidarity. "And that is why I am here, Niko. You understand their technology, their history. I understand their energetic signature. Together, we can peel back the layers of their deception."

Her sensitivity was proving to be an invaluable asset. While Niko could analyze the physical remnants of OmniCorp's presence, Kira could discern the intentions behind them. She was like a living, breathing lie detector, her senses attuned to the subtle energetic vibrations that betrayed the truth. This was crucial. OmniCorp wouldn't leave a place like this – a world of unique biological resources – without laying the groundwork for future exploitation, or at least, for ensuring no one else could exploit it without their knowledge.

"I remember the 'Project Nightingale' incident on Cygnus X-1," Niko recounted, his mind drifting back to one of OmniCorp's more audacious operations. "They claimed to be developing a new atmospheric purification system for arid worlds. The public face was benevolent environmentalism. But the reality? They were using the purification process to extract rare atmospheric isotopes, which were then refined into a powerful, albeit highly addictive, stimulant. They built massive, aesthetically pleasing towers that looked like natural geological formations, but internally, they were complex industrial facilities. The energy signatures were masked to mimic geothermal activity. Most of the local population, desperate for economic opportunity, welcomed them. They never suspected the true purpose until the 'purification' process began to actively deplete the atmosphere of vital trace elements, causing widespread respiratory illnesses, while OmniCorp shipped out shiploads of the refined isotopes."

He paused, letting the weight of that memory settle. "I was on the periphery of that project, analyzing atmospheric samples. Even then, something felt off. The readings were too consistent, too...*curated*. I never got to the bottom of it, but the unease has stayed with me. Your perception, Kira, it confirms what I suspected then: that their operations are always built on a scaffold of lies."

Kira's response was a soft, resonant hum, a sound that conveyed understanding and a shared sense of purpose. "The energetic signature of

Project Nightingale," she murmured, her eyes closed as if recalling a distant sensation, "would have been a tapestry of feigned purity and underlying avarice. A shimmering facade over a greedy heart. I can sense that same subtle dissonance here, though perhaps on a smaller scale, more like a scouting mission than a full-scale operation."

This was what made their partnership so potent. Niko's scientific rigor, honed by years of field research and corporate-induced skepticism, provided the framework for understanding the 'how' and 'what' of OmniCorp's actions. Kira's innate empathic and energetic sensitivity provided the 'why,' revealing the true intentions and the ethical vacuum at the core of their methodology. She could sense the subtle energetic signatures of hidden cameras, passive sensors, and even carefully laid bio-traps designed to collect samples or tag indigenous life forms.

"They often employ 'chameleon technology'," Niko explained, recalling the internal jargon. "Devices that mimic natural energy patterns, blend into the local bio-electric fields, or emit frequencies that actively suppress the senses of sensitive organisms. They don't want their activities to be detected. Detection means risk, and risk means reduced profit margins."

"And this 'chameleon technology'," Kira purred, her gaze fixed on a tangled mass of what appeared to be native vines, "it doesn't fool me. It's like trying to hide a shout in a cacophony. The effort to maintain the illusion, the energetic strain of the mimicry, creates its own unique ripple. A ripple of... *forced silence*. It's the sound of something trying too hard to be unnoticed."

She cautiously approached the vines, sniffing the air with intense concentration. Niko watched, his hand hovering over his multi-tool, ready to assist if needed. Kira reached out a paw, gently touching one of the thicker tendrils. A faint, almost imperceptible shimmer rippled across its surface, a momentary disruption in its otherwise natural appearance.

"Here," Kira announced, her voice taking on a sharper edge. "This vine... it's been enhanced. The OmniCorp signature is faint, but it's there. It's a passive data collector. It will be transmitting information about atmospheric conditions, soil composition, and perhaps even bio-signatures of passing fauna back to a central hub."

Niko carefully extended a sensor from his gauntlet, calibrating it to detect subtle artificial energy emanations. The device chirped, indicating a low-level energy output, far below what would typically register on standard scans, but undeniably artificial. "You're right, Kira. There's a dormant transmission node embedded within the cellular structure of the plant. It's incredibly sophisticated; it's designed to draw power directly from the plant's own metabolic processes."

He looked around, a new sense of unease creeping in. If one vine was enhanced, how many others were? Were entire sections of this forest subtly integrated into an OmniCorp surveillance network? The thought was chilling. This wasn't just about identifying discarded equipment; it was about recognizing a potentially pervasive, hidden infrastructure designed to monitor and report on every aspect of Veridia's ecosystem.

"They are like a creeping vine themselves," Niko murmured, the metaphor hitting home with newfound relevance. "Insidious, pervasive, and designed to choke out the native life if left unchecked. They infiltrate, they adapt, and they drain the host of its vitality."

"And they leave behind a residue of their presence, even when they are gone," Kira added, her gaze now sweeping across the wider clearing. "The soil remembers. The air remembers. And I can read those memories." She moved with fluid grace, her senses guiding her through the undergrowth, a living testament to the interconnectedness that OmniCorp so callously disregarded. She paused near a cluster of strange, phosphorescent fungi. "These, too," she indicated with a subtle flick of her tail, "bear the faint imprint of their passage. Not a direct enhancement, but a disruption. A suppression of their natural luminescence. It's as if they didn't want even the fungi to shine too brightly, lest they attract unwanted attention to their clandestine activities."

Niko activated his scanner again, focusing on the fungi. The luminescence was indeed dimmer than the surrounding specimens, and the spectral analysis showed a slight distortion in their usual light-emitting chemical compounds. It was a subtle manipulation, designed to reduce visibility, to make the forest floor seem less active, less alive. It was a testament to OmniCorp's strategy of managing perception, of shaping the environment to serve their own hidden agendas.

"They want to control what is seen and what is hidden," Niko deduced. "They don't want natural phenomena to reveal their presence or their activities. It's all about maintaining their operational secrecy. They operate in the shadows, and they try to turn the entire world into their shadow."

Kira let out a soft sigh, a sound that carried a weight of ancient wisdom. "The natural world is honest, Niko. It reveals itself. It communicates its needs, its strengths, its vulnerabilities. OmniCorp thrives on the opposite: on concealment, on exploitation, on silencing the authentic voice of life. Their technology is a tool for that silencing, and their energetic residue is the echo of their lies."

She looked up at Niko, her luminous eyes reflecting a deep understanding. "You were right to leave them. Your integrity is a far greater asset than any of their advanced technology. And my senses... they are a mirror to the truth they try to bury. Together, we are a force that can see through their shadows."

Niko met her gaze, a surge of gratitude and renewed purpose flowing through him. He had walked away from OmniCorp burdened by guilt and the cynicism of experience. But with Kira by his side, he felt a flicker of hope. She was not just a companion; she was a vital sensor for the truth, an anchor to the natural world, and a constant reminder that even in the face of overwhelming corporate deception, authentic perception and unwavering integrity could still prevail. The fight against the corporate shadow was not just a battle of technology or resources; it was a battle for the very essence of truth and honesty, and Kira was an invaluable ally in that crucial struggle. The abandoned equipment was not merely debris; it was a tangible testament to the insidious nature of their deception, a silent hum of untruth that Kira's senses could decipher, and Niko could now, with her guidance, begin to dismantle.

The realization settled over Niko like a shroud, a chilling echo of past deceptions now amplified by Kira's acute senses. OmniCorp wasn't merely present; they were actively *mining* the essence of Veridia, their objective far more insidious than simple resource extraction. The discarded machinery, the subtly altered flora, the energetic imprints of their clandestine operations – they all pointed to a singular, avaricious purpose: to siphon the planet's vital energies, its unique biological signatures, and its resonant frequencies for their own profit, regardless of the catastrophic impact on the delicate ecosystem. The urgency that had been a low thrum in Niko's mind now became a pounding drumbeat. They were no longer just observers; they were guardians, tasked with a mission that transcended mere documentation. It was a race against time, a desperate attempt to preempt the irreparable scarring of a world still awakening to its own potential.

Kira, her posture rigid, her usually fluid movements now laced with a nervous tension, vocalized his unspoken fears. "They seek the deep resonance, Niko. The hum of life that is unique to Veridia. It is... potent. A source of raw power that OmniCorp craves. They do not understand it, not truly, but they can sense its value. They will strip it bare, leaving only silence and a hollow shell." Her words painted a grim picture, a stark contrast to the vibrant symphony of life that had greeted them upon arrival. The very air seemed to vibrate with the unspoken threat, a palpable tension that coiled in Niko's gut. This wasn't just another corporate terraforming project gone awry; this was an active, calculated plunder of a world's very soul.

Niko's mind raced, piecing together the fragmented clues. He recalled the OmniCorp's internal memos he'd accessed years ago, detailing their insatiable hunger for novel energy sources. Veridia, with its unique geological formations, its complex bio-luminescent life, and its seemingly anomalous atmospheric phenomena, would have been a prime target. They would have seen it not as a living, breathing entity, but as a vast, untapped reservoir of raw, exploitable power. The 'environmental surveys' and 'geological assessments' he'd dismissed as standard OmniCorp procedure now took on a sinister new light. They weren't just gathering data; they were mapping out the veins of Veridia's lifeblood, identifying the most potent nodes of energy for their insatiable machines.

"The energy cells I detected," Niko murmured, his voice low with grim realization, "they weren't just for powering their equipment. They were conduits. Designed to channel and amplify the planet's natural energetic output. They've been trying to tap into Veridia's resonant frequencies, to draw them out, perhaps to synthesize them, or even to weaponize them." The implications were staggering. OmniCorp's pursuit of profit had always been rapacious, but this transcended mere resource depletion. They were attempting to fundamentally alter the planet's energetic equilibrium, a reckless act that could have cascading and devastating consequences for the delicate web of life.

Kira let out a soft, mournful sound, a vibration that resonated deep within Niko's chest. "They are blind to the interconnectedness," she communicated, her empathy a tangible presence. "They see only the prize, not the price. The harmony they seek to disrupt is the very thing that sustains Veridia. To take from it without giving back, without understanding its intricate balance, is to invite destruction. I can feel the distress of the ancient trees, the subtle tremor of fear in the smallest creatures. They sense the violation."

Niko knelt beside her, his hand resting on the rough bark of a colossal, moss-laden tree. It felt ancient, wise, and now, vulnerable. He could almost feel the faint pulse of life within it, a slow, steady beat that spoke of millennia of growth and resilience. OmniCorp's operations, even if they had been physically removed, left behind an energetic scar, a disruption that the planet was struggling to heal. This was why they had to act. Observation was no longer sufficient. They had to understand the full extent of the damage, to find a way to mitigate any lingering harm, and most importantly, to gather irrefutable evidence of OmniCorp's transgressions.

"We need to map their extraction points," Niko stated, his mind already formulating a plan. "Identify the specific locations where they were trying to siphon energy. We need to document the technology they deployed, the residual signatures, anything that can serve as undeniable proof of their intent. This information is crucial not only to understand the potential long-term impact on Veridia but also to expose OmniCorp to the wider galactic community." The thought of bringing OmniCorp to justice, of holding them accountable for their rapacious greed, fueled a fire within him. He had seen firsthand the damage they could inflict, the lives they had ruined, and the ecosystems they had decimated.

Kira nodded, her gaze sweeping across the dense canopy. "The energetic currents will guide us. They are like scars on the planet's skin, faint but discernible to those who know how to look. Where their machines were most active, the natural resonance will be distorted, weakened, or unnaturally amplified. It will be like a discordant note in Veridia's song." She paused, her ears swiveling, catching a subtle shift in the ambient energy. "There is a stronger signature to the north-east, near the crystalline mesa. It pulses with a frantic energy, a desperate attempt to draw in that which is not its own."

"The crystalline mesa," Niko mused, pulling up a topographical scan of the region on his gauntlet's display. "It's known for its unique piezoelectric properties. The crystals amplify and store ambient energy. If OmniCorp was targeting Veridia's energy reserves, that would be a prime location. They could have been using the mesa as a natural amplifier, a giant receiver for their siphoning operations." The pieces were falling into place with alarming speed, painting a picture of calculated exploitation on a grand scale.

"The energetic signature there is... violent," Kira communicated, a shiver rippling through her fur. "It is the sound of something being torn from its source. The crystals are not inherently distressed, but the forces being exerted upon them are causing immense strain. It is a violation of their natural function, a forced overextension."

Niko's hand tightened on his multi-tool. The weight of his past with OmniCorp pressed down on him. He had been a cog in their machine, an analyst who had unwittingly provided data that had led to destruction. This time, he would be different. This time, he was on the side of the planet, of its life, of its inherent right to exist undisturbed. The responsibility was immense, but so was the conviction. He looked at Kira, her presence a silent testament to the very essence of Veridia that OmniCorp sought to exploit. Her sensitivity, her connection to the natural world, was not just a unique ability; it was a vital weapon against the soulless machinations of corporate greed.

"We need to move quickly," Niko urged, his voice firm. "If they are still active, even remotely, any delay could mean further damage. We have to assess the extent of their interference, document what we can, and then... then we have to find a way to shut down whatever residual systems they might have left behind. We can't let them win, Kira. Not this time."

Kira met his gaze, her luminous eyes reflecting a shared resolve. "The forest has its own defenses, Niko," she said, her voice laced with a quiet strength. "Its resilience is profound. But even the strongest defenses can be overwhelmed by a relentless assault. We are here to help it withstand that assault, to be its voice when it cannot cry out for itself."

The journey to the crystalline mesa was a testament to Veridia's untamed beauty, a landscape sculpted by forces far older and grander than any corporate ambition. Yet, beneath the surface of this pristine wilderness, the insidious tendrils of OmniCorp's exploitation were beginning to reveal themselves. As they moved deeper into the terrain, the subtle energetic disturbances that Kira perceived became more pronounced. The air itself seemed to thrum with a low-grade, artificial hum, a discordant note beneath the natural symphony of the forest. Niko's sensors, calibrated to detect even the faintest anomalies, began to register scattered residual energy signatures, faint but undeniably present, remnants of the vast network OmniCorp had once established.

"There are traces of discarded atmospheric processors," Niko reported, pointing to a cluster of metallic shards half-buried in the loam, their surfaces pitted and scarred by time and weather. "Their function was to regulate atmospheric composition, ostensibly for environmental stability. But I suspect they were also designed to mask the unique energetic frequencies of this planet, to create a sonic and energetic camouflage for their deeper operations." Kira's ability to sense the "dishonesty" of the environment now made perfect sense. OmniCorp hadn't just built machines; they had woven a tapestry of deception, a carefully constructed illusion of normalcy to mask their true intentions.

Kira nudged a gnarled root with her nose, her sensitive whiskers twitching. "This soil," she communicated, a faint tremor in her voice, "it remembers the pressure. The artificial compaction from their heavy machinery. It is struggling to breathe, to allow the natural flow of nutrients. They did not merely tread upon the land; they *imprisoned* it." Her words underscored the fundamental disrespect that OmniCorp held for living systems. They viewed the planet not as a dynamic, interconnected entity, but as a static resource to be manipulated and exploited.

As they approached the foothills of the mesa, the landscape began to change. The vegetation grew sparser, the earth drier, and the crystalline structures that gave the mesa its name started to emerge, shimmering with an internal light. These were not mere geological formations; they were vibrant, living conduits of energy, pulsating with the very essence of Veridia. And here, the energetic disturbances that Kira sensed were no longer subtle whispers but a cacophony of distress.

"The mesa," Kira breathed, her gaze fixed on the colossal crystalline spires that pierced the sky, "it is in pain. The resonance is being strained to its breaking point. They have forced it to channel an unnatural flow, to absorb and redirect energies it was not designed to contain. It is like a heart being forced to beat at a thousand times its natural rhythm."

Niko's gauntlet buzzed, a barrage of alerts flooding his display. "I'm detecting massive residual energy signatures," he announced, his voice tight with urgency. "Concentrated around the base of the largest crystalline formations. It appears they installed massive energy siphoning arrays, designed to draw power directly from the piezoelectric properties of the crystals. The technology is still partially active, buried beneath the surface, leaching energy even now."

He ran a more detailed scan, his brow furrowed in concentration. "They were sophisticated. They used bio-integrated conduits, woven into the crystalline matrix itself, to maximize energy transfer. They weren't just extracting; they were actively *integrating* their technology with the planet's natural systems. It's a parasitic relationship, designed to drain the host dry." The sheer audacity of their methods was breathtaking. OmniCorp's modus operandi was always to appear as a benevolent force of progress, while secretly embedding their destructive technology within the very fabric of the environment they claimed to protect.

Kira moved with a newfound determination, her senses focused on a particular cluster of crystals that seemed to thrum with a more intense, discordant energy. "Here," she indicated with a flick of her tail. "Beneath this formation. The energy flow is strongest, and the disruption is most severe. It feels like a wound, a raw opening where Veridia's lifeblood is being siphoned away."

Niko knelt by the indicated crystals, his scanners working overtime. "You're right. There's a massive subterranean installation. Energy conduits, power converters, and what looks like a central processing unit, all designed to harness and transmit Veridia's resonant energy. It's still drawing power, a trickle now, but a trickle nonetheless. And it's destabilizing the entire crystalline structure." He pointed to a faint, hairline fracture snaking across the surface of a nearby crystal. "If this continues, the entire mesa could fracture. The resulting energy surge could be catastrophic, not just for Veridia, but for the surrounding systems."

The weight of their discovery pressed down on them. This wasn't just an environmental crime; it was a potential ecological disaster in the making. OmniCorp's reckless pursuit of profit had pushed Veridia to the brink. Their mission had shifted from documentation to active intervention. They had to find a way to disable this installation, to sever the parasitic connection before it was too late.

"We need to disable the core processing unit," Niko stated, his mind already racing through possible scenarios. "It's the nexus of their operation. If we can shut that down, the siphoning will stop, and the crystals can begin to heal." He looked at Kira, his expression grim. "But getting to it won't be easy. OmniCorp always builds in redundancies, fail-safes. There will likely be automated defenses, traps."

Kira met his gaze, her eyes glowing with an unwavering resolve. "I can sense them, Niko. The energetic signatures of their hidden defenses. They are like knots in the flow, subtle distortions that betray their presence. Where you see technology, I see intent. And their intent is to protect their plunder."

The race against exploitation had taken on a terrifying new dimension. It was no longer just about uncovering the truth; it was about actively protecting Veridia from an imminent and catastrophic threat. The fate of the crystalline mesa, and perhaps much more, rested on their ability to outmaneuver OmniCorp's insidious technology and to sever the connection that was slowly bleeding Veridia dry. The corporate shadow had revealed its true, rapacious face, and Niko and Kira were now its only obstacle.

Chapter Five

THE RESONANT DIVIDE

The weight of OmniCorp's actions had always been a heavy burden on Niko, a constant reminder of his past complicity. Now, that weight had intensified, morphing into a tangible threat that pulsed beneath the very soil of Veridia. The subterranean installation they had discovered at the crystalline mesa was not merely a scar; it was an active wound, a parasitic leech siphoning the planet's life force. And it was destabilizing the intricate network that bound Veridia together. Kira's subtle tremors and Niko's readings painted a grim picture: the mesa, a critical nexus in the planet's bio-energetic grid, was on the verge of collapse. The implications sent a shiver down Niko's spine – a cascade failure, a ripple effect that could potentially unmake vast swathes of the ecosystem, perhaps even destabilize connections beyond Veridia itself.

"It's worse than we thought," Niko stated, his voice heavy with an exhaustion that went beyond physical fatigue. He gestured towards the intricate energy schematics flickering on his gauntlet's display. "The siphoning arrays, even in their current diminished state, are overloading the primary conduits connected to this mesa. The crystals are acting as an immense capacitor, storing an unsustainable amount of energy that's being pumped into them. If they can't discharge it, if the network can't absorb it, the whole nexus point will fail. And that," he looked up, meeting Kira's concerned gaze, "could trigger a chain reaction."

Kira let out a low, guttural sound, a vibration that resonated with the distress of the planet. She pressed closer to Niko, her sleek fur brushing against his arm, an unspoken offering of comfort and shared burden. "The imbalance is growing," she communicated, her senses attuned to the subtle shifts in Veridia's energetic hum. "It feels like a taut string, stretched to its absolute limit. The creatures here, the plants... they are all feeling it. A deep unease, a premonition of something shattering."

Niko's team, the Resonant Pack, had always operated under a strict code of non-interference. Their mandate was to observe, to document, to understand the myriad forms of life and their delicate interdependencies, and to share that knowledge without imposing their own will. It was a principle born from centuries of observation, a recognition of the hubris inherent in assuming any species possessed the right or the wisdom to unilaterally alter another's path, no matter how noble the intention. Yet, here they were, confronted with a situation where inaction carried the potential for catastrophic destruction. OmniCorp, in their relentless pursuit of profit, had inadvertently, or perhaps recklessly, pushed Veridia to the precipice of ecological collapse.

"We have a directive," Anya's voice, usually crisp and decisive, held a note of uncertainty as she addressed Niko, her holo-projection shimmering beside him. "We are not to meddle. We are witnesses, not architects of fate." She ran a hand through her short, practical haircut, her brow furrowed. "But this... this isn't just meddling, is it? This is about preventing an active, ongoing harm that OmniCorp initiated. A harm that, if left unchecked, will cause irreparable damage, far beyond what we are authorized to passively observe."

Dr. Aris Thorne, the pack's xenobotanist, a man who often found solace in the quiet contemplation of flora, added his voice, his tone measured. "The interconnectedness of Veridia's bio-network is far more intricate than our initial surveys suggested. Kira's insights have been invaluable, revealing a level of energetic symbiosis that is fundamental to the planet's stability. If this nexus point fails, it's not just a localized ecological disaster. The energetic currents, the very lifeblood of this world, could be rerouted in ways that are unpredictable and devastating. We're talking about potential extinctions, habitat loss on an unprecedented scale, and the disruption of processes we may not even fully comprehend yet."

Niko closed his eyes, the hum of the crystalline mesa a low thrumming in his own bones. He could feel the distress, a palpable ache that seemed to emanate from the very air. He thought of the creatures they had encountered, the sentient flora, the sheer vitality of Veridia. To stand by and watch it crumble felt like a profound betrayal, not just of their burgeoning connection to this world, but of a more universal ethical imperative.

"But where do we draw the line?" Niko countered, his voice resonating with the internal struggle. "If we intervene here, what about the next time? What about other worlds where industrial exploitation leads to ecological imbalance? Do we become the galaxy's perpetual repair crew? It's a slippery slope, Anya. One that could compromise the very principle that guides us, the principle of respecting a world's inherent right to evolve on its own terms."

Kira shifted, nudging his hand again. Her communication was subtle, more of a feeling than a direct thought.

The wound bleeds, she conveyed, a simple, poignant statement that cut through the complex ethical debate. *It needs mending. Not for us, but for itself.*

"Kira's right," Niko said, his gaze fixed on the pulsating mesa. "Our directive is paramount, but it was designed to protect worlds from external interference, not to paralyze us in the face of active, ongoing devastation initiated by others. OmniCorp's actions have created this crisis. They left behind this... this energetic cancer. And it's spreading. Allowing it to fester would be a dereliction of our responsibility, a failure to protect something we have come to understand and value."

Anya's projection flickered, a subtle acknowledgment of the gravity of his words. "So, we're considering direct intervention. Actively disabling the siphoning arrays, perhaps attempting to stabilize the nexus point ourselves?"

"We have to," Niko confirmed, his voice firm, the internal conflict beginning to resolve into a clear path forward. "We can't stand idly by and watch Veridia suffer. We have the technology, and Kira has the insight to guide us. We can do this surgically, with minimal disruption, aiming only to neutralize the immediate threat and allow Veridia's natural resilience to take over. We are not imposing a solution; we are removing an impediment. We are not dictating a new path; we are restoring the original one."

Dr. Thorne nodded slowly. "My concern is the downstream effects. If we disrupt the flow in a way that the planet's natural systems aren't prepared for, we could inadvertently create new problems. However, the alternative – allowing the cascade failure – is undeniably worse. We must proceed with extreme caution, focusing on a complete and immediate shutdown of the OmniCorp technology, then observing closely to ensure Veridia can reassert its own equilibrium."

"And what if OmniCorp has other systems in place?" Anya raised a crucial point. "Fail-safes, automated defenses that could react to our intervention? They wouldn't want their investment, even a failing one, to be destroyed."

"That's where Kira's abilities become critical," Niko stated. "She can sense the residual energy signatures of their technology, their hidden traps. We'll move with her guidance, targeting the primary nexus of the siphoning operation. Our objective is to sever the connection, to starve the parasitic conduits, and to shut down the central processing unit that's driving the overload. We're not here to wage war; we're here to perform an emergency amputation."

The ethical tightrope they walked was precarious. The non-interference directive was not a rigid rule to be followed blindly, but a guiding principle designed to foster respect and prevent unintended consequences. In this instance, however, the consequences of *inaction* were far more dire and demonstrably caused by an external, exploitative force. To adhere strictly to the directive in this scenario would be to condone destruction, to allow the damage initiated by OmniCorp to fester and spread unchecked. It was a subtle but vital distinction. They weren't imposing their will on Veridia; they were attempting to remove the imposition that OmniCorp had already made.

Niko looked at Kira, who remained pressed against his side, her large, luminous eyes reflecting a mixture of apprehension and unwavering resolve. He could feel her empathy, a constant, gentle current that mirrored his own emotional landscape. She felt the planet's pain, the fear of its inhabitants, and the immense pressure of their decision. Her presence was a silent anchor, a reminder of what they were fighting for – the inherent right of Veridia to exist, to thrive, to resonate with its own unique song.

"This is not a decision we make lightly," Niko addressed his team, his voice clear and firm, cutting through the holographic haze. "We are stepping beyond our usual boundaries, but we are doing so to uphold a higher principle: the preservation of life and the integrity of a world that is actively being harmed. We will act with precision, with respect for Veridia's own systems, and with a singular focus on neutralizing OmniCorp's destructive legacy. Our goal is to create the conditions for Veridia to heal itself, not to dictate its future."

He turned his attention back to the shimmering mesa, its internal light now seeming to flicker with an urgent plea. The decision had been made. The weight of responsibility was immense, the potential for unforeseen repercussions a constant shadow, but the imperative to act was undeniable. They were the Resonant Pack, and Veridia's song was in danger of fading into silence. They could not, would not, let that happen. The ethical crossroads had been navigated, and the path forward, though fraught with peril, was clear. It was a path of intervention, of desperate repair, and of unwavering hope that Veridia's inherent resilience would prevail. The symphony of life on this world deserved a chance to continue, unmarred by the discordant echoes of corporate greed.

The air around the crystalline mesa hummed with a palpable tension. It wasn't just the ambient energy of Veridia, but an artificial discord, a jarring note introduced by OmniCorp's parasitic technology. Niko, flanked by Kira and the holographic projections of Anya and Dr. Thorne, felt the immensity of the decision they had just made. The non-interference directive, the bedrock of their mission, had been pushed to its absolute limit, bent and reshaped by the undeniable reality of active ecological devastation.

"We need a plan of action," Niko stated, his voice carrying the weight of their collective agreement. "Kira, can you pinpoint the exact locations of the conduits and the central processing unit you sensed? We need to be as surgical as possible."

Kira tilted her head, her sensitive ears twitching, her gaze fixed on a section of the mesa where the crystalline structures seemed to twist and strain against an invisible force. "The primary surge is originating from beneath that largest spire," she communicated, a faint tremor running through her. "The conduits are like veins, burrowing deep into the crystal matrix. They converge there. The control nexus... it feels like a knot of tangled, artificial energy. It is actively drawing, forcing the flow. I can also sense... other signatures. Smaller, dispersed units. Likely auxiliary power regulators and defensive nodes."

Dr. Thorne's projection flickered. "Auxiliary nodes and defensive systems. Just as Anya feared. OmniCorp would have ensured redundancy. Our approach needs to account for potential automated responses. We cannot afford to trigger a full-scale defensive protocol that could further destabilize the mesa or cause an uncontrolled energy discharge."

"That's where caution comes in," Niko replied, his eyes scanning the intricate geological data overlaid with Kira's energetic readings. "We isolate and disable the main conduits first. Starve the beast at its source. Then, we move to the central nexus. Kira, if you can identify the weakest points in their defensive network, the less robust energetic signatures, we can prioritize those. We bypass the heavy defenses and aim for a swift shutdown of the core system. The goal is to remove the artificial pressure, not to engage in a prolonged conflict."

Anya's projection appeared more concerned. "Niko, have you considered the ethical implications of actively manipulating Veridia's energy systems, even with the intent of repair? Our directive is clear: observe, do not interfere. We are not scientists of this world; we are outsiders. What if our intervention, however well-intentioned, introduces a novel stressor that Veridia's natural resilience cannot overcome?"

"Anya, I understand your concern," Niko said, his gaze steady. "But consider this: OmniCorp *has* interfered. They have actively manipulated Veridia's energy systems, and their actions have created a threat that Veridia itself may not be able to overcome on its own. We are not imposing a new system; we are removing an imposed one. Think of it like removing a tumor. The surgeon's intervention is a form of interference, but it's done to preserve the patient's life. Our goal is to remove OmniCorp's parasitic technology, to sever the connection that is bleeding Veridia dry, and then to step back. We will monitor, of course, but the ultimate healing will be Veridia's own."

Kira nudged his hand again, her thoughts a gentle stream of reassurance.

The planet trusts us, Niko. It feels our intent. It knows we seek to help it breathe again.

"Her intuition is a powerful guide," Dr. Thorne added, his voice thoughtful. "And it aligns with our understanding of emergent symbiotic networks. While our physical actions are external, Kira's ability to sense and interpret the energetic flow allows us to integrate our intervention with Veridia's natural processes. We are not forcing a solution; we are facilitating its own recovery."

Niko nodded, a renewed sense of purpose settling over him. The ethical dilemma, while profound, had been met with a pragmatic and compassionate response. They were not acting out of a desire for control, but out of a deep-seated respect for life and a responsibility to mitigate harm, especially harm initiated by the kind of rapacious greed that had defined OmniCorp for so long.

"Our priority is to disable the main siphoning arrays first," Niko reiterated. "Kira, lead us to the most accessible conduit nexus points. Anya, Dr. Thorne, you'll be monitoring Veridia's overall energetic state, looking for any signs of cascading instability. If we see anything that suggests our intervention is causing undue stress, we pull back immediately and re-evaluate."

The team acknowledged his command, their holographic forms resolute. The weight of their actions was heavy, but the alternative – inaction – was unthinkable. Veridia's resonant song was faltering, its vibrant melody threatened by the jarring intrusion of OmniCorp's technology. They were here to help it find its harmony once more, to restore the delicate balance that allowed life to flourish. The path ahead was uncertain, fraught with technological and ethical complexities, but their resolve was firm. They were the Resonant Pack, and they would not let Veridia's song be silenced. The ethical crossroads had led them to a path of intervention, a path guided by compassion and a profound respect for the interconnected web of life.

The Resonant Pack's operational mandate was etched into their very beings: observe, understand, and document. The principle of non-interference was not a mere guideline; it was the bedrock of their existence, a sacred trust forged over millennia of intergalactic exploration. It was born from the hard-won wisdom that the most profound ecological disasters often stemmed not from malice, but from an arrogant overestimation of one's own understanding and the right to impose one's will upon another world's natural trajectory. Yet, here they stood, on the precipice of a situation that threatened to shatter that foundational tenet, a situation where adherence to their deepest principle might, paradoxically, lead to the very destruction they sought to prevent.

Niko ran a gloved hand over the cool, smooth surface of his gauntlet, bringing up the detailed schematics of their emergency intervention protocols. These were procedures reserved for the direst of circumstances, the celestial equivalent of last resorts, requiring not just a majority vote, but the unanimous consent of every member of the pack. The process itself was designed to be a crucible, forcing an agonizing level of introspection and consensus-building that mirrored the planet's own delicate equilibrium. Each protocol was a testament to their commitment to minimal impact restoration, a surgical approach focused on alleviating immediate threats without usurping the planet's own inherent capacity for recovery. The emphasis was always on 'restoration,' not 'control.' They were to be the gentlest of hands, nudging a damaged system back towards its natural rhythm, rather than forcibly re-engineering it.

"The protocols are clear," Niko murmured, his voice a low rumble in the charged atmosphere around the crystalline mesa. "We're not to introduce foreign variables unless absolutely necessary. No permanent alterations, no imposing our own energy signatures, and certainly no technological solutions that create a dependency. The goal is to remove the disruptive element, to create space for the ecosystem to heal itself." He tapped a section of the display, highlighting the 'Resonant Harmonic Re-alignment Sequence.' "This is for situations where a planet's natural energetic frequencies have been thrown out of sync. It involves broadcasting harmonizing frequencies, carefully modulated to match the planet's baseline resonance. It's designed to encourage cellular regeneration and re-establish bio-energetic pathways."

Kira, sensing the weight of his contemplation, nudged his hand with her head. Her thoughts, a blend of empathic resonance and focused observation, echoed his concerns.

The disruption is too great, Niko. It is not a gentle nudge. It is a violent tear. The healing requires more than just removing the tear; it requires mending the ragged edges.

Niko nodded, acknowledging her insight. "Precisely. The 'Harmonic Re-alignment' might be too subtle here. OmniCorp hasn't just created a subtle disharmony; they've installed a drain, a siphon that is actively bleeding Veridia's life force. This isn't about re-tuning; it's about severing a parasite. That brings us to the 'Symbiotic Severance Procedure.'" He scrolled to another section. "This is where things get... complicated."

The Symbiotic Severance Procedure was the most extreme of their emergency measures, a protocol developed after a near-catastrophic intervention on a world where a fungal blight, inadvertently introduced by a mining colony, had begun to consume the planet's sentient forest. It involved the precise, targeted disabling of an invasive organism or technology that was actively degrading the ecosystem. The key word was 'precise.' It was not a broad-spectrum cleansing, but a highly localized and temporary incapacitation of the foreign element.

"The procedure requires us to Identify the invasive element's energetic anchor points," Niko explained, his gaze sweeping over the holographic diagrams of the mesa's complex internal structure. "Kira, you've already identified the primary conduits feeding into the crystalline matrix. These are our anchor points. The procedure then calls for the deployment of localized null-field projectors. These projectors generate a temporary, contained field that disrupts the specific energetic frequencies of the invasive technology, effectively rendering it inert for a defined period."

Dr. Thorne's holo-projection shimmered into sharper focus. "The critical aspect here, Niko, is 'temporary.' We are not destroying OmniCorp's technology. We are incapacitating it. The null-field is designed to decay naturally, to dissipate within a specific timeframe, leaving the planet's own systems to reassert themselves without the persistent interference."

"And the duration is crucial," Anya added, her voice measured. "If the field decays too quickly, OmniCorp's systems could reactivate before Veridia has had a chance to stabilize. If it lasts too long, we risk creating a different kind of energetic vacuum, an absence that the planet might not be immediately equipped to fill. It's a delicate balance."

Niko's jaw tightened. "That's where the 'Adaptive Monitoring and Gradual Dissipation' component comes in. The null-field projectors are linked to our central monitoring system, which, in turn, is receiving real-time data from Kira's bio-energetic readings. If we detect any signs of instability or distress in Veridia's natural systems as the field begins to decay, we can initiate a controlled extension or a more rapid dissipation, depending on what the readings indicate."

He paused, the silence in the command module amplifying the unspoken question hanging in the air. This was far beyond observation. This was active, albeit temporary, manipulation of an alien world's energetic infrastructure. This was the very definition of interference.

"The protocol also includes contingency measures for defensive responses," Niko continued, pushing aside his own burgeoning unease. "OmniCorp would have likely implemented fail-safes. The procedure outlines methods for circumventing or temporarily disabling automated defenses without triggering a wider alarm or escalating the situation. This would involve precise energy dampeners and targeted frequency disruptions, again, designed for minimal collateral impact."

Kira nudged him again, a stronger pressure this time, conveying a sense of urgency.

The knot is tightening, Niko. The drawing... it is accelerating. The crystalline structures are groaning.

Niko's attention snapped back to the pulsating mesa. Kira's sensory input was not just a tool; it was a direct line to Veridia's suffering. He could feel it, too – a low-grade hum of distress that was steadily intensifying. The ethical tightrope they were walking felt less like a stable pathway and more like a frayed rope over a chasm.

"The fundamental challenge," Niko stated, his voice low and deliberate, "is the potential for unintended consequences. Even with the most sophisticated protocols, we are dealing with systems and energies that are, to a degree, beyond our complete comprehension. Our understanding of Veridia's bio-energetic grid is still incomplete. What if the null-field, even with its careful calibration, creates a resonance that proves harmful to the native lifeforms? What if the severance, even if temporary, disrupts a crucial symbiotic relationship that has evolved over millennia?"

Dr. Thorne responded, his voice calm and reassuring. "These are valid concerns, Niko, and they are addressed within the protocol itself. We are trained to anticipate such possibilities. The initial deployment of the null-field would be at its lowest effective intensity. We would monitor Veridia's response for a standard cycle – that's a period of six local rotations – before increasing the field strength or initiating the dissipation sequence. This allows us to observe the immediate impact on the indigenous life and energy flows without committing to a full-scale, potentially irreversible, intervention."

Anya's projection added, "And our withdrawal would be immediate if any critical threshold is breached. The protocol explicitly states that the preservation of the world's inherent integrity supersedes the completion of the intervention. We would rather leave OmniCorp's technology in place and find another solution, if one exists, than cause irreparable harm through our own actions."

Niko nodded, the rigorous nature of their training and the inherent caution built into their procedures offering a sliver of reassurance. These were not the hasty, profit-driven decisions of OmniCorp. These were decisions born from a deep respect for life and a profound understanding of the delicate balance of interconnectedness.

"We also need to consider the 'Exigent Re-stabilization Protocol'," Niko continued, his gaze fixed on the schematics. "If, during or after the severance, Veridia's energetic grid experiences a sudden, critical imbalance – a cascade failure, as we feared – this protocol outlines immediate, albeit limited, interventions. This might involve deploying localized energy regulators to buffer extreme fluctuations, or even a carefully controlled transfer of stabilizing energy from our ship's reserves, but only as a last, desperate measure."

The prospect of using their ship's energy reserves sent a ripple of apprehension through the team. It was akin to a doctor using their own life force to sustain a patient – a profoundly intimate and draining act. It was a commitment that went far beyond a simple repair.

"The energy transfer is a double-edged sword," Anya commented, her brow furrowed. "It could save Veridia in a critical moment, but it could also create a dependency, a reliance on external energy sources. It would be the ultimate violation of the non-interference principle, short of outright terraforming."

"Which is why it's at the absolute end of the emergency protocols," Niko agreed. "A truly exigent circumstance, where the alternative is total collapse. We would need absolute certainty that Veridia's own systems are incapable of recovery. And even then, the transfer would be designed to be a temporary crutch, a bridge to allow its own systems to regain functionality, not a permanent power source."

He paused, taking a deep breath. The weight of the decision pressed down on him. They had the knowledge, the technology, and now, the potential authorization to act. But the act itself was a transgression of their most fundamental beliefs.

"The critical point," Niko emphasized, his voice resonating with conviction, "is that these protocols are not about imposing our will. They are about

removing an imposition. OmniCorp has already intervened, and their intervention is actively destructive. We are not creating a new order; we are attempting to restore the old one. We are not rewriting Veridia's song; we are silencing the jarring, discordant note that OmniCorp has introduced. And if we must use the Symbiotic Severance Procedure, it will be with the utmost surgical precision, always with the intent of stepping back and allowing Veridia to reclaim its own narrative."

Kira's presence was a constant, grounding force. She communicated a sense of shared responsibility, a silent understanding that their purpose extended beyond mere observation when faced with such blatant harm.

The world weeps, Niko. It reaches out. It asks for relief from the pain. To ignore that plea would be a greater violation than any intervention.

"Kira's right," Niko said, his voice firm. "Our directive is to protect life. Sometimes, protection requires more than passive observation. It requires decisive, yet gentle, action. We have explored every angle, debated every potential consequence. The risk of inaction – of allowing OmniCorp's technology to continue its destructive course – is far greater than the calculated risks of these emergency protocols."

He looked at his team, their holographic forms steady and resolute. "We are not usurping Veridia's autonomy. We are defending it against an external force that is systematically dismantling it. When these protocols are activated, it is not because we believe we know better than Veridia. It is because Veridia is being denied its right to exist as itself, due to the avarice of an outside entity."

The crystalline mesa pulsed, a silent testament to the immense power contained within and the precariousness of its balance. The hum of OmniCorp's technology was a palpable thrum, a discordant vibration that grated against Niko's very senses. He could feel the strain on the crystalline lattice, the desperate effort of the planet's natural systems to resist the unnatural drain. The decision to even consider activating these protocols was a heavy one, a testament to the unique and terrible circumstances they faced. It meant confronting the possibility of their own hubris, of misjudging the intricate web of life they sought to protect.

"The 'Adaptive Monitoring and Gradual Dissipation' component of the Symbiotic Severance Procedure is our primary safeguard," Niko reiterated, his gaze sweeping over the complex algorithms displayed on his gauntlet. "The null-field projectors are designed to be responsive. They're not crude tools. They can be modulated in real-time, their decay rate adjusted based on Kira's input. If Veridia shows any signs of distress – a dip in its core energetic signature, a disruption in its natural cycles, a ripple of pain through its interconnected lifeforms – we'll have the capacity to either slow the decay and maintain the incapacitation longer, or, if necessary, to initiate an emergency shutdown of the field itself and withdraw."

He looked towards Kira, who remained focused on the mesa, her senses extended like delicate antennae. "Kira, you will be our eyes and ears, our bio-energetic barometer. You will be the one to tell us when the balance is tipping, when our presence, however temporary, is causing undue strain. And if that happens, we pull back. No debate, no hesitation. The protocol explicitly states that our intervention is only justified if it leads to a net positive for Veridia's long-term health."

Anya's projection appeared beside him, her expression grave. "And what if OmniCorp's systems, despite our efforts, manage to reassert themselves before Veridia can fully recover? The null-field is temporary. Their technology, if reactivated, could be more aggressive, more ingrained. We might be leaving them with a damaged system that is then subjected to an even more potent attack."

"That is a calculated risk," Niko admitted, his voice tight. "But it is a risk we must take. We are not attempting to permanently disable OmniCorp's technology; that would be beyond our mandate and potentially create even greater unforeseen consequences. Our objective is to provide Veridia with a window of respite, a chance to re-establish its equilibrium without the constant, debilitating drain. We are severing the connection, not destroying the instrument of violation. The hope is that in that window, its natural resilience can reassert itself, strengthening its systems against future intrusions."

Dr. Thorne chimed in, his voice a steadying presence. "It's important to remember the inherent resilience of complex ecosystems, Niko. Veridia has existed for eons, evolving its intricate bio-energetic network. Our intervention, while disruptive, is intended to remove an artificial stressor that is preventing this natural resilience from functioning. We are essentially removing a tumor to allow the body to heal itself. The healing process will be Veridia's own; we are merely clearing the path."

Niko nodded, the imagery of a tumor and a surgeon's scalpel resonating with the difficult truth of their situation. They were not conquerors, nor were they deities. They were, at best, emergency medical personnel for a wounded planet.

"The 'Exigent Re-stabilization Protocol'," Niko continued, his voice firming with a renewed sense of purpose, "is our final safeguard. It is the absolute last resort, a measure to be employed only when all other options have failed and a catastrophic, irreversible collapse of Veridia's bio-energetic grid is imminent. The controlled energy transfer from the *Odyssey* is the core of this protocol. It is a desperate measure, a temporary infusion of stabilizing energy to prevent a total shutdown. But it comes with the explicit understanding that our goal would be to withdraw that energy as soon as Veridia's own systems show any sign of regaining coherence."

He met the gaze of each of his team members, his holographic projections and Kira's physical presence forming a tight circle of resolve. "We have reviewed the protocols. We understand the risks. We understand the profound ethical implications of deviating from our non-interference mandate. But we also understand the catastrophic consequences of inaction. OmniCorp's avarice has created a crisis that threatens the very existence of this vibrant world. We are not acting out of a desire to control or to impose. We are acting out of a responsibility to preserve, to defend, and to restore."

Kira let out a soft chuff, a sound that conveyed a mixture of apprehension and a deep, abiding hope. She nudged Niko's hand again, her message clear and resonant:

The song must not be silenced, Niko. We must help it find its voice again.

"We will proceed with caution, with precision, and with a profound respect for Veridia's own intrinsic systems," Niko declared, his voice carrying a new, unwavering conviction. "Our primary objective is to disable the OmniCorp siphoning arrays using the Symbiotic Severance Procedure. Kira will guide us to the optimal deployment points for the null-field projectors. Anya and Dr. Thorne will monitor Veridia's overall energetic health, ready to alert us to any anomalies. If we encounter insurmountable resistance, or if Veridia's systems show signs of critical distress, we will disengage. But if the situation allows, we will provide Veridia with the opportunity to heal, to breathe freely once more. This is not a choice we make lightly, but it is a choice we must make. The Resonant Pack will not stand idly by while a world is bled dry." The decision, though agonizing, had been made. The weight of the universe, and the responsibility for its smallest, most vibrant songs, rested heavily upon their shoulders.

The tension in the command module was a palpable force, a thick, suffocating blanket woven from the threads of uncertainty and the immense weight of their potential actions. Niko felt it coiling in his gut, a familiar knot of apprehension that tightened with every flicker of the holographic displays. The Symbiotic Severance Procedure, a necessary evil born of desperation, loomed large, demanding a precision and restraint that felt almost impossible to maintain when faced with the sheer scale of OmniCorp's transgression. He ran a gauntlet-clad hand over his brow, a gesture of weariness that betrayed the immense pressure he was under. The responsibility for Veridia's fate rested squarely on his shoulders, a burden amplified by the knowledge that even the most carefully calibrated intervention carried inherent risks.

It was in these moments, when the logical processors of his mind began to fray under the strain of ethical dilemmas and the sheer magnitude of the task, that Kira's presence became an indispensable anchor. She sensed his turmoil, the subtle shifts in his bio-signature, the micro-expressions that flitted across his face. Without a word, she moved, her lithe form gliding across the deck. She approached Niko, her large, intelligent eyes fixed on his. A gentle nudge of her head against his arm, a soft, melodic whine that resonated with a deep, comforting frequency, served as a silent balm. It was more than just a physical touch; it was a transfusion of calm, a wordless reassurance that they were not alone in this struggle.

Kira's empathic link wasn't a crude biological broadcast, but a nuanced symphony of emotional resonance. It was the ability to perceive the subtle energetic currents that flowed between sentient beings, to understand the unspoken language of fear, doubt, and hope. When she nudged Niko, it was as if she were gently smoothing the rough edges of his anxieties, weaving a thread of peace through the tangled fabric of his thoughts. He found himself unconsciously relaxing his grip on the console, the tightness in his chest easing ever so slightly. He met her gaze, and in those liquid depths, he saw not just understanding, but a shared resolve, a silent affirmation that they would navigate this treacherous path together.

Her attention then shifted to Anya, whose holographic projection flickered with an almost imperceptible tremor. Anya, ever the pragmatist, was grappling with the potential cascading failures, the 'what-ifs' that gnawed at the edges of their carefully constructed plan. Kira moved towards Anya's projection, her form becoming almost translucent as she focused her empathic energies. She didn't touch Anya's projection directly, but rather bathed it in a field of quiet assurance. The tremor in Anya's form subsided, her posture straightening, her gaze becoming more focused, less clouded by doubt. It was a subtle shift, a testament to the profound impact of Kira's non-verbal communication.

Even Dr. Thorne, usually a bastion of scientific equanimity, exhibited a faint furrow in his brow, a testament to the intellectual challenge of balancing intervention with observation. Kira approached him next, her whines deepening into a low, resonant hum that seemed to vibrate at a frequency that soothed the very core of his being. He looked down at her, a small, grateful smile touching his lips. "Thank you, Kira," he murmured, his voice a touch steadier than before. "Your presence is... remarkably grounding."

This was the essence of the Resonant Pack's strength, a unique synergy forged between advanced intellect and primal intuition. It was a reminder that solutions were not solely the domain of logic and technology. Sometimes, the most crucial element in overcoming overwhelming challenges was the quiet strength of empathy, the unspoken understanding that bridged the gap between species and dissolved the isolating grip of fear. Kira, with her keen senses and her profound connection to the emotional currents of her packmates, was the living embodiment of this vital principle. She was not merely an observer; she was an active participant in their emotional well-being, a silent guardian who ensured that their resolve remained unbroken, their focus unwavering, even when facing the abyss. Her ability to sense and subtly influence emotional states was not just a biological quirk; it was a crucial component of their operational success, providing not just practical guidance but also the essential emotional resilience needed to confront the daunting, often terrifying, realities of their mission. The delicate dance of their decision-making process, fraught with the potential for error and regret, was rendered navigable by the silent, steadying influence of their empathic anchor.

The journey to the nexus point was a descent into a fractured dreamscape. As their shuttle pierced the upper atmospheric layers of Veridia, the familiar verdant tapestry gave way to an unsettling, volatile spectacle. Below, the landscape shimmered, not with the steady, life-affirming glow of healthy bioluminescence, but with a feverish, disoriented pulse. The air, when they finally landed a safe distance from the epicentre of the disturbance, was thick with an almost tangible static. It wasn't the clean, sharp crackle of a distant storm, but a deeper, more resonant hum that seemed to vibrate in the very marrow of their bones.

Niko, disembarking with his diagnostic tools humming to life, felt an immediate prickle of unease crawl across his skin. The ground beneath his boots was a spongy, yielding carpet of flora, but its usual vibrant hues were muted, overlaid with an erratic, flickering luminescence. Patches of deep violet, usually a sign of healthy nutrient uptake in the subterranean fungal networks, now flashed with an angry, insistent crimson. Lumina vines, typically a soft, ethereal blue that pulsed in gentle waves, sputtered and died in rapid succession, leaving behind brief, dark scars on the glowing undergrowth. It was a symphony of light gone horribly wrong, a chaotic light show dictated by an unseen, destructive conductor.

Kira, ever attuned to the subtle shifts in their environment, was the first to betray the true extent of the anomaly. Her usual calm, a steady beacon of empathic presence, began to fray. Her fur, normally sleek and lustrous, bristled at irregular intervals, and a low, guttural whine, a sound Niko had rarely heard from her, rumbled in her chest. Her bio-resonance readings, projected onto Niko's wrist-mounted display, were no longer a steady green but a jagged, spiking red. She pressed herself closer to Niko's leg, her large, intelligent eyes wide with a distress that transcended mere observation. It was a primal alarm, a visceral reaction to the profound wrongness of the place. Niko instinctively placed a reassuring hand on her head, his gloved fingers tracing the agitated fur. "Easy, girl," he murmured, his own senses picking up the unsettling discord. "We're here. We'll figure this out." But even as he spoke, a part of him echoed Kira's silent distress. The air here didn't just crackle; it throbbed, a sickly, irregular heartbeat that spoke of a system in profound disarray.

He began his documentation, his holographic scanner sweeping across the immediate vicinity. OmniCorp's signature was all too evident, not in the crude physical destruction of machinery, but in the insidious poisoning of the very lifeblood of Veridia. The targeted disruption of the nexus point, designed to siphon off its unique dimensional energies, had unleashed a cascade of unforeseen ecological consequences. The bio-luminescent flora, so intricately woven into the planet's energy grid, was the first casualty. The Lumina vines, which acted as natural conduits, were fraying at the molecular level, their light-emitting organelles malfunctioning under the stress of fluctuating interdimensional currents. The fungal networks beneath the soil, the true circulatory system of Veridia's flora, were similarly afflicted. Niko zoomed in on a section of the ground where a vibrant network of mycelial threads was meant to be pulsing with a healthy, interconnected glow. Instead, he saw gaping chasms of darkness, where the fungal hyphae had withered and died, leaving behind sterile, inert soil.

"Look at this," he said, turning to Anya, who was meticulously analyzing the atmospheric composition on her own console. "OmniCorp's primary extraction nexus was positioned directly over a major convergence point for the subterranean fungal mycelia. They've effectively severed the planet's circulatory system in this region." He pointed his scanner at a cluster of flora he identified as 'Whisperblossoms,' delicate, bell-shaped flowers that usually emitted a soft, soothing hum. Here, they were contorted, their petals blackened at the edges, their hum replaced by a high-pitched, discordant whine that grated on the nerves. "These Whisperblossoms rely on specific vibrational frequencies from the mycelia to regulate their growth cycles and emit their harmonic compounds. Without that stable input, they're essentially screaming in distress."

The visual spectacle was undeniably dramatic. Patches of the ground seemed to shift and writhe, not with the movement of creatures, but with the violent, unpredictable flares of bioluminescence. A patch of what looked like moss, normally a uniform emerald glow, erupted in a series of strobe-like pulses, shifting from green to an unnerving electric blue, then to a sickly yellow, before abruptly going dark. The effect was disorienting, like staring into a fractured mirror reflecting a dying world. The sheer scale of the devastation was disheartening. This wasn't just a localized problem; it was a wound in the heart of Veridia, a wound that was actively festering.

Dr. Thorne, usually so stoic, let out a low sigh as he observed the readings. "The dimensional energy instability is far more pronounced than our simulations predicted," he stated, his voice tinged with concern. "It appears OmniCorp's extraction process has not only disrupted the bio-energetic pathways but has also created a feedback loop, amplifying the inherent dimensional flux. This nexus point is meant to be a stable junction, a calm eddy in the larger dimensional currents. Now, it's a maelstrom." He gestured towards a particularly violent flare of light that erupted from a cluster of what looked like crystalline growths, usually a soft, milky white. They were now emitting sharp, jagged shards of pure white light that seemed to cut through the surrounding gloom. "These Crystallite formations are highly sensitive to dimensional harmonics. Their current state indicates extreme energetic overloads. They're essentially becoming unstable capacitors, on the verge of catastrophic discharge."

Niko focused his scanner on a patch of what appeared to be a thick, moss-like growth, its usual gentle emerald glow now fractured by sporadic, violent flashes of electric blue. This was the 'Veridian Velvet,' a crucial part of the soil's composition, known for its ability to absorb and neutralize toxins. But here, it was malfunctioning, its bioluminescence flickering like a dying ember. He zoomed in on the cellular structure, his display showing a chaotic disruption of its chloroplasts, the very engines of its photosynthetic and luminescent processes. "The Velvet is breaking down," Niko reported, his voice tight with frustration. "It's not just failing to neutralize the energy fluctuations; it's actively reacting to them in a destructive feedback loop. The OmniCorp tech seems to have saturated the surrounding environment with exotic particle radiation, destabilizing the very molecular structure of the flora. The bio-luminescence is acting as a visual symptom of cellular death."

He continued his survey, documenting the cascading effects. The 'Gloomweed,' a plant that typically absorbed ambient light and re-emitted it as a deep, calming indigo, was now emitting a chaotic, flickering pattern of blues and greens, its normally soothing glow replaced by an aggressive, pulsing light that seemed to induce a sense of unease. Niko's bio-signature analysis confirmed it; prolonged exposure to this corrupted light caused a measurable spike in stress hormones. Even the 'Embermoss,' a typically resilient species that thrived in the planet's more geothermally active regions, was showing signs of distress. Its usual warm, flickering red glow was muted, interspersed with streaks of an alarming, sickly yellow, indicating a severe metabolic imbalance.

The beauty of the nexus point, once a testament to Veridia's vibrant, interconnected ecosystem, was now a haunting spectacle of decay. The air itself seemed to hum with an almost audible sorrow, a mournful lament for what had been lost. The ethereal dance of light that usually characterized this region, a silent language of life and energy, had devolved into a chaotic, flickering death rattle. Niko felt a pang of profound sadness. He had studied this place in simulations, marveled at its intricate bio-energetic dance from afar. To see it in such a state, ravaged by the greed of a corporation that saw only resources to be exploited, was a visceral blow. The delicate balance, the millennia of evolution that had sculpted this unique biome, had been shattered in a matter of cycles.

Kira, sensing Niko's growing despair, nudged his hand again, her whine now a low, mournful thrum. Her empathic link was usually a source of comfort, but here, in this zone of immense energetic distortion, it was like trying to tune a finely-calibrated instrument in the midst of a hurricane. She was picking up not just the distress of her packmates, but the echoes of the planet's own agony. The bio-luminescent flora, in its erratic flickering, was not just a visual display; it was a manifestation of the planet's suffering, a primal scream translated into light. The energy signatures were so distorted that Kira's internal compass, her natural affinity for navigating and understanding Veridia's energetic flows, was thrown into disarray. Her normally keen senses were struggling to process the cacophony of dissonant frequencies.

Niko knelt beside her, running a gloved hand over her trembling flank. "I know, girl," he whispered, his voice rough. "It's bad. Worse than we thought." He activated his handheld environmental scanner, focusing its sensitive array on a patch of ground where the bio-luminescent fungi, normally a vibrant network of interconnected glowing threads, were now visibly dying. The delicate hyphae, the planet's natural circulatory system, were brittle and fractured, their glow extinguished. "OmniCorp's extraction process is creating localized dimensional rifts, destabilizing the quantum fields that underpin this ecosystem," Niko explained to Anya, his voice grim. "The fungi are not just dying; they are disintegrating at a subatomic level. The light you're seeing is the residual energy bleed-off from this process. It's like watching cells die in fast-forward."

He continued his documentation, meticulously recording the spectral analysis of the erratically pulsing flora. The Lumina vines, which normally pulsed with a steady, calming blue, were now flickering with an aggressive, almost angry, violet. The Embermoss, usually a warm, comforting red, was now interspersed with jarring streaks of acidic yellow. Niko cross-referenced the readings with the known bio-signatures of the native flora. "The color shifts indicate a fundamental alteration in the energy absorption and emission spectrum of these organisms," he stated. "OmniCorp's technology is forcing them to absorb and re-emit energy in frequencies that are toxic to their internal structures. It's like forcing a plant to photosynthesize infrared light; it's fundamentally incompatible with its biology."

The air itself felt charged, not with the invigorating energy of a healthy planet, but with a volatile, unstable power. Sparks of emerald and sapphire light arced erratically between patches of glowing flora, and the ground beneath their boots vibrated with an unsettling hum. Kira whined again, a deeper, more distressed sound this time. Her bio-readings spiked even higher, showing a significant increase in her stress hormones. She pressed herself against Niko's leg, her usually confident posture now one of vulnerability. Niko, despite his own rising apprehension, managed a reassuring stroke of her head. "It's okay, Kira," he soothed. "We're protected. We'll get through this."

He turned his attention back to the landscape, his gaze sweeping across the scene. The beauty of the nexus point was undeniable, even in its current state of disarray. Luminescent flowers, some shaped like delicate bells, others like intricate stars, dotted the landscape, their light normally a gentle, harmonious glow. Now, their pulses were erratic, their colors shifting in a chaotic, disorienting dance. A patch of what looked like bioluminescent moss, normally a vibrant emerald, was now flashing with an intense, almost blinding, sapphire. Niko's scanner identified the specific flora: 'Starpetal Blooms,' known for their ability to regulate the local energy field through synchronized light emissions. Their current erratic behavior was a clear indicator of severe energetic disruption.

"The Starpetal Blooms are key regulators of this nexus," Niko explained to Anya, his voice tight. "Their synchronized luminescence usually creates a stable, harmonic field. OmniCorp's interference has shattered that synchronization. They're pulsing independently now, and the frequencies are clashing, creating this chaotic energy discharge." He pointed his scanner towards a cluster of 'Gloomcaps,' a type of bioluminescent fungus that typically emitted a soft, indigo light. Here, the Gloomcaps were pulsing with a jarring, almost neon, pink. "Even the Gloomcaps are affected. Their light spectrum has shifted drastically. This isn't just cosmetic; it's a sign of deep cellular stress. The energy OmniCorp is siphoning is fundamentally incompatible with Veridia's biological systems."

The air itself seemed to vibrate, a low, resonant hum that was both unnerving and strangely beautiful. It was the sound of a planet in pain, a symphony of dying light. Kira, her senses overwhelmed by the discordant energies, began to tremble. Her usual calm, her innate ability to project soothing resonance, was faltering. Niko felt a wave of her distress wash over him, a chilling echo of the planet's own suffering. He placed a reassuring hand on her flank, his touch a small anchor in the overwhelming storm of chaotic energy. "Easy, girl," he murmured, his gaze fixed on the spectacle before them. "We're here. We'll find a way to fix this." The sheer scale of the degradation was breathtaking, a stark reminder of the destructive potential of unchecked technological ambition. The once vibrant nexus point was a dying star, its light flickering erratically, a beautiful, tragic testament to the fragility of life.

The air thrummed, a symphony of suffering that resonated not just in their ears, but in the very fabric of their beings. Niko, his brow furrowed in concentration, watched the fluctuating bio-resonance readings on his wrist-mounted display. Kira, normally a beacon of unwavering calm, paced restlessly at his side, her tail tucked low, her whines a soft counterpoint to the planet's agitated pulse. Anya, her fingers flying across her console, her face illuminated by the holographic projections, presented a grim tableau of atmospheric and energetic instability. Dr. Thorne, his usual stoic demeanor strained, observed the data with a heavy heart. The nexus point, once a vibrant heart of Veridia's life force, was now a gaping wound, its light a fevered, chaotic dance of decay.

"The resonant frequencies are degrading exponentially," Anya reported, her voice tight. "The Lumina vines are not just flickering; their core energetic structures are collapsing. We're seeing localized chronal distortions around major nodes where the fungi have completely died off."

Niko ran a hand through his hair, the gritty texture of the Veridian dust clinging to his glove. "Chronal distortions? That's... unexpected. It suggests the dimensional energy OmniCorp tapped into isn't just raw power; it's intrinsically linked to Veridia's temporal stability." He glanced at Kira, her distress a palpable wave he could feel even through their empathic link. Her internal compass, her innate understanding of the planet's energetic flows, was wildly askew. She wasn't just sensing the pain of the flora; she was feeling the planet unraveling on a fundamental level.

"The simulations predicted instability, but not this level of systemic collapse," Dr. Thorne admitted, his gaze fixed on a particularly violent burst of crimson light erupting from a cluster of what should have been healthy Gloomcaps. "OmniCorp's extraction method has created a cascade failure. The bio-harmonic feedback loop is accelerating, tearing at the planet's very essence."

Niko knelt beside Kira, stroking her agitated fur. "She feels it too," he murmured. "The dissonance is overwhelming her. It's like trying to hear a whisper in a rock concert." He looked at Anya, then at Thorne. The weight of their mission pressed down on him. They were here to observe, to document, to understand. But understanding had led them to this horrific spectacle, and observation felt increasingly like complicity.

"We can't just stand here," Anya stated, her voice firm, cutting through the tension. "We have protocols, yes. Non-interference is paramount. But if non-interference means allowing this entire biome to be annihilated, then our mandate needs to be re-evaluated."

"Re-evaluated how, Anya?" Thorne asked, his voice weary. "Intervention carries its own immense risks. We've seen the projections. A misstep here could shatter the nexus entirely, creating a dimensional implosion that could destabilize this entire sector."

"But doing nothing guarantees its destruction!" Niko countered, his voice rising with a frustration he hadn't felt in cycles. "Look at Kira. She's suffering. This planet is suffering. OmniCorp has already violated every ethical boundary. Are we going to compound that by adhering to a protocol that condemns an entire world?"

He stood, pacing the small, disturbed clearing. The flickering lights, once a source of wonder, now seemed like malevolent eyes watching their indecision. He remembered the initial reports, the satellite imagery of the nexus point, a vibrant tapestry of life and energy. Now, it was a scarred, dying thing, its breath coming in ragged, erratic gasps of light.

"Our primary objective was to understand OmniCorp's technology and its impact," Thorne reminded them, his tone measured, but his eyes held a deep concern. "Intervention was always a contingency, a last resort, with a vanishingly small probability of success and an astronomically high risk of catastrophic failure."

"And what if this is that last resort?" Anya challenged. "What if the risk of inaction is now greater than the risk of intervention? We have the bio-harmonic resonators. They were designed for precisely this kind of scenario – to gently guide destabilized ecosystems back towards equilibrium."

Niko stopped pacing, his mind racing. The resonators. He had helped design them, had poured over their theoretical applications for years. They were sophisticated instruments, capable of emitting precise bio-harmonic frequencies designed to resonate with and recalibrate the planet's natural energetic pathways. They could, in theory, coax the damaged flora back into a state of coherence, to re-establish the lost connections within the fungal network. But the theory was one thing; the reality of this fractured nexus was another.

"The energy field here is too volatile," Thorne argued. "The resonators are designed for ambient fluctuations, not for the kind of interdimensional chaos OmniCorp has unleashed. Introducing their frequencies could be like trying to tune a delicate instrument in the middle of an earthquake. It could amplify the instability, causing a feedback loop that would tear the nexus apart."

"But we can calibrate them," Niko said, a spark of hope igniting within him. He looked at Kira, who had finally settled beside him, her trembling subsiding slightly as he spoke. Her presence, her innate connection to Veridia, was the key. "Kira's readings. They're not just showing distress; they're showing the precise nature of the disruption. We can use her bio-signature, her understanding of Veridia's healthy resonant state, to fine-tune the resonators. We can create a counter-frequency, a harmonic pulse that speaks directly to the planet's original song."

He pulled up a holographic display of the resonator schematics, his fingers tracing the complex patterns of their internal matrix. "The resonators aren't just emitters; they're also highly sensitive receivers. We can synchronize them with Kira's bio-resonance, creating a living feedback loop. As the nexus attempts to destabilize, Kira will react, and the resonators will adjust in real-time, guided by her instincts and our analysis."

Anya nodded, her eyes alight with a similar surge of calculated optimism. "That's... elegant, Niko. It leverages our unique advantages. It shifts the risk profile. Instead of imposing a potentially alien frequency, we're using Veridia's own intrinsic resonance, amplified and stabilized."

Thorne remained silent for a long moment, his gaze sweeping over the chaotic landscape, then back to Niko and Kira. The decision weighed heavily on him. He had spent his career studying the delicate balance of planetary ecosystems, the catastrophic consequences of even minor disruptions. The idea of actively interfering with such a complex and volatile system, even with the best intentions, was terrifying. But he also saw the undeniable truth in Niko's words, the desperate plea in Kira's mournful eyes, the dying light of the nexus.

"The parameters of the intervention would need to be strictly defined," Thorne said finally, his voice firm. "We wouldn't be attempting a full re-stabilization, not at first. We'd initiate a limited recalibration, focusing on the most critical nodes – the primary fungal convergence points and the Lumina vine conduits. A gentle nudge, not a forceful shove."

"Agreed," Niko confirmed, relief flooding through him. "We'd deploy a network of micro-resonators, strategically placed to create a stabilizing field. They'd work in conjunction with the primary resonators, creating a layered harmonic dampening effect. We'd start with a minimal power output, gradually increasing it only as the data confirms a positive trend."

"And Kira?" Anya asked, looking at the psionic canine. "Can she handle the strain? The linked resonance could be... intense."

Niko looked at Kira, who met his gaze with an unwavering intensity. Her distress had not vanished, but it was now mingled with a sense of purpose, a readiness. He felt a surge of affection and a profound sense of responsibility. "She'll be at my side, directly linked. I'll monitor her readings constantly. If she shows signs of critical overload, we abort immediately. Her safety, and the integrity of our link, is non-negotiable."

Thorne let out a slow breath. "This is a significant deviation from our original protocol. The decision carries immense weight. If we fail, we could irrevocably damage this nexus, and potentially create even greater instabilities. OmniCorp will be accountable, but the immediate consequences will be ours to bear."

"We understand the risks, Doctor," Anya said, her voice steady. "But the potential reward – saving this ecosystem, proving that intervention can be guided by ecological understanding and compassion – outweighs the danger of inaction."

Niko met Thorne's gaze, a silent understanding passing between them. This was no longer just about OmniCorp. It was about their own principles, their own capacity for action in the face of devastation. It was about the inherent value of life, whether biological or energetic, and their responsibility as stewards, not just observers.

"We proceed," Thorne declared, his voice resonating with a newfound resolve. "But with extreme caution. Every step must be calculated. Every adjustment made with absolute precision. Niko, you will lead the deployment and management of the resonators, with Anya providing real-time atmospheric and energetic analysis. I will oversee the overall mission parameters and contingency planning." He looked at Kira, who offered a soft, almost imperceptible rumble of affirmation. "And Kira," he added, a hint of respect in his tone, "you will be our guide. Your connection to Veridia is our most valuable tool."

The decision, once made, settled upon them with a palpable shift in the atmosphere. The anxiety remained, a low hum beneath their resolve, but it was now tempered by a focused purpose. They were no longer passive witnesses to destruction. They were about to engage, to attempt the delicate dance of healing on a wounded world. The line between observation and intervention had been irrevocably crossed, and the future of the nexus point, and perhaps their own mission, hung precariously in the balance. The complex machinery of the bio-harmonic resonators, dormant and theoretical until this moment, now held the weight of their hope. It was a gamble, a desperate, necessary gamble, born from the understanding that sometimes, to preserve life, one must be willing to risk everything.

CHAPTER SIX

MENDING THE THREADS

The transport hummed softly, a stark contrast to the chaotic symphony of Veridia's dying heart. Within its confines, the air was thick with a different kind of tension, one born not of fear, but of focused intent. Niko, his fingers meticulously adjusting the finely tuned calibration on a bio-harmonic resonator, felt the familiar prickle of adrenaline. These weren't weapons, nor were they tools of brute force. They were instruments of subtle persuasion, designed to whisper to the damaged bio-network of Veridia, to remind it of its own inherent song.

"Frequency alignment is nominal across all primary units," Anya's voice, calm and precise, emanated from her comm unit. She was overseeing the atmospheric and energetic readouts from the transport's command center, a crucial role that allowed Niko to concentrate on the delicate physical placement of the resonators. "Kira's empathic signature is stable, indicating a lower stress baseline than predicted, at least for now."

Niko glanced at Kira, who sat beside him, her large, intelligent eyes fixed on the landscape blurring past the reinforced viewport. Her tail gave a slow, deliberate thump against the transport's floor, a subtle but significant sign of her own quiet determination. The close-range bio-resonance scanner integrated into her harness was relaying a constant stream of data to

Niko's wrist-mounted display. It wasn't just a visual representation; it was a visceral echo of Veridia's ailing pulse, filtered through Kira's unique psionic sensitivity. She was not merely sensing the planet's pain; she was actively participating in its recalibration, acting as the living, breathing nexus between their technology and the planet's natural energetic flows.

Dr. Thorne's voice, deep and steady, joined the comm channel. "Remember, Niko, the objective is not to impose a new resonance, but to reawaken the existing one. These resonators are designed to be a gentle nudge, a harmonic echo that encourages self-correction. Think of it as a tuning fork for a symphony that has fallen out of tune."

"Understood, Doctor," Niko replied, his gaze sweeping over the rugged terrain. They were approaching one of the designated deployment zones, a region characterized by the unnerving stillness of the once-vibrant Lumina vines. Their tendrils, usually a cascade of soft, pulsating light, were now dull and brittle, their energetic core seemingly extinguished. This was where the damage was most pronounced, where OmniCorp's reckless exploitation had created a void that was rapidly expanding.

The transport descended with a soft hiss, settling onto a patch of ground that felt strangely inert, devoid of the usual vibrant hum of life. The moment the ramp lowered, the true nature of their task became apparent. The air, while breathable, carried a faint, cloying scent, a byproduct of the decaying fungal networks. The silence was profound, a heavy blanket broken only by the faint, mournful sigh of the wind through the skeletal remains of what had once been a flourishing ecosystem.

"This is Node Seven," Niko announced, stepping out of the transport. The ground beneath his boots felt unnaturally firm, as if the very soil had become desiccated and resistant to any organic processes. Kira followed, her movements economical and deliberate, her senses already engaged with the subtle energetic currents – or lack thereof – in the immediate vicinity.

He unslung the first resonator from its protective casing. It was a sleek, metallic cylinder, roughly the size of a large flask, etched with intricate patterns that glowed with a faint, internal luminescence. These were the primary resonators, the backbone of their intervention. Each was equipped with a micro-matrix of harmonic emitters, capable of generating a precise spectrum of frequencies. The truly groundbreaking aspect, however, was their adaptive learning capability, designed to synchronize with and amplify an organism's natural resonant patterns.

"Kira, focus," Niko murmured, his voice a low rumble meant only for her. He placed a hand on her flank, feeling the subtle tremor of her concentration. Her eyes flickered, scanning the immediate area, her internal bio-resonance compass working overtime. The data streamed onto his display: fluctuating energy signatures, void zones where the fungal network should have been a vibrant web, and unsettling pockets of chronal instability that Anya had warned them about.

"The fungal network here is almost entirely severed," Niko reported, his voice tight. "The Lumina vines are drawing residual energy from the substrate, but it's like trying to sustain life on stale water. There's a significant void emanating from approximately fifty meters northeast of our position. That's where the primary disruption occurred."

"Acknowledged," Anya's voice crackled. "We're seeing a localized de-phasing in the atmospheric energetic field. The chronal distortions are minor but present. Be mindful, Niko. The echoes of OmniCorp's technology are still potent."

With deliberate precision, Niko walked towards the area Kira indicated. The ground became even more barren, the silence more oppressive. He reached the epicenter of the void, a small clearing where the soil was cracked and dry. This was it. The heart of the wound. He knelt, the resonator cradled in his gloved hands, and initiated the deployment sequence.

"Primary resonator, Node Seven, initiating synchronization protocol," he stated into his comm unit. The resonator pulsed softly, its internal light intensifying. Kira nudged his hand, her gaze fixed on a particular point on the ground. Niko followed her lead, his fingers digging into the desiccated earth.

"Target sub-surface fungal convergence point identified," he confirmed, and then, with a final, gentle push, he embedded the resonator into the soil. The moment it made contact, a faint shimmer rippled across its surface, and its luminescence deepened, syncing with Kira's bio-signature. A wave of complex, harmonic frequencies, tuned to Veridia's original, healthy resonant state, began to emanate outwards. It wasn't a sound, not in the traditional sense, but a palpable vibration that seemed to seep into the very essence of the earth.

"Initial resonance transmission successful," Niko reported, watching his display. "Kira's readings show a slight increase in localized energetic coherence. It's a small ripple, but it's a positive one."

"Small ripples can become waves," Dr. Thorne responded, his voice carrying a note of cautious optimism. "Continue to the secondary deployment points. Remember the network effect. Each resonator strengthens the field for the others."

The process was painstaking. They moved from Node Seven to Node Eight, then Node Nine, and so on, across the afflicted landscape. Each deployment was a meticulous dance of observation, Kira's psionic intuition, and Niko's technical precision. They were guided by Kira's heightened senses, which could detect even the faintest vestiges of Veridia's former vitality, pinpointing areas where the fungal hyphae, though damaged, still held a faint energetic imprint. These became the anchor points for the resonators, the places where the planet's natural melody was weakest but not yet entirely silenced.

At Node Twelve, the situation was particularly dire. The Lumina vines here were not just dull; they were fragmented, their ethereal glow completely extinguished. The ground was a mosaic of brittle, dessicated matter. Kira whined softly, a low, mournful sound that resonated with the desolation around them.

"The network is almost completely collapsed here," Niko observed, his brow furrowed. "The chronal distortions are more pronounced. Anya, can you give me a precise reading on the energetic void?"

"The void is a significant gradient, Niko," Anya replied. "It's not a single point, but a region of diffuse energetic depletion. The resonators will need to work harder here, establishing a broader harmonic field."

This deployment required a different approach. Instead of a single primary resonator, Niko opted for a cluster of three, strategically placed to create a more encompassing stabilizing field. He worked swiftly, his movements efficient, as Kira continued to guide him, nudging his arm towards specific points in the ground.

"Placement adjusted based on Kira's proximity readings," he reported. "We're trying to blanket the area, to create a sympathetic resonance that will encourage the fragmented hyphae to reconnect."

As the resonators hummed to life, a faint, almost imperceptible shimmer began to coalesce in the air around them. It was like watching a heat haze, but with an ethereal quality, a subtle distortion of light that hinted at the energetic currents being stirred. Kira's tail gave a tentative, slow sweep. Her distress hadn't vanished, but a new layer had been added – a flicker of hope, a faint echo of the planet's former vitality that the resonators were beginning to coax back into existence.

"I'm detecting a shift," Niko breathed, watching his display. "The energetic gradient is still steep, but the rate of depletion has slowed. And... there's a faint signal returning from the Lumina vine conduit. It's weak, but it's there."

"That's the beauty of these devices," Dr. Thorne mused over the comms. "They don't force a change; they enable it. They create the optimal conditions for Veridia's own healing mechanisms to kick in. It's a collaborative effort between our technology and the planet's inherent resilience."

The hours that followed were a testament to their dedication. They moved through desolate plains and hushed, dying groves, deploying resonators like seeds of hope in a barren land. Each unit was carefully placed, each frequency finely tuned. Kira remained their unwavering guide, her psionic senses acting as the ultimate arbiter, ensuring that their interventions were aligned with the subtle, intricate patterns of Veridia's bio-energetic field. There were moments of intense concentration, of painstaking calibration, and moments of quiet awe as they witnessed the subtle, yet profound, changes beginning to manifest.

At one point, they encountered a patch of what should have been bioluminescent moss, now rendered a dull, ashen grey. Niko hesitated, unsure of the best placement. Kira, without prompting, began to circle a small, unassuming rock, her whine a soft query. Niko followed her gaze, and upon closer inspection, he saw it – a single, infinitesimally small spore clinging to the rock's surface, a remnant of life clinging to existence.

"Kira's found a micro-resilient pocket," he reported, a smile touching his lips. "This is where the Lumina vines will eventually draw their initial sustenance. It needs to be protected." He carefully placed a micro-resonator, a smaller, more localized version of the primary units, directly beside the spore. Its hum was almost inaudible, a gentle lullaby designed to nurture the fragile spark of life.

"The deployment is proceeding as planned, Doctor," Niko said, his voice imbued with a growing sense of purpose. "We've covered eighty percent of the primary nexus points. Kira's readings indicate a subtle but consistent improvement in energetic coherence across the deployed zones."

"Excellent work, Niko, Anya, and Kira," Thorne responded. "The data is encouraging. We're seeing a reduction in the rate of degradation, and in some areas, a stabilization of the chronal distortions. It's a testament to your skill and to the efficacy of the bio-harmonic resonators."

The sun, a diffused disc behind Veridia's hazy atmosphere, began its slow descent, painting the sky in hues of muted orange and violet. The light, once so vibrant and life-giving, now seemed tinged with a melancholic beauty. But as the resonators pulsed with their subtle, life-affirming frequencies, a new kind of light began to emerge – not the dazzling spectacle of the Lumina vines, but a gentler, more pervasive glow, emanating from the very earth itself. It was the quiet return of hope, the nascent hum of a world beginning to mend. The delicate threads of Veridia's bio-network, frayed and torn, were slowly, painstakingly, being rewoven.

Kira's role transcended mere observation; she was the living compass, the sensitive barometer of Veridia's reawakening. As Niko meticulously calibrated the output of a primary resonator, ensuring its harmonic frequencies were perfectly attuned to the spectral signature of the desiccated fungal network, it was Kira's low, resonant hum that provided the crucial real-time feedback. Her tail, usually a barometer of her emotional state, now seemed to pulse with an almost independent rhythm, a subtle indication of the energetic tides she was experiencing. Niko watched the bio-resonance scanner integrated into her harness, a complex weave of optical fibers and psionic conduits, as it translated her subtle somatic cues into actionable data. Her large, intelligent eyes, pools of liquid amber, followed the invisible currents of energy that flowed, or rather, *failed* to flow, across the barren landscape.

"The coherence is wavering again, Niko," Anya's voice cut through the comm channel, a thread of concern weaving through her usual professional detachment. "We're seeing a localized dip in the resonance field strength, approximately thirty meters to your west."

Niko acknowledged the warning, his hands moving with practiced efficiency. He adjusted a dial on the resonator, a minute shift that felt infinitesimally small in the face of Veridia's profound ailment, yet held the weight of their entire mission. He glanced at Kira, who had already turned, her gaze fixed on a point beyond a cluster of brittle, greyed flora. She emitted a soft, guttural whine, a sound that was not of distress, but of guidance. It was a specific pitch, a nuanced inflection that Niko had come to understand intimately. It meant: *there*.

"She's indicating a flux point, Anya," Niko reported, already moving in the direction Kira indicated. "Her signature is... it's like a tremor in the energy flow. The resonator's output might be too direct, too assertive for this specific node. We need to broaden the harmonic spread, encourage a gentler convergence."

He reached the spot, a seemingly unremarkable patch of cracked earth. But Kira stood beside him, her body subtly vibrating. Her psionic sensors, far more sensitive than any manufactured instrument, were picking up on an anomaly – a subtle eddy in the weakened energetic field, a pocket where the imposed frequencies were creating a discordant ripple rather than a gentle resonance. The ground here felt different, a subtle textural shift that hinted at a deeper energetic imbalance.

"The existing fungal hyphae are fragmented to a critical degree here," Niko observed, consulting his wrist-mounted display. The readings, now cross-referenced with Kira's psionic input, painted a clearer picture. "The resonator's direct wave is causing micro-fractures in the already compromised network. Kira's right, we need a softer approach. A diffusion of the harmonic energy, rather than a focused beam."

He knelt, his gloved fingers tracing the faint outlines of desiccated root structures beneath the surface. Kira nudged his hand, then let out a series of short, almost musical barks, her tail giving a decisive flick towards a specific area. It was an instinctive gesture, born of millennia of interspecies communication and amplified by their current, extraordinary circumstances. She wasn't just sensing the problem; she was articulating the solution.

"She's suggesting a peripheral dispersion pattern," Niko relayed to Anya and Dr. Thorne, his voice laced with a growing respect for Kira's intuitive prowess. "Instead of a single point of emission, we'll use a series of micro-emitters, arrayed in a circular pattern around the core node. The goal is to create a gentle, encompassing resonance that encourages reconnection without further disruption."

He worked quickly, deploying a cluster of smaller, more discreet resonators. These were designed for delicate work, for coaxing rather than commanding. As each unit was activated, its faint luminescence pulsed in sync with Kira's subtle energy emissions. The air around them seemed to thicken, not with pollution, but with a nascent, palpable energy. Niko watched his display intently. The readings were shifting, the erratic fluctuations smoothing out. The dip Anya had detected was receding, replaced by a more stable, albeit still weak, energetic coherence.

"The coherence is stabilizing," Niko announced, a note of triumph in his voice. "The micro-emitter array is proving effective. Kira, good work."

Kira responded with a soft chirp, her tail giving a slow, contented sweep. It was a small victory, a single thread rewoven in the vast, intricate tapestry of Veridia's bio-energetic network. But it was a victory nonetheless, and it was largely thanks to Kira's unparalleled sensitivity.

Later, as they navigated a particularly desolate region where the chronal distortions were beginning to manifest as faint visual shimmering, a new challenge arose. The readings from their instruments became erratic, the data streams fluctuating wildly, rendering them almost useless. Anya reported a significant interference from the ambient chronal field, a byproduct of OmniCorp's reckless temporal manipulation.

"I'm losing lock on the primary resonance signature," Niko reported, his voice tight with frustration. "The distortion field is scrambling my readings. I can't get a clear fix on the optimal frequency modulation."

It was then that Kira stepped forward. She moved with an unusual grace, her large eyes seemingly focused on something beyond the visible spectrum. She began to emit a low, continuous hum, a sound that seemed to vibrate not just in the air, but within the very fabric of reality. It was a deeply resonant tone, one that Niko recognized from their initial bonding exercises – a frequency of pure, unadulterated empathy.

"She's... she's creating her own resonant field," Anya said, her voice filled with awe. "She's using her empathic signature to anchor herself against the chronal interference. Niko, can you try to lock onto *her* field? Her bio-resonance is providing a stable baseline."

Niko's fingers flew across his console. He recalibrated his equipment, shifting from the erratic external readings to the stable, pure signal emanating from Kira. It was like switching from a crackling, static-filled radio broadcast to a crystal-clear symphony. The chronal distortions still shimmered around them, a disorienting visual phenomenon, but Kira's empathic hum cut through the chaos, providing a true north for their efforts.

"I've got it," Niko breathed, his focus sharpening. "Her signature is acting as a conduit, filtering out the temporal noise. I can now modulate the resonators with precision. It's... it's extraordinary. Her psionic field is acting as a natural dampener for the chronal instability."

Kira continued to hum, her steady presence a beacon in the swirling temporal eddies. She was not just an animal; she was an integral part of their technologically advanced intervention, her innate biological and psionic capabilities proving indispensable. The team had designed the bio-harmonic resonators with sophisticated adaptive algorithms, but they had never fully anticipated the profound synergy that would emerge when those algorithms were interfaced with a sentient, empathic being.

"This is precisely what Dr. Thorne envisioned," Anya commented, her voice calmer now. "A true partnership. Our technology provides the framework, the precision, but Kira provides the intuitive understanding, the vital spark that allows us to adapt to the unforeseen. She's not just sensing Veridia's pain; she's actively healing it, in her own way, by providing a stable point of reference amidst the chaos."

The process of deploying the resonators became a rhythmic dance between Niko's technical expertise and Kira's intuitive guidance. She would often pause, her ears twitching, before issuing a soft vocalization or a subtle postural shift that directed Niko's attention to a specific area. These weren't random actions; they were precise indications of minute energetic imbalances, of subtle shifts in the dimensional threads that the instruments, however sophisticated, were failing to register.

At one particularly critical node, where the fungal network had been almost entirely obliterated, leaving behind a gaping void of corrupted energy, the resonators struggled to establish a stable connection. Niko made several attempts, adjusting frequencies, recalibrating power outputs, but the energy field remained stubbornly discordant.

"It's too unstable," Niko reported, frustration creeping into his tone. "The void is too large; it's actively repelling the harmonic frequencies. We need to create a localized sympathetic resonance, but I can't find the anchor point."

Kira whined, a low, guttural sound of concern. She nudged Niko's leg, then moved a few steps away, her gaze fixed on a patch of ground that appeared no different from its desolate surroundings. She pawed at the earth once, twice, then settled into a crouch, her tail sweeping slowly, deliberately.

Niko followed her gaze, his instruments providing no definitive reading of any anomaly. Yet, he trusted Kira implicitly. He knelt and began to gently clear away the loose, desiccated soil where she indicated. Beneath the surface, he found it: a single, dormant spore, encased in a protective bio-membrane, clinging to life with an almost impossible tenacity. It was an infinitesimal spark in a vast darkness.

"Found it," Niko announced, a sense of reverence in his voice. "A dormant spore. This is the anchor. Kira's detected the faint energetic signature of its potential, its inherent blueprint for re-growth. We need to harmonize the resonator's output directly with that potential."

He carefully placed a micro-resonator beside the spore, its delicate emitters aimed at the microscopic source of life. He then initiated a complex recalibration sequence on the primary resonator, using Kira's psionic field as a stabilizing reference. The goal was not to impose a frequency, but to coax the dormant spore's own bio-harmonic signature into becoming a broadcasting point, a tiny beacon that could then amplify the resonator's signal.

"Initiating localized harmonic attunement," Niko murmured, his eyes glued to his display. The readings began to shift, slowly at first, then with increasing speed. The chaotic energy of the void began to coalesce, drawn towards the nascent signature of the spore. The micro-resonator pulsed softly, its light intensifying, not with an aggressive glow, but with a gentle, nurturing warmth.

"It's working," Anya breathed over the comms. "The void is contracting. The energetic signature is... it's expanding outwards from that point. Kira's psionic field is acting as a sympathetic amplifier, strengthening the spore's inherent resonance."

Kira let out a soft, contented sigh, her tail giving a slow, steady thump against the ground. She had felt the dormant life, recognized its potential, and guided their technology to nurture it. It was a profound demonstration of their interconnectedness, a testament to the idea that healing wasn't about imposing will, but about facilitating growth, about reminding life of its own inherent strength. The single spore, bathed in the carefully orchestrated harmonic frequencies, began to emit a faint, almost imperceptible shimmer, a promise of what was to come. The threads, however fragile, were beginning to mend, guided by a partnership of science and soul.

The oppressive, chaotic symphony of Veridia's bio-luminescence began to recede, its jagged, erratic pulses softening into a gentler, more rhythmic cadence. Where once there had been a jarring, almost violent strobe of amethyst light, now a more harmonious, undulating glow began to assert itself. It was as if the planet itself was taking a slow, deep breath, its very essence settling into a more balanced state. Niko watched, mesmerized, as the spectral analysis on his monitor shifted from a cacophony of discordant frequencies to a more ordered, coherent spectrum. The jagged peaks and troughs were smoothing out, replaced by a series of gentle, oscillating waves. This wasn't a sudden, dramatic cure, but a subtle, yet profound, transition. It was the planetary equivalent of a fever breaking.

He traced a finger across the cool surface of the display, his gaze fixed on the shifting patterns. The subterranean fungal network, the very circulatory system of Veridia's life force, was exhibiting a renewed vigor. The energy flow, which had been sputtering and intermittent, was becoming more consistent, more robust. It was akin to observing a sluggish river suddenly finding its channel, its currents strengthening, its flow becoming purposeful. The data streams, once fragmented and unreliable, now painted a picture of gradual, yet undeniable, recovery. He noted with particular satisfaction the re-establishment of micro-currents within previously inert zones, like tiny capillaries rejoining the main arterial pathways. These were the nascent signs of reconnection, the initial whisperings of a revitalized ecosystem.

Kira, sensing the shift in the ambient resonance, uncoiled herself from her watchful posture. The agitated tension that had thrummed through her body, a palpable manifestation of the planet's distress, began to dissipate. Her tail, which had been held stiffly, began to wag with a slow, steady rhythm, each sweep a quiet affirmation of the calming energies. A soft, contented sigh escaped her, a sound of profound relief that echoed the internal landscape of Niko's own weary heart. The agitated thrum that had permeated their surroundings, a constant undercurrent of cosmic static, was being replaced by a gentle, harmonizing hum. It was a palpable shift, a tangible easing of pressure that allowed their own psionic senses to unfurl, to finally feel a sense of peace.

He carefully logged the observed changes, his fingers moving with a practiced economy of motion. Each data point was crucial, a piece of the intricate puzzle of Veridia's healing. He documented the widening bandwidth of the recovered energy flows, the increasing coherence of the spectral signatures, and the gradual normalization of the planetary bio-energetic field. There were still areas of significant damage, vast scars on the planet's energetic skin, but the overall trend was overwhelmingly positive. The intervention, guided by Dr. Thorne's theoretical frameworks and amplified by Kira's intuitive connection, was proving to be more than just effective; it was demonstrating a profound understanding of Veridia's fundamental energetic architecture.

"Anya, readouts are stabilizing," Niko reported, his voice a low rumble of cautious optimism. "The primary network is showing sustained coherence. The secondary nodes are beginning to synchronize. It's... it's working. The resonance cascade is dissipating, and the harmonic reintegration is proceeding as predicted, albeit at a slightly accelerated pace." He hesitated, then added, "Kira's influence is undeniable. Her psionic anchor is stabilizing the entire system."

Anya's voice, when it came through the comms, was tinged with a similar relief. "Excellent, Niko. Dr. Thorne is reviewing the preliminary telemetry. He's... he's very pleased. The simulation models didn't quite capture the dynamic adaptability Kira brings to the equation. It's a testament to her unique connection with Veridia. She's not just a tool; she's a partner in this recovery."

Niko glanced at Kira, who was now lying on the ground, her head resting on her paws, her eyes half-closed, but still tracking the subtle shifts in the light around them. Her breathing was deep and even, a stark contrast to the shallow, rapid breaths she had taken when the planetary distress was at its peak. The subtle vibrations that had emanated from her, a constant hum of empathic resonance, had subsided into a gentle, almost imperceptible thrum. She was a living barometer, and the storm had passed.

The amethyst glow that permeated the landscape was no longer a frantic, disorienting flicker. Instead, it pulsed with a slow, steady beat, like the gentle rhythm of a healthy heart. It was a light that spoke of restoration, of life returning to weakened tissues. The energy wasn't merely flowing; it was *circulating*, nourishing the desiccated flora that dotted the landscape, stirring the dormant seeds buried deep within the soil. Niko could almost feel the nascent life stirring beneath his boots, a subtle awakening that mirrored the reawakening of the fungal network.

He decided to conduct a series of localized environmental scans, focusing on areas that had previously exhibited the most severe signs of energetic depletion. He deployed a small swarm of micro-drones, their optical sensors tuned to the newly established harmonic frequencies. As they fanned out across the terrain, their feeds began to populate his console with images of subtle but significant transformations. Small, hardy mosses, previously bleached and brittle, were now showing hints of green, their cellular structures seemingly rehydrating under the influence of the ambient resonance. Tiny, almost microscopic fungi, barely visible to the naked eye, were beginning to sprout from the cracks in the parched earth, their nascent mycelial threads reaching out to reconnect with the recovering subterranean network.

"The flora is responding," Niko announced, a thrill of discovery in his voice. "It's not just the fungal network; the surface vegetation is showing signs of recovery. We're seeing chlorophyll regeneration in some of the less damaged species. The micro-drones are picking up increased bio-electric potential in the root systems." He zoomed in on one of the drone feeds, showcasing a cluster of what had been grey, lifeless stalks. Now, a faint blush of color was returning to their surfaces, and the faint, almost imperceptible shimmer of bio-energy was beginning to pulse within their vascular tissues. It was a fragile rebirth, but a rebirth nonetheless.

Kira let out a soft yip, nudging Niko's hand with her nose. She then trotted a short distance away, towards a cluster of what appeared to be petrified wood, remnants of a forest long gone. She circled the area, her tail giving a slow, inquisitive wag, before settling down and looking back at him. Intrigued, Niko followed, his instruments still active. As he approached, he noticed something his initial scans had missed. Encased within the petrified wood were faint, fossilized imprints, not of leaves or branches, but of intricate, almost crystalline structures.

"What is this, Kira?" he murmured, kneeling down to examine the fossil. Kira nudged his hand again, then pawed gently at the base of the petrified wood. Niko's instruments, calibrated to detect subtle energetic signatures, began to register a faint, residual resonance emanating from the fossilized material. It was a memory of energy, a ghost of a once-vibrant life form.

"It's... it's unlike anything in our databases," Niko reported to Anya, his voice hushed with a sense of wonder. "These aren't plant fossils in the traditional sense. They appear to be the fossilized remains of some kind of crystalline flora, something that was deeply integrated with Veridia's energetic network. Kira's detected a faint energetic imprint. It's like a harmonic echo."

He carefully deployed a specialized resonator, designed for excavating delicate energetic signatures from inert materials. He adjusted its frequency, aiming to coax any latent resonance from the fossil. As the resonator hummed to life, a faint, ethereal light began to emanate from the crystalline imprints within the petrified wood. The amethyst glow of Veridia's ambient energy seemed to concentrate around the fossil, drawn to it as if to a long-lost relative.

"Remarkable," Anya breathed over the comms. "The crystalline flora... Dr. Thorne theorized about their existence in his initial hypotheses. He believed they played a crucial role in regulating and amplifying Veridia's bio-energetic field. Their extinction, or rather, their dormancy, would have had a profound destabilizing effect on the planet's ecosystem."

The resonance from the fossil grew stronger, a complex series of interwoven frequencies that spoke of a profound, intricate connection to the planet's core. It was a song of crystal and energy, a melody that had been silenced for millennia. Kira watched intently, her ears twitching, as if she could hear the silent music that was now resonating through the air.

"Kira is reacting strongly to this," Niko observed. "Her empathic field is intensifying in response to the fossil's resonance. It's almost as if she's... remembering it. Or perhaps, she's recognizing a fundamental harmonic principle that she herself embodies."

He continued to fine-tune the resonator, slowly amplifying the extracted frequencies. The light from the fossil pulsed in time with Kira's own subtle bio-energetic field, creating a feedback loop of remarkable synergy. He felt a profound sense of connection, not just to Kira, but to the ancient life form whose energetic ghost they were now communing with. This was not just about restoring a fungal network; it was about rediscovering Veridia's lost heritage, about reawakening the forgotten players in its intricate ecological drama.

The data streaming from the resonator was unlike anything they had encountered before. It wasn't just a simple energy signature; it was a complex tapestry of harmonic interactions, a blueprint for a form of life that had integrated itself with the very fabric of the planet. Niko realized that the crystalline flora might have been the primary conduits for Veridia's energy, acting as natural amplifiers and distributors, their intricate structures capable of resonating with and modulating the planet's core frequencies. Their demise, therefore, would have crippled the entire system, leaving it vulnerable to the chaotic surges and imbalances that had plagued it for so long.

"Niko, I'm picking up a correlating pattern," Anya's voice cut through his focus. "The harmonic signatures from that fossilized structure are mirroring some of the higher-frequency resonances we've been detecting in the most stable areas of the fungal network. It's not a direct match, but the underlying mathematical principles are eerily similar. It suggests that the fungal network, in its own way, is attempting to replicate the function of the crystalline flora."

This was a revelation. The fungal network wasn't just a passive recipient of energy; it was an active, adaptive system, striving to compensate for the loss of its original energetic architects. It was a testament to the resilience of life, its innate drive to find a way, to adapt and to endure. And now, with the introduction of the bio-harmonic resonators and Kira's empathic guidance, they were essentially providing the fungal network with the missing pieces of the puzzle, the harmonic keys that would allow it to unlock its full potential.

Niko carefully collected a sample of the petrified wood, encasing it in a stasis field. This would be crucial for further study, for understanding the intricate bio-energetic architecture of the lost crystalline flora. He looked at Kira, who had risen and was now standing beside him, her amber eyes reflecting the soft amethyst glow of the recovering world. She let out a soft, contented chirp, a sound that resonated with a sense of accomplishment and peace.

"We're not just mending threads, Kira," Niko murmured, stroking her sleek fur. "We're weaving them back together, using the echoes of the past to build a stronger future."

The process of healing was multi-layered, extending beyond the immediate restoration of the fungal network. The success in re-establishing energy flow was already beginning to have a cascading effect on the surface flora. Niko deployed additional sensors, designed to monitor atmospheric composition and soil nutrient levels. The initial readings were promising. The increased bio-electric activity within the root systems was not only facilitating the uptake of water and minerals but was also stimulating a series of complex biochemical processes.

He noticed that the desiccated, almost mineralized soil was beginning to show subtle signs of organic enrichment. Microbes, previously dormant due to the lack of energy and moisture, were reawakening, their metabolic activity accelerating. These microbial communities were the unsung heroes of any ecosystem, tirelessly breaking down organic matter, releasing essential nutrients, and forming symbiotic relationships with plant roots. Their resurgence was a critical indicator of Veridia's gradual return to health.

"The soil microbiomes are showing significant increases in activity," Niko reported to Anya, pointing to a series of charts on his display. "We're seeing a rise in nitrogen-fixing bacteria and mycorrhizal fungi. This is exactly what we hoped for. The enhanced energy flow from the network is essentially jump-starting the nutrient cycle."

Kira, meanwhile, had wandered towards a patch of ground where only sparse, brittle, greyed vegetation had managed to cling to existence. She lowered her head, sniffing the dry, cracked earth, and then began to paw at a specific spot. Niko, trusting her intuition implicitly, followed. He found nothing immediately visible, just more of the same desiccated landscape. But Kira persisted, her paws digging with a focused intensity.

"She's indicating something," Niko said, pulling out a hand-held scanner. The scanner, however, registered nothing out of the ordinary. Yet, Kira's insistence was undeniable. He decided to trust her instinct and began to carefully excavate the area she was indicating. Beneath a thin layer of desiccated topsoil, he discovered a small, seed-like object, remarkably well-preserved despite the harsh conditions. It was unlike any seed he had ever seen, its outer shell a deep, iridescent purple, shimmering faintly even in the subdued light.

"Found something," Niko announced, his voice filled with a growing sense of awe. "A seed. Kira found it. It's unlike anything cataloged in our botanical surveys. It's radiating a faint, yet distinct, bio-energetic signature."

He carefully collected the seed, placing it in a specialized containment unit designed to maintain optimal environmental conditions. The unit was equipped with micro-sensors that would monitor the seed's metabolic activity and energetic output. As the containment unit hummed to life, a faint glow emanated from within, and the seed's iridescent shell seemed to deepen in color, as if responding to the gentle surge of energy.

"This is extraordinary, Niko," Anya responded, her voice laced with excitement. "This could be a key to understanding Veridia's original flora, the species that were most deeply integrated with its energetic core. If we can coax this seed to germinate, it could provide us with a direct link to the planet's past, and perhaps, a blueprint for its future."

Kira nudged the containment unit with her nose, then let out a soft, resonant hum, a sound that seemed to vibrate with a sense of anticipation. It was as if she understood the significance of their discovery, recognizing the potential for life held within that small, iridescent seed.

The success with the fungal network was more than just a scientific achievement; it was a profound vindication of their approach. It demonstrated that by working in harmony with Veridia's natural energetic systems, rather than imposing artificial solutions, they could facilitate a true and lasting recovery. The interventions were not about dominance, but about partnership, about understanding the intricate dance of life and energy that defined the planet.

As the amethyst glow continued to stabilize, the world around them began to transform in subtle yet significant ways. The air, once heavy with the scent of decay and dust, now carried a faint, earthy aroma, reminiscent of rain on dry soil. The silence, which had been oppressive and absolute, was now punctuated by the faint rustling of nascent vegetation and the almost imperceptible hum of reawakening microbial life. It was a symphony of small miracles, each one a testament to the planet's enduring capacity for regeneration.

Niko took a moment to simply observe, to absorb the palpable shift in the atmosphere. Kira, sensing his reflective mood, leaned against his leg, her presence a warm, comforting anchor. Her tail wagged a slow, steady rhythm, a silent acknowledgement of the progress they had made. The agitated energy that had once pulsed through her, mirroring Veridia's distress, had been replaced by a calm, steady resonance, a quiet confidence in the unfolding healing process.

He knew that the journey was far from over. Vast swathes of Veridia still bore the deep wounds inflicted by OmniCorp's recklessness. But for the first time since their arrival, a genuine sense of hope had taken root. The threads of life, so brutally torn, were being meticulously rewoven, not by force, but by a gentle, harmonizing touch, guided by science, amplified by empathy, and ultimately, initiated by the planet's own indomitable will to survive. The flora was responding, not just to their technology, but to the reawakened pulse of Veridia itself, a pulse that Kira, in her profound connection, helped to amplify and stabilize. The slow, steady hum of the planet was becoming a melody of recovery, and they were privileged to be its witnesses, and its humble facilitators.

The amethyst glow that now pulsed with a steady, life-affirming rhythm across Veridia's surface was a testament to their success. The bio-harmonic resonators, guided by Kira's unwavering psionic anchor, had indeed managed to coax the planet's vital energetic network back from the brink. The fungal mycelium, once a fractured and sputtering conduit of life, now hummed with a revitalized flow, its currents strengthening, its reach extending into areas long thought to be irrecoverably dead. Niko watched the data streams with a profound sense of quiet triumph, the jagged peaks of despair on his monitors smoothed into gentle, undulating waves of recovery. Micro-drones, dispatched to monitor the reawakening flora, sent back feeds of verdant shoots pushing through parched earth, of chlorophyll regenerating in the leaves of once-barren shrubs, and of microscopic life stirring within the soil, re-establishing the intricate nutrient cycles that were the bedrock of any thriving ecosystem. It was a symphony of rebirth, orchestrated by science, amplified by intuition, and ultimately, driven by the planet's own indomitable will to survive.

Yet, as Niko meticulously logged the myriad indicators of Veridia's healing, a subtle, persistent shadow lingered. It wasn't a flaw in the data, nor a failure of their intervention. It was something far more insidious, a testament to the enduring, often irreversible, damage inflicted by OmniCorp's rapacious exploitation. In certain pockets of the landscape, the recovery was not a complete restoration, but a fractured echo of what once was. These were the areas where the bio-harmonic resonance seemed to falter, where the amethyst light, though present, held a dimmer, more desultory hue. Here, the soil remained stubbornly compacted, its texture unnaturally coarse, as if the very earth had been leached of its inherent pliability. The flora, where it managed to sprout at all, often bore the hallmarks of permanent molecular scarring. Their leaves, even as they unfurled, possessed a certain brittle translucence, and the regeneration of chlorophyll seemed to stall at a suboptimal level, leaving them perpetually a pale, washed-out green.

Niko knelt, his gloved hand tracing the outline of a patch of ground that felt unnaturally rough beneath his fingertips. It was as if the earth itself had been subjected to a harsh, chemical etching, a permanent alteration at a cellular level. Kira, ever attuned to the subtle energetic currents, approached the area with a hesitant step. She lowered her head, her sensitive snout twitching, not with the curious exploration she displayed in the recovering zones, but with a faint, almost imperceptible unease. She let out a low whine, a soft, rumbling sound that spoke of apprehension, and nudged Niko's hand with her nose, her gaze flicking towards the damaged terrain.

"I feel it too, Kira," Niko murmured, his voice laced with a weariness that had nothing to do with his physical exertion. He activated a localized atmospheric and soil composition analyzer, its small sensors extending to probe the very fabric of the damaged earth. The readings confirmed his suspicions. While the overall levels of harmful toxins had been significantly reduced by the planet's natural processes and their own clean-up efforts, there were residual molecular abnormalities that their current technology could not fully rectify. Certain complex organic compounds had been irrevocably altered, their molecular structures warped by OmniCorp's industrial processes, leaving them incapable of reintegrating into the natural biogeochemical cycles. It was the energetic equivalent of scar tissue, a permanent blemish on Veridia's vibrant ecological tapestry.

He stood and walked a few paces away, towards a cluster of low-lying shrubs. These plants, while showing signs of life, were clearly struggling. Their leaves were misshapen, exhibiting a peculiar asymmetry, and their growth patterns were stunted, their branches twisting at unnatural angles. Niko carefully detached a single leaf, placing it under a portable microscopic scanner. The cellular structure was distorted, the chloroplasts appearing abnormally small and irregular in shape. It was clear that these organisms, while surviving, would never achieve their full biological potential, their photosynthetic efficiency permanently compromised.

"It's like a chemical memory etched into their very being," Niko explained, his voice soft, almost regretful. He projected the microscopic imagery onto his wrist-mounted display for Anya to see. "OmniCorp's waste products didn't just poison the immediate environment; they fundamentally altered the genetic and molecular blueprints of some of Veridia's flora. Even with the harmonic resonance restoring the planet's energy flow, these molecular changes are proving to be remarkably resilient. It's a permanent scar, a reminder of their recklessness."

Kira approached one of the damaged shrubs, her tail giving a slow, hesitant wag. She sniffed at the leaves, her body language conveying a mixture of curiosity and a lingering sense of concern. She then nudged Niko again, her amber eyes meeting his, a silent question in their depths.

"What happened here, Kira?" he answered softly, stroking her fur. "They did something... irreversible. Something that even the planet's natural healing cannot entirely mend. It's a consequence of exploitation, my friend. A harsh lesson in the enduring impact of unchecked greed."

He activated his data recorder, initiating a detailed scan of the area. He began to meticulously document every instance of such permanent damage. Each observation was a testament, a piece of evidence building a case against

OmniCorp. He recorded the specific molecular alterations in the soil, the compromised cellular structures of the flora, the subtle but significant deviations from optimal bio-energetic signatures in these affected zones. He cross-referenced these findings with historical atmospheric and geological data, identifying the likely sources of OmniCorp's most egregious pollutions – abandoned processing plants, illegal waste disposal sites, and areas of intense, unregulated resource extraction.

"We're documenting the 'ghosts' of OmniCorp's passage," Niko reported to Anya, his voice tight with a controlled anger. "Areas where the healing is incomplete, where the scars remain. The bio-harmonic resonators are mending the energetic network, but they can't rewrite molecular damage. This is what we have to present. This is the irrefutable evidence of their destructive legacy."

He pointed to a section of his display that showed a thermal imaging sweep. Even with the ambient amethyst glow, these damaged areas registered a slightly lower thermal signature, a subtle but consistent drop in their energy output. It was as if these patches of land were perpetually cooler, perpetually less vibrant, a physical manifestation of their depleted vitality.

"It's like a faint fever that never quite breaks," Niko elaborated. "The planet's overall temperature is normalizing, but these zones... they remain sluggish. The microbial activity is present, but it's less robust, less diverse. The entire ecosystem in these pockets is functioning at a significantly reduced capacity. It's a localized ecological depression, a direct consequence of OmniCorp's actions."

Kira moved ahead, her steps more determined now, as if drawn by an invisible thread towards a specific point. Niko followed, his instruments constantly active. She stopped at the edge of what appeared to be a shallow ravine, its sides eroded and scarred. The usual growth of hardy, low-lying Veridian mosses was absent here, replaced by a thin, dusty layer of inorganic sediment. The air itself seemed to carry a faint, acrid undertone, barely perceptible to Niko's enhanced senses, but evidently strong enough to register on Kira's.

"This looks like an old waste conduit," Niko mused, scanning the ravine. "Possibly a discharge point for industrial effluent. The soil composition here is particularly anomalous – high concentrations of heavy metals and complex synthetic polymers, far beyond what we've seen in even the moderately damaged areas." He zoomed in on a section of the ravine wall, where the rock strata had been visibly discolored and warped. "The geological formations themselves show signs of thermal and chemical stress. This wasn't just dumping; they were processing and discharging here."

Kira whined again, her gaze fixed on a particular spot near the base of the ravine. Niko knelt, his scanner humming. It registered a faint, intermittent energy signature, unlike the steady hum of the recovering network. It was erratic, almost sputtering, like a dying ember. He carefully dug away some of the loose sediment. Beneath the surface, he unearthed a cluster of what looked like petrified fragments, fused together into an unidentifiable mass. The fragments, when touched, felt unnaturally smooth and unnaturally dense, as if they had been subjected to immense heat and pressure.

"What is this?" he whispered, his brow furrowed in concentration. He brought a fine-tipped manipulator arm from his multi-tool to gently scrape at one of the fragments. A faint, almost metallic scent, sharp and chemical, wafted into the air. "The molecular structure is unlike anything I've encountered. It's a complex lattice of inorganic compounds, but it exhibits a residual, albeit weak, bio-electric potential. It's almost as if... as if this material was once integrated with a biological system, but has been fundamentally altered, mineralized by OmniCorp's processes."

He recalled Dr. Thorne's initial hypotheses about Veridia's ancient crystalline flora, their unique bio-energetic architecture. Could these fused fragments be remnants of a similar, but far more ancient, form of life, corrupted and fossilized by OmniCorp's waste? The thought sent a shiver down his spine. It was a chilling possibility, that OmniCorp had not only destroyed the living ecosystems but had also irrevocably tainted the very echoes of Veridia's deep past.

"This is evidence of irreparable contamination," Niko stated, his voice firm and resolute. He carefully collected a sample of the fused fragments, sealing it in a specialized containment unit designed for highly volatile and altered materials. "These aren't just scars on the land; they are monuments to OmniCorp's disregard for life in all its forms, living and ancient."

Kira nudged the containment unit, her tail giving a slow, almost mournful sweep. She then looked back at the ravine, her gaze lingering on the scarred earth, a silent testament to the damage that had been inflicted. Niko understood her unease. It was the animal instinct recognizing a profound wrongness, a lingering miasma of toxicity that even the planet's most robust healing couldn't fully erase.

"We need to ensure these areas are clearly demarcated and isolated," Niko continued, his fingers flying across his console, inputting the coordinates and damage assessments. "Even with our efforts, complete recovery here might be impossible. These will serve as permanent reminders, not just for us, but for anyone who comes after, of the catastrophic consequences of unchecked corporate greed and the profound responsibility we have to protect worlds like Veridia."

He stood back, taking in the panoramic view of the ravine and the sparse, struggling vegetation on its periphery. The amethyst light, though present, seemed to struggle to fully penetrate the lingering shadows of industrial residue. It was a stark contrast to the vibrant, pulsating glow in the areas they had successfully revitalized. This was the lingering trace of OmniCorp, a ghostly imprint on the planet's energetic and molecular landscape, a somber footnote in the story of Veridia's hard-won recovery.

The data they were compiling was more than just scientific observation; it was a narrative of destruction and resilience. It told of a planet pushed to the brink, of life clinging tenaciously to existence, and of the enduring damage left behind by those who saw only resources to be plundered, not a living world to be cherished. Niko felt a deep sense of responsibility to ensure that this narrative was heard, that the full extent of OmniCorp's actions, both immediate and long-lasting, was brought to light. The permanent scars, the molecular damage, the lingering unease that Kira sensed – these were not mere footnotes; they were central chapters in the unfolding story of Veridia's survival, and a crucial part of their report to the Interstellar Ecological Council. They were the irrefutable, tangible proof of OmniCorp's devastating impact, a testament to the fact that some wounds, even on a planetary scale, might never truly heal. And in acknowledging these permanent traces, they were honoring not just the planet's resilience, but also the memory of what had been lost.

The shimmering amethyst glow, once a beacon of desperate healing, now settled into a steady, rhythmic pulse. It was a visual manifestation of the planet's reawakening, a vibrant tapestry woven from scientific precision and the innate resilience of life. Niko, his eyes still scanning the complex arrays of data streaming across his holographic displays, felt a profound wave of relief wash over him. The bio-harmonic resonators, their delicate frequencies precisely calibrated to Veridia's weakened energetic network, had performed beyond their most optimistic projections. The planet's vital conduits, once fractured and sputtering, now hummed with a revitalized flow, their mycelial tendrils extending, strengthening, and reclaiming swathes of land that had been declared lost. He watched, captivated, as the jagged peaks of despair on his monitors smoothed into gentle, undulating waves of recovery, each crest a testament to the life force reasserting its dominion. Micro-drones, dispatched like tiny emissaries of hope, relayed images of verdant shoots pushing through the formerly parched earth, of chlorophyll regenerating in the leaves of trees that had stood skeletal and barren for cycles, and of microscopic organisms stirring within the soil, re-establishing the intricate nutrient cycles that formed the very bedrock of a thriving ecosystem. It was a symphony of rebirth, a grand overture conducted by science, amplified by intuition, and fundamentally driven by Veridia's own indomitable will to survive.

Yet, even as Niko meticulously logged the myriad indicators of Veridia's recuperation, a subtle, persistent shadow lingered. It was not a flaw in the data, nor a failure of their intervention. It was something far more insidious, a stark reminder of the enduring, often irreversible damage inflicted by OmniCorp's rapacious exploitation. In certain pockets of the landscape, the recovery was not a complete restoration, but a fractured echo of what once was. These were the zones where the bio-harmonic resonance seemed to falter, where the amethyst light, though present, held a dimmer, more desultory hue. Here, the soil remained stubbornly compacted, its texture unnaturally coarse, as if the very earth had been leached of its inherent pliability. The flora, where it managed to sprout at all, often bore the hallmarks of permanent molecular scarring. Their leaves, even as they unfurled, possessed a certain brittle translucence, and the regeneration of chlorophyll seemed to stall at a suboptimal level, leaving them perpetually a pale, washed-out green.

Niko knelt, his gloved hand tracing the outline of a patch of ground that felt unnaturally rough beneath his fingertips. It was as if the earth itself had been subjected to a harsh, chemical etching, a permanent alteration at a cellular level. Kira, ever attuned to the subtle energetic currents, approached the area with a hesitant step. She lowered her head, her sensitive snout twitching, not with the curious exploration she displayed in the recovering zones, but with a faint, almost imperceptible unease. She let out a low whine, a soft, rumbling sound that spoke of apprehension, and nudged Niko's hand with her nose, her gaze flicking towards the damaged terrain.

"I feel it too, Kira," Niko murmured, his voice laced with a weariness that had nothing to do with his physical exertion. He activated a localized atmospheric and soil composition analyzer, its small sensors extending to probe the very fabric of the damaged earth. The readings confirmed his suspicions. While the overall levels of harmful toxins had been significantly reduced by the planet's natural processes and their own clean-up efforts, there were residual molecular abnormalities that their current technology could not fully rectify. Certain complex organic compounds had been irrevocably altered, their molecular structures warped by OmniCorp's industrial processes, leaving them incapable of reintegrating into the natural biogeochemical cycles. It was the energetic equivalent of scar tissue, a permanent blemish on Veridia's vibrant ecological tapestry.

He stood and walked a few paces away, towards a cluster of low-lying shrubs. These plants, while showing signs of life, were clearly struggling. Their leaves were misshapen, exhibiting a peculiar asymmetry, and their growth patterns were stunted, their branches twisting at unnatural angles. Niko carefully detached a single leaf, placing it under a portable microscopic scanner. The cellular structure was distorted, the chloroplasts appearing abnormally small and irregular in shape. It was clear that these organisms, while surviving, would never achieve their full biological potential, their photosynthetic efficiency permanently compromised.

"It's like a chemical memory etched into their very being," Niko explained, his voice soft, almost regretful. He projected the microscopic imagery onto his wrist-mounted display for Anya to see. "OmniCorp's waste products didn't just poison the immediate environment; they fundamentally altered the genetic and molecular blueprints of some of Veridia's flora. Even with the harmonic resonance restoring the planet's energy flow, these molecular changes are proving to be remarkably resilient. It's a permanent scar, a reminder of their recklessness."

Kira approached one of the damaged shrubs, her tail giving a slow, hesitant wag. She sniffed at the leaves, her body language conveying a mixture of curiosity and a lingering sense of concern. She then nudged Niko again, her amber eyes meeting his, a silent question in their depths.

"What happened here, Kira?" he answered softly, stroking her fur. "They did something... irreversible. Something that even the planet's natural healing cannot entirely mend. It's a consequence of exploitation, my friend. A harsh lesson in the enduring impact of unchecked greed."

He activated his data recorder, initiating a detailed scan of the area. He began to meticulously document every instance of such permanent damage. Each observation was a testament, a piece of evidence building a case against

OmniCorp. He recorded the specific molecular alterations in the soil, the compromised cellular structures of the flora, the subtle but significant deviations from optimal bio-energetic signatures in these affected zones. He cross-referenced these findings with historical atmospheric and geological data, identifying the likely sources of OmniCorp's most egregious pollutions – abandoned processing plants, illegal waste disposal sites, and areas of intense, unregulated resource extraction.

"We're documenting the 'ghosts' of OmniCorp's passage," Niko reported to Anya, his voice tight with a controlled anger. "Areas where the healing is incomplete, where the scars remain. The bio-harmonic resonators are mending the energetic network, but they can't rewrite molecular damage. This is what we have to present. This is the irrefutable evidence of their destructive legacy."

He pointed to a section of his display that showed a thermal imaging sweep. Even with the ambient amethyst glow, these damaged areas registered a slightly lower thermal signature, a subtle but consistent drop in their energy output. It was as if these patches of land were perpetually cooler, perpetually less vibrant, a physical manifestation of their depleted vitality.

"It's like a faint fever that never quite breaks," Niko elaborated. "The planet's overall temperature is normalizing, but these zones... they remain sluggish. The microbial activity is present, but it's less robust, less diverse. The entire ecosystem in these pockets is functioning at a significantly reduced capacity. It's a localized ecological depression, a direct consequence of OmniCorp's actions."

Kira moved ahead, her steps more determined now, as if drawn by an invisible thread towards a specific point. Niko followed, his instruments constantly active. She stopped at the edge of what appeared to be a shallow ravine, its sides eroded and scarred. The usual growth of hardy, low-lying Veridian mosses was absent here, replaced by a thin, dusty layer of inorganic sediment. The air itself seemed to carry a faint, acrid undertone, barely perceptible to Niko's enhanced senses, but evidently strong enough to register on Kira's.

"This looks like an old waste conduit," Niko mused, scanning the ravine. "Possibly a discharge point for industrial effluent. The soil composition here is particularly anomalous – high concentrations of heavy metals and complex synthetic polymers, far beyond what we've seen in even the moderately damaged areas." He zoomed in on a section of the ravine wall, where the rock strata had been visibly discolored and warped. "The geological formations themselves show signs of thermal and chemical stress. This wasn't just dumping; they were processing and discharging here."

Kira whined again, her gaze fixed on a particular spot near the base of the ravine. Niko knelt, his scanner humming. It registered a faint, intermittent energy signature, unlike the steady hum of the recovering network. It was erratic, almost sputtering, like a dying ember. He carefully dug away some of the loose sediment. Beneath the surface, he unearthed a cluster of what looked like petrified fragments, fused together into an unidentifiable mass. The fragments, when touched, felt unnaturally smooth and unnaturally dense, as if they had been subjected to immense heat and pressure.

"What is this?" he whispered, his brow furrowed in concentration. He brought a fine-tipped manipulator arm from his multi-tool to gently scrape at one of the fragments. A faint, almost metallic scent, sharp and chemical, wafted into the air. "The molecular structure is unlike anything I've encountered. It's a complex lattice of inorganic compounds, but it exhibits a residual, albeit weak, bio-electric potential. It's almost as if... as if this material was once integrated with a biological system, but has been fundamentally altered, mineralized by OmniCorp's processes."

He recalled Dr. Thorne's initial hypotheses about Veridia's ancient crystalline flora, their unique bio-energetic architecture. Could these fused fragments be remnants of a similar, but far more ancient, form of life, corrupted and fossilized by OmniCorp's waste? The thought sent a shiver down his spine. It was a chilling possibility, that OmniCorp had not only destroyed the living ecosystems but had also irrevocably tainted the very echoes of Veridia's deep past.

"This is evidence of irreparable contamination," Niko stated, his voice firm and resolute. He carefully collected a sample of the fused fragments, sealing it in a specialized containment unit designed for highly volatile and altered materials. "These aren't just scars on the land; they are monuments to OmniCorp's disregard for life in all its forms, living and ancient."

Kira nudged the containment unit, her tail giving a slow, almost mournful sweep. She then looked back at the ravine, her gaze lingering on the scarred earth, a silent testament to the damage that had been inflicted. Niko understood her unease. It was the animal instinct recognizing a profound wrongness, a lingering miasma of toxicity that even the planet's most robust healing couldn't fully erase.

"We need to ensure these areas are clearly demarcated and isolated," Niko continued, his fingers flying across his console, inputting the coordinates and damage assessments. "Even with our efforts, complete recovery here might be impossible. These will serve as permanent reminders, not just for us, but for anyone who comes after, of the catastrophic consequences of unchecked corporate greed and the profound responsibility we have to protect worlds like Veridia."

He stood back, taking in the panoramic view of the ravine and the sparse, struggling vegetation on its periphery. The amethyst light, though present, seemed to struggle to fully penetrate the lingering shadows of industrial residue. It was a stark contrast to the vibrant, pulsating glow in the areas they had successfully revitalized. This was the lingering trace of OmniCorp, a ghostly imprint on the planet's energetic and molecular landscape, a somber footnote in the story of Veridia's hard-won recovery.

The data they were compiling was more than just scientific observation; it was a narrative of destruction and resilience. It told of a planet pushed to the brink, of life clinging tenaciously to existence, and of the enduring damage left behind by those who saw only resources to be plundered, not a living world to be cherished. Niko felt a deep sense of responsibility to ensure that this narrative was heard, that the full extent of OmniCorp's actions, both immediate and long-lasting, was brought to light. The permanent scars, the molecular damage, the lingering unease that Kira sensed – these were not mere footnotes; they were central chapters in the unfolding story of Veridia's survival, and a crucial part of their report to the Interstellar Ecological Council. They were the irrefutable, tangible proof of OmniCorp's devastating impact, a testament to the fact that some wounds, even on a planetary scale, might never truly heal. And in acknowledging these permanent traces, they were honoring not just the planet's resilience, but also the memory of what had been lost.

As the planet's vital energetic network stabilized, a new kind of assessment began, one focused not on the sprawling landscapes but on a point of convergence, a singularity of immense energetic significance: the nexus where the interdimensional gateway was anchored. This was the delicate linchpin of their entire operation, the point of entry and exit for energies and phenomena that defied terrestrial comprehension. For cycles, the fluctuations and anomalies emanating from this nexus had been a source of profound concern. The risk of a cascade failure, of the very fabric of reality fraying at the edges, had loomed large, a spectral threat casting a long shadow over their efforts to mend Veridia.

Niko directed a battery of sophisticated scanners towards the nexus, their beams of modulated energy probing the anomaly with unprecedented precision. Kira, her head tilted, her ears swiveling, was their primary biosensor, her psionic sensitivity an invaluable tool in navigating the esoteric energies at play. Her low, steady hum of contentment, a sound that had become synonymous with Veridia's gradual recovery, now resonated with a new depth. She moved with an assured grace, her paws treading the familiar, yet always awe-inspiring, ground around the gateway's anchoring point. The usual subtle crackle of displaced quantum foam, the faint shimmer of temporal distortion, the almost imperceptible scent of ozone laced with something akin to starlight – all these familiar signatures of the gateway were present, but they were different. They were *settled*.

"Kira, report," Niko's voice was a calm, measured tone, projecting confidence he now felt deep within his bones. He watched her, his gaze unwavering.

Kira met his eyes, and a wave of pure, unadulterated stability washed over Niko. It wasn't just a visual or auditory cue; it was a direct, psionic transmission. The chaotic energy patterns that had previously characterized the nexus were gone, replaced by a baseline resonance that mirrored the healthy, rhythmic pulse of Veridia's restored ecosystem. The chaotic oscillations, the sharp spikes of uncontrolled energy that had threatened to destabilize the gateway's very existence, had smoothed out. The intervention at the nexus, a delicate balancing act of energy redirection and harmonic dampening, had been a resounding success. The critical threat of a cascade failure, a scenario that could have torn a permanent wound in spacetime and unleashed unpredictable dimensional bleed-through, had been averted.

"The gateway is stable, Niko," Kira's telepathic voice was clear, resonant, and filled with a quiet triumph. "The vibrations are harmonized. The flow is consistent. It's like... like a perfectly tuned instrument, singing its true song."

Niko let out a breath he hadn't realized he'd been holding for weeks. He ran a final diagnostic sweep, cross-referencing Kira's psionic readings with the complex metrics generated by the gateway's energy regulators. The data confirmed it. The temporal displacement fields were within acceptable parameters. The dimensional containment layers were holding firm. The quantum entanglement links, the invisible threads that tethered the gateway to its anchor point in their reality, were robust and unwavering.

"Confirmed," Niko announced, his voice tinged with elation. He turned to Anya and the rest of the pack, a wide smile spreading across his face. "Gateway stability confirmed. The nexus is secure. We've done it. We've stabilized the gateway."

A chorus of relieved exclamations rippled through the group. The weight that had pressed down on them, the unspoken fear of an unimaginable catastrophe, began to lift. They could breathe again. They could focus. Their mission, to understand and, if possible, to mend the damage inflicted upon Veridia, could now proceed with a renewed sense of purpose and confidence. The immediate threat of dimensional instability had receded, leaving them free to confront the remaining challenges.

However, the relief was tempered by a profound understanding of the forces they were dealing with. The ease with which OmniCorp had manipulated and destabilized such a critical nexus point was a chilling reminder of the immense power they had wielded, and the utter disregard they had shown for the consequences. The gateway, once a source of wonder and scientific pursuit, had become a weapon, a tool for exploitation and, potentially, for devastating destruction.

"This means we can proceed with the full analysis of the dimensional bleed-through patterns," Anya stated, her voice regaining its professional edge. "Now that the gateway is stable, we can collect data on the interdimensional incursions without risking further destabilization."

Niko nodded, though a somber note had entered his voice. "Yes. But it also means we understand the true scale of the threat OmniCorp posed. They weren't just polluting a planet; they were tampering with the fundamental architecture of reality. The fact that they could even *reach* this nexus, let alone destabilize it, speaks volumes about their ambition and their recklessness."

Kira, usually buoyant after a success, let out a soft, almost mournful sigh. She nudged Niko's hand, her amber eyes reflecting the stable, pulsing glow of the gateway. Her psionic echo carried a new layer of understanding, a nascent awareness of the broader cosmic implications of OmniCorp's actions.

The gateway was stable, but the knowledge of its vulnerability, and the potential for such power to be misused, had cast a long shadow. They had mended one thread, a critical one, in the tapestry of Veridia's survival, but the broader picture, the complex and dangerous interplay of interdimensional forces, remained a daunting and sobering prospect. Their mission had just taken on a new, and far more profound, dimension. The immediate crisis had passed, but the awareness of the immense, volatile forces they were now capable of interacting with had irrevocably altered their perspective.

The universe, they now understood with stark clarity, was far more interconnected, and far more fragile, than they had ever imagined. And OmniCorp had proven, with terrifying efficacy, how easily such fragility could be exploited.

CHAPTER SEVEN

WHISPERS OF SENTIENCE

The amethyst glow of Veridia's nascent recovery continued to bathe the landscape, a constant reminder of the delicate balance they had fought so hard to restore. Niko, Anya, and Kira moved through the revitalized flora, their senses finely tuned to the subtle shifts in the environment. The data flowing from Niko's instruments painted a picture of ecological health, of systems reawakening and re-establishing their ancient rhythms. Yet, with each passing cycle, a new layer of complexity was unfolding, one that transcended the mere restoration of biological functions. It was a subtle stirring, a whisper of something more profound, that had begun to captivate Niko's scientific curiosity and challenge his fundamental understanding of Veridia's inhabitants.

The initial surveys had classified the native fauna as primarily instinct-driven, their behaviors dictated by the primal imperatives of survival, reproduction, and territoriality. While impressive in their adaptations to Veridia's unique environment, they had been categorized within the established parameters of known biological complexity. However, as they ventured further into the recovering zones, these parameters began to blur. Niko found himself frequently pausing, his brow furrowed in thought, as he observed interactions that defied simple explanation.

One such observation occurred near a cluster of bioluminescent flora that had recently re-emerged, their gentle, pulsating light a welcome sight against the deepening twilight. A group of the six-limbed, crystalline-shelled creatures, initially encountered near the dormant bio-pods, were engaged in an activity that was far from random foraging. They moved with a deliberate, coordinated purpose, their chitinous bodies clicking softly as they navigated the uneven terrain. Niko recognized the distinct pattern of their movements; it was not the haphazard search for sustenance, but a structured approach to a problem.

A fallen branch, thick and heavy, lay partially obstructing a pathway that led to a rich patch of nutrient-rich moss. Individually, the creatures had attempted to dislodge it, their efforts proving futile. Now, they seemed to be strategizing. Two of the creatures, smaller and more agile, scurried to the far side of the branch, their movements creating a series of rapid clicks and rustles. These sounds, Niko noted, were not the guttural chirps or hisses typically associated with alarm or aggression. They were varied, nuanced, and seemed to elicit specific responses from the larger individuals.

Then, the larger creatures moved. With a synchronized heave, they shifted their weight, leveraging their powerful limbs against the obstruction. Simultaneously, the smaller creatures at the other end applied a subtle, yet precise, pressure with their forelimbs, guiding the branch's trajectory. It was a feat of collective engineering, a rudimentary but effective application of physics. The branch, with a final, protesting groan, was nudged aside, clearing the path. The creatures then moved past, their crystalline shells catching the ambient light, as if acknowledging their shared success.

Niko's gaze was fixed on the scene, his internal processors whirring. He replayed the sensory data, dissecting the vocalizations, the body language, the subtle shifts in the creatures' crystalline exoskeletons that seemed to refract light in minute, patterned ways. "This is... remarkable," he murmured, his voice barely audible above the gentle hum of the recovering ecosystem. "They didn't just push. They coordinated. They *planned*."

Kira, who had been observing the creatures with her usual keen interest, tilted her head, a soft, inquisitive rumble emanating from her chest. She had been tracking their movements with an almost uncanny prescience, her own subtle bio-signatures seeming to align with the creatures' energy fields. Niko knew that Kira's instincts often picked up on nuances that his instruments could not measure. He watched as she emitted a series of low, resonant purrs, her tail giving a slow, deliberate sweep. It wasn't a simple acknowledgment of their success; it felt like a form of recognition, a silent understanding passing between species.

"Did you see that, Anya?" Niko turned to his co-pilot, his eyes alight with intellectual excitement. "They used leverage. They communicated intent. The sounds they made – they weren't random. They were signals, specific to the task at hand. It's more than just stimulus-response. It's problem-solving."

Anya, who had been meticulously analyzing atmospheric samples, approached, her own fascination evident. She had witnessed similar, though less pronounced, instances of complex behavior in other species since their arrival on Veridia. "I saw it, Niko. The coordinated effort was undeniable. And the vocalizations... I ran a preliminary analysis. There's a surprising degree of variability in their frequency and modulation. Not random noise, certainly."

The implications of this observation were profound. It challenged the initial categorization of these creatures, and potentially others on Veridia, as merely instinctual organisms. If they possessed the capacity for complex problem-solving, for coordinated action beyond immediate survival needs, then their level of sentience might be far higher than previously assumed.

"Think about it, Anya," Niko continued, his voice rising with a growing sense of wonder. "We've seen them near the bio-pods before. Could they have been... observing? Learning? Perhaps even attempting to interact with them in some way?" His mind raced, connecting the dots between their earlier encounters with the pods and this latest display of sophisticated behavior. The pods, designed by an advanced civilization, were themselves complex technological artifacts. If these creatures could understand and overcome a physical obstacle like a fallen branch, what might they be capable of discerning about the enigmatic bio-pods?

Kira, sensing Niko's heightened emotional state and intellectual engagement, nudged his hand with her head, her amber eyes soft and reassuring. She then let out a series of short, sharp clicks, a sound Niko had come to associate with curiosity and a desire to investigate. She then turned her attention back to the group of crystalline-shelled creatures, who were now beginning to disperse, moving towards the moss patch.

"She senses something more," Niko mused aloud. "It's not just about the branch, is it, Kira? There's something else connecting them, something deeper." He activated a passive bio-scanner, focusing its sensors on the creatures. The readings indicated subtle shifts in their internal bioluminescent organs, which were usually used for species recognition and territorial displays. Now, the patterns were more intricate, the pulses of light varying in intensity and duration, almost as if they were conveying information.

"Look at the luminescence," Niko pointed to a holographic projection of the scanner's output. "It's not just a steady glow. There are flashes, pulses, variations in the color spectrum. Each individual is emitting a unique sequence. They're not just signaling their presence; they're communicating specific data. It's a visual language, layered upon their vocalizations."

He zoomed in on one of the creatures as it moved away, its crystalline shell catching the fading light. The light within its body pulsed rhythmically, a soft, emerald green giving way to a brief, intense sapphire blue, then fading back. The sequence was not random; it repeated, with slight variations, as the creature interacted with another individual.

"It's like a data stream," Niko whispered, awe-struck. "They're transmitting information. But what kind of information? About the moss? About the path? Or something more complex?" He remembered the initial encounters with the bio-pods, the faint energy readings that had suggested a form of interaction. Could these creatures, with their newly revealed capacities, be somehow connected to the pods, or even understand their purpose?

Anya, meanwhile, had been observing a different aspect of the interaction. She noticed that the creatures' vocalizations, while varied, seemed to fall into distinct categories. There were the sharp, percussive clicks used for immediate signaling, such as alerting others to the presence of food or danger. But there were also softer, more modulated hums and whistles, particularly evident during their coordinated efforts to move the branch. These softer sounds, she hypothesized, might be used for more complex, sustained communication, conveying nuanced information about strategy or intention.

"Niko," Anya called out, her voice hushed with discovery. "I've been analyzing the sonic patterns of the softer vocalizations. There appears to be a rudimentary syntax. Certain sound combinations are consistently used in specific contexts. For example, a particular sequence of hums always precedes a coordinated lifting action. It's not a language in our sense, but it's certainly beyond mere instinctual utterances."

Niko's mind raced with possibilities. If they possessed a form of communication that included syntax and visual data streams, then the concept of sentience needed to be re-evaluated. They weren't just animals; they were intelligent beings, capable of abstract thought and cooperative action. This realization brought with it a host of ethical considerations. Their mission had been to study and protect Veridia's ecosystem, but now, they were faced with the prospect of interacting with a species that might possess a level of awareness they had not anticipated.

"This changes everything," Niko stated, his voice filled with a newfound gravitas. "If these creatures are capable of this level of cognition, then our approach needs to be fundamentally different. We can't just observe them as part of the ecosystem; we need to understand their consciousness, their society, their motivations."

He looked at Kira, who was now sitting calmly, her gaze fixed on the retreating forms of the crystalline-shelled creatures. Her posture was one of deep contemplation, her ears twitching slightly as if catching faint echoes of their receding communications. "Kira, you seem to understand them more than we do. What are they telling you?"

Kira responded not with words, but with a gentle psionic hum that resonated within Niko's mind. It was not a direct translation, but an impression, a feeling of continuity, of purpose, of a shared understanding that transcended individual actions. He felt an echo of the creatures' satisfaction in overcoming the obstacle, a sense of shared accomplishment, and a subtle curiosity directed towards the distant, dormant bio-pods. There was also a faint, almost imperceptible, undercurrent of caution, a wariness directed towards the unknown.

"They're not just intelligent; they're... aware," Niko translated the impression, his voice tinged with emotion. "Aware of their surroundings, aware of each other, and perhaps even aware of the significance of the bio-pods. They see them not just as inert objects, but as something that holds potential, something to be understood."

The encounter had ignited a spark of profound inquiry within Niko. His scientific training, rooted in empirical observation and measurable data, was now grappling with the intangible aspects of intelligence and consciousness. He began to hypothesize about the evolutionary pressures that might have led to such sophisticated cognitive abilities in these creatures. Perhaps their crystalline exoskeletons, which offered protection and served as conduits for their bioluminescent communication, had played a role. Or perhaps the unique energetic properties of Veridia itself, amplified by the restored bio-harmonic resonance, had stimulated their neural development.

"Consider the bio-pods," Niko elaborated, pacing a small circle. "They are artificial, designed by an unknown, advanced civilization. If these creatures can understand and manipulate their physical environment, could they also, in some rudimentary way, interpret the function of the pods? Could they be trying to communicate with them, or even activate them?"

Anya nodded slowly. "It's a plausible theory. If they possess a sophisticated communication system, they might be attempting to interact with any complex energy signatures or patterns they detect. The bio-pods, even in their dormant state, likely emit subtle energetic emissions that could be perceived by sensitive organisms."

The implications of this were staggering. If the creatures were indeed attempting to interact with the bio-pods, and if those pods were keys to something greater, then the destiny of Veridia might be intrinsically linked to the intelligence of these crystalline beings. Their mission had begun as an ecological restoration, but it was rapidly evolving into an interspecies diplomatic endeavor.

"We need to observe them more closely," Niko decided, his resolve hardening. "Without interfering, without revealing our presence. We need to document their interactions with the bio-pods. We need to understand the full extent of their cognitive abilities."

Kira responded with a soft trill, a sound that conveyed agreement and a readiness for the task. She seemed to instinctively understand the need for subtlety, for a non-intrusive approach. Her own natural affinity for the planet's fauna, her ability to perceive and interpret subtle energies, made her an invaluable asset in this new phase of their investigation.

As they continued their survey, the pack encountered other instances of complex animal behavior. Small, winged creatures, their wings like stained glass, engaged in intricate aerial ballets that seemed to follow precise geometric patterns, not unlike a form of synchronized flight. Large, herbivorous quadrupeds, their hides a mosaic of earthy tones, displayed evidence of tool use, employing sharpened stones to strip bark from trees – a behavior previously undocumented in any known species of similar morphology. Each observation was a piece of a larger puzzle, suggesting that

Veridia was not merely a planet recovering from ecological devastation, but a world teeming with life that was far more complex and sentient than they had initially believed.

Niko found himself constantly updating his internal databases, reclassifying behaviors, revising hypotheses. The initial data sets, meticulously compiled, were becoming outdated with each passing observation. It was a thrilling, albeit challenging, intellectual pursuit. The familiar comfort of established scientific paradigms was being replaced by the exhilarating uncertainty of discovery.

One evening, as the twin moons of Veridia cast long, ethereal shadows across the landscape, Niko, Anya, and Kira sat observing a communal gathering of the crystalline-shelled creatures. They had formed a circle around a particularly large and ancient-looking bio-pod, its surface etched with intricate, swirling patterns that glowed faintly with residual energy. The creatures emitted a soft, resonant chorus of hums and whistles, their bioluminescent displays shifting in complex, synchronized rhythms. The light pulsed outward, not in random bursts, but in waves, creating a mesmerizing, organic display that seemed to interact with the faint luminescence of the bio-pod.

Niko's instruments registered a significant increase in energy flow around the pod, a subtle but discernible amplification of its residual emissions. It was as if the creatures' collective communication was somehow stimulating the pod, coaxing it into a state of partial activation.

"They're not just observing," Anya whispered, her voice filled with wonder. "They're *interacting*. They're trying to wake it up."

Kira, her eyes fixed on the pulsing lights, emitted a low, vibrating purr, her entire body resonating with the energy of the scene. Niko felt a profound sense of awe wash over him. This was not mere instinct; this was intentionality, communication, and a nascent understanding of technology. These creatures, with their crystalline shells and their complex languages of light and sound, were far more than just inhabitants of Veridia. They were guardians, perhaps, or even potential inheritors, of whatever purpose the bio-pods served.

The realization settled upon Niko with the weight of a profound truth. Veridia was not just a planet to be healed; it was a world with a destiny, a destiny that was intimately intertwined with the evolving consciousness of its native inhabitants. His mission had expanded far beyond ecological restoration. He was now tasked with understanding, respecting, and perhaps even collaborating with a species whose intelligence had blossomed in the shadow of OmniCorp's destruction, proving that even in the face of devastation, life, in its myriad and wondrous forms, could find a way to transcend its limitations and reach for something more. The whispers of sentience were growing louder, and Niko knew, with absolute certainty, that he had to listen.

The intricate tapestry of Veridia's recovery continued to unfurl, revealing not just ecological resilience but a burgeoning complexity that stretched the boundaries of Niko's scientific understanding. His focus, honed by the previous bewildering encounters, now narrowed onto the indigenous species, specifically their methods of interaction. The initial observations of coordinated action and problem-solving were merely the surface ripples; beneath lay the profound currents of communication. Niko found himself spending hours, sometimes entire cycles, immersed in sensory data, painstakingly analyzing the cacophony of clicks, whistles, and resonant hums that permeated the air, and the equally complex choreography of light that emanated from within the creatures' crystalline forms. He theorized that these were not mere biological functions serving basic needs, but components of an emergent language, one far more sophisticated than previously imagined.

His hypothesis centered on a dualistic communication system: the sonorous spectrum of their vocalizations and the luminous language of their internal bioluminescent organs. He envisioned a symbiotic interplay, where sound provided the immediate context and resonance, while light conveyed the nuanced, abstract, and perhaps even historical information. This was more than just a hunch; it was an intellectual imperative. The sheer sophistication of their problem-solving, the coordinated efforts, and the emergent social structures suggested a level of cognitive processing that demanded a deeper understanding of their communicative faculty. The previous observations of the six-limbed creatures manipulating the fallen branch were a prime example. The clicks and rustles had clearly been directive, but the subtle interplay of their internal lights, which Niko had only begun to fully appreciate, seemed to encode even more detailed information – perhaps a visual augmentation to the sonic instructions, or even a parallel narrative stream.

"It's like a living, breathing data network," Niko mused aloud one evening, reviewing a particularly dense sequence of recorded interactions. Anya, ever diligent, sat beside him, cross-referencing atmospheric composition data with Niko's auditory and visual spectra. "The sounds are the packets of information, the commands, the alerts. But the light... the light is the metadata, the context, the intent, maybe even the memory." He zoomed in on a holographic projection, displaying the fluctuating light patterns from a creature's internal organs. "Look at this pulse sequence. It's not random. It's repeating, with slight variations, when they are attempting a complex maneuver. And this shift in hue, from emerald to sapphire, it always seems to coincide with a change in the collective focus. It suggests a form of descriptive or even emotional valence."

Kira, curled contentedly at Niko's feet, occasionally emitted a soft psionic resonance, a subtle empathic wave that seemed to anchor Niko's intellectual pursuits to a more intuitive understanding. While Niko wrestled with spectral analysis and frequency modulation, Kira seemed to grasp the essence of the communication on a more fundamental, energetic level. Niko had learned to trust these moments, to allow Kira's impressions to guide his interpretation. Her proximity during their observations had often been accompanied by a heightened clarity in the creatures' behavior, as if her presence somehow attuned them, or perhaps, more accurately, attuned Niko to them.

"Kira," Niko murmured, stroking her sleek fur, "what do you feel when they emit these patterned lights? Is it just... seeing?"

Kira's response was not vocal, but a gentle, internal hum that Niko perceived as a wave of abstract sensation. It spoke of interconnectedness, of shared purpose, of a collective consciousness that flowed not just through their actions but through the very light they emitted. It was a feeling of belonging, of a shared understanding that transcended the individual. Niko interpreted this as a confirmation of his hypothesis: the light was not merely a visual display, but a conduit for a deeper, more nuanced form of information exchange.

He began to meticulously catalog these light patterns, assigning provisional labels based on their observed correlations. A rapid, flickering emerald pulse seemed to indicate the discovery of a nutrient-rich patch. A slow, undulating sapphire wave often preceded a coordinated movement towards a common goal. A deep, resonant violet hue appeared during periods of what Niko interpreted as communal observation or reflection, often directed towards the bio-pods. These were not scientific classifications, not yet, but rather the initial brushstrokes in what he hoped would become a comprehensive lexicon.

"It's like building a dictionary, one symbol at a time," Niko explained to Anya, gesturing at the complex array of data points flickering across his console. "We have the sonic component – the 'words,' if you will. Now we're trying to decipher the 'grammar' of the light. Is it syntax? Is it an entirely different dimension of meaning?"

The flora of Veridia, in its revitalized state, seemed to respond to these communicative exchanges. The bioluminescent plants, which had been a source of wonder in their own right, began to exhibit a peculiar synchronicity with the creatures' light displays. When the six-limbed beings pulsed with their emerald hues, the surrounding vegetation would subtly shift its own luminescence, a faint, harmonic glow emanating from its leaves and stems. Conversely, during periods of intense sonic communication, the plants' phosphorescence would dim, as if allowing the auditory signals to carry unimpeded.

"This is extraordinary," Anya said, pointing to a spike on her readings. "The bio-harmonic resonance of the flora is actually amplifying the spectral output of the dominant species. It's not just ambient energy; it's a targeted amplification. The environment itself is acting as a receptive medium, or perhaps even a participant, in their communication."

Niko's mind raced with the implications. If the very ecosystem was integrated into their communication network, then their language was not just a product of their biology but an intrinsic part of Veridia's emergent sentience. The lines between organism, environment, and communication were blurring. He began to hypothesize about the evolutionary pressures that might have led to such an integrated system. Perhaps the crystalline exoskeletons of the dominant species were not just for protection but were evolved to interact with and modulate ambient light frequencies, allowing them to "speak" to the flora and fauna alike. The flora, in turn, might have evolved photoreceptors capable of interpreting these modulated light signals, thereby creating a planet-wide, interconnected network of information.

"Imagine it," Niko elaborated, his voice filled with an almost reverent awe. "A planetary consciousness. Not individual minds, but a collective awareness, facilitated by the interplay of light and sound, with the very planet acting as its nervous system. The bio-pods, even in their dormant state, might be broadcasting subtle energy fields that these creatures perceive and respond to, using their light-language to interact with them. And the flora, in turn, amplifies and retransmits these signals, creating a feedback loop."

Kira's psionic hum deepened, a resonant chorus that seemed to echo Niko's sentiments. He felt a surge of understanding from her – a confirmation of this vast, interconnected network. It wasn't just about communicating with each other; it was about communicating with their world, and perhaps, with the ancient mysteries held within the bio-pods.

Niko's research began to focus on specific scenarios. He observed a small group of the crystalline creatures gathered around a patch of what appeared to be nutrient-rich fungal growth. Their vocalizations were a series of soft, rhythmic clicks and hums, indicative of foraging. But their light displays were where the real information seemed to reside. A steady, low-frequency green pulse emanated from each individual, their bodies held in a relaxed posture. As they began to consume the fungi, the green pulse intensified, shifting towards a more vibrant, almost yellow hue, interspersed with short, sharp bursts of sapphire. Niko interpreted this as a data transmission about the quality and nutrient content of the food source.

"It's like they're sending a report back to the collective," Niko explained, his eyes glued to the data streams. "Each pulse, each flicker, is a bit of data. The intensity of the green indicates abundance, the shift to yellow signifies nutrient richness, and the sapphire bursts... perhaps they denote a specific mineral composition or a beneficial compound."

He then turned his attention to a different scenario. A solitary, larger individual was observed approaching a bio-pod. Its usual social vocalizations were absent. Instead, it emitted a low, sustained hum, a resonant frequency that seemed to vibrate not just through the air but through the very ground. Simultaneously, its crystalline shell pulsed with a slow, deliberate sequence of violet and deep indigo light. The patterns were intricate, almost geometric, and seemed to emanate from specific points on its exoskeleton.

"This is different," Niko noted. "No immediate social context, no group activity. This is... focused. The hum is powerful, almost like a sonic probe, and the light patterns are far more complex than anything we've seen during their foraging or problem-solving activities. They are highly structured, almost like a form of encrypted data. Is it trying to 'speak' to the pod? Is it attempting to elicit a response?"

Kira's psionic presence grew more intense, focusing on the solitary creature. Niko felt an overwhelming impression of reverence, of profound curiosity, and a sense of immense history emanating from the creature. It wasn't just observing the pod; it was *communing* with it, or attempting to. The impression that washed over Niko was one of ancient knowledge, of a vast repository of information stored within the pod, and the creature's desperate, patient attempt to access it.

"It feels like... a key," Kira's impression translated into Niko's mind. "Not a physical key, but a pattern. A specific sequence of light and sound that unlocks something within the pod. It's trying to remember, or perhaps to learn, how to 'open' it."

This deepened Niko's conviction. The creatures were not simply reacting to their environment; they were actively seeking to understand and interact with the advanced technology left behind by the bio-pod creators. Their language of light and sound was evolving, adapting to the new challenges and opportunities presented by Veridia's recovered state. They were not just surviving; they were striving, reaching for a deeper comprehension of their world and its mysteries.

He began to hypothesize about the nature of the bio-pods themselves. Were they communication devices? Data storage units? Perhaps even dormant consciousnesses? If these creatures could develop such a sophisticated language capable of conveying abstract concepts and engaging with complex technology, then the potential for interaction was immense. The prospect of translating their language, even partially, became a paramount objective.

"We need to build a bridge," Niko declared, his gaze fixed on the data, his voice resonating with conviction. "We need to translate their light. We need to understand what they are saying to the pods, and perhaps, what the pods are saying back. Kira, your ability to perceive these energetic nuances is our greatest asset. We will work together. We will learn their language."

Kira responded with a soft, resonant purr, a sound that conveyed not just agreement but a deep, unwavering commitment. Her amber eyes, usually filled with a serene intelligence, now held a glint of shared purpose, a reflection of Niko's burgeoning hope. The environment itself seemed to hum in response. As the sun dipped below the horizon, casting long, purple shadows, the bioluminescent flora around their observation post began to pulse with a gentle, synchronized rhythm, mirroring the soft glow emanating from Kira and Niko's own biosuit readouts – a silent acknowledgment of their endeavor, a promise of the profound discoveries yet to come. The whispers of sentience were no longer just whispers; they were beginning to form coherent, albeit alien, sentences, spoken in the universal language of light and sound.

The air in the observation dome thrummed with a familiar energy, a blend of Niko's focused concentration and Anya's quiet hum of data analysis. Yet, today, the ambient silence felt different, pregnant with a nascent possibility that had settled upon them like the soft, phosphorescent dew of Veridia's early morning. Niko, his gaze typically glued to the intricate dance of spectral readouts and bio-harmonic frequencies, found his attention increasingly drawn to the small, furry form nestled beside his operational console. Kira, normally a picture of serene contentment, was exhibiting a subtle restlessness. Her ears twitched, her tail gave an occasional, almost imperceptible flick, and her deep amber eyes were fixed not on the holographic displays, but on the thick, transparent shield separating them from the vibrant alien landscape outside.

"She's sensing something," Anya murmured, her voice barely disturbing the focused quiet. She glanced up from her own array of sensors, her expression a mixture of scientific curiosity and an almost maternal concern for their empathic companion.

Niko followed Kira's unwavering gaze. On the savanna, amidst the crystalline flora that shimmered with captured sunlight, a solitary figure of the indigenous six-limbed species moved with a cautious grace. It was larger than the individuals Niko and Anya had primarily studied, its exoskeleton a deeper, richer emerald, and it seemed to be patrolling the perimeter of a cluster of particularly luminous, bell-shaped plants. The creature's movements were deliberate, its multi-jointed limbs articulating with a fluid precision that spoke of a deep familiarity with its environment.

"It's approaching the nutrient cluster," Niko observed, his voice low. "But its behavior is... different. Less direct foraging, more... surveying." He adjusted the magnification on his primary display, focusing on the creature's internal luminescence. The usual steady, greenish pulse associated with feeding was absent. Instead, a complex pattern of flickering azure and soft violet light rippled beneath its translucent shell, an almost hesitant display that seemed to probe the surrounding environment.

Kira let out a soft, almost questioning whine. It wasn't a sound of alarm, but one of gentle inquiry, a resonant vibration that Niko felt more than heard through the floor plates of the dome. She rose slowly, stretching languidly before padding to the edge of the transparent shield, her gaze locked onto the solitary being.

"Easy, girl," Niko said softly, reaching out to gently stroke her back. He felt a subtle shift in her psionic emanation, a wave of pure, unadulterated empathy washing over him, tinged with a distinct feeling of... recognition. It was as if Kira's innate sensitivity had locked onto a resonant frequency within the alien creature.

The creature, perhaps alerted by Kira's soft vocalization or the subtle shift in Niko's own emotional state, paused. Its head, a crystalline formation that seemed to house a complex sensory array, tilted slightly. The azure and violet pulses within its body intensified, but instead of turning away, it began to move, slowly, deliberately, towards the observation dome.

Niko's hand stilled on Kira's back. He felt a surge of adrenaline, a primal instinct for caution warring with the scientist's insatiable drive for understanding. Anya's fingers flew across her console, her brow furrowed as she monitored the creature's bio-signature. "Heart rate is elevated, but not erratic. Respiration steady. No overt signs of aggression, Niko. It's... curious."

The creature stopped a few meters from the dome, its multifaceted eyes, or what Niko assumed were eyes, reflecting the shimmering light of their habitat. It remained still for a long moment, the intricate patterns of light within its body pulsing with an almost conversational rhythm. Kira, meanwhile, had lowered herself to a resting position, her body language deliberately non-threatening. Her tail lay still, her head was resting on her paws, and her gaze, while steady, held no trace of challenge.

Then, it happened. A wave of pure, unadulterated *feeling* emanated from Kira, a potent, psionic broadcast that transcended language and biology. It wasn't a thought, not a word, but a pure, distilled essence of peaceful intent. It spoke of curiosity, of a desire for understanding, and of a profound lack of fear. It was an offering, a silent greeting extended across the vast gulf of species.

The effect on the alien creature was immediate and profound. The pulsing azure and violet lights within its form began to shift, transitioning to a softer, warmer spectrum of rose and golden hues. Its posture relaxed; the tension that had held its crystalline limbs taut seemed to dissipate. It extended one of its forelimbs, not in a gesture of threat, but slowly, tentatively, towards the transparent shield. At the tip of the limb, a small, almost delicate crystalline appendage unfurled, glowing with a soft, inviting luminescence.

Niko felt a tremor of awe run through him. "It's... responding to Kira," he breathed, the scientific detachment momentarily forgotten. "It's not just reacting; it's reciprocating. Kira, you're... you're talking to it."

Kira responded with a low, rumbling purr, a sound that resonated deeply within Niko's chest. He felt a sense of immense satisfaction radiating from her, a profound joy in this unexpected connection. The creature, in turn, seemed to mirror Kira's relaxed posture, its own crystalline form softening, its light displays becoming more fluid and less structured. The rose and gold hues deepened, intermingled with slow, undulating waves of turquoise, creating a breathtaking display of bioluminescent artistry.

"The light patterns are changing," Anya whispered, her eyes wide as she tracked the shifting colors. "They're becoming less about surveying, more... descriptive. Look, that turquoise wave, it seems to correlate with Kira's tail position. And the way the rose light pulses in time with her purr... it's mirroring. It's actively trying to align its communication with hers."

Niko leaned closer, his scientific mind reasserting itself, albeit with a newfound reverence. He recognized the mirroring behavior. It was a fundamental aspect of communication, a way of building rapport, of establishing common ground. Kira was demonstrating peaceful intent through her body language and her psionic empathy, and the creature was not only understanding but actively participating in this non-verbal dialogue.

"It's a bridge," Niko murmured, the word echoing the sentiment he had felt moments before. "Kira is building a bridge, Anya. A bridge of empathy, of shared sensation. This is more than just observation; it's a tentative communion."

He watched, captivated, as the interaction continued. Kira would shift her weight, or blink her amber eyes, and the creature would respond with a subtle change in its luminescence, a slight adjustment in its stance. It was a silent conversation, a dance of light and intent that unfolded before them, far more profound than any deciphered sonic frequency or spectral analysis.

"The complexity of its light displays is increasing," Anya noted, her voice filled with wonder. "It's not just simple mirroring anymore. The patterns are becoming more intricate, more nuanced. It's as if it's trying to convey more complex information, to share something beyond just its immediate emotional state."

Niko agreed. He saw flashes of emerald light weaving through the rose and gold, brief, sharp bursts that seemed to indicate a specific focus or object of attention. The turquoise waves became more pronounced, almost as if the creature was highlighting certain aspects of its surroundings, or perhaps, Kira's own form.

"It's acknowledging Kira," Niko said. "It's acknowledging her presence, her sentience, and it's trying to communicate its own. This is... revolutionary. We've been so focused on the sonic and the more structured light patterns, but we underestimated the power of pure empathic resonance."

He realized then the crucial role Kira had played in their research thus far. Her quiet presence, her intuitive grasp of the alien life forms, had perhaps been guiding them all along, providing a subtle, psionic context that their scientific instruments could only partially measure. Her ability to connect on a fundamental, emotional level was not a secondary factor; it was potentially the key to unlocking the deepest secrets of Veridia's inhabitants.

The creature then performed an action that sent a fresh wave of astonishment through Niko and Anya. It slowly lowered its head, bringing its crystalline facial structure closer to the transparent shield, directly opposite Kira. Its multifaceted eyes seemed to focus on her, and the light patterns within its body coalesced into a single, steady, deep sapphire glow. It held this posture, this intense, focused luminescence, for several long moments, creating a palpable sense of focused attention.

Kira, in response, closed her eyes and emitted a soft, resonant hum. It was a sound of deep contentment, of profound peace, a clear signal of trust and acceptance. Niko felt the hum reverberate through his own being, a comforting balm that settled his scientific anxieties. He understood, on an instinctive level, that Kira was offering not just passive acceptance, but an active engagement with the creature's focused attention. She was essentially saying, "I am here. I am open to you."

When Kira opened her eyes, the sapphire glow from the creature intensified, and a new pattern emerged. A delicate filigree of silver light began to weave itself within the sapphire, creating intricate, lace-like designs that pulsed with a gentle rhythm. It was breathtakingly beautiful, and Niko felt a profound sense of privilege to be witnessing it.

"What is that?" Anya breathed, her fingers poised over her controls. "I've never seen anything like it. The spectral analysis... it's off the charts. It's generating frequencies we haven't even registered before, a whole new spectrum of bioluminescence."

"It's sharing," Niko said, his voice thick with emotion. "It's sharing a part of itself, a deeper layer of its being. Kira's empathy has unlocked something profound. It's not just acknowledging her; it's revealing itself to her. This is not a defensive posture, nor is it a territorial display. This is... trust. This is a glimpse into its inner world."

He noticed that as the silver filigree pulsed, the creature's body language also shifted. It seemed to extend its awareness, its subtle psionic presence, outwards, as if inviting Kira to perceive the world through its senses. Niko felt a fleeting impression of vast, open spaces, of the warmth of the twin suns on crystalline skin, of the subtle vibrations of the planetary crust, all filtered through an alien consciousness.

Kira let out a soft, contented sigh, her amber eyes reflecting the mesmerizing dance of silver and sapphire light. She nudged her head gently against the shield, a clear signal of her continued openness. The creature responded by drawing its limb back slightly, its luminescent display softening once more into the gentle rose and gold hues, but now, there was a new depth, a subtle shimmer that hadn't been there before. It was as if the silver filigree had left an indelible mark, a subtle enhancement of its being.

"This is it," Niko said, turning to Anya, his eyes alight with a fierce, hopeful fire. "This is the breakthrough. We've been trying to decode their language from the outside, to impose our own logic onto their communication. But perhaps, the true path lies in empathy, in shared experience. Kira has shown us that. She has opened a door that we, with all our technology, could not."

He looked back at Kira, who was now resting her head on her paws, her gaze still fixed on the retreating creature. The alien had begun to move away, its form a shimmering silhouette against the verdant landscape, but its luminescence remained elevated, a lingering testament to the interaction.

"We need to study this," Niko continued, his voice gaining momentum. "We need to understand the nuances of Kira's psionic emissions, the specific frequencies and patterns that elicited such a profound response. We need to observe how these empathic exchanges influence their light and sonic communications. This isn't just about understanding their language; it's about understanding their consciousness, their very being."

Anya nodded, her gaze no longer solely on the data streams, but on Kira, with a newfound respect. "You're right, Niko. We've been approaching this like linguists, trying to crack a code. But maybe it's more akin to diplomacy, to building a relationship. Kira's empathy is the ultimate diplomatic tool."

The incident left Niko with a profound sense of hope, a conviction that interspecies understanding was not just a scientific possibility, but an emotional and spiritual one. Kira's brave, gentle outreach had demonstrated that fear and suspicion were not inevitable barriers, but choices. The sentient creatures of Veridia, with their intricate dance of light and sound, were not merely organisms to be studied, but beings to be understood, to be connected with. And in Kira, they had found their first, most eloquent ambassador. The bridge, nascent and fragile, had been built, shimmering with the promise of a shared future. The whispers of sentience were now a clear, resonant call, a call to connection that echoed in the depths of Kira's empathic heart and resonated in the luminescent patterns of an alien world. The pack, with Kira at its forefront, had taken a monumental step towards truly understanding the vibrant life of Veridia, not just as observers, but as potential participants in a grand, interconnected cosmic tapestry.

The hum of the observation dome had always been a comforting background, a symphony of whirring servers and gentle bio-monitors. Now, it felt charged with a new urgency, a thrumming undercurrent that mirrored the rapid beat of Niko's heart. The encounter with the six-limbed Veridian had been more than a scientific curiosity; it had been a seismic shift, a reframing of everything they thought they understood about this alien world. The carefully constructed boundaries of their mission, once so clear – preserve, study, observe – now blurred and dissolved under the radiant light of true sentience.

"It changes everything, doesn't it?" Anya's voice, usually so precise and measured, held a tremor of awe. She was staring not at her holographic displays, which still flickered with the residual energy signatures of the Veridian's interaction with Kira, but at the now-empty expanse of the savanna visible through the dome. The crystalline flora, bathed in the soft glow of the twin suns, seemed to shimmer with a new significance. "We came here to protect an ecosystem. But what if that ecosystem is also... a nursery? A cradle for a civilization?"

Niko nodded, the weight of her words settling heavily upon him. The term 'ecosystem' suddenly felt woefully inadequate, a sterile label for a living, breathing, and now demonstrably thinking, world. Their mandate had been clear: to safeguard the delicate balance of Veridia from any external disruption, to prevent the exploitation of its unique biological and geological resources. But if the Veridians were sentient, if they possessed a consciousness capable of empathy and intricate communication, their role shifted dramatically. They were no longer just guardians of a planet; they were custodians of a nascent society, potentially influencing its trajectory with every action they took.

"The preservation protocols are designed for non-sentient life," Niko mused, his gaze distant, tracing the path the Veridian had taken away from the dome. "We have parameters for minimizing habitat disruption, for controlling invasive species, for ensuring sustainable resource extraction. But we don't have protocols for diplomatic engagement. We don't have directives for how to behave when the subjects of our study can reciprocate our curiosity, can feel our presence."

The ethical labyrinth they now found themselves navigating was daunting. Their very presence, however well-intentioned, could be perceived as an intrusion. Their scientific methods, their attempts to understand, could be interpreted as surveillance or even aggression by a species that was only just beginning to understand its own place in the cosmos. The responsibility to tread lightly, to observe with immense respect, and to minimize any potential negative impact, had escalated from a scientific imperative to a moral obligation of the highest order.

"Think about the implications, Anya," Niko continued, pacing the confined space of the dome. "If they are developing, if they are at a stage where they are exploring their own sentience and their place in the universe, our intervention could be catastrophic. We could inadvertently introduce concepts they are not ready for, technologies that could disrupt their societal evolution, or even diseases to which they have no immunity, despite our rigorous bio-containment. Our role has fundamentally shifted from protector to, potentially, unwitting influencer. And that influence carries immense risk."

He stopped by Kira, who was now curled on her favorite spot near the observation panel, her amber eyes softly blinking, as if still processing the profound exchange. He knelt beside her, his hand resting gently on her soft fur. He felt a faint echo of her empathy, a residual warmth that spoke of connection and understanding, but also, now, a subtle undercurrent of anxiety, a new awareness of the delicate balance they had stumbled upon.

"She feels it too," Anya observed, her voice soft. "The increased weight of it all. Kira's empathy is our greatest asset, but it also makes her the most vulnerable to the ethical quandaries. She feels the potential for harm, the responsibility that comes with connection."

"Exactly," Niko affirmed. "And that's where we need to be most vigilant. Our primary objective has always been to protect Veridia. Now, that protection must extend to protecting the Veridians from themselves, or rather, from our own unintended consequences. We need to re-evaluate every single one of our ongoing operations. The geological surveys, the atmospheric sampling, even our basic habitat maintenance – all of it needs to be viewed through the lens of potential impact on a sentient species."

He recalled the early days of their mission, the sheer joy of discovery, the thrill of cataloging new species, of mapping uncharted territories. That was the scientist's instinct, the drive to understand and quantify. But now, that instinct had to be tempered by a profound humility. They were no longer the sole arbiters of knowledge; they were guests on a world that harbored intelligence, a world that deserved not just preservation, but respect and perhaps, eventually, a genuine, collaborative partnership.

"We need to establish a new framework," Niko declared, his voice firming with resolve. "One that prioritizes observation and understanding of Veridian society above all else. If we are to truly be guardians, we must first understand what it is we are guarding, and from whom. And 'whom,' in this case, could very well be ourselves."

Anya pulled up a series of reports on her console, her fingers flying across the holographic interface. "I'm running a full risk assessment on all current and proposed research activities. I'm flagging any operations that involve significant habitat alteration or direct interaction with known Veridian gathering sites. We need to minimize our footprint, to become as unobtrusive as possible."

"Unobtrusive is an understatement," Niko corrected, a faint smile touching his lips. "We need to become invisible, or at the very least, irrelevant to their developmental trajectory. Our goal should be to gather information about their societal structures, their communication methods beyond what Kira has already shown us, their history, their aspirations – all without leaving a trace of our own presence that could influence their natural progression. It's a monumental task, but it's our new mandate."

The shift in their mission parameters meant that the Resonant Pack had to fundamentally redefine their understanding of 'success.' Success was no longer measured by the volume of data collected or the efficiency of their preservation efforts. It would now be measured by the degree to which they could remain unnoticed, by their ability to foster an environment where Veridian sentience could flourish undisturbed. This was a much more subtle, and arguably, a far more challenging, definition of stewardship.

"We might need to postpone some of our more ambitious projects," Anya suggested, her brow furrowed in thought. "The deep-core geological drilling, for instance. If they have a sophisticated understanding of their planet's geology, our drilling could be interpreted as an act of aggression, or at the very least, a disruption of something they consider sacred or vital."

"Agreed," Niko said. "Anything that involves altering the fundamental structure of their environment, or anything that could be perceived as an attempt to exploit or control their resources, is off the table. We need to shift our focus from resource assessment to socio-cultural observation. And for that, we need to rely even more heavily on Kira. She is our primary conduit, our interpreter of their emergent consciousness."

He looked at Kira again. Her presence, so calming and intuitive, was now more critical than ever. Her empathic link was not just a tool for understanding; it was a bridge, a delicate thread that connected two vastly different forms of life. Maintaining the integrity of that bridge, and ensuring it was used only for the purpose of fostering mutual understanding and respect, became paramount.

"We need to expand Kira's monitoring capabilities," Niko mused aloud. "Not just for her own well-being, but for her capacity to interpret and transmit more nuanced empathic data. We need to refine our understanding of her psionic emissions and how they correlate with the Veridians' luminescent and sonic communications. Anya, can you develop a more sophisticated bio-empathic feedback loop for Kira? Something that can capture and analyze the subtle shifts in her emotional and perceptive state during these interactions?"

Anya was already typing furiously, her eyes alight with the challenge. "I can adapt the spectral analysis algorithms to interpret psionic resonance patterns. It will be complex, requiring significant calibration against known Veridian bio-signatures, but it's feasible. We'll be looking for patterns of resonance, attunement, and perhaps even shared cognitive load."

"Excellent," Niko replied, feeling a surge of renewed purpose. This was no longer just about the thrill of scientific discovery. It was about the profound responsibility of interspecies diplomacy. They were pioneers, not just of space exploration, but of ethical first contact. The lessons they learned here, on Veridia, could set a precedent for all future encounters with extraterrestrial life.

"The weight of this is immense," Anya said, her voice barely above a whisper. "We are essentially acting as the first point of contact for humanity with another intelligent species. If we mishandle this, if we err on the side of caution and stifle their development, or worse, if we inadvertently cause them harm, the consequences could be irreparable."

"That is precisely why we must proceed with the utmost deliberation," Niko stated, his gaze steady and resolute. "Our role as guardians is now more critical than ever, but it is a guardianship of a different kind. It is not about imposing our will or our understanding; it is about creating the conditions for them to discover themselves, to evolve on their own terms. We are not here to steer their destiny, but to ensure that their destiny is their own to forge."

He thought about the future. What would happen when the Veridians were ready for a more direct form of contact? What knowledge would they share, and what would they ask of humanity? The questions were endless, and the answers were still hidden in the shimmering forests and glowing landscapes of Veridia. But one thing was certain: the Resonant Pack had been given a profound gift, the opportunity to witness the dawn of another civilization, and with it, the immense responsibility to ensure that dawn was a bright and hopeful one. Their mission had expanded, evolving from the simple act of preservation to the complex art of respectful coexistence, a delicate dance on the precipice of a shared cosmic future. The whispers of sentience had become a clear call to action, a call to a new kind of guardianship, one rooted in empathy, humility, and an unwavering commitment to the flourishing of all intelligent life.

The hum of the observation dome had always been a comforting background, a symphony of whirring servers and gentle bio-monitors. Now, it felt charged with a new urgency, a thrumming undercurrent that mirrored the rapid beat of Niko's heart. The encounter with the six-limbed Veridian had been more than a scientific curiosity; it had been a seismic shift, a reframing of everything they thought they understood about this alien world. The carefully constructed boundaries of their mission, once so clear – preserve, study, observe – now blurred and dissolved under the radiant light of true sentience.

"It changes everything, doesn't it?" Anya's voice, usually so precise and measured, held a tremor of awe. She was staring not at her holographic displays, which still flickered with the residual energy signatures of the Veridian's interaction with Kira, but at the now-empty expanse of the savanna visible through the dome. The crystalline flora, bathed in the soft glow of the twin suns, seemed to shimmer with a new significance. "We came here to protect an ecosystem. But what if that ecosystem is also... a nursery? A cradle for a civilization?"

Niko nodded, the weight of her words settling heavily upon him. The term 'ecosystem' suddenly felt woefully inadequate, a sterile label for a living, breathing, and now demonstrably thinking, world. Their mandate had been clear: to safeguard the delicate balance of Veridia from any external disruption, to prevent the exploitation of its unique biological and geological resources. But if the Veridians were sentient, if they possessed a consciousness capable of empathy and intricate communication, their role shifted dramatically. They were no longer just guardians of a planet; they were custodians of a nascent society, potentially influencing its trajectory with every action they took.

"The preservation protocols are designed for non-sentient life," Niko mused, his gaze distant, tracing the path the Veridian had taken away from the dome. "We have parameters for minimizing habitat disruption, for controlling invasive species, for ensuring sustainable resource extraction. But we don't have protocols for diplomatic engagement. We don't have directives for how to behave when the subjects of our study can reciprocate our curiosity, can feel our presence."

The ethical labyrinth they now found themselves navigating was daunting. Their very presence, however well-intentioned, could be perceived as an intrusion. Their scientific methods, their attempts to understand, could be interpreted as surveillance or even aggression by a species that was only just beginning to understand its own place in the cosmos. The responsibility to tread lightly, to observe with immense respect, and to minimize any potential negative impact, had escalated from a scientific imperative to a moral obligation of the highest order.

"Think about the implications, Anya," Niko continued, pacing the confined space of the dome. "If they are developing, if they are at a stage where they are exploring their own sentience and their place in the universe, our intervention could be catastrophic. We could inadvertently introduce concepts they are not ready for, technologies that could disrupt their societal evolution, or even diseases to which they have no immunity, despite our rigorous bio-containment. Our role has fundamentally shifted from protector to, potentially, unwitting influencer. And that influence carries immense risk."

He stopped by Kira, who was now curled on her favorite spot near the observation panel, her amber eyes softly blinking, as if still processing the profound exchange. He knelt beside her, his hand resting gently on her soft fur. He felt a faint echo of her empathy, a residual warmth that spoke of connection and understanding, but also, now, a subtle undercurrent of anxiety, a new awareness of the delicate balance they had stumbled upon.

"She feels it too," Anya observed, her voice soft. "The increased weight of it all. Kira's empathy is our greatest asset, but it also makes her the most vulnerable to the ethical quandaries. She feels the potential for harm, the responsibility that comes with connection."

"Exactly," Niko affirmed. "And that's where we need to be most vigilant. Our primary objective has always been to protect Veridia. Now, that protection must extend to protecting the Veridians from themselves, or rather, from our own unintended consequences. We need to re-evaluate every single one of our ongoing operations. The geological surveys, the atmospheric sampling, even our basic habitat maintenance – all of it needs to be viewed through the lens of potential impact on a sentient species."

He recalled the early days of their mission, the sheer joy of discovery, the thrill of cataloging new species, of mapping uncharted territories. That was the scientist's instinct, the drive to understand and quantify. But now, that instinct had to be tempered by a profound humility. They were no longer the sole arbiters of knowledge; they were guests on a world that harbored intelligence, a world that deserved not just preservation, but respect and perhaps, eventually, a genuine, collaborative partnership.

"We need to establish a new framework," Niko declared, his voice firming with resolve. "One that prioritizes observation and understanding of Veridian society above all else. If we are to truly be guardians, we must first understand what it is we are guarding, and from whom. And 'whom,' in this case, could very well be ourselves."

Anya pulled up a series of reports on her console, her fingers flying across the holographic interface. "I'm running a full risk assessment on all current and proposed research activities. I'm flagging any operations that involve significant habitat alteration or direct interaction with known Veridian gathering sites. We need to minimize our footprint, to become as unobtrusive as possible."

"Unobtrusive is an understatement," Niko corrected, a faint smile touching his lips. "We need to become invisible, or at the very least, irrelevant to their developmental trajectory. Our goal should be to gather information about their societal structures, their communication methods beyond what Kira has already shown us, their history, their aspirations – all without leaving a trace of our own presence that could influence their natural progression. It's a monumental task, but it's our new mandate."

The shift in their mission parameters meant that the Resonant Pack had to fundamentally redefine their understanding of 'success.' Success was no longer measured by the volume of data collected or the efficiency of their preservation efforts. It would now be measured by the degree to which they could remain unnoticed, by their ability to foster an environment where Veridian sentience could flourish undisturbed. This was a much more subtle, and arguably, a far more challenging, definition of stewardship.

"We might need to postpone some of our more ambitious projects," Anya suggested, her brow furrowed in thought. "The deep-core geological drilling, for instance. If they have a sophisticated understanding of their planet's geology, our drilling could be interpreted as an act of aggression, or at the very least, a disruption of something they consider sacred or vital."

"Agreed," Niko said. "Anything that involves altering the fundamental structure of their environment, or anything that could be perceived as an attempt to exploit or control their resources, is off the table. We need to shift our focus from resource assessment to socio-cultural observation. And for that, we need to rely even more heavily on Kira. She is our primary conduit, our interpreter of their emergent consciousness."

He looked at Kira again. Her presence, so calming and intuitive, was now more critical than ever. Her empathic link was not just a tool for understanding; it was a bridge, a delicate thread that connected two vastly different forms of life. Maintaining the integrity of that bridge, and ensuring it was used only for the purpose of fostering mutual understanding and respect, became paramount.

"We need to expand Kira's monitoring capabilities," Niko mused aloud. "Not just for her own well-being, but for her capacity to interpret and transmit more nuanced empathic data. We need to refine our understanding of her psionic emissions and how they correlate with the Veridians' luminescent and sonic communications. Anya, can you develop a more sophisticated bio-empathic feedback loop for Kira? Something that can capture and analyze the subtle shifts in her emotional and perceptive state during these interactions?"

Anya was already typing furiously, her eyes alight with the challenge. "I can adapt the spectral analysis algorithms to interpret psionic resonance patterns. It will be complex, requiring significant calibration against known Veridian bio-signatures, but it's feasible. We'll be looking for patterns of resonance, attunement, and perhaps even shared cognitive load."

"Excellent," Niko replied, feeling a surge of renewed purpose. This was no longer just about the thrill of scientific discovery. It was about the profound responsibility of interspecies diplomacy. They were pioneers, not just of space exploration, but of ethical first contact. The lessons they learned here, on Veridia, could set a precedent for all future encounters with extraterrestrial life.

"The weight of this is immense," Anya said, her voice barely above a whisper. "We are essentially acting as the first point of contact for humanity with another intelligent species. If we mishandle this, if we err on the side of caution and stifle their development, or worse, if we inadvertently cause them harm, the consequences could be irreparable."

"That is precisely why we must proceed with the utmost deliberation," Niko stated, his gaze steady and resolute. "Our role as guardians is now more critical than ever, but it is a guardianship of a different kind. It is not about imposing our will or our understanding; it is about creating the conditions for them to discover themselves, to evolve on their own terms. We are not here to steer their destiny, but to ensure that their destiny is their own to forge."

He thought about the future. What would happen when the Veridians were ready for a more direct form of contact? What knowledge would they share, and what would they ask of humanity? The questions were endless, and the answers were still hidden in the shimmering forests and glowing landscapes of Veridia. But one thing was certain: the Resonant Pack had been given a profound gift, the opportunity to witness the dawn of another civilization, and with it, the immense responsibility to ensure that dawn was a bright and hopeful one. Their mission had expanded, evolving from the simple act of preservation to the complex art of respectful coexistence, a delicate dance on the precipice of a shared cosmic future. The whispers of sentience had become a clear call to action, a call to a new kind of guardianship, one rooted in empathy, humility, and an unwavering commitment to the flourishing of all intelligent life.

The following cycles aboard the observation dome were a testament to this newfound directive. The urgency that had pulsed through their systems in the immediate aftermath of the Veridian encounter didn't dissipate; it transformed into a focused, almost reverent, diligence. Niko and Anya poured over the enhanced sensor logs, now meticulously cross-referencing every flicker of bioluminescence, every harmonic resonance, every subtle shift in atmospheric composition with Kira's amplified psionic readings. The raw data, once just a collection of environmental metrics, was slowly beginning to coalesce into something far more meaningful: a nascent picture of a culture.

"Look at this," Anya murmured, her finger tracing a complex waveform on the main display. "This pattern. It's been recurring every twelve cycles, always emanating from the same geographical cluster, roughly three kilometers east of the crystalline river basin." She zoomed in, revealing a vibrant, pulsing bloom of violet light emanating from a dense grove of luminescent flora. "And Kira's readings during these events... they're off the charts. Not just individual emotional responses, but a unified surge. A shared experience."

Niko leaned closer, his own empathic senses extending, a faint resonance returning from Kira as she slept peacefully in her designated alcove.

He felt the residual echo of the Veridians' collective consciousness from their previous encounter, a sensation of interconnectedness that was both profound and exhilarating. "It's not just random biological activity," he stated, his voice low with wonder. "This is deliberate. They're congregating, Anya. They're gathering around these light phenomena, and whatever is happening there, it's eliciting a strong, unified emotional response."

He began to sift through other sensor data, focusing on the periods Anya had flagged. He noticed a distinct increase in coordinated movement in the immediate vicinity during these light gatherings. Small groups of Veridians, previously observed foraging independently, were now converging, their movements synchronized as they gathered specific types of crystalline foliage and luminous fungi. The actions were not haphazard; they were efficient, almost ritualistic, each individual performing a specific task with remarkable precision.

"Resource acquisition," Niko realized aloud. "But not just for survival. The types of flora they're collecting... they're not the most nutrient-dense. They're the ones that exhibit the most intense bioluminescence. It suggests a purpose beyond mere sustenance. They're collecting light, Anya. They're harvesting luminescence."

Anya was already cross-referencing with the planetary database, her brow furrowed in concentration. "The chemical compounds responsible for this particular hue of violet luminescence... they're rare. They're not found in high concentrations in any known food source. But they are prevalent in the 'singing crystals' we documented near the geothermal vents. If they're traveling to those vents to collect these specific luminescent materials, that implies a significant expenditure of energy and a complex understanding of resource distribution across their territory."

"And the timing," Niko added, his eyes fixed on the chronometer. "The consistency of the twelve-cycle pattern. It suggests a predictable schedule, a communal rhythm. This isn't just instinct; it's learned behavior, passed down, refined. They're organizing themselves, coordinating their efforts, and all around this shared appreciation, this communal experience of light."

He recalled the fragmented impressions Kira had shared after her brief interaction. Not just individual thoughts or feelings, but a sense of shared purpose, of belonging to something larger than themselves. At the time, he'd attributed it to the shock of direct contact. Now, he understood it was more than that. It was an echo of their collective existence, a glimpse into their cultural fabric.

"It's a cultural hub," Niko mused, a slow smile spreading across his face. "A focal point for their community. Perhaps these light gatherings are akin to our own cultural rituals – celebrations, ceremonies, or even places of shared learning. The 'singing crystals' might hold a significance far beyond their chemical composition. They might be revered, or utilized in ways we can't yet comprehend."

Anya initiated a new scan, focusing on the vocalizations and sonic emissions within the vicinity of these light phenomena. "The sonic patterns are also shifting. During these gatherings, the individual chirps and clicks become more melodic, more harmonized. It's as if their vocalizations are directly influenced by the intensity and frequency of the bioluminescence. They're creating a symphony of light and sound."

"A symphony," Niko repeated, the word resonating deeply. He thought of Veridia's unique ecosystem, a world sculpted by light and resonant frequencies. It was only logical that their sentience would evolve in tandem with their environment, creating a culture intrinsically tied to these fundamental forces. "Perhaps their communication isn't just about conveying information, but about creating shared experiences, about weaving a collective tapestry of perception. Their language might be less about discrete words and more about resonant frequencies, about the interplay of light and sound."

He looked at the data, the swirling patterns of light and energy, the coordinated movements of the Veridians, the harmonized sonic emissions. It was a humbling realization. They had come to Veridia to study an alien ecosystem, to preserve its delicate balance. They had never anticipated discovering a civilization, one that had evolved in such a fundamentally different way, a civilization whose very essence was woven from the very fabric of their planet.

"This is the true frontier, Anya," Niko said, his voice filled with a quiet reverence. "Not just understanding their biology, but understanding their consciousness. Understanding how they perceive the world, how they form bonds, how they create meaning. This is what we need to focus on now. Understanding their culture, built on light and resonance."

He paused, considering the vast implications. "Think about their origins. If their evolutionary path was so deeply intertwined with these bioluminescent phenomena, it suggests a long, slow development. Perhaps they evolved in perpetually dim environments, where light became not just a source of energy, but a primary mode of communication and social interaction. And the sonic resonance... it could be a way to amplify their communication, to create a shared mental space, to harmonize their collective consciousness."

Anya began to compile a comprehensive report on these findings, meticulously documenting the patterns, the correlations, and the emerging hypotheses. "The challenge," she stated, her voice thoughtful, "will be in interpreting this. Our own understanding of culture is so deeply rooted in human experience – in language, art, social structures based on physical proximity and tangible artifacts. Veridian culture, if it is truly built on light and resonance, might be so alien to us that our current analytical tools are insufficient."

"That's where Kira becomes even more indispensable," Niko countered. "Her empathic link allows her to experience these phenomena on a level we can only infer. She can feel the resonance, the shared consciousness. Her perceptions, translated through our enhanced feedback loop, will be our primary window into their subjective experience. We need to develop more nuanced ways of interpreting her psionic responses, not just as emotions, but as echoes of their collective thought processes, their cultural narratives."

He envisioned a future where the observation dome was not just a research station, but a hub for interspecies cultural exchange. A place where the Resonant Pack could learn from the Veridians, not just about their planet, but about entirely new ways of experiencing existence. The possibilities were staggering, and the responsibility that came with them equally so.

"We need to be incredibly careful not to project our own cultural biases onto their behavior," Niko warned, more to himself than to Anya. "What appears to be a simple gathering of light-seeking creatures might, in fact, be a complex philosophical discourse. What seems like a coordinated effort to gather resources could be an act of profound artistic expression. We have to shed our assumptions and approach this with an open, receptive mind."

He looked out at the Veridian landscape, now bathed in the soft, ethereal glow of the twin suns setting on the horizon. The crystalline flora pulsed with a gentle luminescence, casting long, dancing shadows across the savanna. It was a world alive with subtle energies, a world that had developed its own unique form of intelligence, its own nascent civilization, entirely independent of humanity.

"This discovery changes the very definition of 'life' as we know it," Niko said, his voice tinged with awe. "It pushes the boundaries of what we thought was possible for consciousness to evolve. We're not just preserving a planet; we're witnessing the genesis of a new cultural paradigm, a paradigm that could teach us so much about ourselves, about the universe, and about the infinite potential of life."

The mission had taken an unexpected turn, from the meticulous cataloging of flora and fauna to the profound study of an alien psyche. The ethical considerations remained paramount, but they were now intertwined with a new, exhilarating imperative: to understand.

To listen to the whispers of sentience and to patiently, respectfully, learn the language of light and resonance, a language that promised to unlock the deepest secrets of Veridia and, perhaps, of life itself. The exploration of their culture, built on the very essence of their world, was the new, awe-inspiring frontier.

Chapter Eight
ECHOES OF HOME

The hum of the observation dome, once a source of comfort, now carried a subtle dissonance, a low thrum that vibrated not just through the metallic structure, but through Niko's very being. It was the sound of distance, of separation, a constant reminder of the gulf that lay between him and the world he called home. Veridia, with its incandescent flora and resonant harmonies, was a marvel, a testament to the boundless creativity of the universe. Yet, as he watched the twin suns dip below the horizon, painting the sky in hues of amethyst and gold, a familiar ache settled in his chest. It was the pang of nostalgia, a yearning for a world etched into the very fibers of his soul.

He found himself drifting, his gaze unfocused, lost in the shimmering tapestry of memories. He remembered the scent of damp earth after a spring rain, the dense, verdant embrace of ancient redwood forests, their colossal trunks stretching towards an unseen sky. He recalled the salty spray of ocean waves crashing against rugged coastlines, the endless expanse of blue mirroring the vastness of his own thoughts. He envisioned the silent majesty of snow-capped mountains, their peaks piercing the clouds, a stark beauty that spoke of enduring resilience. These were not just landscapes; they were sensory anchors, grounding him to a reality that felt increasingly distant, a dream fading with each passing cycle on Veridia.

Kira, sensing the shift in his emotional state, nudged his hand with her velvety muzzle. Her amber eyes, so full of an alien wisdom, met his, and in their depths, he saw a reflection of his own quiet sadness. She was attuned to the subtle currents of his feelings, a living barometer of his internal world. He stroked her fur, the familiar texture a small comfort against the vastness of his longing. She offered no judgment, no platitudes, only a silent, unwavering presence, a testament to the profound bond that had formed between them. Her empathy, once a tool for understanding Veridia, now served as a quiet solace for his own homesickness.

"It's the quiet, isn't it?" Anya murmured, her voice soft, as if afraid to shatter the fragile peace of the moment. She had been observing Niko's reverie, her own gaze distant, perhaps tracing her own memories of Earth. "The absence of the familiar cacophony. The constant hum of a billion lives, the distant roar of traffic, the laughter, the arguments... the sheer, unyielding press of humanity."

Niko nodded, his throat tight. Anya was right. It wasn't just the absence of the natural world, but the absence of human connection, the vibrant, messy, often chaotic tapestry of terrestrial life. Here, on Veridia, their mission demanded a singular focus, an unwavering dedication to observation and preservation. Their existence was a finely tuned instrument, calibrated for scientific inquiry, for the delicate dance of interspecies stewardship. But life, he was realizing, was more than data streams and bio-signatures. It was the shared warmth of a crowded room, the comfort of a familiar voice, the bittersweet melancholy of an old song.

"I miss the rain," Niko confessed, the words feeling inadequate to convey the depth of his sentiment. "The way it washes everything clean. The smell of ozone, the way the world seems to hold its breath just before it falls. And the sheer, overwhelming green of it all. The infinite variations of chlorophyll, the way life fights its way through concrete, through rock, through any obstacle." He gestured vaguely towards the alien landscape outside the dome, a panorama of crystalline structures and bioluminescent flora. "Veridia is beautiful, breathtakingly so. But it's a different kind of beauty. It's...

organized. Precise. Earth's beauty is wild, untamed, a magnificent, chaotic explosion of life."

Anya sighed, a sound that resonated with a shared understanding. "I find myself cataloging the mundane. The way sunlight filters through leaves. The sound of wind rustling through tall grass. The feeling of sand between my toes. Things I never even noticed when I was there, things I took for granted as simply 'being.' Now, they are treasures, precious fragments of a life that feels like it belongs to someone else."

The ethical weight of their mission was immense, a responsibility that weighed heavily on their shoulders. They were guardians, caretakers of a nascent civilization, tasked with ensuring their development was unhindered by external influence. This duty demanded a level of detachment, a scientific objectivity that was increasingly at odds with the primal human need for connection, for the comfort of familiarity. They were scientists, explorers, diplomats, but they were also, fundamentally, beings who had left behind families, friends, a home that pulsed with the rhythm of their own species.

"It's the paradox of our existence here," Niko mused, his fingers tracing the condensation forming on the observation panel. "We are tasked with preserving an entire world, a world teeming with a unique and evolving form of sentience. That's a profound honor, a calling that defines our purpose. But that purpose requires us to be... removed. To exist in a state of perpetual observation, always on the periphery, never fully immersed." He glanced at Kira, who had settled her head on his lap, her gentle purr a steady vibration against his thigh. "Even Kira, with her extraordinary connection to Veridia, carries the imprint of Earth within her. That quiet yearning in her eyes when she dreams... it's a reflection of our shared origins, a reminder of the world we left behind."

He recalled the training simulations, the rigorous psychological evaluations designed to prepare them for the rigors of deep space and extended isolation. They had been drilled on maintaining focus, on prioritizing the mission above personal comfort. But no simulation, however realistic, could truly replicate the slow, insidious erosion of spirit that came with profound distance. The vastness of the cosmos, while awe-inspiring, was also an isolating force, dwarfing individual lives and amplifying the sense of being adrift.

"I think about my younger sister," Anya said, her voice barely audible. "Her wedding is next year. I'll miss it. And her first child... I might never meet my niece or nephew. These are the sacrifices, aren't they? The intangible costs of this grand endeavor. We gain a universe of knowledge, but we risk losing pieces of ourselves, pieces of our personal histories."

Niko squeezed Kira's flank, a silent acknowledgment of their shared burden. "That's where the duty comes in, Anya. It's what keeps us going. The knowledge that what we are doing here matters. That the preservation of Veridia, and the careful nurturing of its sentient inhabitants, will have a ripple effect, not just on this planet, but potentially on humanity's understanding of life itself. We are pioneers, charting not just new worlds, but new ethical landscapes. That knowledge, that responsibility, must be enough to anchor us."

He knew it was a constant balancing act. The scientist within him craved the objective data, the analytical interpretation of Veridia's wonders. But the human in him yearned for the familiar, for the grounding influence of his home world. He found solace in the small rituals of their isolated existence: the carefully prepared meals, the shared moments of quiet contemplation, the shared responsibility for Kira. These acts, however mundane, were threads that connected him to a sense of normalcy, to the broader human experience.

"Sometimes," Niko admitted, his voice barely a whisper, "I wonder if the isolation is a necessary component of our role. Perhaps true objectivity requires a degree of emotional distance from any world, including our own. If we were too deeply invested in Earth's affairs, too emotionally entangled, could we truly act as impartial guardians for Veridia?"

Anya considered this, her brow furrowed. "It's a valid question. But I believe there's a difference between impartiality and emotional sterility. We can be objective without being devoid of feeling. Our connection to Earth, our memories of its beauty and its people, can fuel our desire to protect Veridia, to ensure that such wonders are not lost elsewhere. It can serve as a constant reminder of what is at stake, of the preciousness of all life, in all its myriad forms."

He thought of the vast, interconnected web of life on Earth, the delicate balance that had taken billions of years to evolve. Veridia, in its own unique way, was a parallel masterpiece, a testament to the universe's capacity for creating complexity and beauty. To protect this nascent sentience, to ensure its path was its own, was to honor the very principle that had given rise to life on his own planet.

"I miss the smell of pine needles after a summer storm," Niko said, a faint smile touching his lips. "And the feel of worn leather in an old book. And the sound of my mother's laughter. These are the fragments I hold onto. They are the echoes of home that I carry with me, the reminders of what I am fighting for, not just here, but for all worlds that hold the promise of life."

He looked out at the alien stars, a dusting of unfamiliar constellations against the cosmic black. They were beautiful, certainly, but they lacked the comforting familiarity of Orion, the steady glow of Polaris. They were a constant reminder of his displacement, of the immense distance that separated him from everything he had ever known. Yet, within that vast expanse, he found a flicker of hope. The universe was vast, teeming with possibilities, and humanity, in its quest for understanding and connection, was reaching out, not just to conquer, but to comprehend, to protect, to co-exist. The mission on Veridia, with all its challenges and sacrifices, was a testament to that evolving aspiration. It was a testament to the enduring power of duty, tempered by the deep, resonant ache of a homesick heart. He drew a deep breath, the recycled air of the dome filling his lungs, a sterile substitute for the fresh breezes of Earth, but a breath nonetheless, fueling the resolve that propelled him forward, a sentinel on the frontier of a new cosmic dawn.

The silent hum of the observation dome, a constant companion since their arrival, seemed to deepen its tone, resonating not just through the metallic hull, but through the very marrow of Niko's bones. It was a sound he had grown accustomed to, a lullaby of isolation, yet tonight, it felt imbued with a new layer of meaning. It was the sound of distance, of separation, a physical manifestation of the immeasurable gulf that lay between him and the vibrant, chaotic symphony of Earth. Veridia, with its phosphorescent flora that pulsed with an internal light and its intricate, melodic soundscapes, was a marvel, a testament to the boundless creativity of the universe. But as the twin suns, Sola and Lumina, began their slow descent, bleeding hues of molten amethyst and burnished gold across the alien sky, a familiar ache, a persistent thrum of nostalgia, settled deep within his chest.

He found his gaze drifting, not to the data streams or the bio-signatures being meticulously logged, but to the shimmering, intangible tapestry of memory that unfurled behind his eyes. He could almost feel the cool, damp earth beneath his bare feet after a spring rain, the dense, verdant embrace of ancient redwood forests, their colossal trunks soaring towards a sky that felt impossibly close. He conjured the sting of salty spray from ocean waves crashing against rugged, time-worn coastlines, the endless expanse of sapphire blue mirroring the boundless, restless expanse of his own thoughts. He envisioned the stark, silent majesty of snow-capped mountains, their jagged peaks piercing the ethereal wisps of clouds, a raw, untamed beauty that spoke of an enduring, almost defiant resilience. These were not mere landscapes, he realized, but visceral anchors, grounding him to a reality that felt increasingly like a half-forgotten dream, a fading echo with each passing Veridian cycle.

Kira, her velvety muzzle nudging his hand with an almost imperceptible pressure, broke through his reverie. Her amber eyes, pools of an ancient, alien wisdom, met his, and in their luminous depths, he saw a perfect, melancholic reflection of his own quiet sorrow. She was an empathic marvel, attuned to the subtle currents of his emotional state, a living, breathing barometer of his internal world. He stroked her silken fur, the familiar texture a small, solid comfort against the overwhelming vastness of his longing. She offered no judgment, no facile reassurances, only a silent, unwavering presence, a living testament to the profound, unspoken bond that had woven itself between them. Her extraordinary empathy, once a tool honed for understanding Veridia's complex ecosystems and its nascent sentient life, now served as a quiet, profound solace for his own encroaching homesickness.

"It's the quiet, isn't it?" Anya murmured, her voice a soft whisper, as if afraid to shatter the fragile, poignant peace of the moment. She had been observing Niko's silent communion with his memories, her own gaze distant, perhaps tracing the contours of her own deeply personal recollections of Earth. "The sheer absence of the familiar cacophony. The constant, overwhelming hum of a billion lives intertwined, the distant, persistent roar of traffic, the laughter, the arguments, the unspoken anxieties... the sheer, unyielding press of humanity all around you."

Niko nodded, his throat constricting with an emotion he couldn't quite articulate. Anya was profoundly right. It wasn't merely the absence of Earth's vibrant natural world, but the gnawing void of human connection, the messy, complex, often chaotic tapestry of terrestrial life. Here, on Veridia, their meticulously defined mission demanded a singular, unwavering focus, an absolute dedication to observation and the delicate art of non-interference. Their existence had become a finely tuned instrument, calibrated for rigorous scientific inquiry, for the intricate, ethical dance of interspecies stewardship. But life, he was beginning to understand with a startling clarity, was so much more than data streams and bio-signatures. It was the shared warmth of a crowded, boisterous room, the comforting resonance of a familiar voice calling his name, the bittersweet melancholy that clung to the air after an old, beloved song had faded.

"I miss the rain," Niko confessed, the words feeling woefully inadequate to convey the sheer depth of his sentiment, the primal longing that the sound and smell of rain evoked. "The way it washes everything clean, leaving the world glistening and new. The sharp, clean scent of ozone that hangs in the air, the way the entire world seems to hold its breath in anticipation, just before the first drops fall. And the sheer, overwhelming, riotous green of it all. The infinite, breathtaking variations of chlorophyll, the tenacious, irrepressible way life fights its way through concrete, through solid rock, through any obstacle imaginable." He gestured vaguely towards the alien landscape visible through the observation dome, a panorama of impossibly intricate crystalline structures and bioluminescent flora that pulsed with an otherworldly light. "Veridia is beautiful, breathtakingly so. But it's a different kind of beauty. It's... organized. Precise. Almost mathematically perfect. Earth's beauty is wild, untamed, a magnificent, chaotic, glorious explosion of life."

Anya sighed, a soft sound that resonated with a profound, shared understanding, a quiet acknowledgment of their mutual isolation. "I find myself meticulously cataloging the mundane. The way sunlight filters through the broad leaves of the native flora. The gentle sound of the wind rustling through the tall, feathery grasses. The utterly simple feeling of sand between my toes on a beach. Things I never even consciously noticed when I was there, things I took for granted as simply... being. Now, they are treasures, precious, irreplaceable fragments of a life that feels increasingly like it belongs to someone else entirely."

The ethical weight of their mission was immense, a responsibility that settled heavily upon their shoulders, a constant, pressing burden. They were guardians, caretakers of a nascent civilization, tasked with ensuring its organic development remained unhindered by any external influence, by any unintended consequence of their presence. This profound duty demanded a level of detachment, a rigorously maintained scientific objectivity that was increasingly at odds with the fundamental, primal human need for connection, for the deep comfort of familiarity. They were scientists, explorers, diplomats, but they were also, at their core, beings who had left behind families, friends, a home that pulsed with the unique, insistent rhythm of their own species.

"It's the inherent paradox of our existence here," Niko mused, his fingers tracing the delicate condensation that had formed on the cool surface of the observation panel. "We are tasked with the monumental responsibility of preserving an entire world, a world teeming with a unique and evolving form of sentience. That's an honor of immeasurable significance, a calling that defines our very purpose. But that purpose, by its very nature, requires us to be... removed. To exist in a state of perpetual observation, always on the periphery, never fully immersed, never truly a part of the tapestry we are sworn to protect." He glanced down at Kira, who had settled her head on his lap, her gentle, rumbling purr a steady, comforting vibration against his thigh. "Even Kira, with her extraordinary, almost mystical connection to Veridia, carries the imprint of Earth within her. That quiet, almost imperceptible yearning in her eyes when she dreams... it's a reflection of our shared origins, a constant, poignant reminder of the world we left behind."

He recalled the rigorous training simulations, the exhaustive psychological evaluations meticulously designed to prepare them for the immense rigors of deep space travel and extended periods of profound isolation. They had been drilled relentlessly on maintaining unwavering focus, on prioritizing the mission above all personal comfort, above all personal desires. But no simulation, however realistic, however well-crafted, could truly replicate the slow, insidious erosion of spirit that came with an almost unimaginable distance. The sheer vastness of the cosmos, while undeniably awe-inspiring, was also a profoundly isolating force, dwarfing individual lives and amplifying the disorienting sense of being utterly adrift in an infinite ocean of stars.

"I think constantly about my younger sister," Anya said, her voice barely audible, a fragile thread of sound in the quiet dome. "Her wedding is scheduled for next year. I know I'll miss it. And her first child... the birth of my niece or nephew. I might never have the chance to meet them. These are the sacrifices, aren't they? The intangible, often unacknowledged costs of this grand, cosmic endeavor. We gain a universe of knowledge, an unprecedented understanding of alien life, but we risk losing irreplaceable pieces of ourselves, precious pieces of our personal histories, our familial bonds."

Niko gently squeezed Kira's flank, a silent, instinctive acknowledgment of their shared emotional burden, their mutual longing. "That's where the duty comes in, Anya. It's what keeps us going, what propels us forward when the longing becomes almost unbearable. The absolute knowledge that what we are doing here, on this distant world, matters. That the careful preservation of Veridia, and the deliberate, ethical nurturing of its sentient inhabitants, will have a profound ripple effect, not just on this singular planet, but potentially on humanity's entire understanding of life itself, of its infinite possibilities. We are pioneers, charting not just new worlds, but entirely new ethical landscapes, forging pathways for future generations. That knowledge, that immense responsibility, must be enough to anchor us."

He knew, with a certainty born of experience, that it was a constant, precarious balancing act. The scientist within him, the rational, analytical mind, craved the objective data, the precise, unemotional interpretation of Veridia's myriad wonders. But the human in him, the deeply feeling being, yearned for the familiar, for the grounding, stabilizing influence of his home world, for the simple comfort of what was known. He found solace in the small, established rituals of their isolated existence: the carefully prepared, nutritionally balanced meals, the shared moments of quiet, contemplative silence, the shared responsibility for Kira's well-being. These acts, however mundane, were essential threads that connected him to a sense of normalcy, to the broader, richer human experience he had left behind.

"Sometimes," Niko admitted, his voice barely a whisper, lost in the hum of the dome, "I wonder if the isolation is not just a consequence, but a necessary component of our role here. Perhaps true objectivity, the kind required for such a delicate mission, demands a degree of emotional distance from any world, including our own. If we were too deeply invested in Earth's affairs, too emotionally entangled with its ongoing dramas, could we truly act as impartial, unbiased guardians for Veridia?"

Anya considered this, her brow furrowed in deep thought, her gaze fixed on the swirling patterns of light outside the dome. "It's a valid question, Niko. A deeply troubling one, perhaps. But I believe there's a fundamental difference between impartiality and emotional sterility. We can be objective without being entirely devoid of feeling. Our connection to Earth, our cherished memories of its profound beauty and the people we love, can actually fuel our desire to protect Veridia, to ensure that such wonders, such unique expressions of life, are not lost to the vast indifference of the cosmos. It can serve as a constant, potent reminder of what is truly at stake, of the inherent preciousness of all life, in all its countless, wondrous forms."

He thought of the vast, intricate, and astonishingly interconnected web of life on Earth, the delicate, millennia-honed balance that had taken billions of years to evolve and stabilize. Veridia, in its own profoundly unique and alien way, was a parallel masterpiece, a testament to the universe's seemingly boundless capacity for creating breathtaking complexity and exquisite beauty. To protect this nascent sentience, to ensure its evolutionary path was its own, uncorrupted and unfettered, was to honor the very principle that had given rise to life on his own cherished planet.

"I miss the smell of pine needles after a summer storm," Niko said, a faint, wistful smile touching his lips, a ghost of a memory. "And the distinct feel of worn leather in an old, beloved book. And the sound of my mother's laughter, a sound so full of warmth and life. These are the fragments I hold onto, the anchors in the storm of longing. They are the echoes of home that I carry with me, the silent reminders of what I am fighting for, not just here, in this distant corner of the galaxy, but for all worlds that hold the fragile, extraordinary promise of life."

He looked out at the alien stars, a scattered dusting of unfamiliar constellations against the inky, cosmic blackness. They were beautiful, undeniably so, a spectacle of cosmic grandeur, but they lacked the comforting, reassuring familiarity of Orion, the steady, guiding glow of Polaris. They were a constant, unavoidable reminder of his displacement, of the immense, crushing distance that separated him from everything he had ever known, everything he had ever loved. Yet, within that vast, indifferent expanse, he found a flicker of resilient hope. The universe was vast, endlessly so, teeming with unimaginable possibilities, and humanity, in its relentless, evolving quest for understanding and connection, was reaching out, not merely to conquer or to exploit, but to comprehend, to protect, to co-exist. The mission on Veridia, with all its profound challenges and personal sacrifices, was a testament to that evolving, hopeful aspiration. It was a testament to the enduring, indomitable power of duty, tempered by the deep, resonant ache of a homesick heart, a heart that still beat to the rhythm of a distant, beloved world. He drew a slow, deep breath, the recycled air of the dome filling his lungs, a sterile, artificial substitute for the fresh, invigorating breezes of Earth, but a breath nonetheless, fueling the quiet, persistent resolve that propelled him forward, a solitary sentinel on the luminous frontier of a new cosmic dawn.

He realized, with a sudden, profound clarity, that memories were not merely passive recordings of past events. They possessed an energy, a resonance, an energetic signature that was as unique and as tangible as any physical object. And emotions, those ephemeral, often overwhelming currents that swept through him, were not confined to the biological confines of his own mind. They too, he suspected, carried their own distinct vibratory frequencies, their own energetic resonances. He began to wonder, with a sense of profound wonder, if these deeply personal resonances, these echoes of lived experience, could somehow traverse the unfathomable distances between dimensions. Were they tethered irrevocably to their origin point, or did they possess a subtle, unseen ability to journey beyond the confines of space and time?

This introspection, this sudden, startling leap from the personal to the cosmic, began to paint his understanding of their mission in entirely new hues. He contemplated how his own emotional state, amplified and perhaps even focused by Kira's innate empathy, might be subtly influencing the very fabric of the gateway, the ephemeral conduit that had brought them to Veridia. Could their collective longing, their shared homesickness, their deep-seated yearning for Earth, be subtly destabilizing its delicate equilibrium? Or, conversely, could it be imbuing it with a unique resonance, a signature that would forever mark it as a bridge between worlds?

He looked at Kira, her amber eyes reflecting the soft glow of the Veridian flora outside. Her very presence, a bridge between species and worlds, was a constant reminder of the interconnectedness he was beginning to perceive. He felt the gentle thrum of her purr against his thigh, a physical manifestation of her empathetic state, a vibration that seemed to harmonize with the low hum of the observation dome. It was a symphony of subtle energies, a cosmic dance of consciousness and matter. He imagined their emotions, their memories, not as fleeting sparks, but as persistent waves of energy, rippling outwards, interacting with the fundamental forces that governed the multiverse.

Perhaps, he mused, the gateway wasn't merely a passive portal, a hole punched through spacetime. Perhaps it was a living entity, a complex construct that responded to the energetic signatures of those who interacted with it. And perhaps, he dared to think, their own emotional resonances, their deeply ingrained memories of Earth, were not just a source of personal solace, but an integral component of the gateway's own energetic signature. They were not just observers, he was beginning to believe; they were, in some profound and subtle way, active participants in the very mechanics of interdimensional travel. The emotional echoes of home, it seemed, were not just fading memories, but potent forces, capable of resonating across the vast, unknowable expanse of the cosmos, subtly shaping the very fabric of reality.

Kira's velvety muzzle nuzzled against Niko's hand, a familiar, comforting gesture that grounded him in the present moment. Her amber eyes, usually so alert and inquisitive, held a soft, distant glaze, reflecting the flickering bioluminescent flora outside the observation dome. Niko recognized the subtle shift in her demeanor, a nearly imperceptible languor that had crept into her posture over the past few Veridian cycles. It was a quiet echo of his own longing, a testament to the profound, unspoken empathy that bound them together. She was, in many ways, a mirror to his own soul, a living barometer of their shared experience on this alien world.

He stroked the silken fur along her spine, feeling the gentle rise and fall of her breath. Kira, ever the adaptable companion, had mastered the intricacies of Veridia's environment with remarkable ease. Her senses, honed by generations of selective breeding for keen observation and unwavering loyalty, had adapted to the subtly different atmospheric pressures, the unique spectral qualities of the twin suns, and the complex, layered scents of this verdant, alien landscape. She navigated the crystalline terrain with a confident gait, her paws, so accustomed to the varied textures of Earth, now treading with a measured grace across the phosphorescent mosses and silicate-rich soil. Yet, beneath this veneer of adaptation, Niko sensed a deeper, more primal current of remembrance, a quiet yearning for the familiar textures and aromas of their terrestrial home.

There were moments, usually when Niko's own melancholy deepened, that a soft, almost inaudible whine would escape Kira's throat. It was a sound so subtle, so laced with a primal innocence, that it could easily be missed amidst the ambient hum of the observation dome. But Niko, attuned to her every nuance, never failed to hear it. He understood that these were not random vocalizations, but gentle laments, triggered by the faint resonances of his own memories that subtly permeated the shared space. Perhaps it was the phantom scent of damp earth after a spring shower that he conjured in his mind, or the remembered crispness of autumn air, or even the subtle, underlying scent of human habitation – the faint, comforting aroma of laundry detergent, woodsmoke, or the specific musk of their own dwelling. These intangible olfactory memories, as potent and evocative as any visual cue, seemed to stir a corresponding wistfulness in Kira.

He recalled the vast, sprawling forests of Earth, the ancient trees that had stood for centuries, their bark rough and furrowed, smelling of decay and new life in equal measure. He remembered the thrill of tracking deer through dense undergrowth, the scent of crushed pine needles and damp loam a heady perfume. Kira, too, had reveled in those scents, her nose a finely tuned instrument, deciphering the complex narratives written in the invisible language of pheromones and microbial traces. Here, on Veridia, the dominant scents were different – a sharp, metallic tang from the crystalline structures, a sweet, almost cloying perfume from the bioluminescent flora, and an underlying earthy scent that was alien, though not unpleasant. Kira explored these new olfactory landscapes with curiosity, her tail wagging tentatively, but Niko could see the subtle, almost imperceptible pauses, the moments when her nostrils would flare, seeking something... familiar.

He remembered their walks in the park back on Earth. The manicured lawns, the fallen leaves crunching underfoot, the distant sound of children's laughter. Kira would chase squirrels with boundless enthusiasm, her powerful legs propelling her through the dappled sunlight, her wet nose nudging his hand for praise. Those were simpler times, filled with the uncomplicated joys of shared outdoor adventures. Now, their 'adventures' were carefully controlled scientific excursions, meticulously planned and executed within the parameters of their non-interference directive. The thrill of the chase had been replaced by the quiet intensity of observation, the joyous abandon of a run in the park by the measured discipline of traversing alien terrain.

One evening, as Niko was replaying old audio logs of Earth's natural soundscapes – the mournful cry of a lone wolf, the rhythmic crashing of ocean waves, the gentle chirping of crickets on a summer night – Kira had lifted her head from her slumber. She had let out a soft, prolonged whine, her body trembling slightly. Niko had paused the playback, his heart aching with a sudden surge of empathy for his loyal companion. He had knelt beside her, wrapping his arms around her, murmuring reassurances. She had licked his hand, her tail giving a weak thump against the floor, a gesture of comfort and reassurance that belied her own distress. It was then that he understood, with a profound clarity, that Kira was not merely adapting; she was actively *missing* the sensory tapestry of their home.

Her loyalty, a fierce and unwavering flame that had guided her through countless experiences with Niko, extended beyond simple obedience. It was a deep, intrinsic bond, woven from shared experiences, mutual affection, and an almost telepathic understanding. This bond, he realized, was intrinsically tied to their shared origin. Kira's very being, her instincts, her deeply ingrained responses, were all shaped by her life on Earth. Even as her intellect and senses adjusted to Veridia, her primal, emotional core retained the indelible imprint of her homeland.

He recalled a specific instance, not long after their arrival. Niko had been meticulously cleaning his geological sampling tools, the sharp, metallic scent of the cleaning solvent momentarily filling the air. Kira, who usually displayed an intense interest in his equipment, had recoiled, sneezing and shaking her head, her amber eyes wide with an expression that seemed to convey a deep, visceral displeasure. It wasn't the scent itself that bothered her, Niko theorized, but the unfamiliarity. On Earth, such chemical smells were often associated with the sterile, controlled environments of labs or workshops, or the less pleasant aspects of urban pollution. Here, the air was pristine, devoid of such manufactured odors. The sudden intrusion of a scent so fundamentally terrestrial, so out of place in the alien symphony of Veridia, had clearly been jarring to her refined senses.

Her favorite scratching post, a sturdy piece of driftwood that had been a gift from a friend, now sat unused in a corner of their habitat module. Kira showed no interest in it, though back on Earth, she had spent hours diligently sharpening her claws against its weathered surface, leaving behind faint, comforting scent markers. The Veridian flora provided no comparable texture, no satisfying resistance for her claws. She simply didn't have the need, or perhaps the instinct, to engage with it. It was a small thing, perhaps, but indicative of the deeper connections she had to her terrestrial past, connections that transcended mere practicality.

Niko found himself observing her more closely now, noting the subtle cues that betrayed her inner state. The way she would sometimes lie with her head on her paws, her gaze fixed on the distant, star-dusted horizon visible through the observation dome, a look of profound introspection in her eyes. It reminded him of his own quiet moments of contemplation, when the sheer distance from Earth would press down on him, heavy and inescapable. He saw in her a resilience he admired, a capacity to adapt and to endure, but he also recognized the quiet melancholy that accompanied it.

He understood that Kira's presence was more than just that of a loyal pet or a highly trained research assistant. She was a living testament to the enduring power of home, a furry embodiment of the concept of belonging. Even in the face of extraordinary circumstances, of a journey that defied all conventional understanding, the resonance of her origins remained. Her loyalty to him, to their shared mission, was undeniable, but it was a loyalty rooted in a history, a shared past that had been forged on the familiar soil of Earth.

Sometimes, when he felt particularly overwhelmed by the weight of their responsibilities or the sheer isolation of their existence, he would find himself talking to Kira, not in commands or scientific directives, but in the quiet, intimate language of shared memories. He would describe the taste of fresh-baked bread, the feel of sand between his toes, the sound of rain drumming on the roof of their old house. He would watch her ears perk up, her tail give a gentle wag, as if she too, in her own way, was re-experiencing those sensory delights. It was a form of communion, a way of reinforcing their shared connection to the world they had left behind, a world that continued to live within them, a vibrant, indelible echo.

He recalled the time he had found a small, iridescent beetle scurrying across the floor of their habitat. It was a Veridian native, its exoskeleton shimmering with an otherworldly luminescence. Kira, usually fascinated by any small, moving creature, had approached it with a hesitant curiosity, sniffing it delicately. Then, to his surprise, she had let out a low, soft whine, and had stepped back, leaving the beetle undisturbed. Niko wondered if, in that moment, she had unconsciously compared it to the common dung beetles or scarabs she had encountered on Earth, their familiar, earthy scents so different from the sharp, mineral aroma of the Veridian insect. It was a subtle rejection, a quiet preference for the known over the new, a testament to the deep-seated affiliations forged in her formative years.

The theme of home, of belonging, was not merely a backdrop to their scientific endeavors; it was an integral part of their experience. Kira, with her unwavering devotion and her subtle expressions of longing, served as a constant reminder of this fundamental human, and indeed animal, need. She was a living embodiment of the concept that even the most adaptable creatures carry the indelible resonance of their origins. Her presence, far from being a distraction, was a source of strength, a reminder of the fundamental values they were striving to uphold – the protection of life, the respect for diverse ecosystems, and the profound, intrinsic worth of every living being, no matter how alien or distant. In Kira's quiet sighs and her searching gaze, Niko found not just a reflection of his own homesickness, but a deeper understanding of the universal drive to connect, to belong, and to carry the echoes of home, no matter how far one might journey into the vast, unknown reaches of the cosmos. Her loyalty was not just to him, but to the shared world that had shaped them, a world that continued to pulse in their hearts, a vibrant, enduring symphony of memories.

The hum of the habitat's life support systems, usually a comforting thrum that lulled Niko into a sense of security, felt... off. It was a subtle dissonance, a faint tremor beneath the surface of the familiar sonic landscape of Veridia. Kira, curled at his feet, her usual vigil of alertness momentarily softened by sleep, twitched an ear. Niko paused in his meticulous calibration of the atmospheric sensors, his gaze drawn to the communications console. It had been quiet for so long, a silence that had become a balm, a respite from the cacophony of signals and chatter that had defined their initial exploration phases. Now, a faint, almost imperceptible pulse emanated from the unit, a ghost of a signal struggling to break through the immense gravitational and energetic barriers that separated them from Earth.

He initiated the diagnostic sequence, his fingers flying across the holographic interface with practiced efficiency. The console responded, a cascade of diagnostic readouts blooming into existence, each line of code a testament to the ingenuity and desperation of those who had engineered this lifeline across the void. The signal was weak, fragmented, and heavily attenuated, a whisper in the cosmic wind. But it was there. A faint thread, woven from quantum entanglement and bolstered by a network of resonance-dampened relays, designed to slip through the gaps in the fabric of spacetime, unseen and unheard.

Kira, sensing the shift in his attention, stirred. She rose, stretching languidly, her amber eyes now fully open and fixed on the console. There was a flicker of recognition in them, a primal understanding that this humming box, this nexus of light and data, represented a connection to a place she, too, held dear. She padded softly to his side, her warm flank pressing against his leg, a silent anchor in the face of the approaching deluge of information.

"Easy, girl," Niko murmured, stroking her head. "Looks like we've got some visitors."

The console chirped, a more robust tone now, indicating the successful establishment of a handshake protocol. The message, delayed by weeks, perhaps even months, of cosmic transit and temporal distortions, was finally ready for decryption. A proprietary encryption algorithm, designed to resist even the most sophisticated interdimensional decryption attempts, began to unravel, revealing the layered complexities of the communication. This wasn't a casual update; it was a carefully constructed, highly secure dispatch, a testament to the precariousness of their situation and the forces at play far beyond the tranquil surface of Veridia.

The first packets of data materialized on the screen, not as text, but as a series of abstract visual representations, a language designed to convey complex political and security concerns without the risk of linguistic misinterpretation or interception. Niko's brow furrowed as he began to decipher the evolving patterns. The visual language spoke of shifting alliances, of a growing unease within the established interdimensional framework. The dominant players, familiar from countless briefings and strategic simulations, were reconfiguring their positions, their diplomatic dances now fraught with a palpable tension.

The symbols denoting OmniCorp, the monolithic conglomerate that had long been a shadow lurking at the periphery of human expansion, now pulsed with a malevolent red. Their influence, once contained within the more conventional dimensions, had begun to spill over, their insatiable hunger for resources and control extending into the nascent parallel worlds they were exploring. The visual metaphors were stark: tendrils of dark energy snaking outwards, encroaching upon the established gateways, disrupting the delicate equilibrium that had been painstakingly maintained.

Niko's breath hitched as a sequence of symbols flashed across the screen, directly referencing the gateway security protocols. The message was clear: the interdimensional portals, the very conduits that allowed for their exploration and connection, were becoming increasingly vulnerable. Not just to accidental breaches or natural phenomena, but to deliberate sabotage. The threat wasn't merely to the exploration missions; it was to the structural integrity of their own reality, a chilling reminder that the borders they believed they were crossing were, in fact, the very walls protecting their home.

Kira let out a soft whine, her head nudging his hand. She seemed to sense the gravity of the information, her usual playful demeanor replaced by a quiet, watchful stillness. Niko met her gaze, offering a reassuring scratch behind her ears. "It's... complicated, girl," he admitted, his voice low. "But we'll figure it out. We always do."

He continued to process the data stream, each new visual abstract a piece of a larger, more disturbing puzzle. The message detailed covert OmniCorp operations, aimed at destabilizing nascent dimensional ecosystems, not for scientific curiosity or resource acquisition, but for outright subjugation. Their advanced technology, honed through decades of unchecked exploitation on Earth, was being repurposed for more insidious ends. The intent was not just to control, but to corrupt, to twist the natural order of these alien worlds for their own nefarious purposes.

There were also, interspersed within the dire political updates, concerning reports from Earth itself. Not about OmniCorp's direct actions in the parallel worlds, but about the growing internal anxieties and governmental paralysis back home. The message hinted at political infighting, at factions within the ruling council that were either complicit with OmniCorp or too indecisive to take meaningful action. The very entities responsible for safeguarding humanity's future seemed to be actively undermining it, either through negligence or design.

This wasn't just about protecting alien worlds; it was about protecting the very concept of a shared future, a future built on cooperation and ethical exploration, rather than on corporate greed and interdimensional conquest. The message underscored the immense responsibility that rested on their shoulders, not just as scientists and explorers, but as guardians of a fragile network of worlds.

The communication concluded with a series of highly classified security alerts, detailing potential methods of interdimensional infiltration. The emphasis was on resonance dampening and quantum decoherence, technologies that the pack had themselves helped to develop. It was a grim irony that the very tools they had created to ensure their own safety were now being used to highlight the escalating threats. The message was a stark reminder that in the vast expanse of dimensions, privacy was a fleeting commodity, and vigilance was the only true currency.

Niko leaned back, the holographic displays shimmering before him. The faint, comforting hum of the habitat now seemed to carry a new weight, a subtle undercurrent of dread. He looked at Kira, her tail thumping a slow, steady rhythm against the floor. Her presence, her unwavering loyalty, was a beacon in the encroaching darkness. She represented the simple, pure essence of home, the connection to something real and untainted by the machinations of interdimensional politics and corporate avarice.

He initiated a reply sequence, composing a concise, encrypted acknowledgment of receipt. He didn't have the full picture, not yet, but he understood the implications. Their mission, once a purely scientific endeavor, had become something far more significant, far more dangerous.

They were not just observers; they were participants, players on a cosmic stage where the stakes were higher than they had ever imagined. The echoes of home, the distant whispers from Earth, had arrived, not with reassurance, but with a grim warning. The void between worlds was not empty; it was teeming with unseen threats, and the fight for their home, and for the myriad worlds they had come to understand, had just begun.

He initiated a further sub-protocol, designed to sweep the local subspace for any residual resonance patterns that might indicate eavesdropping attempts. The process was painstaking, involving the meticulous analysis of quantum foam fluctuations and the subtle distortions in the local spacetime fabric. It was a testament to the paranoia, and perhaps the prescience, of the intelligence operatives back on Earth, who had gone to such lengths to ensure the message's integrity. Even the handshake protocol itself had been designed to mimic a random cosmic event, a burst of quantum noise that would dissipate without a trace in the background radiation of the universe.

Kira, sensing his continued focus, nudged his hand again, her soft muzzle warm against his skin. He looked down at her, a profound sense of gratitude washing over him. In her, he saw the embodiment of everything they were fighting for. Her simple needs, her uncomplicated affection, her deep-seated connection to the terrestrial world – these were the fundamental truths that OmniCorp, with its insatiable drive for power and control, sought to extinguish. The message from Earth wasn't just about political tensions and security breaches; it was a stark reminder of the values at stake, the inherent worth of life, and the profound beauty of the natural order that OmniCorp so readily trampled.

He began to access the secondary data streams, a series of detailed reports on OmniCorp's technological capabilities. These were not mere estimations; they were derived from high-risk infiltration missions, from the daring exploits of agents who had risked everything to gather intelligence. The reports spoke of sophisticated resonance-nullifying technology, capable of masking their presence within the interdimensional currents. They detailed advanced energy weapons, capable of destabilizing the very fabric of spacetime, creating localized tears that could be exploited for rapid transit or, more ominously, for the extraction of exotic matter from nascent realities.

The implication was clear: OmniCorp was not merely seeking to exploit resources. They were actively developing the means to weaponize interdimensional travel, to turn the very pathways of exploration into instruments of conquest. The parallel worlds, with their unique biospheres and nascent civilizations, were seen not as wonders to be studied and protected, but as ripe fruit to be plucked and consumed.

Niko activated a simulated environmental impact assessment based on the reported OmniCorp activities. The holographic projection bloomed into a swirling vortex of ecological collapse. Entire ecosystems, delicately balanced over millennia, imploded under the sudden, violent intrusion of OmniCorp's destructive technologies. The unique fauna and flora of these worlds, evolved in isolation, were unable to withstand the abrupt introduction of unfamiliar energy signatures and invasive alien materials. The vibrant colors of Veridia, the very lifeblood of this world, flickered and dulled, replaced by sterile, monochromatic desolation.

Kira whined softly, her eyes fixed on the disturbing projections. She had a keen sense of ecological balance, a primal understanding of the interconnectedness of life. The visual representation of such widespread destruction seemed to physically distress her, her body tensing as if bracing for an unseen impact. Niko gently placed a hand on her back, offering silent reassurance. "We won't let that happen," he vowed, his voice firm, though he knew the weight of that promise was immense.

The communication also included intelligence on emerging interdimensional political factions. It was a complex web of newly formed alliances and deeply entrenched rivalries, a testament to the chaotic nature of interdimensional politics. Some factions were actively seeking to establish robust security protocols, advocating for stricter oversight of gateway operations and greater transparency in interdimensional resource management. Others, however, were aligning themselves with OmniCorp, lured by the promise of advanced technology and the potential for accelerated expansion, blind to the catastrophic consequences.

Niko felt a familiar pang of weariness. The sheer scale of the political machinations, the endless cycles of ambition and betrayal, were exhausting to contemplate. It was a stark contrast to the relative simplicity of their scientific objectives on Veridia. Here, the challenges were tangible: understanding atmospheric composition, cataloging indigenous lifeforms, and ensuring their own survival. Back on Earth, and in the broader interdimensional political landscape, the challenges were abstract, insidious, and infinitely more complex.

He opened another data packet, this one detailing the security vulnerabilities of Earth's primary gateway nexus. The information was highly classified, revealing the blind spots and theoretical weak points in the planetary defense grid. It was a chilling testament to OmniCorp's intelligence-gathering capabilities, and a stark indicator of the internal threats that plagued humanity's own defenses. The message was not merely an alert; it was a desperate plea for vigilance, a signal that the enemy was not only at the gates of the parallel worlds, but also within their own bastions of power.

The communication ended with a cryptic, but undeniably urgent, directive: "Secure the resonance echoes. They are the key." Niko pondered the meaning of this final instruction. Resonance echoes. What did they refer to? Were they physical artifacts, remnants of interdimensional transit? Or were they something more abstract, echoes of consciousness, perhaps, imprinted on the very fabric of spacetime? The ambiguity was unsettling, adding another layer of mystery to an already complex and alarming message.

He decided to initiate a broad-spectrum scan of their immediate vicinity, utilizing their advanced resonance detection equipment. The instruments, usually employed to chart the subtle energetic signatures of Veridia's unique flora and fauna, were now repurposed for a more clandestine purpose. The process was slow, methodical, each scan a deep probe into the local quantum field. He was searching for anomalies, for faint traces of energy that might indicate a clandestine presence, or for any residual resonance patterns that might align with the enigmatic directive.

Kira, sensing his renewed focus on the console, settled back down at his feet, her presence a comforting weight. He glanced at her, her amber eyes reflecting the glow of the holographic displays. Her quiet strength, her unwavering loyalty, was a constant source of solace. She was a reminder of what truly mattered – the simple bonds of connection, the inherent value of life, and the enduring echo of home that resonated within them all. Even amidst the encroaching darkness and the cosmic political intrigues, her presence was a beacon, a silent affirmation that they were not alone. The fight was far from over, and the path ahead was fraught with peril, but with Kira by his side, Niko felt a renewed sense of purpose. They would face whatever came next, together, carrying the echoes of home as their guide.

The resonance detection sweep began to yield results, subtle fluctuations appearing on the secondary displays. These weren't random cosmic noise. They were faint, ephemeral imprints, fleeting traces of energy that seemed to echo a complex, underlying pattern. The signature was unlike anything they had encountered on Veridia. It was structured, almost deliberate, as if someone, or something, had intentionally imprinted a message onto the local spacetime.

Niko meticulously began to isolate and amplify these faint signals, feeding them into the decryption algorithms. The process was agonizingly slow, each amplification step risking the loss of the delicate resonance. He imagined the source of these echoes – perhaps a distant probe, a relay drone, or even a deliberately left message from one of the nascent dimensional factions mentioned in the dispatch. The possibility of OmniCorp involvement was, of course, a chilling consideration, but the nature of the echoes felt less like a threat and more like a... legacy.

As the amplified signals coalesced, a new set of visual data began to form on the console. These were not political diagrams or security alerts. They were abstract representations of energy flow, of resonant frequencies aligning and diverging. It was a language of pure physics, a representation of forces that governed the interdimensional currents. As Niko delved deeper, a startling realization began to dawn: the patterns were not merely descriptive; they were prescriptive.

The echoes were, in essence, a set of instructions. They detailed a method for stabilizing and even amplifying the very resonance dampening technology that protected their communication channels. It was a countermeasure, a way to reinforce their defenses against potential eavesdropping and infiltration. The message wasn't just a warning; it was an offering, a technological gift from an unknown benefactor.

Niko's mind raced. Who would provide such advanced knowledge, and why? The political landscape described in the earlier message was a maelstrom of competing interests. Was this a gambit by a rival faction, seeking to bolster their own allies? Or was it a desperate attempt by a rogue element within Earth's own intelligence agencies, operating outside the established channels to provide them with a critical advantage? The ambiguity was unsettling, yet the potential benefit was undeniable.

He initiated a controlled simulation, applying the principles described by the resonance echoes to their existing communication hardware. The results were immediate and profound. The previously faint and tenuous signal from Earth strengthened exponentially, its clarity and stability increasing by orders of magnitude. The background noise, the ever-present static of interdimensional transit, was effectively silenced, leaving a pristine, unwavering connection.

Kira, who had been watching the simulations with an almost unnerving focus, let out a contented sigh. Even she seemed to sense the shift, the palpable increase in security and connection. Niko stroked her flank, his heart filled with a mixture of relief and profound curiosity. "They understood, girl," he whispered. "They knew we needed help. And they gave it to us."

He continued to analyze the resonance echoes, discovering that they also contained encrypted schematics for a portable resonance amplifier. This device, if constructed, could potentially allow them to transmit more powerful and secure messages across vast interdimensional distances, and perhaps even to actively probe for other secure channels or hidden threats. It was a game-changer, a tool that could fundamentally alter their operational capabilities.

The implications of this discovery were staggering. The delayed communication from Earth had been a grim harbinger of danger, but this unexpected gift, delivered through the very void that separated them, offered a ray of hope. It suggested that they were not entirely alone in their struggle against the encroaching darkness of OmniCorp and the political instability back home. There were others, unseen and unknown, who were working to protect the integrity of the interdimensional framework.

He began to compile a detailed report of his findings, meticulously documenting the process of identifying, amplifying, and interpreting the resonance echoes. He included the proposed schematics for the portable amplifier, a testament to the ingenuity of their anonymous benefactor. As he worked, he couldn't shake the image of Kira's steady gaze, her quiet presence a constant reminder of the fundamental values they were fighting to preserve. The technological advancements, the political machinations, the existential threats – they all paled in comparison to the simple, profound truth of their connection. The echoes of home had arrived, not just as a message of warning, but as a promise of resilience, a testament to the enduring power of cooperation, even across the vast, silent expanse of the cosmos. The fight for their future, and the future of the worlds they explored, had just become a little less daunting.

The weight of the incoming transmission settled upon Niko like a shroud. The encrypted data streams, once a lifeline, now felt like harbingers of a deepening crisis. The nuanced visuals and coded warnings painted a stark picture: OmniCorp was not merely probing the edges of interdimensional exploration; they were actively seeking to control it, to exploit the nascent worlds and their unique ecosystems for their own insatiable growth. The threat wasn't just to the exploratory missions themselves, but to the very concept of ethical expansion, of respectful coexistence between species and across dimensions. The message from Earth had been clear: the gateways, once seen as pathways to discovery, were becoming battlegrounds.

Niko leaned back, the cool metal of the console a stark contrast to the warmth of Kira's body pressed against his leg. Her presence was a constant, a grounding force in the swirling chaos of interdimensional politics and corporate ambition. He had been so focused on calibrating the habitat's atmospheric processors, on the meticulous cataloging of Veridia's bioluminescent flora, that he had almost become insulated from the larger, more dangerous currents at play. Now, those currents had surged, carrying with them a stark, undeniable message: their small corner of the universe was no longer a sanctuary. It was a frontier, and frontiers were always contested.

The communication had contained more than just a dire assessment of OmniCorp's accelerating aggression. Woven into the security alerts and political analyses were subtle, yet insistent, undercurrents suggesting a need for greater military presence, for fortified gateways, for a more aggressive stance. The term "reinforcements" had appeared, not as a direct request to Niko's team, but as a general consensus forming amongst the fractured factions on Earth, a growing understanding that passive observation was no longer an option. This, Niko knew, was the crux of the problem. How did one deploy reinforcements across dimensions? The very act of interdimensional transit was fraught with peril, a carefully orchestrated dance of quantum mechanics and energy manipulation that was far from foolproof. To even consider sending additional personnel, equipment, and support would require a monumental undertaking, one that could destabilize the very gateways they were trying to protect.

He traced the glowing lines of a complex probability matrix on the console, projecting potential OmniCorp incursions into Veridia's delicate ecosystem. The simulations were grim. Even a small, targeted deployment of OmniCorp's notorious 'terraforming disruptors' could irrevocably damage the delicate mycorrhizal networks that sustained Veridia's towering flora. The vibrant hues of the native life, the symphony of chirps and rustles that usually filled the habitat's air, could be replaced by a sterile silence, a monochrome landscape devoid of the life they had worked so painstakingly to understand and protect. The thought sent a chill down his spine. Their mission had always been about observation, about learning, about coexisting. But it seemed the universe, or at least a significant portion of it, was poised to force them into a role they had never envisioned: defenders.

Kira stirred, sensing the shift in his mood. She nudged his hand with her nose, her amber eyes fixed on his face, her tail giving a slow, questioning thump against the floor. She understood the change in the atmosphere, the subtle tension that had entered their once-serene existence. Her instincts, honed by millennia of evolution to sense danger and harmony, were finely tuned to the subtle shifts in Niko's emotional state. He met her gaze, offering a reassuring scratch behind her ears. "It's okay, girl," he murmured, though the words felt hollow even to him. "Just thinking about... things."

The "things" were monumental. The message from Earth had not explicitly asked for his return, but the implication hung heavy in the air. Their specialized knowledge of Veridia, their deep understanding of its unique biology and its potential for terraforming – or, as it was increasingly becoming apparent, for defending – was precisely what a more aggressive Earth would now crave. They were, in essence, on the front lines of a conflict that was escalating far beyond the immediate scope of their scientific inquiry. But to leave Veridia now... it felt like a betrayal. They had spent cycles establishing a rapport with the indigenous fauna, learning their communication patterns, understanding the intricate web of life that bound this world together. To abandon that, to retreat to the relative safety of Earth's fortified orbitals or even the heavily guarded research stations, would leave Veridia vulnerable, an easy target for OmniCorp's rapacious ambition.

He projected a holographic map of their current location, the swirling nebulae and distant star clusters a stark reminder of the vastness of the cosmos and the isolation of their position. Then, he overlaid it with a projection of Earth's known interdimensional gateway network. The nodes, marked by glowing points of light, were concentrated, heavily defended, and, according to the recent transmission, increasingly under threat. The idea of reinforcements arriving at Veridia, of a veritable armada descending upon this tranquil world, seemed both fantastical and terrifying. The disruption to the local environment would be immense, potentially more damaging than a targeted OmniCorp strike.

"What do you think, Kira?" he whispered, more to himself than to the loyal canine. "Should we pack up and head home? Should we be part of the 'reinforcements'?"

Kira responded with a soft whine, her gaze fixed not on the holographic map, but on the viewport that overlooked Veridia's alien landscape. The twin moons cast an ethereal glow upon the shimmering foliage, and the air pulsed with the soft, rhythmic bioluminescence of the nocturnal flora. It was a world teeming with life, a testament to the power of natural evolution, a stark contrast to the sterile, manufactured environments of Earth's orbital stations. Her attention, her deep, instinctive connection, remained with Veridia.

Niko understood. Her reaction was a silent, profound argument for staying. She embodied the essence of home, not the distant, troubled planet they had left behind, but the vibrant, living world they had found. To protect Veridia was to protect a new kind of home, a home that represented the hope for a future where humanity could coexist with other worlds, rather than conquer them.

The message had also hinted at the possibility of smaller, more specialized units being deployed. Not necessarily large military fleets, but highly trained teams, equipped for interdimensional infiltration and defense. This was a more palatable prospect. A small, well-equipped team, working in conjunction with their existing knowledge of Veridia, could provide the necessary deterrent without causing significant ecological disruption. But who would they be? And would they truly understand the delicate balance they were tasked with protecting, or would they view Veridia as just another strategic asset, another piece on the cosmic chessboard?

He initiated a secondary data retrieval, focusing on the specific security protocols related to interdimensional transit of military personnel and equipment. The information was dense, filled with acronyms and technical jargon that spoke of quantum entanglement stabilizers, resonance dampening fields, and temporal displacement metrics. It was clear that the technological hurdles were significant, but not insurmountable. The primary challenge, as always, was not the science, but the politics. The decision to deploy such forces would have to be made at the highest levels of government, levels that were, according to the transmission, deeply fractured and susceptible to OmniCorp's influence.

The thought of facing OmniCorp directly, not as observers but as combatants, was a daunting one. Their technological superiority, their ruthless efficiency, and their utter disregard for collateral damage made them a formidable adversary. Niko wasn't a soldier; he was an ecologist, a scientist. His expertise lay in understanding and preserving life, not in destroying it. Yet, the possibility of Veridia falling under OmniCorp's control, of its unique biodiversity being systematically eradicated or exploited, was a far greater threat than any direct confrontation.

He looked at Kira again. Her tail gave another gentle thump. She was ready for whatever came next, her loyalty unwavering. She was a constant reminder of the primal, intrinsic value of life, a value that OmniCorp seemed determined to obliterate in its pursuit of unchecked expansion. The echoes of home, the whispers from Earth, had indeed brought a warning. But they had also brought something else: a choice. A choice between retreating to safety and abandoning a world that had become, in its own unique way, a part of them, or standing their ground, defending not just their mission, but the very principle of interdimensional harmony.

The implications of the message were far-reaching. If OmniCorp was escalating its activities to this degree, it meant that the threat was no longer theoretical. It was imminent. And if reinforcements were being discussed, it implied a recognition of this imminent threat by those back on Earth. But how quickly could these reinforcements be mobilized? And would they arrive in time? The vast distances and the complexities of interdimensional travel meant that "soon" could still translate to "too late" in the grand scheme of things.

He began to draft a preliminary report, detailing his assessment of the situation on Veridia and outlining the potential risks and benefits of various response scenarios. He focused on the ecological impact of a potential military deployment, advocating for smaller, specialized teams if any were to be sent. He also highlighted the importance of maintaining a continuous scientific presence, even if additional security measures were implemented. The knowledge they had gained on Veridia was too valuable to abandon, and the protection of its unique biosphere was paramount.

As he worked, he couldn't help but reflect on the irony of it all. They had ventured into the interdimensional unknown seeking knowledge, seeking to expand humanity's understanding of the universe. Now, they were facing the very real possibility of becoming unwilling participants in an interdimensional conflict, a conflict sparked by greed and a lust for power. The path of exploration, it seemed, was rarely a peaceful one.

Kira yawned, a soft, breathy sound that seemed to punctuate the gravity of his thoughts. She stretched, her muscles rippling beneath her fur, before settling back down, her head resting on her paws. Her quiet presence was a constant anchor. She was a reminder of what was truly at stake: the simple, unadulterated beauty of life, in all its myriad forms. The whispers from Earth had brought a call to action, a potential call for reinforcements. But for Niko and Kira, on the vibrant, living world of Veridia, the call was also a call to protect the home they had found, and to stand firm against the encroaching darkness. The decision weighed heavily on him, a moral and strategic calculus with consequences that would ripple across dimensions.

CHAPTER NINE
THE SHIFTING THRESHOLDS

The subtle tremors began not with a jolt, but with a disconcerting whisper. Niko, engrossed in recalibrating the habitat's atmospheric scrubbers, barely registered the initial shift. It was Kira, however, who reacted first. Her low growl, a sound rarely heard outside of territorial warnings or particularly unsettling meteor showers, rumbled in her chest. Her ears, usually perked in attentive curiosity, flattened against her skull, and her tail tucked tightly between her legs. She whined, a soft, pleading sound, and pressed herself closer to Niko's side, her body rigid with an apprehension he hadn't witnessed since their initial descent into Veridia's chaotic, storm-ridden canyons.

He paused, his hand hovering over a complex array of conduits. "What is it, girl?" he murmured, his voice laced with concern. He scanned the habitat's internal diagnostics. Air pressure: nominal. Gravitational field: stable. Ambient temperature: within optimal parameters. Nothing on the readouts suggested any cause for alarm. Yet, Kira's distress was palpable, a tangible wave emanating from her that set his own teeth on edge. It was more than just an animal's heightened senses; it was a primal scream against an unseen threat. He remembered the preliminary xenobiological reports, the theories regarding the potential for certain sentient or highly evolved species to possess a form of resonance sensitivity, an ability to perceive subtle energetic shifts in their environment, particularly those related to dimensional or quantum fluctuations. Kira, with her unique lineage and deep connection to Veridia, was proving to be far more than just a companion; she was an early warning system.

He knelt, stroking her sleek, dark fur. "Easy, girl. What are you feeling?" He tried to project calmness, but a knot of unease began to tighten in his own stomach. Kira's sensitivity was usually a source of comfort, a subtle barometer of Veridia's serene rhythms. Now, it felt like a klaxon blaring in the darkness. She shivered, her amber eyes wide and fixed on the primary viewport, her gaze seemingly piercing through the reinforced transparisteel to the alien landscape beyond. The vibrant amethyst hues of the Veridian flora, usually a source of visual delight, now seemed to hold a sinister undertone, as if the very light was beginning to flicker with instability.

He followed her gaze. The twin moons, their ethereal glow a constant presence in Veridia's twilight sky, seemed to shimmer with an unnatural intensity. It was subtle, almost imperceptible, but once he focused on it, he couldn't unsee it. A wavering, like heat haze rising from asphalt, seemed to distort the edges of the celestial bodies. He accessed the external atmospheric sensors, cross-referencing them with the habitat's chronometers. Everything appeared to be within established parameters, yet the visual anomaly persisted.

"Gateway diagnostics," he commanded the habitat's AI. "Run a full spectrum analysis. Focus on energy signatures and dimensional flux."

The AI's synthesized voice responded with its usual calm efficiency, a stark contrast to the growing tension in the room. "Initiating full spectrum analysis of Gateway Alpha. Initial readings indicate a steady, stable energy flow, consistent with baseline parameters."

Kira whined again, a more insistent sound this time, and nudged his hand with her wet nose, her gaze darting from the viewport to the main console where the gateway readings were displayed. It was a silent, desperate plea. He trusted her instincts implicitly. If she was this agitated, something was fundamentally wrong. He zoomed in on the gateway schematics on the console, scrutinizing the intricate web of energy conduits and resonance stabilizers that kept their portal to Earth ajar.

Then he saw it. Amidst the steady hum of the gateway's operational cycle, there were minute, almost imperceptible spikes. They were random, fleeting, and entirely out of character for the meticulously controlled interdimensional transit system. It was as if tiny hiccups were occurring in the fabric of spacetime itself, infinitesimal tears that briefly disrupted the flow of energy. He magnified the readings, isolating the anomalies. They were short-lived, lasting only milliseconds, but their frequency was increasing.

"Show me historical data for Gateway Alpha," Niko instructed, his voice tightening. "Compare current flux readings against established norms for the past three cycles."

The AI processed the request, and a new graph appeared on the screen, overlaying the real-time data with historical averages. The contrast was stark. While the historical data showed a smooth, almost monotonous line of stability, the current readings were a jagged, erratic mess. The spikes were no longer infinitesimal; they were clearly defined bursts of energy, brief but potent, that seemed to ripple outwards from the gateway's core.

"What is causing these fluctuations?" Niko pressed.

"Analysis inconclusive," the AI replied. "The energy signatures are anomalous. They do not correspond to known interdimensional transit phenomena, nor do they match signatures associated with external environmental factors within expected ranges. There are also localized distortions in the dimensional fabric, extremely brief and minute, appearing in proximity to the gateway's nexus point."

Localized distortions. Brief. Minute. The words echoed in Niko's mind, each one a hammer blow against the precarious stability of their situation.

He recalled the OmniCorp transmissions, the veiled threats, the hints of advanced, disruptive technologies. Had their previous interference, the subtle probes they had conducted with their cloaked drones, somehow left a lingering residue? Or was this something far more profound, something inherent to the very act of interdimensional traversal that they had not yet fully understood? The gateways were not simply portals; they were delicate bridges built on the quantum entanglement of disparate realities. Any disruption to that delicate balance could have catastrophic consequences.

He looked back at Kira. Her distress had intensified. She was now pacing the habitat, a low, guttural whine escaping her throat, her tail still tucked, her body tense. She was more than just sensing danger; she was actively recoiling from it, as if the very air around the gateway was becoming toxic. This was not just a technical problem; it was an existential one.

"Run a resonance sensitivity correlation," Niko commanded, a desperate hope rising within him. "Cross-reference Kira's agitation levels with the gateway's flux readings."

The AI's response was almost immediate. "Correlation established. Kira's physiological stress indicators, specifically elevated heart rate and neural resonance frequencies, directly align with the detected energy spikes and localized distortions within Gateway Alpha. The intensity of her distress appears to be proportional to the magnitude of the gateway anomalies."

It was a confirmation he both dreaded and needed. Kira's advanced sensitivity was acting as a magnified lens, translating the imperceptible shifts in the gateway into a language of pure, unadulterated fear. The gateway wasn't just malfunctioning; it was actively *hurting* her, or at least, causing her immense discomfort. This meant the anomalies were not just fleeting technical glitches; they were significant enough to affect a being as attuned to Veridia's energetic symphony as Kira.

Niko brought up a visual representation of the gateway's nexus. Instead of the smooth, flowing lines of interdimensional energy he was accustomed to seeing, the visualization was now peppered with tiny, ephemeral flickers of discordant color, brief flashes of static that disrupted the otherwise harmonious flow. It was like watching a perfect, crystalline structure begin to fracture.

"Can you isolate the source of these energy spikes?" Niko asked, his voice low and strained.

"The spikes appear to be originating from within the gateway's stabilization matrix," the AI reported. "However, the energy signatures are unlike any known operational or diagnostic frequencies. There are also indications of temporal displacement anomalies occurring in conjunction with the energy bursts, though the duration is within femtoseconds."

Temporal displacement. The phrase sent a shiver down Niko's spine. It suggested that the gateway wasn't just experiencing energy fluctuations; it was momentarily stuttering in time, brief pauses or accelerations in its temporal flow. This was far beyond anything that should be happening. It hinted at a fundamental instability, a breakdown in the very physics that underpinned their interdimensional connection. The implications were terrifying. A gateway that was unstable in both energy and time was not a reliable conduit; it was a potential trap, a doorway that could unpredictably snap shut, fragment, or even, in the worst-case scenario, deposit travelers in an unknown point in spacetime, or worse, in a state of quantum de-coherence.

He thought back to the OmniCorp transmissions. They had spoken of "gateway stabilization protocols" and "resonance disruption technologies." Had OmniCorp's earlier, seemingly minor incursions been a prelude to a more direct attack, not on Veridia itself, but on the very access point that connected it to Earth? The idea that they could weaponize the gateways, destabilizing them to the point of rendering them unusable or dangerously unpredictable, was a chilling prospect. It would effectively cut off any reinforcements, any support, and strand them here, isolated and vulnerable.

"Niko," Kira whined, nudging his hand again, her large eyes pleading. He looked down at her, her distress a mirror of his own growing fear. He knew he had to do something. He couldn't stand by and watch as the portal, their only link to home and their only hope for additional resources, devolved into a source of chaos and danger.

He initiated a deeper diagnostic scan, pushing the AI to analyze the harmonic resonance frequencies of the gateway's core components. "I need to know if there's any degradation in the quantum entanglement anchors," he stated, his voice firm despite the tremor of anxiety that ran through him. "And I want a predictive model for gateway stability over the next seventy-two hours, assuming current anomaly trends continue."

The AI's response was a cascade of data, complex waveforms and probability matrices that painted a grim picture. "Analysis of quantum entanglement anchors indicates a subtle but progressive decoherence. The initial stability factor was at 0.9998. It has now decreased to 0.9972. Predictive model suggests a 63.7% probability of critical gateway instability within seventy-two hours, manifesting as unpredictable energy surges and localized spacetime distortions of significant magnitude."

Sixty-three point seven percent. That was more than a coin flip. It was a clear and present danger. The gateway was not just showing anomalies; it was actively degrading. The unique vibrational signature of Veridia, the very essence of its being that the gateway was designed to resonate with, was perhaps being overwhelmed or distorted by something external. OmniCorp's interference was a strong candidate, but the thought lingered: could Veridia itself, in its own profound and alien way, be reacting to something? Had their presence, or OmniCorp's actions, somehow disturbed a deeper, more fundamental layer of this interdimensional nexus?

He looked out at the amethyst landscape. The vibrant colors, once a symbol of life and wonder, now seemed to pulse with an unsettling energy. The air, usually alive with the gentle hum of biological processes, felt charged, expectant. The beautiful, tranquil world had suddenly acquired a sharp, dangerous edge, and the gateway, their lifeline, was becoming the epicenter of that peril. The shifting thresholds were not merely political or strategic; they were physical, manifesting in the very fabric of reality that bound Veridia to their own. The amethyst hues outside now seemed tinged with a dangerous unpredictability, a warning that the very doors of perception were beginning to warp. This was no longer just about defense; it was about survival, and the immediate threat was at their very doorstep, or rather, at their very nexus point. The anomaly readings were a symphony of chaos, and Kira, the most sensitive instrument in their possession, was conducting the terrifying overture.

The faint, almost imperceptible tremors had escalated. Niko had been meticulously reinforcing the atmospheric seals around the habitat's primary observation dome, a task that had become routine following the initial Gateway fluctuations. Kira, however, was anything but routine. Her usual curiosity had curdled into a perpetual state of alert. A low, guttural rumble was now her constant companion, a sound that emanated from her chest whenever the ambient energy readings spiked, however minutely. Her amber eyes, once pools of serene intelligence, now darted constantly towards the viewport, tracking unseen disturbances in the twilight air.

It had started with visual anomalies. Fleeting shimmers at the periphery of vision, like heat haze dancing over an unseen fire. Then came the auditory intrusions – a high-pitched whine that seemed to resonate from beyond the habitat's hull, or a series of sharp, percussive clicks that defied any logical source within Veridia's established ecosystem. Niko had initially attributed them to sensory overload, a cumulative effect of prolonged exposure to an alien biosphere coupled with the stress of the Gateway's instability. But Kira's reactions were too specific, too visceral, to be dismissed. She would tense, her hackles rising, a low growl building in her throat, her gaze fixed on a point in the distance, as if confronting an invisible assailant.

One cycle, while Niko was calibrating the nutrient dispensers for the hydroponic flora, a soft, resonant chime echoed through the habitat. It was melodic, ethereal, and utterly alien. It lasted only a second, but it was enough to send Kira into a frenzy. She lunged towards the viewport, barking, her body a coiled spring of defensive energy. The pack, usually so stoic, responded in kind. Barkar, the grizzled veteran, let out a series of sharp, warning barks, his massive frame tensed. Luna, normally the most placid of the group, emitted a distressed yelp, pressing close to Niko's legs. Even the normally aloof Kaelen whined, his ears swiveling towards the source of the sound, a bewildered confusion in his intelligent eyes.

Niko rushed to the viewport, his heart pounding. He scanned the amethyst landscape, looking for any visual cue, any disturbance that could explain Kira's extreme reaction. The twin moons cast their familiar, gentle glow, and the phosphorescent flora pulsed with its steady rhythm. Nothing. Yet, Kira's agitation was undeniable. She paced the habitat, a low growl vibrating in her chest, her gaze unwavering, as if an invisible entity was still taunting them from beyond the reinforced transparisteel.

"What is it, girl?" Niko murmured, kneeling to try and soothe her. He ran a hand over her sleek fur, feeling the tension in her muscles. "What did you see?"

Kira whined, nudging his hand, then turned her head back towards the viewport, her amber eyes wide with a primal fear. It was then that Niko noticed it, not through his own eyes, but through Kira's focused gaze. A subtle distortion, like a ripple in water, had momentarily appeared in the sky, directly above the jagged peaks of the Crimson Spires. It was gone as quickly as it had appeared, but Kira's reaction confirmed its reality.

He brought up the external atmospheric and energy sensors. They registered no significant anomalies. No atmospheric pressure changes, no unusual energy signatures, no temporal displacements beyond the minuscule fluctuations that had become disturbingly common. Yet, the 'bleed-through' events, as he had begun to call them, were increasing in frequency and intensity. It was as if the dimensional barriers, once thought to be robust and impenetrable, were becoming porous, allowing ephemeral fragments of other realities to intrude upon their own.

"Gateway diagnostics," Niko commanded, his voice tight with a new urgency. "Run a comparative analysis of ambient sensory data with historical records from pre-Gateway fluctuations. Focus on localized, transient phenomena."

The habitat's AI responded, its synthesized voice a calm counterpoint to the rising dread in Niko's gut. "Analysis complete. Detected a series of non-localized, transient auditory and visual anomalies. These events exhibit characteristics inconsistent with known Veridian environmental phenomena. Power signatures are negligible, temporal deviation is within previously established parameters of femtosecond fluctuation. However, a correlation has been established between these detected anomalies and elevated stress indicators in the domesticated Canid subjects."

In simpler terms: the strange sounds and sights were real, not imagined, and they were clearly affecting Kira and the pack. The 'bleed-through' wasn't just a theoretical concept anymore; it was a tangible phenomenon, a ghostly whisper from another dimension that was unnerving the very creatures most attuned to Veridia's natural rhythms.

Niko's mind raced, piecing together the fragmented data. The Gateway Alpha, their link to Earth, was the focal point of these instabilities. The energy spikes, the temporal hiccups, and now these sensory intrusions – they were all symptoms of a deepening malaise. He recalled OmniCorp's veiled threats, their boasts of advanced technologies capable of "destabilizing nexus points." Had their previous interference, their attempts to probe and potentially manipulate the Gateway, created hairline fractures in the interdimensional membrane?

He activated the habitat's external visual recorders, scrubbing through the logs from the past few cycles. He found them: fleeting moments of iridescent light, impossible geometric shapes that flickered into existence for a nanosecond, and then vanished. Once, he even detected a faint, melancholic melody, a sound that seemed to tug at a forgotten memory, before it was swallowed by the Veridian wind. Each intrusion was subtle, easily dismissed as a trick of the light or a quirk of atmospheric conditions, but in retrospect, they painted a disturbing picture of a reality under siege.

Kira, sensing his renewed focus, nudged his hand again, her growl subsiding into a low, questioning whine. Niko knelt and stroked her head. "It's okay, girl," he said, though he didn't entirely believe it himself. "We're going to figure this out. We have to."

He initiated a containment protocol, a series of measures designed to reinforce the habitat's internal shielding and minimize any potential for external sensory bleed-through. It was a temporary fix, a band-aid on a rapidly growing wound, but it was all he could do with the resources at hand. The pack seemed to understand. They moved with a renewed sense of purpose, their initial fear replaced by a quiet vigilance. Barkar took up a position near the main airlock, his low growl a constant deterrent. Luna and Kaelen patrolled the perimeter of the habitat's interior, their senses on high alert. Kira, however, remained by Niko's side, her amber eyes fixed on the viewport, a silent sentinel against the encroaching strangeness.

"The dimensional barriers are not as stable as we presumed," Niko mused aloud, more to himself than to the AI. "The act of maintaining a stable interdimensional connection... it must require a constant, immense expenditure of energy, a delicate balancing act. And any disruption, any external force, can cause those balances to falter."

He thought about the theoretical physics behind the Gateway technology. It relied on quantum entanglement, on a delicate resonance between two distinct points in spacetime. It was a bridge built on the very fabric of reality, and like any bridge, it was vulnerable to stress. OmniCorp's interference had clearly put that stress on the system, causing the initial fluctuations. But now, it felt like something more. The bleed-through events, the subtle yet persistent intrusions, suggested that the stress was not just confined to the Gateway itself, but was beginning to warp the dimensional fabric surrounding it, creating fleeting apertures into adjacent realities.

He remembered a lecture from his xenobotanist days, discussing how certain deep-sea organisms could perceive electromagnetic fields far beyond the human spectrum. They lived in a world of unseen forces, a symphony of energy that dictated their existence. Veridia, in its own way, was just as complex, just as filled with unseen energies. And the Gateway was a focal point, a place where those energies converged and, perhaps, began to break down.

The next few cycles were a tense ballet of vigilance and containment. The sensory intrusions continued, some more unnerving than others. A brief, spectral fog that smelled faintly of ozone and something metallic. A chorus of whispers that seemed to emanate from the very walls of the habitat, speaking in a language that was utterly incomprehensible, yet filled with a palpable sense of sorrow. Kira, in particular, bore the brunt of it. Her growls became more frequent, her sleep fitful. She would often wake with a start, a low whine escaping her, her body trembling as if she had witnessed a nightmare made real.

Niko noticed a subtle change in her behavior. She began to spend more time near the Gateway's containment field, not out of curiosity, but out of a strange, almost protective instinct. She would sit for hours, her gaze fixed on the shimmering energy nexus, as if trying to understand or perhaps even mend the tears in reality that were manifesting there. It was a profound display of her connection to the very fabric of their existence.

One evening, as Veridia's twilight deepened, a particularly disturbing anomaly occurred. A section of the habitat's secondary viewport flickered, and for a brief, terrifying moment, the amethyst landscape outside was replaced by a scene of stark, skeletal trees under a sky the color of dried blood. A single, crimson sun hung low on the horizon, casting long, ominous shadows. The air within the habitat grew cold, and a scent of decay, acrid and primal, filled the space.

Kira let out a piercing howl, a sound of pure terror that echoed through the habitat. Barkar responded with a series of thunderous roars, his teeth bared, his body a rigid wall of muscle. Luna and Kaelen cowered behind Niko, their whines a chorus of distress. The pack, despite their training and their resilience, were clearly overwhelmed.

Niko felt a primal fear grip him. This wasn't just a visual glitch; it was an invasion, a glimpse into a hostile, alien reality that had momentarily breached their defenses. He fumbled for the emergency override, his fingers clumsy with adrenaline. He slammed his hand down on the button, initiating a full-spectrum energy surge to reinforce the viewport's shielding.

The spectral landscape vanished as quickly as it had appeared, replaced by the familiar, albeit now unsettling, amethyst hues of Veridia. The chilling cold receded, and the acrid smell dissipated, leaving behind only the faint scent of recycled air and the lingering tang of fear. Kira, her body still trembling, pressed herself against Niko's leg, her low growls a constant, reassuring rumble.

He looked at the pack, their amber eyes wide with a shared trauma. They had faced down meteor showers, navigated treacherous canyons, and endured the psychological toll of isolation, but this was different. This was an assault on their very sense of reality, a constant, insidious erosion of the boundaries that kept them safe.

"The bleed-through is escalating," Niko stated, his voice grim. "We can't just reinforce the habitat. We need to understand what's causing it, and more importantly, how to stop it."

He knew, with a chilling certainty, that the Gateway Alpha was not merely malfunctioning. It was becoming a conduit for something far more chaotic, a bridge between worlds that were not meant to be crossed. OmniCorp's actions, whether intentional or not, had destabilized the delicate equilibrium, and now, the very foundations of their reality were beginning to fray. The dimensional thresholds were shifting, not gradually, but with terrifying, unpredictable lurches, and the consequences of these breaches were only just beginning to manifest. He looked at Kira, her steady gaze a silent testament to her unwavering loyalty and her keen perception. She was their early warning system, their living barometer of the encroaching darkness, and her fear was a stark reflection of the danger they all faced. The beautiful, alien world of Veridia, once a sanctuary, was becoming a battleground, and the enemy was not an external force, but the very fabric of existence itself. The subtle tremors had become violent shudders, and the whispers were growing into a cacophony that threatened to shatter their fragile existence.

The growing unease within the habitat had, for Niko, coalesced into a stark, chilling suspicion. The 'bleed-through' events, the ephemeral breaches in reality that were unsettling Kira and the pack, were becoming too frequent, too pronounced, to be mere accidents of quantum entanglement gone awry. He found himself replaying OmniCorp's past actions, their insistent probing of the Gateway, their thinly veiled threats regarding the 'strategic importance' of the nexus point. Their technology, developed for resource extraction and planetary subjugation, was inherently crude, a blunt instrument designed to force nature into submission rather than work in harmony with it. Was it possible that their previous attempts to manipulate the Gateway had not just caused temporary instability, but had inflicted lasting damage, like a clumsy surgeon leaving behind a permanent weakness?

He considered the sheer audacity of OmniCorp's corporate philosophy. They operated on a principle of dominance, viewing every new frontier not as a marvel to be understood, but as a resource to be exploited. The interdimensional nexus, the Gateway Alpha, represented an unimaginable power source, a potential key to unlocking technologies that could dwarf anything humanity had ever conceived. It was a prize worth any risk, and for a corporation like OmniCorp, conventional risks were merely calculated expenditures. But what if they weren't just gambling? What if they were actively exacerbating the problem?

Niko envisioned their engineers, hunched over consoles, monitoring the Gateway's energy fluctuations. They would have seen the initial instabilities, the localized spacetime distortions, the subtle temporal anomalies. Instead of retreating, instead of acknowledging the delicate nature of what they were dealing with, they might have seen it as an opportunity. An opportunity to push further, to force the Gateway open, or to destabilize it to a point where only *their* specialized technology could "stabilize" it – and thus, control it. The idea was terrifyingly plausible. OmniCorp had a history of creating crises and then presenting themselves as the sole solution.

He began to correlate the increased frequency of the bleed-through events with OmniCorp's known operational timelines. Their orbital presence had been significantly amplified in the weeks leading up to the most severe anomalies. Their scout ships, cloaked and seemingly idle, were in constant proximity to the Gateway's projected energy signature. It was too coincidental. It felt less like the random hiccups of a damaged system and more like deliberate, targeted interference.

"AI," Niko began, his voice low, "Run a comparative analysis of OmniCorp orbital telemetry data with the timestamps of the most significant dimensional bleed-through events. Focus on any correlated sensor readings or energy emissions from OmniCorp vessels in the vicinity of the Gateway nexus."

The AI hummed, its processing units whirring softly. "Analysis in progress. Cross-referencing OmniCorp flight logs, active sensor sweeps, and passive energy signatures against localized temporal-spatial anomaly records. Preliminary findings indicate a statistically significant correlation between periods of high OmniCorp sensor activity and increased frequency and intensity of detected interdimensional bleed-through phenomena."

Niko's gut tightened. The AI's measured, objective language was more chilling than any expletive he could have uttered. It wasn't just a hunch; it was data. OmniCorp was actively involved, their presence a catalyst for the very instability they had likely created in the first place. This was no longer just about survival; it was about defending their small corner of reality from deliberate aggression.

The nature of the threat had shifted. It was no longer an abstract concern about the fragility of dimensions or the unintended consequences of advanced technology. It was a direct confrontation, albeit one fought on a battlefield of quantum mechanics and esoteric energies. OmniCorp, with its insatiable hunger for power and control, saw the Gateway not as a bridge, but as a weapon, or at the very least, a unique and exploitable resource. Their approach, blunt and exploitative, was anathema to the intricate, almost organic balance that seemed to govern the interdimensional nexus.

He thought about the pack, their reactions to the anomalies. Kira's terror, Barkar's protective roars, Luna and Kaelen's distress. They were sensitive to these shifts, their instincts screaming that something was profoundly wrong. They weren't just reacting to spooky phenomena; they were reacting to a violation. A violation of the natural order, a disruption of the subtle energies that held their reality together. And now, Niko understood that this violation was not solely the result of a damaged system, but a deliberate act of aggression.

"The stakes have changed," Niko murmured, running a hand through his hair. "It's not just about the Gateway failing. It's about OmniCorp *making* it fail. Or worse, making it work in a way that benefits them, no matter the cost to us, or to Veridia."

The implications were staggering. If OmniCorp was actively manipulating the Gateway, they might possess the means to control the bleed-through events, to direct them, or even to weaponize them. Imagine, Niko thought, a reality's edge being pushed, a neighboring dimension's hostile environment being projected onto their own, not as a fleeting glimpse, but as a sustained invasion. It was a terrifying prospect, and one that made their small habitat feel even more vulnerable.

He looked at Kira, who was watching him with an intelligent intensity in her amber eyes. She seemed to sense the gravity of his thoughts, the shift in his focus from passive observation to active defense. Her growl, usually a low rumble of unease, now carried a distinct edge of defiance. She was not merely a victim of these anomalies; she was a guardian, a sentinel attuned to the subtle shifts in their reality.

Niko initiated a new series of protocols, not just for containment, but for active defense. He began recalibrating the habitat's energy shielding, not to simply block external intrusions, but to actively counter and repel specific energy signatures. It was a long shot, based on theoretical physics and an educated guess about OmniCorp's methods, but it was a necessary step. He was no longer just an explorer; he was a defender of his own reality.

"AI, begin analysis of OmniCorp's known energy projection technologies," Niko commanded, his voice firm. "Specifically, focus on any systems capable of generating localized reality distortions or interdimensional resonance fields. I need to understand how they might be weaponizing the Gateway, or how they might attempt to control its inherent instability."

The AI acknowledged, its synthesized voice a calm counterpoint to the storm brewing in Niko's mind. "Processing query. Accessing OmniCorp R&D archives and theoretical weaponization protocols. Analysis may require significant computational resources and time."

"Time is something we may not have much of," Niko replied, glancing at the viewport. The amethyst landscape of Veridia, once a symbol of hope and discovery, now seemed to hold a hidden tension, a subtle awareness of the encroaching darkness. The pack, sensing his resolve, had shifted from a state of anxious vigilance to one of quiet readiness. Barkar stood by the main airlock, a formidable silhouette of protective readiness. Luna and Kaelen had taken up positions at strategic points, their ears swiveling, their senses extended. Kira remained by his side, a constant, comforting presence, her amber eyes reflecting the glow of the habitat's consoles, a silent promise of unwavering loyalty.

The OmniCorp gambit, as Niko now saw it, was a multi-layered deception. First, they had damaged the Gateway, perhaps accidentally, perhaps through deliberate sabotage. Then, they had allowed the initial instabilities to manifest, creating an atmosphere of concern and uncertainty. Now, they were likely amplifying those instabilities, not only to mask their continued interference but to create a scenario where they could swoop in, claim control, and exploit the Gateway for their own nefarious purposes. They were the arsonists who then offered to sell the fire extinguishers.

He remembered the xenobotanist's lecture again. The deep-sea organisms perceiving unseen forces. Their existence was a testament to the fact that reality was far more nuanced, far more layered, than what could be perceived by conventional senses. The Gateway was a point of connection, a bridge between these layers. To exploit it with OmniCorp's crude methods was akin to trying to reroute a complex river system with a bulldozer. The inevitable result was not control, but chaos, and OmniCorp seemed to be reveling in that chaos, using it as a smokescreen for their own machinations.

The thought of OmniCorp wielding such power, of them being able to dictate the very fabric of reality, sent a shiver down his spine. They represented the worst of humanity's tendencies: greed, unchecked ambition, and a profound disregard for the natural world, whether terrestrial or otherworldly. Their interference wasn't just a threat to their mission; it was a threat to the very possibility of coexisting with Veridia, with its unique biosphere and its unfathomable secrets.

Niko knew that their mission had irrevocably changed. It was no longer solely about scientific exploration or establishing a foothold for humanity. It was about preservation. Preservation of their habitat, preservation of the delicate balance of Veridia, and perhaps, in a larger sense, preservation of a reality that had been threatened by the avarice of a single corporation. The pack looked to him, their trust absolute, their reliance on his leadership unwavering. He couldn't let them down. He had to unravel OmniCorp's gambit, to expose their destructive machinations, and to protect the gateway, not as a prize to be claimed, but as a wonder to be understood and respected. The shifting thresholds were not just a natural phenomenon; they were a battlefield, and OmniCorp had just declared war.

The low thrum of the habitat's life support systems, once a comforting lullaby, had begun to grate on Kira's nerves. It was more than just the pervasive hum; it was the subtle, almost imperceptible discordance that had crept into everything. A dissonant undertone beneath the familiar symphony of their artificial environment. For weeks, it had been a whisper, a fleeting sensation that flickered at the edges of her awareness, easily dismissed as stress or fatigue. But now, the whisper had become a persistent buzz, a constant, irritating static that seemed to permeate the very air she breathed.

Her sleep, once deep and restorative, was now fractured. Nightmares, not of predators or territorial disputes, but of shimmering, unstable geometries and a gnawing sense of wrongness, plagued her rest. She would wake with a jolt, her heart hammering against her ribs, her fur bristling, not from any immediate threat, but from the lingering echo of the disquiet that had seeped into her dreams. The edges of her vision seemed to shimmer, as if the very fabric of reality was thinning, allowing glimpses of something... other. It was disorienting, unsettling, and exhausting.

During their waking hours, the intensified bleed-through events were more than just visual or auditory disturbances; they were visceral experiences for Kira. The brief, flickering incursions from other dimensional strata would send waves of disquiet through her. A sudden chill that had nothing to do with the habitat's temperature, a phantom scent of ozone and decay, or a fleeting visual distortion that made the familiar walls of their living space momentarily warp and twist. These weren't just fleeting anomalies for her; they were assaults on her senses, each one leaving her more drained than the last.

Her once razor-sharp senses, honed by generations of instinct and attuned to the subtle nuances of Veridia's alien ecology, were being blunted by the sheer energetic noise. The rich tapestry of scents that usually told her the story of the habitat – the faint metallic tang of the recycling unit, the earthy notes of the hydroponic gardens, the individual bio-signatures of Niko and the others – was now muddled, overlaid with an alien, disquieting aroma that defied categorization. It was like trying to listen to a whispered conversation in the middle of a thunderclap. The individual sounds were lost in the overwhelming cacophony.

Niko noticed the change with a growing knot of concern in his stomach. He watched Kira's once fluid movements become slightly more hesitant, her typically vibrant amber eyes clouded with a weariness that no amount of rest seemed to alleviate. She would often lie curled in her designated spot, her breathing shallow, her ears occasionally twitching as if trying to pinpoint a sound that wasn't there, or perhaps one that was too pervasive to ignore. The playful nips and nudges she offered him were fewer, and when she did engage, there was a noticeable lack of her usual enthusiastic vigor.

"Kira?" he would murmur, stroking her sleek, dark fur. "Are you alright, girl?"

She would lift her head, her gaze meeting his, and he would see a flicker of the familiar intelligence and trust, but it was always shadowed by that pervasive fatigue. A soft whine would escape her, a sound more of distress than complaint, and she would press closer to him, seeking solace in his proximity. It was in these moments that Niko felt the weight of his responsibility most acutely. They were a pack, bound by more than just shared living space; they were a symbiotic unit, their well-being intertwined.

He began to adjust her routine, instinctively seeking ways to mitigate the unseen pressures that were clearly affecting her. He increased the duration of her rest periods, ensuring she had uninterrupted time in her favorite, quiet corners of the habitat. He also began a series of specialized treatments, drawing on the limited xenobotanical knowledge he possessed and his understanding of bio-energetic resonance. He synthesized a mild, calming elixir from a locally sourced Veridian moss known for its subtle sedative properties, mixing it with purified water and offering it to her.

"Drink up, Kira," he'd coax, holding the bowl to her muzzle. "This will help you rest."

She would drink, her thirst overriding her lethargy, and he would watch, a silent prayer on his lips that it would bring her some measure of peace. He also implemented stricter protocols for managing the habitat's internal energy fields, attempting to dampen any residual energetic bleed-through that might be agitating her. He rerouted secondary power conduits, installed additional harmonic dampeners salvaged from their initial survey equipment, and even experimented with generating a counter-frequency hum designed to mask the most disruptive alien resonances. It was a painstaking process, a constant fiddling with the habitat's internal environment, an attempt to create a pocket of calm within the encroaching storm.

He found himself spending hours just observing her, analyzing her posture, her breathing patterns, her subtle shifts in temperature. He correlated her periods of heightened agitation with the more pronounced bleed-through events, noting that immediately after a particularly severe anomaly, Kira would be noticeably more withdrawn and listless. Her fatigue wasn't just a personal matter; it was a diagnostic tool, an incredibly sensitive barometer for the escalating crisis at the Gateway Alpha.

This realization struck Niko with a profound sense of awe and trepidation. Kira, and by extension the rest of the pack, were not merely passive observers of the dimensional shifts. Their biological systems, attuned to the subtle energies of their environment, were deeply affected by the instability. Her suffering was a direct, physical manifestation of the Gateway's compromised state. It was a stark, undeniable demonstration of the intricate symbiosis that existed not only between the pack members, but between their very beings and the fundamental forces of their adopted world.

He remembered the xenobotanist's lectures about Veridia's interconnected ecosystems, how every organism, from the colossal sky-whales to the microscopic nutrient-cycling fungi, played a vital role. He had understood it intellectually, but seeing it play out in Kira's health brought a new, urgent dimension to that understanding. Her well-being was not just a matter of companionship; it was intrinsically linked to the stability of the Gateway, and by extension, to the safety of their entire operation, and perhaps even to the very integrity of their localized reality.

The thought was both terrifying and galvanizing. If Kira's health was a direct indicator, then her declining state was a flashing red siren, screaming that the situation was far worse than he had initially feared. OmniCorp's interference, whatever its current manifestation, was not just creating abstract disruptions; it was actively harming the living beings they had come to protect and understand. It was an ethical violation as much as a scientific one.

He began to see Kira not just as his companion, but as a living embodiment of the Gateway's fragility. Her psychic strain was not an isolated incident, but a symptom of a larger disease that was afflicting their reality. The more she suffered, the more the Gateway was being pushed, the more the barriers between dimensions were being eroded. Her fatigue was the cost of those breaches, her anxiety the echo of alien energies bleeding into their own.

"AI," Niko said, his voice low, his gaze fixed on Kira, who was now peacefully, though still shallowly, breathing on her resting mat. "Initiate a comparative study. Track Kira's physiological data – heart rate, neural activity, stress hormone levels – against the recorded intensity and frequency of dimensional bleed-through events. I want to see the precise correlation."

The AI responded with its usual measured cadence. "Processing. Cross-referencing Kira's bio-metric logs with Gateway anomaly datasets. Establishing baseline metrics for energetic stress tolerance. This analysis will require significant comparative processing power."

"Do it," Niko commanded, his jaw tightening. "Every bit of data helps. Her health is not just about her; it's about understanding the damage being done. It's about quantifying the cost of OmniCorp's recklessness."

He knelt beside Kira, gently stroking her head. She stirred slightly, a soft sigh escaping her. He could feel the faint tremor of her muscles beneath his fingertips, a sign of underlying tension even in her sleep. The soft glow of the habitat's internal lights reflected in her closed eyelids. He imagined the chaotic energies swirling outside, the invisible battle being waged at the nexus, and how it was all funneled through Kira, amplified and translated into physical distress.

He recalled the scientific principle of sympathetic resonance, how objects could vibrate in response to external frequencies, even without direct contact. Kira was a living antenna, her sophisticated biological system picking up the discordant frequencies emanating from the destabilized Gateway, responding to them with distress. It was a profound, albeit painful, testament to her connection to Veridia and its foundational energies.

The thought of her suffering, however, fueled a new resolve within him. He couldn't stand by and watch her weaken, knowing that her decline was a direct symptom of an external, malicious force. His mission had always been one of discovery and understanding, of forging a peaceful coexistence. But now, that mission had a new, urgent imperative: protection. Protection of Kira, protection of the pack, and protection of the delicate balance that OmniCorp seemed intent on shattering.

He considered the ethical implications of their presence. Had their own activities, however well-intentioned, contributed to the Gateway's instability? He tried to push the thought away, focusing on the immediate threat. OmniCorp's actions were demonstrably deliberate, their past behavior a clear indicator of their exploitative nature. They weren't just probing a phenomenon; they were actively weaponizing it, or at the very least, recklessly destabilizing it for their own gain, and Kira was bearing the brunt of that reckless assault.

He decided to implement more rigorous containment protocols, not just for the habitat's external shielding, but for Kira's immediate environment. He began creating a small, localized 'calm zone' within their living quarters, using materials that had demonstrated a higher degree of energetic dampening. He carefully arranged polished obsidian-like rocks, known for their absorptive properties, around her resting area, and suspended a precisely tuned harmonic resonator, a device originally designed for planetary surveying, above her mat, set to emit a low, steady frequency intended to counter the disruptive alien wavelengths.

"Just a little peace for you, girl," he whispered, adjusting the resonator.

Kira's breathing seemed to deepen almost imperceptibly. Her ears twitched, but instead of the usual anxious flick, they settled back, a subtle sign of relaxation. It was a small victory, but in the face of overwhelming odds, any small victory was a cause for hope.

Niko understood that Kira's health was not just a personal concern; it was a critical warning. The Gateway's stability was not an abstract concept for scientists in labs; it was a tangible force that had direct, immediate consequences for the living beings attuned to it. Her psychological and physical strain was a direct, undeniable measure of how close they were to a catastrophic breach. The symbiotic link between Kira and the Gateway was a powerful, and terrifying, testament to the interconnectedness of all things on Veridia. He knew then that his efforts to heal Kira, to restore her peace, were not just acts of compassion; they were essential steps in the larger fight to stabilize the Gateway and protect their reality from the encroaching chaos. The fate of their habitat, and perhaps much more, was inextricably bound to the quiet suffering of his loyal companion.

The silence in the habitat had become a heavy, oppressive blanket. It wasn't the absence of sound, but the pregnant pause between the increasingly erratic surges of dimensional bleed-through. Each lull in the storm offered a brief, deceptive respite, only to be shattered by another violent ripple that sent tremors through their reality, and through Kira's increasingly frayed nervous system. Niko watched her, his heart a leaden weight in his chest. Her amber eyes, once pools of vibrant curiosity, were now dulled by a constant, low-grade anxiety, her fur often standing on end with no discernible external stimulus. Her fatigue was a palpable aura, a testament to the invisible war being waged just beyond the thin veil of their existence.

"We can't keep this up, Niko," Elara's voice was barely a whisper, yet it cut through the tense quiet of the main chamber. She was studying the holographic projections that flickered with an alarming instability, the arcs of energy that represented the Gateway Alpha behaving less like a stable conduit and more like a fractured mirror. "Her distress is a constant. Every energy spike, every localized distortion, it's amplified through her. She's our canary, but she's dying in the mine."

Niko nodded, his gaze lingering on Kira, who was currently curled into a tight ball on her mat, her breathing shallow and punctuated by soft, almost imperceptible tremors. He had tried everything within his limited xenobotanical and bio-energetic knowledge. The calming tinctures, the harmonic resonators, the meticulously crafted 'calm zones' – they offered fleeting moments of reprieve, but the encroaching tide of instability was too powerful, too persistent. Kira was absorbing the brunt of it, her finely tuned Veridian physiology acting as a distress beacon for the entire operation.

"I've been running simulations," he admitted, turning to face Elara and Jax, who was silently observing the increasingly erratic readings. Jax, ever the pragmatist, had been monitoring the integrity of their habitat's structural and life-support systems, his face a mask of grim concentration. "The harmonic dampeners are reaching their saturation point. They can only absorb so much before they begin to resonate with the disruptive frequencies, amplifying them instead of nullifying them."

"Which means we're essentially just delaying the inevitable," Jax stated flatly, his voice devoid of emotion, a stark contrast to the turmoil he must have been feeling. He gestured to a particularly violent oscillation on Elara's display. "Look at that. It's a Class-4 resonance cascade, localized within the Gateway itself. If that propagates outward... well, our little sanctuary won't be so little anymore. It'll be atomized, or worse."

A heavy silence descended. The "worse" hung in the air, unspoken but understood. Worse meant unimaginable horrors, dimensional rifts tearing open, realities bleeding into each other in ways that defied comprehension, or worse still, complete non-existence.

"We need to consider more... definitive solutions," Elara said, her voice regaining a sliver of its usual resolve. She met Niko's gaze, her own filled with a mixture of apprehension and grim determination. "The simulations indicate that a temporary shutdown of the primary energy conduits feeding the Gateway might be our only viable option to prevent a full-scale collapse. We could isolate the Gateway, let the energies stabilize on their own, perhaps even allow the natural regenerative processes of Veridia to mend the breach."

Niko's stomach clenched. A shutdown. The word itself felt like a betrayal. Their entire mission was predicated on understanding and coexisting with the Gateway, on harnessing its potential for interstellar travel. To shut it down, even temporarily, felt like severing a lifeline, like abandoning the very purpose of their presence here.

"A shutdown," Niko repeated slowly, the implications sinking in. "What are the projected risks, Elara?"

Elara turned back to her console, her fingers flying across the holographic interface. "The immediate risk is significant energy feedback. The system is currently under immense strain. A sudden disconnection could cause a massive discharge, potentially destabilizing the localized chroniton field, leading to unpredictable temporal distortions. We could find ourselves flung forward or backward in time, or perhaps worse, fractured across multiple temporal streams."

"In layman's terms?" Jax prompted, his eyes never leaving the readouts.

"We could cease to exist in any coherent form," Elara admitted, her voice tight. "Or we could find ourselves in a Veridia that is centuries older, or younger, than we are now. The ecosystem might be unrecognizable, the atmospheric composition altered, our habitat rendered uninhabitable or simply... gone."

Niko ran a hand over his face, the rough texture of his fur a small comfort. "And the long-term consequences?"

"That's the greater unknown," Elara replied, her brow furrowed. "The Gateway is a nexus, a point of intersection for multiple dimensional strata. By severing the energy flow, we're not just turning off a machine; we're fundamentally altering the energetic dynamics of this entire region. It's possible that the inherent forces that maintain the dimensional boundaries could be irrevocably weakened. We might be preventing a catastrophic breach now, only to pave the way for a more pervasive, uncontrollable bleed-through in the future, one that could engulf entire star systems."

"Or," Jax interjected, his voice a low rumble, "it might allow the natural healing process to occur. Veridia's biosphere is incredibly resilient. The xenobotanists always said that the planet itself possessed an intrinsic ability to regulate and stabilize these energetic phenomena. Perhaps by removing our artificial influence, we allow that natural regulatory system to reassert itself."

"And what about Kira?" Niko asked, his voice rough with emotion. "If we shut down the Gateway, will her symptoms subside?"

"The data suggests it's highly probable," Elara confirmed. "Her distress is directly correlated to the Gateway's instability. Removing the source of that instability should, in theory, allow her to recover. But there's no guarantee. The energies that have already permeated her system might have caused lasting neurological or physiological changes. We can't be certain she'll ever be completely free of the effects, even if the Gateway stabilizes."

The thought of Kira being permanently scarred by their presence, by OmniCorp's reckless meddling, was a bitter pill to swallow. She was more than just a barometer; she was a sentient being, a member of their pack, and her suffering was a moral indictment of their situation.

"Rerouting energy flows," Niko mused, looking at the complex schematics Elara had projected. "Could we channel the excess energy into a more stable, contained system? Perhaps a deep-space capacitor bank, or even an artificial dimensional sink, if we had the technology."

"We don't have that technology, Niko," Jax said, his voice pragmatic. "Not here, not now. And even if we did, the sheer volume of energy involved is astronomical. Attempting to contain it would be like trying to catch a supernova in a teacup. The risk of containment failure and an even more catastrophic release would be immense."

Elara sighed, the sound heavy with the weight of their predicament. "The options are stark. We can continue as we are, watching Kira deteriorate and risking a full-scale Gateway collapse that could have unimaginable consequences for this sector of the galaxy, or we can attempt a controlled shutdown. The shutdown carries its own set of terrifying risks – temporal displacement, permanent dimensional instability, and the potential for unknown, cascading ecological shifts on Veridia. And then there's the ethical dimension. We came here to study, to understand, to coexist. Shutting down the Gateway feels like an admission of failure, a blunt instrument where precision is needed."

Niko walked over to Kira, gently resting his hand on her flank. She stirred, a faint purr rumbling in her chest, a sound that was both comforting and heart-wrenching given her current state. He could feel the subtle vibrations of her internal systems, the constant, low-level hum of her bio-energetic field, now undoubtedly struggling to maintain equilibrium against the encroaching alien energies.

"OmniCorp's interference has pushed us to this," Niko said, his voice low and steady. "They are the architects of this crisis. We are simply trying to mitigate the damage they have caused. We have a responsibility to Kira, to our mission, and to whatever life might exist beyond this immediate vicinity. The potential for widespread destruction, for the unraveling of our reality, outweighs the risks of a temporary shutdown, however significant they may be."

He looked at Elara and Jax, his gaze unwavering. "We need to prepare for the shutdown. We need to identify the optimal window, calculate the necessary energy dissipation protocols, and ensure we have contingency plans for every conceivable temporal and dimensional anomaly. We do this not as an act of defeat, but as a desperate measure to preserve what we can. We aim to minimize the damage, to give Veridia a chance to heal, and to give Kira a chance to be whole again."

Jax nodded, his expression one of grim acceptance. "I'll start running the structural integrity simulations for the shutdown sequence. We'll need to reinforce critical systems and prepare for potential energy surges."

Elara turned to her console, her fingers already moving with renewed purpose. "I'll begin recalibrating the temporal stabilizers and contingency protocols. We'll need to be ready to react instantly to any deviation from the projected outcomes."

Niko knelt beside Kira, stroking her head, the familiar warmth of her fur a stark contrast to the chilling uncertainties that lay ahead. He felt a profound sense of responsibility, the weight of their decision pressing down on him. They were not just scientists or explorers anymore. They were guardians, forced to make impossible choices in the face of an existential threat. The shifting thresholds of the Gateway had brought them to the precipice of the unknown, and the only way forward was to step into the void, hoping to find solid ground on the other side. The gamble was immense, the stakes unimaginable, but the alternative – to stand by and watch their world, and Kira, crumble – was no longer an option. The time for desperate measures had arrived. He could only hope they were desperate enough, and wise enough, to survive the consequences.

CHAPTER TEN

THE NAVIGATOR'S HEART

The hum of the Gateway Alpha had always been a reassuring presence, a low thrum that resonated deep within Niko's bones, a constant reminder of the immense power they were attempting to understand. But now, that hum was faltering. It was no longer a steady bass line, but a hesitant, reedy note, punctuated by disconcerting silences. The holographic projections that tracked the Gateway's energetic signature, once vibrant and dynamic, now flickered with a desperate instability, the arcs of light that represented its resonance field shrinking and contorting like dying embers. Elara's brow was furrowed in concentration, her fingers dancing over the console, but even her practiced movements seemed tinged with a growing unease.

"The resonance field is collapsing," she stated, her voice tight, devoid of its usual academic detachment. "The stabilization matrix is showing overload. It's... it's trying to hold onto something that's no longer there."

Niko felt a cold dread seep into his gut, a sensation far more profound than the anxiety that had been a constant companion since their arrival. This was different. This was a fundamental shift, a warning sign that their entire endeavor, their hope of understanding the very fabric of existence, was about to unravel. He looked at Kira. She was no longer curled in distress; she was alert, her head tilted, her large amber eyes fixed on the faltering energy projections. Her ears twitched, not with fear, but with a peculiar, focused attention. Her breathing, which had been shallow and ragged, now seemed to deepen, taking on a rhythm that was almost... deliberate.

Jax, ever stoic, pointed to a particularly alarming dip on the main display. "We're approaching critical mass. If that field collapses entirely, the Gateway... it might just wink out of existence. Permanently."

The implications of that statement hung heavy in the recycled air. Permanently. Not a temporary shutdown, not a controlled redirection, but an irretrievable closure. The bridge between worlds, the potential for so much more, gone in an instant. The carefully laid plans, the years of research, the very reason for their presence on Veridia, rendered obsolete.

"Standard stabilization protocols are failing," Elara reported, her voice strained. "The energy feedback loop is too volatile. We can't force it open any longer. The system is actively rejecting our attempts to maintain its integrity."

Niko felt a flicker of despair. They had exhausted their technological solutions. The harmonic dampeners were saturated, the energy conduits were pushed to their absolute limits, and now, the very structure of the Gateway was rebelling against their interference. They were like children trying to force open a locked door, their efforts only serving to jam it tighter.

He walked over to Kira, his heart aching at the sight of her. She was no longer trembling. Instead, a strange calm had settled over her. She met his gaze, and for the first time in weeks, he saw a spark of her old curiosity, a subtle flicker of understanding that transcended their shared language of gestures and vocalizations. She nudged his hand with her head, a soft, insistent pressure. It wasn't a plea for comfort, but something else. A communication.

He remembered the old Veridian texts, the ones that OmniCorp had dismissed as myth and superstition, the obscure theories whispered in hushed tones by xenolinguists and fringe theorists. The concept of 'navigational resonance.' It spoke not of physical forces or energetic currents, but of a deeper, more fundamental connection. It suggested that the very act of conscious intent, when amplified by a profound, symbiotic bond, could influence the fabric of spacetime, could... guide.

He had dismissed it, of course. It was too intangible, too unscientific for his pragmatic mind. But now, looking at Kira, at the subtle shift in her posture, the focused intensity in her eyes, he wondered. Was it possible that their technological approach had been too narrow? Had they been so focused on manipulating the physical forces that they had overlooked the power of the intangible?

"The resonance field is too weak to maintain a stable connection," Elara said, her voice tinged with a resignation that sent a shiver down Niko's spine. "We can't force it. It's like trying to keep a drowning person afloat by pushing them underwater."

Niko knelt beside Kira, his hand resting on her flank. He could feel the subtle tremors that still ran through her, not of distress, but of immense, focused effort. He felt a faint, almost imperceptible pulse emanating from her, a resonance that seemed to echo the faltering hum of the Gateway.

"Navigational resonance," he murmured, the words tasting strange and alien on his tongue.

Elara looked up from her console, her expression one of bewilderment. "What was that, Niko?"

"The old theories," he said, his voice gaining a new, hesitant strength. "The ones about consciousness influencing dimensional pathways. About a symbiotic link creating a... a beacon. A guide."

Jax scoffed softly, though without his usual biting sarcasm. "Niko, we're dealing with fundamental physics here, not telepathic spirit guides. We need concrete solutions, not wishful thinking."

"But what if our concrete solutions have led us to this impasse?" Niko argued, his gaze fixed on Kira. She let out a soft chuff, a sound that seemed to acknowledge his words. "We've tried to *force* the Gateway open, to *stabilize* it with our technology. But what if it's not about force? What if it's about... alignment? About a directed consciousness?"

He looked at Elara. "The Gateway is a nexus, a point where realities intersect. It's not just an energy conduit; it's a pathway. And pathways can be navigated. The texts spoke of pairs, of beings with a deep, innate connection, who could synchronize their consciousness to 'sing' a path through the dimensional strata."

Elara's eyes widened slightly, a flicker of something akin to hope, or perhaps just desperate curiosity, surfacing. "You're suggesting... using Kira and yourself as a form of biological navigator? To guide the Gateway's resonance field?"

"It's the only thing we haven't tried," Niko said, his voice firm. "Our technology is failing. We're running out of options. Kira's physiology is incredibly sensitive to dimensional flux. Her distress was a symptom of the Gateway's instability. But what if that sensitivity can be... repurposed? What if her attuned senses, combined with my focus, can create a stable enough energetic imprint to coax the Gateway back into alignment, even temporarily?"

He stood up, his resolve hardening. He would not let Kira suffer any longer, nor would he stand by and watch their mission, their hopes, crumble into dust. "The simulations show a catastrophic collapse is imminent. We can't prevent it with conventional means. But if these ancient theories hold any truth... if there's a way to influence the Gateway not with brute force, but with... intention... then we have to try."

He extended a hand to Kira, his own internal compass spinning wildly, but his purpose clear. "I believe that her connection to the Gateway is not just passive, but active. She is feeling its weakening, its imminent closure. And I believe that together, we can transmit a different kind of signal. Not one of panic or desperation, but one of purpose. A signal that says, 'This path is still viable. This connection is still important. Come back to us.'"

Elara was already tapping rapidly on her console. "The harmonic dampeners are being purged. We'll need to reconfigure them to act as amplifiers, not suppressors. We'll need to reroute primary power to... well, to you two. Essentially, you'll become the conduit, the locus of control."

Jax, surprisingly, didn't object. He simply observed the readouts, his expression unreadable. "The risk of feedback is still astronomical. If your combined consciousness falters, or if the Gateway rejects your signal, the resulting discharge could be... instantaneous and absolute. You could be vaporized, scattered across dimensions, or worse."

"Worse is what we're facing if we do nothing," Niko retorted, his gaze unwavering. He looked at Kira, who was now standing, her body radiating a subtle, almost visible energy. Her amber eyes met his, and in their depths, he saw not just his own reflection, but a vast, shimmering expanse of possibility. "We're not trying to force it open anymore. We're going to try and persuade it. To resonate with it."

He took a deep breath, the scent of ozone and something akin to ancient earth filling his lungs. "This is it, then. The last resort. We move beyond the circuits and the equations, and into... the navigator's heart." He turned to Kira, a silent question in his eyes. She responded with a soft, confident purr, a sound that vibrated not just through his hand, but through the very core of his being. It was an affirmation. A commitment. The journey into the unknown had just begun, and it would be navigated not by instruments, but by the profound, untamed power of a connected consciousness. The Gateway's fading signal was a call to a deeper, more primal form of exploration, a testament to the idea that the greatest discoveries might lie not in what we can build, but in what we can become, together. The hum of the failing Gateway was a dirge, but their shared intent was a nascent melody, a song sung against the encroaching silence. This was their only hope: to become the navigators of their own destiny, guided by a resonance that transcended mere physics, a resonance born of trust, empathy, and the unshakeable bond between a man and his Veridian companion.

The hum of the Gateway Alpha, once a reassuring constant, had become a stuttering, mournful sigh. Niko knelt beside Kira, his hand resting on the smooth, velvety fur of her flank. The subtle tremors that ran through her were not of fear, but of an immense, focused exertion. He could feel a faint, almost imperceptible pulse emanating from her, a resonance that seemed to echo the faltering hum of the Gateway, a faint whisper against the encroaching silence.

"Navigational resonance," he murmured, the words tasting strange and alien on his tongue. Elara looked up from her console, her expression a mixture of bewilderment and an almost desperate scientific curiosity. "What was that, Niko?"

"The old theories," he explained, his voice gaining a hesitant strength, amplified by the palpable energy radiating from Kira. "The ones about consciousness influencing dimensional pathways. About a symbiotic link creating a... a beacon. A guide."

Jax, ever the pragmatist, scoffed softly, though the edge of his usual sarcasm was dulled by the gravity of their situation. "Niko, we're dealing with fundamental physics here, not telepathic spirit guides. We need concrete solutions, not wishful thinking."

"But what if our concrete solutions have led us to this impasse?" Niko countered, his gaze unwavering, fixed on Kira. She let out a soft chuff, a sound that seemed to acknowledge his words, a low rumble of understanding that vibrated through his hand. "We've tried to *force* the Gateway open, to *stabilize* it with our technology. But what if it's not about force? What if it's about... alignment? About a directed consciousness?"

He turned to Elara, his mind racing, piecing together the fragmented texts and Kira's intuitive reactions. "The Gateway is a nexus, a point where realities intersect. It's not just an energy conduit; it's a pathway. And pathways can be navigated. The texts spoke of pairs, of beings with a deep, innate connection, who could synchronize their consciousness to 'sing' a path through the dimensional strata."

Elara's eyes widened, a flicker of something akin to hope, or perhaps just the thrill of a novel hypothesis, surfacing. "You're suggesting... using Kira and yourself as a form of biological navigator? To guide the Gateway's resonance field?"

"It's the only thing we haven't tried," Niko stated, his resolve hardening with each passing second. The simulations flashing on the main display indicated a catastrophic collapse was imminent. Their sophisticated technology, their years of meticulous research, had brought them to this precipice, only to reveal its limitations. "Our technology is failing. We're running out of options. Kira's physiology is incredibly sensitive to dimensional flux. Her distress was a symptom of the Gateway's instability. But what if that sensitivity can be... repurposed? What if her attuned senses, combined with my focus, can create a stable enough energetic imprint to coax the Gateway back into alignment, even temporarily?"

He stood up, his decision made, the weight of their collective future pressing down on him. He would not let Kira suffer any longer, nor would he stand by and watch their mission, their hopes, crumble into dust. "The simulations show a catastrophic collapse is imminent. We can't prevent it with conventional means. But if these ancient theories hold any truth... if there's a way to influence the Gateway not with brute force, but with... intention... then we have to try."

He extended a hand to Kira, his own internal compass spinning wildly, but his purpose clear, a single point of focus amidst the chaos. "I believe that her connection to the Gateway is not just passive, but active. She is feeling its weakening, its imminent closure. And I believe that together, we can transmit a different kind of signal. Not one of panic or desperation, but one of purpose. A signal that says, 'This path is still viable. This connection is still important. Come back to us.'"

Elara was already tapping rapidly on her console, her fingers a blur of motion. "The harmonic dampeners are being purged. We'll need to reconfigure them to act as amplifiers, not suppressors. We'll need to reroute primary power to... well, to you two. Essentially, you'll become the conduit, the locus of control."

Jax, surprisingly, offered no objection. He simply observed the readouts, his expression unreadable, a statue of stoic contemplation. "The risk of feedback is still astronomical. If your combined consciousness falters, or if the Gateway rejects your signal, the resulting discharge could be... instantaneous and absolute. You could be vaporized, scattered across dimensions, or worse."

"Worse is what we're facing if we do nothing," Niko retorted, his gaze unwavering. He looked at Kira, who was now standing, her body radiating a subtle, almost visible energy. Her amber eyes met his, and in their depths, he saw not just his own reflection, but a vast, shimmering expanse of possibility, a universe reflected in miniature. "We're not trying to force it open anymore. We're going to try and persuade it. To resonate with it."

He took a deep breath, the scent of ozone and something akin to ancient earth filling his lungs, a primal aroma that resonated deep within him. "This is it, then. The last resort. We move beyond the circuits and the equations, and into... the navigator's heart." He turned to Kira, a silent question in his eyes, a plea for shared understanding. She responded with a soft, confident purr, a sound that vibrated not just through his hand, but through the very core of his being. It was an affirmation. A commitment. The journey into the unknown had just begun, and it would be navigated not by instruments, but by the profound, untamed power of a connected consciousness. The Gateway's fading signal was a call to a deeper, more primal form of exploration, a testament to the idea that the greatest discoveries might lie not in what we can build, but in what we can become, together. The hum of the failing Gateway was a dirge, but their shared intent was a nascent melody, a song sung against the encroaching silence. This was their only hope: to become the navigators of their own destiny, guided by a resonance that transcended mere physics, a resonance born of trust, empathy, and the unshakeable bond between a man and his Veridian companion.

The ancient texts, once relegated to the dusty shelves of xenolinguistic archives and dismissed as poetic fancy, now shimmered with a potent, irrefutable truth. They spoke of a symbiotic resonance, a phenomenon that transcended the conventional understanding of physics and biology. It was not merely about shared vocalizations or synchronized body language; it was about a deep, interwoven tapestry of consciousness, a shared energetic field that could, under specific conditions, interact with the very fabric of spacetime. The Veridian texts, in particular, described this phenomenon in terms of an "empathic beacon," a concept that hinted at the possibility of influencing dimensional currents through sheer force of emotional and cognitive alignment.

Niko had spent countless hours poring over these obscure documents, his initial skepticism slowly eroding under the weight of mounting anomalies. The Veridians, a species known for their profound connection to their planet and its unique energetic signature, had apparently developed a sophisticated understanding of interdimensional travel long before the advent of advanced propulsion systems. Their methods, however, were not mechanical but organic, rooted in the cultivation of profound interspecies bonds. The canine-like Veridians, with their heightened sensory perception and innate capacity for empathic communication, were central to this ancient science.

It was believed that certain species, particularly those with a naturally strong empathic capacity, could attune themselves to the subtle vibrations of the universe. When paired with a sentient being capable of focused intent, this attunement could be amplified, creating a unique energetic signature capable of interacting with dimensional frequencies. This was the essence of the "Navigator's Heart" – not a biological organ, but a state of being, a convergence of emotional depth, unwavering trust, and focused mental energy.

Kira, with her exceptionally sensitive auric field and her innate ability to perceive shifts in dimensional pressures, was a perfect candidate for such a role. Her distress had been an involuntary alarm, a biological response to the Gateway's imminent collapse. But Niko now understood that this sensitivity could be harnessed, channeled, transformed. Her ability to perceive the weakening of the Gateway's resonance was, in essence, her perceiving a disruption in the flow of dimensional currents.

Their bond, forged through shared hardship and mutual reliance, had developed beyond simple companionship. It was a profound symbiosis, a mirroring of consciousness that allowed them to communicate on a level that transcended spoken words. Niko could feel Kira's emotional state as if it were his own, and he suspected she could do the same for him. This shared awareness, this constant feedback loop of empathy, was the bedrock upon which their navigational potential was built.

The scientific community had long debated the existence and mechanics of such phenomena. Theories ranged from quantum entanglement operating on a macro scale to subtle energy fields that were as yet unmeasurable by conventional instruments. The OmniCorp doctrine, however, had always favored a purely empirical, materialistic approach, dismissing anything that could not be quantified or replicated in a laboratory setting. The Veridian texts, with their talk of 'soul echoes' and 'resonant consciousness,' were readily categorized as primitive superstition.

But here, on the precipice of dimensional collapse, faced with the tangible failure of all their technological solutions, the ancient wisdom offered the only glimmer of hope. The Gateway, as an interdimensional nexus, was not merely a construct of exotic matter and manipulated energy fields; it was a point of intersection, a doorway that responded not just to brute force but to nuanced influence. It was a pathway, and pathways, by their very nature, could be navigated.

Niko focused on Kira, her breathing now calm and steady, a testament to her own inner strength. He could feel a subtle hum emanating from her, a low-frequency vibration that seemed to synchronize with his own heartbeat. This was the beginning of their connection, the nascent formation of their shared energetic signature. He extended his hand, not to touch her, but to offer his intent, to send a silent message of partnership.

"We're not just trying to control the Gateway, Kira," he murmured, his voice barely a whisper, yet imbued with a newfound certainty. "We're going to *understand* it. We're going to sing with it. You and I, we're going to be its song."

He closed his eyes, visualizing the vast, intricate network of the Gateway, not as a machine, but as a living, breathing entity. He imagined its faltering pulse, its desperate attempt to maintain its connection. He focused on his own emotional state, on the unwavering trust he felt for Kira, on the deep, abiding love that bound them. He allowed that emotion to swell, to become a tangible force, an energetic beacon radiating outwards.

Elara's voice cut through the quiet intensity. "Niko, the power conduits are reconfigured. They're feeding directly into the primary resonance emitters. But we're seeing... anomalies. Your biometrics are spiking, but not in any way we've predicted. It's as if your biological output is... aligning with the Gateway's harmonic frequency."

"That's the point, Elara," Niko replied, his voice laced with a quiet triumph. "We're not fighting the Gateway; we're harmonizing with it. Kira's sensitivity is the key. She's the antenna, picking up the subtlest shifts. And my focus, my intent, is the tuner, bringing our combined energy into alignment with the dimensional currents."

He felt Kira press her head against his arm, a gentle, reassuring weight. He could feel her projecting a sense of calm, of unwavering focus, back at him. It was a feedback loop, a continuous exchange of emotional and energetic information, a dance of consciousness that was slowly, imperceptibly, altering the state of the Gateway.

The ancient Veridian texts spoke of this process as a 'dimensional lullaby,' a way of gently coaxing the fabric of spacetime into a desired configuration. It required immense patience, unwavering trust, and a deep understanding of one's symbiotic partner. It was not about forcing a passage, but about creating an invitation, a resonant invitation that the universe could not ignore.

He pictured the interconnectedness of all things, the subtle threads that wove through the cosmos, binding stars and planets, and indeed, different dimensions, together. He saw their bond with Kira as one such thread, amplified by their shared purpose, now extended to encompass the Gateway itself. Their love, their trust, their shared understanding – these were not merely abstract emotional states. They were palpable forces, capable of interacting with the fundamental energies of existence.

Jax's voice, now a low rumble of surprise, broke through his reverie. "The resonance field... it's stabilizing. Not strengthening, not yet, but the chaotic fluctuations are diminishing. It's like... it's being soothed."

A wave of relief washed over Niko, quickly followed by a surge of exhilaration. They were doing it. They were actually doing it. Their combined consciousness, their "Navigator's Heart," was a tangible force, capable of influencing the very mechanisms of interdimensional travel.

"It's not just soothing, Jax," Elara added, her voice filled with awe. "It's... responding. The Gateway's core frequency is shifting, slowly, but it's moving towards a more coherent pattern. A pattern that seems to be emanating from... from your biometrics, Niko, and Kira's bio-signature."

Niko opened his eyes, meeting Kira's steady gaze. Her amber eyes held a depth that always amazed him, a silent testament to the ancient wisdom that flowed through her lineage. He felt a profound sense of gratitude, not just for her presence, but for the very nature of her being, a being that had unlocked a universe of possibilities simply by being herself.

"It's the trust, Kira," he whispered, his voice thick with emotion. "It's our trust in each other. That's what the Gateway is responding to. It's not just energy it needs; it's intent. It's intention guided by connection."

He felt a faint warmth spreading through his chest, a subtle thrumming that seemed to resonate with the slowly strengthening pulse of the Gateway. This was the Navigator's Heart, not a metaphor, but a very real phenomenon, a testament to the power of interspecies connection and the untapped potential of consciousness itself. They had moved beyond the realm of empirical science, stepping into a new paradigm where empathy and intuition were as vital as any equation. And in doing so, they had not only saved their mission, but had opened a door to a deeper understanding of the universe, a universe where the strongest connections might not be forged in circuits and steel, but in the silent, profound language of the heart. The faltering hum of the Gateway was now a more steady, albeit still weak, melody, a testament to the power of their shared song, a song sung not of force, but of harmony.

Kira's flank vibrated with a soft, rhythmic tremor, a subtle language only Niko could now decipher. She was tired, her breaths coming a little heavier, the amber glow in her eyes a touch dimmer, but her instinct, that ancient, unerring compass, was still sharp. He felt it surge through their interwoven consciousness, a gentle, insistent pressure nudging his own focus. It wasn't a thought, not a directive in the human sense, but a profound *knowing* that rippled from her to him, guiding his mind's eye through the swirling chaos of the Gateway's failing resonance.

"That way, Kira?" he murmured, his own mental visualization of the energy field shifting, aligning with the subtle twitch of her ear, the almost imperceptible tilt of her head. The ancient texts had spoken of 'resonant pathways,' of energetic currents that flowed like unseen rivers through the dimensional strata. The Gateway, in its dying throes, was a maelstrom, its usual predictable channels twisted and broken, yet Kira, with her Veridian heritage, could still sense the ghost of those flows, the faintest whispers of the currents that once were.

He felt her agreement as a warmth spreading through his chest, a comforting counterpoint to the anxiety that still gnawed at the edges of his resolve. Her tail gave a slow, deliberate sweep, a movement that spoke of a clear, defined path opening before them in the flux. It wasn't a broad, open highway, but a narrow, precarious bridge of stabilized energy, a thread woven through the tempest. Niko focused his intent on that thread, drawing on the residual energy that Elara had managed to channel, allowing it to flow through him and, in turn, through Kira.

He envisioned the energy as a tangible substance, a shimmering, opalescent mist. Kira's instincts were guiding him to gather this mist, to condense it, to form it into a coherent beacon at a precise point within the Gateway's fluctuating field. It was like trying to sculpt smoke in a hurricane, but Kira's subtle cues made it possible. A low growl, almost a purr, rumbled in her chest when he approached the correct 'density' of energy, a soft whine if he strayed too far, his focus wavering.

"You feel the eddy here," Niko breathed, his eyes closed, his brow furrowed in concentration. He was experiencing the Gateway not through sight, but through an intricate tapestry of sensation: the prickle of displaced energy on his skin, the phantom scent of ozone mixed with the faint, metallic tang of unstable chronitons, and, most importantly, the guiding vibrations emanating from Kira. She was the seismograph, registering the subtle shifts and tremors of the dimensional currents, and he was the interpreter, translating her instinctual readings into actionable focus.

Kira shifted her weight, her muscles tensing slightly. Niko felt it as a warning. "Too much friction?" he asked, his mind instantly pulling back from the point of focus. Her low chuff was an affirmation. The texts had mentioned the danger of 'dimensional friction,' of trying to force a path where none existed, which could lead to catastrophic feedback loops. It was a delicate dance, a negotiation with forces far beyond their complete comprehension.

He felt Kira's awareness widen, encompassing not just the immediate vicinity of the Gateway, but the subtle atmospheric shifts that indicated the outer hull's integrity was being tested. Her breath hitched for a fraction of a second, a minuscule ripple in their shared awareness, and Niko understood. The ship itself was groaning under the strain. The external stabilizers were struggling, and a breach, however minor, was becoming a real possibility.

"Hold on, Kira," he whispered, not just to her, but to the ship, to the mission, to their very existence. He focused his intent, drawing on the Veridian texts that spoke of 'resonant shielding.' It wasn't about reinforcing the hull with brute force, but about projecting a harmonizing frequency that could, in theory, momentarily smooth out the most violent dimensional stresses. He imagined their combined energy, amplified and directed by Kira's sensitivity, washing over the ship like a calming wave.

Kira responded instantly. She pushed her head against his leg, a solid, grounding presence. He felt her projecting a wave of calm, not just for him, but for the ship itself. It was a curious sensation, as if the very metal of the Gateway Alpha was responding to her empathetic broadcast. The groaning of the hull lessened, the violent vibrations subsiding into a more manageable tremor.

"She's... she's radiating something," Elara's voice crackled over the comms, laced with disbelief. "The stress sensors on the hull are registering a localized dampening field. It's not strong enough to be a permanent solution, but... it's holding. How are you doing that, Niko?"

Niko didn't have the words to explain. He couldn't articulate the complex interplay of instinct and intent, the raw, untamed power that Kira was channeling. "We're... aligning," he managed, focusing back on the task at hand. Kira let out a soft sigh, a sound of exertion, and nudged him again. The 'path' was becoming clearer.

He could feel Kira's focus sharpening, honing in on a specific point of instability within the Gateway's core. It was a knot of chaotic energy, a vortex that threatened to unravel the entire structure. The ancient texts described such points as 'dimensional anchors,' points of extreme instability that could either be collapsed or, if properly understood, utilized as stable points from which to rebuild.

Kira's entire body quivered now, a testament to the immense effort she was expending. Her eyes were fixed on a point in the swirling energies, her gaze unwavering. Niko felt her instinct urging him towards that point, not to attack it, but to *soothe* it. It was like trying to calm a frightened, cornered animal.

"We need to resonate with it, Kira?" he asked, his mind grasping for the Veridian terminology. A soft lick from her against his hand confirmed his understanding. It wasn't about brute force; it was about empathy, about understanding the nature of the instability and offering a harmonizing counter-frequency.

Niko focused his intent, channeling Kira's understanding. He visualized the chaotic energy as a wild, untamed force, a storm raging within the dimensional fabric. He then imagined their combined consciousness, a steady, calm light, reaching out to that storm, not to extinguish it, but to gently guide its currents, to find the underlying pattern within the chaos.

Kira whined softly, a sound of distress. Niko immediately reeled back his focus. "Too much?" he asked, his heart sinking. He felt her answer, not with words, but with a distinct sensation: a feeling of being *pulled* in multiple directions simultaneously, of being torn asunder. The anchor point was not just unstable; it was actively resisting, lashing out with its chaotic energy.

"The texts mentioned 'harmonic redirection'," Niko mused aloud, sifting through the fragmented memories of his research. "Not direct confrontation, but... redirecting the outward flow of its energy."

Kira's tail thumped a slow, steady rhythm against the deck plating. He felt her understanding, her instinct latching onto the concept. Yes, redirection. Not a head-on collision, but a subtle shift in the currents, guiding the destructive energy away from their immediate vicinity, towards a less volatile pocket of spacetime that Kira was now sensing.

He took a deep breath, drawing strength from Kira's unwavering presence. He pictured the chaotic energy like a raging river, and their combined consciousness as a series of strategically placed dams, not to stop the flow, but to channel it, to guide it. Kira was the eyes, seeing the exact placement of these dams, the subtle shifts in the riverbed that would allow for the most effective redirection.

He focused his mental energy, visualizing the containment fields Elara had managed to reconfigure. They were no longer about stabilization, but about redirection. He felt Kira's guidance, a series of precise mental nudges, indicating where to 'place' each containment field, how to shape their output to create the desired effect. It was a delicate ballet of energy manipulation, orchestrated by instinct and intention.

Kira let out a soft grunt of effort. Niko felt a surge of energy flow through him, a controlled release that he directed outward, shaping the containment field according to her unspoken instructions. The chaotic anchor point pulsed, its outward fury momentarily contained, then expertly channeled away from them. It was like watching a wild beast being gently steered into a more manageable enclosure.

"It's working," Elara breathed over the comms. "The resonance field is... reconfiguring. The primary instability is decreasing. Niko, what exactly are you doing?"

"Listening," Niko replied, his voice strained with exertion. "And trusting. Kira's instincts are guiding me. She's the navigator. I'm just... the instrument."

Kira nudged him again, her amber eyes locked on a new anomaly. This one was different, less volatile, but insidious. It was a 'void,' a pocket of absolute nullity that was slowly expanding, threatening to consume the already weakened structure of the Gateway. The Veridian texts described these voids as 'dimensional dead zones,' areas where the fundamental forces of the universe ceased to exist, where reality itself frayed.

"A void?" Niko echoed Kira's silent alarm. He felt the chilling emptiness of it, a gnawing absence that was more terrifying than the raw chaos. "How do we... fill a void?"

Kira's tail gave a slow, deliberate wag. Niko felt her sensing a faint, residual energy signature clinging to the edges of the void, a whisper of what once was. It was like finding a single, unbroken thread in a tapestry that had been torn to shreds.

"We need to draw that residual energy," Niko realized, "and use it to... seed the void. To reintroduce the concept of existence into that null space." It was a monumental task, akin to breathing life into a vacuum.

Kira pulsed with a gentle warmth, a silent encouragement. Niko focused on the faint energy signature, visualizing it as a fragile spark. Kira's instincts were guiding him to gather this spark, to nurture it, to expand it with their own combined consciousness. It wasn't about force, but about a gentle, persistent infusion of intent.

He felt Kira's focus narrowing, her senses extending to encompass the entire Gateway, searching for every last vestige of stable energy that could be coaxed into service. He felt her gathering these scattered remnants, like a cosmic shepherd guiding lost sheep. Then, with a soft, resonant hum that vibrated through his very bones, she began to weave them together, creating a nascent energetic pattern.

"We're going to sing to it, Kira," Niko whispered, his own energy flowing into the growing pattern. "A song of existence."

He felt Kira's response, a deep, resonant chord that echoed his own intent. They were not just navigating the Gateway; they were

rebuilding it, stitch by painstaking stitch, using the very fabric of their connection as the thread. Kira's instincts, honed by millennia of Veridian wisdom, were the blueprint, and Niko's focused consciousness was the hand that brought that blueprint to life. The Gateway, once a symbol of their technological hubris, was slowly transforming into a testament to the profound power of instinct, trust, and the boundless potential of a Navigator's Heart. The journey was far from over, but for the first time, amidst the dying embers of their failing technology, a new dawn, forged in the heart of their unique symbiosis, was beginning to break.

The swirling energies of the Gateway were a tempest, a maelstrom of broken frequencies and fractured dimensional strata. Yet, within the heart of that chaos, a different kind of power was coalescing. Niko sat cross-legged on the deck plating, Kira's massive, scaled body curled protectively around him. Her flank vibrated with a soft, rhythmic tremor, a subtle language only Niko could now decipher. She was tired, her breaths coming a little heavier, the amber glow in her eyes a touch dimmer, but her instinct, that ancient, unerring compass, was still sharp. He felt it surge through their interwoven consciousness, a gentle, insistent pressure nudging his own focus. It wasn't a thought, not a directive in the human sense, but a profound *knowing* that rippled from her to him, guiding his mind's eye through the swirling chaos of the Gateway's failing resonance.

"That way, Kira?" he murmured, his own mental visualization of the energy field shifting, aligning with the subtle twitch of her ear, the almost imperceptible tilt of her head. The ancient texts had spoken of 'resonant pathways,' of energetic currents that flowed like unseen rivers through the dimensional strata. The Gateway, in its dying throes, was a maelstrom, its usual predictable channels twisted and broken, yet Kira, with her Veridian heritage, could still sense the ghost of those flows, the faintest whispers of the currents that once were. He felt her agreement as a warmth spreading through his chest, a comforting counterpoint to the anxiety that still gnawed at the edges of his resolve. Her tail gave a slow, deliberate sweep, a movement that spoke of a clear, defined path opening before them in the flux. It wasn't a broad, open highway, but a narrow, precarious bridge of stabilized energy, a thread woven through the tempest.

Niko focused his intent on that thread, drawing on the residual energy that Elara had managed to channel, allowing it to flow through him and, in turn, through Kira. He envisioned the energy as a tangible substance, a shimmering, opalescent mist. Kira's instincts were guiding him to gather this mist, to condense it, to form it into a coherent beacon at a precise point within the Gateway's fluctuating field. It was like trying to sculpt smoke in a hurricane, but Kira's subtle cues made it possible. A low growl, almost a purr, rumbled in her chest when he approached the correct 'density' of energy, a soft whine if he strayed too far, his focus wavering.

"You feel the eddy here," Niko breathed, his eyes closed, his brow furrowed in concentration. He was experiencing the Gateway not through sight, but through an intricate tapestry of sensation: the prickle of displaced energy on his skin, the phantom scent of ozone mixed with the faint, metallic tang of unstable chronitons, and, most importantly, the guiding vibrations emanating from Kira. She was the seismograph, registering the subtle shifts and tremors of the dimensional currents, and he was the interpreter, translating her instinctual readings into actionable focus. Kira shifted her weight, her muscles tensing slightly. Niko felt it as a warning. "Too much friction?" he asked, his mind instantly pulling back from the point of focus. Her low chuff was an affirmation. The texts had mentioned the danger of 'dimensional friction,' of trying to force a path where none existed, which could lead to catastrophic feedback loops. It was a delicate dance, a negotiation with forces far beyond their complete comprehension.

He felt Kira's awareness widen, encompassing not just the immediate vicinity of the Gateway, but the subtle atmospheric shifts that indicated the outer hull's integrity was being tested. Her breath hitched for a fraction of a second, a minuscule ripple in their shared awareness, and Niko understood. The ship itself was groaning under the strain. The external stabilizers were struggling, and a breach, however minor, was becoming a real possibility. "Hold on, Kira," he whispered, not just to her, but to the ship, to the mission, to their very existence. He focused his intent, drawing on the Veridian texts that spoke of 'resonant shielding.' It wasn't about reinforcing the hull with brute force, but about projecting a harmonizing frequency that could, in theory, momentarily smooth out the most violent dimensional stresses. He imagined their combined energy, amplified and directed by Kira's sensitivity, washing over the ship like a calming wave.

Kira responded instantly. She pushed her head against his leg, a solid, grounding presence. He felt her projecting a wave of calm, not just for him, but for the ship itself. It was a curious sensation, as if the very metal of the Gateway Alpha was responding to her empathetic broadcast. The groaning of the hull lessened, the violent vibrations subsiding into a more manageable tremor. "She's... she's radiating something," Elara's voice crackled over the comms, laced with disbelief. "The stress sensors on the hull are registering a localized dampening field. It's not strong enough to be a permanent solution, but... it's holding. How are you doing that, Niko?"

Niko didn't have the words to explain. He couldn't articulate the complex interplay of instinct and intent, the raw, untamed power that Kira was channeling. "We're... aligning," he managed, focusing back on the task at hand. Kira let out a soft sigh, a sound of exertion, and nudged him again. The 'path' was becoming clearer. He could feel Kira's focus sharpening, honing in on a specific point of instability within the Gateway's core. It was a knot of chaotic energy, a vortex that threatened to unravel the entire structure. The ancient texts described such points as 'dimensional anchors,' points of extreme instability that could either be collapsed or, if properly understood, utilized as stable points from which to rebuild.

Kira's entire body quivered now, a testament to the immense effort she was expending. Her eyes were fixed on a point in the swirling energies, her gaze unwavering. Niko felt her instinct urging him towards that point, not to attack it, but to *soothe* it. It was like trying to calm a frightened, cornered animal. "We need to resonate with it, Kira?" he asked, his mind grasping for the Veridian terminology. A soft lick from her against his hand confirmed his understanding. It wasn't about brute force; it was about empathy, about understanding the nature of the instability and offering a harmonizing counter-frequency.

Niko focused his intent, channeling Kira's understanding. He visualized the chaotic energy as a wild, untamed force, a storm raging within the dimensional fabric. He then imagined their combined consciousness, a steady, calm light, reaching out to that storm, not to extinguish it, but to gently guide its currents, to find the underlying pattern within the chaos. Kira whined softly, a sound of distress. Niko immediately reeled back his focus. "Too much?" he asked, his heart sinking. He felt her answer, not with words, but with a distinct sensation: a feeling of being *pulled* in multiple directions simultaneously, of being torn asunder. The anchor point was not just unstable; it was actively resisting, lashing out with its chaotic energy.

"The texts mentioned 'harmonic redirection'," Niko mused aloud, sifting through the fragmented memories of his research. "Not direct confrontation, but... redirecting the outward flow of its energy." Kira's tail thumped a slow, steady rhythm against the deck plating. He felt her understanding, her instinct latching onto the concept. Yes, redirection. Not a head-on collision, but a subtle shift in the currents, guiding the destructive energy away from their immediate vicinity, towards a less volatile pocket of spacetime that Kira was now sensing. He took a deep breath, drawing strength from Kira's unwavering presence. He pictured the chaotic energy like a raging river, and their combined consciousness as a series of strategically placed dams, not to stop the flow, but to channel it, to guide it. Kira was the eyes, seeing the exact placement of these dams, the subtle shifts in the riverbed that would allow for the most effective redirection.

He focused his mental energy, visualizing the containment fields Elara had managed to reconfigure. They were no longer about stabilization, but about redirection. He felt Kira's guidance, a series of precise mental nudges, indicating where to 'place' each containment field, how to shape their output to create the desired effect. It was a delicate ballet of energy manipulation, orchestrated by instinct and intention. Kira let out a soft grunt of effort. Niko felt a surge of energy flow through him, a controlled release that he directed outward, shaping the containment field according to her unspoken instructions. The chaotic anchor point pulsed, its outward fury momentarily contained, then expertly channeled away from them. It was like watching a wild beast being gently steered into a more manageable enclosure. "It's working," Elara breathed over the comms. "The resonance field is... reconfiguring. The primary instability is decreasing. Niko, what exactly are you doing?"

"Listening," Niko replied, his voice strained with exertion. "And trusting. Kira's instincts are guiding me. She's the navigator. I'm just... the instrument." Kira nudged him again, her amber eyes locked on a new anomaly. This one was different, less volatile, but insidious. It was a 'void,' a pocket of absolute nullity that was slowly expanding, threatening to consume the already weakened structure of the Gateway. The Veridian texts described these voids as 'dimensional dead zones,' areas where the fundamental forces of the universe ceased to exist, where reality itself frayed. "A void?" Niko echoed Kira's silent alarm. He felt the chilling emptiness of it, a gnawing absence that was more terrifying than the raw chaos. "How do we... fill a void?"

Kira's tail gave a slow, deliberate wag. Niko felt her sensing a faint, residual energy signature clinging to the edges of the void, a whisper of what once was. It was like finding a single, unbroken thread in a tapestry that had been torn to shreds. "We need to draw that residual energy," Niko realized, "and use it to... seed the void. To reintroduce the concept of existence into that null space." It was a monumental task, akin to breathing life into a vacuum. Kira pulsed with a gentle warmth, a silent encouragement. Niko focused on the faint energy signature, visualizing it as a fragile spark. Kira's instincts were guiding him to gather this spark, to nurture it, to expand it with their own combined consciousness. It wasn't about force, but about a gentle, persistent infusion of intent.

He felt Kira's focus narrowing, her senses extending to encompass the entire Gateway, searching for every last vestige of stable energy that could be coaxed into service. He felt her gathering these scattered remnants, like a cosmic shepherd guiding lost sheep. Then, with a soft, resonant hum that vibrated through his very bones, she began to weave them together, creating a nascent energetic pattern. "We're going to sing to it, Kira," Niko whispered, his own energy flowing into the growing pattern. "A song of existence." He felt Kira's response, a deep, resonant chord that echoed his own intent. They were not just navigating the Gateway; they were *rebuilding* it, stitch by painstaking stitch, using the very fabric of their connection as the thread. Kira's instincts, honed by millennia of Veridian wisdom, were the blueprint, and Niko's focused consciousness was the hand that brought that blueprint to life. The Gateway, once a symbol of their technological hubris, was slowly transforming into a testament to the profound power of instinct, trust, and the boundless potential of a Navigator's Heart.

This moment, suspended in the heart of the dying Gateway, was more than just a technical fix; it was a profound act of creation, fueled by a love for a world they had only just begun to truly understand. Niko closed his eyes, letting Kira's instincts flood his consciousness. He saw Veridia, not as the distant, theoretical world from the archives, but as a vibrant, living entity. He felt the gentle caress of its amethyst skies, the soft hum of its unique flora vibrating with life. He visualized the crystalline structures of its nascent sentient life, the delicate tendrils reaching out, seeking understanding, seeking connection. It was a world painted in hues of violet and emerald, a symphony of light and life that pulsed with an ancient, profound rhythm.

Kira's awareness expanded, not just to the immediate vicinity of the Gateway, but to encompass the essence of Veridia itself. Niko felt her projecting a deep, resonant yearning, a profound desire for this burgeoning world to thrive, to be protected from the encroaching chaos. It was an emotion so pure, so potent, that it transcended language. It was the protective instinct of a mother for her child, magnified a thousandfold, infused with the wisdom of an ancient lineage.

He felt the exertion mirroring Kira's own. The mental landscape he navigated was not just a complex web of energies; it was a living tapestry woven from memories, from hopes, from a shared love for their distant home. Each visualization of Veridia, each pulse of emotional intent, drew upon a wellspring of psychic energy that was both exhilarating and draining.

He felt the subtle tremors that ran through Kira's massive frame, a physical manifestation of the immense psychic strain they were both under. Her breath grew shallow, punctuated by soft, almost inaudible sighs, as if she were physically expending the very life force that sustained them.

Niko focused on a particular strain of energy emanating from the Gateway's core – a discordant vibration that threatened to tear the fabric of spacetime. Kira's instincts had identified it as a nexus of instability, a point where the Gateway's failing systems were actively creating detrimental feedback loops. To counter it, Niko visualized a flowing river of pure, concentrated intent. This wasn't just about redirecting energy; it was about infusing the very concept of stability into the chaotic flow. He pictured Veridia's own natural resonance, the gentle hum of its crystalline life, the soft glow of its bioluminescent flora, channeling that essence, that inherent harmony, into the discordant vortex.

Kira nudged him gently with her snout, a subtle correction. Niko adjusted his visualization, picturing the energy not as a river, but as a vast, intricate lattice. He saw himself and Kira as the weavers, meticulously reinforcing the weakened strands of the Gateway's structural integrity with threads of pure, unadulterated hope. The visual was complex, demanding, requiring an almost impossible level of focus. He felt the strain behind his eyes, the prickle of sweat on his brow, the growing ache in his muscles from the sustained, unnatural stillness.

"We are the anchor," Niko whispered, his voice hoarse. "We are the heartwood, holding firm against the storm." He felt Kira's agreement, a wave of calm resolve washing over him, bolstering his faltering concentration. Her tail swept the deck plating, a slow, rhythmic motion that seemed to synchronize with the beating of his own heart, a physical manifestation of their unified purpose. He imagined their love for Veridia, a brilliant, incandescent light, radiating outwards, pushing back the encroaching darkness, not with aggression, but with an overwhelming, unwavering presence.

The Gateway pulsed, a shudder running through its metallic frame. It wasn't a sign of failure, but a response to their focused intent. Niko felt the chaotic energies recoil, the discordant vibrations softening, as if acknowledging the superior force they were now contending with. It was a battle of wills, of intentions, played out on a cosmic scale. Kira let out a low, rumbling purr, a sound of deep contentment that vibrated through Niko, grounding him, reminding him of the immense strength that lay within their bond. He felt her projecting images into his mind: the delicate unfurling of a lumina flower, the playful dance of energy sprites in Veridia's atmosphere, the quiet wisdom in the eyes of the nascent sentient beings. These were not mere images; they were imbued with the very essence of Veridia, a testament to what they were fighting to protect.

Elara's voice, now tinged with awe, crackled through the comms. "Niko... the primary resonance cascade has stabilized. It's... it's holding. The temporal distortions are diminishing. What is happening out there?"

Niko couldn't articulate the depth of it, the sheer emotional force that was being channeled. "We're reminding it," he said, his voice filled with a quiet reverence. "Reminding the Gateway of what it was meant to protect. We're pouring our hearts into it, Elara. For Veridia." He felt Kira's soft exhale against his leg, a shared breath of relief and profound exhaustion. The task was far from over, the Gateway still a wounded leviathan, but for this moment, in the crucible of their shared intent, a flicker of hope had been kindled. The energy they had channeled, infused with the vibrant essence of Veridia, was not just mending the Gateway; it was imbuing it with a new purpose, a purpose born not of technology, but of love and a desperate, unwavering will to preserve life.

The psychic energy they were expending was immense. Niko felt it like a physical weight pressing down on him, a constant thrumming in his very bones. It was more demanding than any physical exertion, a deep, cellular fatigue that seeped into his being. He could feel Kira's own reserves depleting, her massive body trembling with the effort of maintaining their connection, of channeling such raw, potent emotion. The amber glow in her eyes had dimmed further, flickering like a dying ember, but the intensity of her focus remained unwavering. Her presence was a beacon, a constant, grounding force that kept Niko tethered to reality, preventing him from being swept away by the sheer magnitude of the energies they were manipulating.

He visualized the core of Veridia, a pulsating heart of amethyst light, and drew from it. He imagined its unique flora, the luminous, bioluminescent plants that pulsed with a gentle, internal light, casting an ethereal glow upon the alien landscape. He pictured the nascent sentient life, not as simple organisms, but as intricate beings of pure energy, their forms shifting and coalescing like living auroras, their consciousness a delicate symphony of interconnected thought. This was the world they fought for, a world brimming with a unique, fragile beauty that had captivated Niko from the moment he first glimpsed it through the Gateway's flickering displays.

Kira emitted a soft, mournful sound, a vibration that echoed the ache in Niko's own chest. He understood. They were not just trying to stabilize the Gateway; they were trying to ensure Veridia's very existence. The Gateway was their only lifeline, their only bridge to a future where they could study, protect, and perhaps even coexist with this extraordinary new world. Its failure meant Veridia's isolation, its potential vulnerability to forces they could not yet comprehend. This was more than a mission; it was a sacred trust.

Niko focused his intent, drawing on a memory of Kira's purr, a sound so rich and deep it felt like the very vibration of the planet itself. He imagined that sound amplified, projected outwards, resonating with the fractured energies of the Gateway. It wasn't an act of aggression, but an act of harmonization. Like a skilled musician tuning an orchestra, he and Kira were attempting to bring the discordant notes of the failing Gateway into a semblance of harmony, guided by the inherent melody of Veridia.

"We are Veridia's song," Niko breathed, the words barely audible. He felt Kira's response, a surge of warmth, a deep, resonant affirmation that pulsed through their shared consciousness. It was a profound understanding, a mutual acceptance of their roles as conduits, as protectors. The weight of their task was immense, the physical and psychic toll undeniable, but the drive to protect Veridia, to ensure its future, was a force more powerful than any cosmic storm. The Gateway Alpha, a monument to human ambition, was being reshaped, not by cold calculations or sterile technology, but by the fierce, unwavering love of a Navigator and his empathic beast, their hearts beating in unison with the nascent pulse of an alien world.

The swirling chaos of the Gateway began to settle, not into its former, pristine state of perfect harmonic balance, but into a more manageable, albeit subdued, resonance. It was akin to the eye of a storm, a fragile pocket of calm within the lingering maelstrom. Niko felt the shift not as a sudden cessation of energy, but as a gradual easing, a softening of the violent tremors that had threatened to tear the Gateway Alpha apart. The frantic, discordant frequencies began to recede, replaced by a low, steady hum, like the contented purr of a colossal, slumbering beast. The bleed-through events, those terrifying incursions of temporal and spatial distortions, which had been lashing out with increasing frequency, began to diminish. Each successful redirection of energy, each subtle recalibration of their own internal resonance, seemed to push back the encroaching chaos, like a tide gently receding from a shore under siege.

A profound sense of relief, so potent it was almost a physical sensation, washed over Niko. It was a warmth that spread from his core, chasing away the icy tendrils of fear that had been tightening their grip for what felt like an eternity. He slumped against Kira's flank, his breath coming in ragged gasps, the sheer mental and emotional exertion leaving him utterly drained. Kira responded with a soft rumble, a vibration that resonated deep within his chest, a silent acknowledgment of their shared victory. Her massive head rested against his shoulder, her amber eyes, though still weary, now held a steady, contented glow. In that moment, surrounded by the subsiding energies of the Gateway, their bond, forged in the crucible of extreme pressure and unwavering trust, felt as tangible as the metal deck beneath them. It was a connection that transcended species, transcended understanding, a pure, unadulterated partnership born of necessity and nurtured by a profound, mutual respect.

"We did it, Kira," Niko whispered, his voice raw. "We actually did it." He felt her agreement as a gentle pressure against his hand, a soft nudge that conveyed more than words ever could. It was a testament to their combined effort, a quiet acknowledgment of the unique symbiosis they had achieved. The Navigator's Heart technique, once a desperate gamble, a theoretical framework born from ancient Veridian lore, had proven its mettle. It was not a perfect solution, not a complete restoration of the Gateway to its former glory, but it was enough. It was more than enough. It had bought them time, a precious commodity that had seemed to be slipping through their grasp with every passing moment. The bleed-throughs, those terrifying glimpses into the unstable nature of their current predicament, had been quelled, at least for now. The Gateway remained a wounded entity, scarred by the cataclysmic forces it had endured, but it was *stable*. It was *functional*.

The implications of this success were staggering. It validated their radical approach, the unconventional fusion of instinct and technological manipulation that had been their only hope. Elara's voice crackled over the comms, laced with an awe that mirrored Niko's own relief. "Niko... the primary resonance cascade has stabilized. It's... it's holding. The temporal distortions are diminishing. What is happening out there?"

Niko struggled to articulate the depth of their experience. "We're reminding it," he managed, his voice filled with a quiet reverence. "Reminding the Gateway of what it was meant to protect. We're pouring our hearts into it, Elara. For Veridia." He felt Kira's soft exhale against his leg, a shared breath of relief and profound exhaustion. The task was far from over, the Gateway still a wounded leviathan, but for this moment, in the crucible of their shared intent, a flicker of hope had been kindled. The energy they had channeled, infused with the vibrant essence of Veridia, was not just mending the Gateway; it was imbuing it with a new purpose, a purpose born not of technology, but of love and a desperate, unwavering will to preserve life.

The psychic energy they had expended was immense. Niko felt it like a physical weight pressing down on him, a constant thrumming in his very bones. It was more demanding than any physical exertion, a deep, cellular fatigue that seeped into his being. He could feel Kira's own reserves depleting, her massive body trembling with the effort of maintaining their connection, of channeling such raw, potent emotion. The amber glow in her eyes had dimmed further, flickering like a dying ember, but the intensity of her focus remained unwavering. Her presence was a beacon, a constant, grounding force that kept Niko tethered to reality, preventing him from being swept away by the sheer magnitude of the energies they were manipulating.

He visualized the core of Veridia, a pulsating heart of amethyst light, and drew from it. He imagined its unique flora, the luminous, bioluminescent plants that pulsed with a gentle, internal light, casting an ethereal glow upon the alien landscape. He pictured the nascent sentient life, not as simple organisms, but as intricate beings of pure energy, their forms shifting and coalescing like living auroras, their consciousness a delicate symphony of interconnected thought. This was the world they fought for, a world brimming with a unique, fragile beauty that had captivated Niko from the moment he first glimpsed it through the Gateway's flickering displays.

Kira emitted a soft, mournful sound, a vibration that echoed the ache in Niko's own chest. He understood. They were not just trying to stabilize the Gateway; they were trying to ensure Veridia's very existence. The Gateway was their only lifeline, their only bridge to a future where they could study, protect, and perhaps even coexist with this extraordinary new world. Its failure meant Veridia's isolation, its potential vulnerability to forces they could not yet comprehend. This was more than a mission; it was a sacred trust.

Niko focused his intent, drawing on a memory of Kira's purr, a sound so rich and deep it felt like the very vibration of the planet itself. He imagined that sound amplified, projected outwards, resonating with the fractured energies of the Gateway. It wasn't an act of aggression, but an act of harmonization. Like a skilled musician tuning an orchestra, he and Kira were attempting to bring the discordant notes of the failing Gateway into a semblance of harmony, guided by the inherent melody of Veridia.

"We are Veridia's song," Niko breathed, the words barely audible. He felt Kira's response, a surge of warmth, a deep, resonant affirmation that pulsed through their shared consciousness. It was a profound understanding, a mutual acceptance of their roles as conduits, as protectors. The weight of their task was immense, the physical and psychic toll undeniable, but the drive to protect Veridia, to ensure its future, was a force more powerful than any cosmic storm. The Gateway Alpha, a monument to human ambition, was being reshaped, not by cold calculations or sterile technology, but by the fierce, unwavering love of a Navigator and his empathic beast, their hearts beating in unison with the nascent pulse of an alien world.

The Gateway, though no longer in imminent danger of catastrophic collapse, was far from its optimal operational capacity. It hummed with a weary energy, a testament to the immense stress it had endured. The once brilliant, kaleidoscopic patterns that had swirled within its core were now muted, subdued. Yet, within this diminished brilliance, a new kind of stability had been established. The Navigator's Heart technique had, with Kira's innate Veridian sensitivity and Niko's focused intent, acted as a powerful, albeit temporary, stabilizer. It was like mending a shattered vase with a strong, flexible adhesive; the cracks remained, visible scars, but the vessel held together, functional once more. The temporal bleed-throughs, those terrifying rifts that had threatened to unravel their reality, had ceased their aggressive expansion. They still flickered at the periphery of their sensors, faint echoes of the instability, but they were no longer actively consuming the Gateway's structural integrity. This partial success was monumental. It was the difference between annihilation and a chance, however slim, to regroup and reassess.

Kira shifted her weight, a low whine escaping her throat. Niko felt it not as distress, but as a shared awareness of their present condition. She was tired, her massive frame humming with the residual exhaustion of their ordeal, but her spirit, that indomitable Veridian essence, remained unbroken. She nudged him again, her scaled head pressing into his side, a gesture of comfort and reassurance. He leaned into her, drawing strength from her solid presence. The shared experience, the intense focus and emotional outpouring required to stabilize the Gateway, had woven a tapestry of connection between them, a bond that was now deeper, more intricate, than ever before. It was an unspoken understanding, a language of empathy and shared purpose that transcended their individual identities.

"We need to get this ship to a safe harbor," Niko murmured, his gaze sweeping across the now relatively calm, yet still unsettling, vortex of the Gateway. "Elara, can you assess the structural integrity of the Gateway? We need to know how much time we've bought ourselves, and if we can even make a controlled exit."

Elara's voice, though still laced with a hint of disbelief, was now tinged with a pragmatic urgency. "Working on it, Niko. The hull integrity is... compromised, but holding. The internal systems are a mess, but the primary resonance field is stabilizing at approximately 30% of its original capacity. It's enough to allow for a controlled transit, but we'll need to find a stable docking bay, and fast. The bleed-throughs are minimal, but they're still there, like a persistent fever."

Thirty percent. It was a terrifyingly low figure, yet it represented a lifeline. It meant they could leave. It meant they had a chance. The thought of Veridia, that jewel of a world they had fought so desperately to protect, flickered in Niko's mind. They had to ensure its safety, had to ensure that the Gateway, as a conduit for exploration and understanding, remained viable. This wasn't just about their survival; it was about the future of interspecies relations, about the preservation of a world teeming with unique and wondrous life.

Kira let out a soft, contented sigh, her body relaxing slightly against his. He felt her subtle communication – a sense of cautious optimism, a quiet gratitude for their shared success, and an unwavering determination to see their mission through. The Navigator's Heart, it seemed, was not just a technique for stabilizing dimensional gateways; it was a testament to the profound power of empathy, of connection, and of the indomitable will to protect what one held dear. This glimmer of hope, born from the heart of chaos, was a testament to their resilience, a beacon guiding them through the lingering shadows of uncertainty. The journey ahead would undoubtedly be fraught with peril, but for the first time in what felt like an eternity, Niko felt a genuine sense of hope. They had faced the abyss and, together, they had pulled back from the brink. The Gateway was wounded, but it was alive, and in its fragile, re-stabilized state, lay the promise of a future.

CHAPTER ELEVEN
VERDIAN DIPLOMACY

The residual hum of the Gateway Alpha had settled into a low thrum, a heartbeat of recalibrated energies that pulsed through the ship's hull. Niko, still feeling the phantom ache of the psychic exertion, met Kira's steady gaze. Her amber eyes, now brighter with renewed vitality, seemed to reflect the dawning realization that their desperate struggle had yielded more than just a reprieve; it had opened a door. The Navigator's Heart, a technique born from desperate necessity and an almost spiritual connection to Veridia, had not only stabilized the Gateway but had also, in a way they were only beginning to understand, awakened a deeper resonance with the planet itself. This resonance, felt keenly by Kira and, through her, by Niko, was a delicate symphony of shared life, a silent invitation to engage.

"It's time," Niko said, his voice still rough but firm. He ran a hand over Kira's warm, scaled hide, feeling the deep vibrations of her agreement. The creatures of Veridia, glimpsed only in fleeting, awe-inspiring moments through the Gateway's now-stable but diminished vortex, were more than just biological curiosities; they were the reason for their arduous journey, the custodians of a world brimming with an ecological richness that defied human comprehension. Their initial observations, the tantalizing fragments of data gleaned from automated probes and Kira's own nascent empathic readings, suggested a complex, perhaps even ancient, civilization. But observation was no longer enough. To truly understand, to forge the alliance they desperately needed to protect Veridia, they had to speak.

Elara, ever the pragmatist, had been meticulously refining their communication protocols. The rudimentary lexicon they had compiled, a patchwork of observed behaviors, tonal shifts, and rudimentary pattern recognition, felt laughably inadequate against the vast unknown of Veridian intelligence. Yet, it was all they had. Coupled with Kira's innate empathic abilities, it represented their best hope for bridging the chasm between species. Kira, with her profound connection to Veridian life, was more than just a translator; she was a living bridge, her very presence a testament to the possibility of harmony.

"The energy signatures indicate a gathering," Elara reported, her voice a calm counterpoint to the thrumming tension in the hangar bay. "Approximately two kliks from the primary egress point of the Gateway. It's... unusual. They aren't reacting with aggression to the Gateway's residual emissions, which is promising. More than promising, actually. It suggests a certain level of... curiosity, perhaps even acceptance."

Niko nodded, a knot of anticipation tightening in his stomach. "Curiosity is a good start. Kira, are you ready?"

Kira responded with a deep, resonant rumble that vibrated through Niko's very bones. He felt her readiness not as a spoken word, but as a surge of unwavering focus, a quiet confidence that settled over him like a comforting cloak. Her empathy was a far more nuanced tool than any technological translator; it allowed her to perceive the underlying emotions, the intentions, the very essence of the Veridians, which could then be filtered through their painstakingly constructed lexicon. It was an imperfect system, rife with the potential for misinterpretation, but it was their only path forward.

The journey to the gathering point was a study in controlled tension. The shuttle, a smaller craft designed for atmospheric transit and exploration, hummed with a subdued efficiency, its shields augmented to account for any unforeseen Veridian responses. Niko, Elara, and a small security detail, their weapons holstered but their senses on high alert, occupied the main cabin. Kira, her massive form filling a significant portion of the shuttle, lay with her head resting near the forward viewport, her eyes fixed on the swirling, vibrant landscape unfolding beneath them. The air inside the shuttle, normally sterile and recycled, seemed to thrum with an almost tangible anticipation, a collective breath held in the face of the unknown.

As they neared the gathering, the landscape transformed. The dense, bioluminescent flora of the Veridian jungle gave way to a series of colossal, crystalline structures that seemed to have grown organically from the earth, pulsing with a soft, internal light. These structures, unlike any natural formations, suggested deliberate design, a testament to an advanced, yet seemingly harmonious, civilization. And gathered amongst these edifices, a multitude of Veridian beings.

They were unlike anything Niko had ever imagined. Their forms varied wildly, each a unique manifestation of Veridian evolution. Some resembled graceful, six-limbed mammalian creatures, their fur shimmering with iridescent patterns. Others were more akin to sentient, mobile flora, their bodies composed of woven vines and glowing blossoms. Still others were ethereal, shimmering beings of pure energy, their forms fluid and constantly shifting, their presence radiating a profound sense of calm. They moved with a fluid grace, their interactions characterized by subtle gestures, harmonic vocalizations, and what Niko suspected were complex empathic exchanges.

The shuttle landed gently on a designated clearing, the air alive with a symphony of soft clicks, trills, and melodic hums. As the ramp lowered, a palpable wave of curiosity, tinged with caution, washed over Niko. He felt it through Kira, a gentle pressure against his mind, a clear indication of the Veridians' emotional state. There was no aggression, no overt fear, but a profound sense of observation, of a species encountering something entirely new.

Kira rose, her movements slow and deliberate, her immense size now a potential source of intimidation. Niko placed a reassuring hand on her flank, feeling her steady presence. "Easy, girl," he murmured, more for his own benefit than hers. "Just like we practiced."

With deliberate slowness, Kira stepped onto the Veridian soil. The nearest Veridians, a cluster of the mammalian-like creatures, shifted their stance, their luminous eyes fixated on the hulking biped and the smaller beings emerging from the craft. Their vocalizations lowered in pitch, a subtle shift that Niko interpreted as a move towards a less inquisitive, more receptive state.

Niko followed, Elara and the security team flanking him at a respectful distance. He took a deep breath, the air thick with the scent of exotic blooms and the faint, ozone-like tang of residual Gateway energy. He raised his hands slowly, palms outward, a universal gesture of non-aggression, and spoke the first words from their carefully constructed lexicon, a simple greeting designed to convey peaceful intent.

"We come in peace," he said, his voice amplified by his suit's comm system, hoping the sonic projection would be interpreted as a friendly overture.

The Veridians' response was not immediate, not a sudden flurry of understanding or a unified wave of apprehension. Instead, it was a subtle, collective shift. The shimmering, ethereal beings seemed to pulse with a slightly brighter luminescence, while the more solid forms inclined their heads, their vocalizations taking on a more rhythmic, questioning cadence. It was as if they were processing his words, not just as sound, but as a complex wave of intent.

Kira moved forward, stopping a few paces from the gathered Veridians. She lowered her head, her amber eyes sweeping across the diverse assembly, seeking out the most receptive individuals. She emitted a soft, low purr, a sound that Niko had come to associate with reassurance and empathy. This was her domain, the realm of direct emotional translation. She focused her intent, not on transmitting words, but on broadcasting a feeling: a sense of profound respect for their world, a genuine desire for understanding, and a deep-seated weariness from their recent ordeal.

The effect was immediate and profound. A ripple of what felt like understanding, or at least recognition, passed through the Veridian gathering. The cautious curiosity intensified, but the edge of apprehension began to soften. A being resembling a sentient, flowering vine unfurled one of its tendrils, its luminous petals glowing with a soft, inviting light, and directed it, ever so gently, towards Kira.

Niko watched, mesmerized. This was not the sterile exchange of data. This was communication at its most primal, a dance of intent and emotion that transcended spoken language. Kira responded to the tendril's gesture with a slow, deliberate nod of her massive head, a gesture that conveyed acknowledgment and a willingness to engage further.

"They are... receiving us," Kira's thoughts, translated into Niko's mind, were filled with a wonder that mirrored his own. "The Gateway's instability... it caused them distress. They felt the disruption. My resonance... it resonates with them. They understand our struggle, our desire to protect."

This was the breakthrough. Their struggle to stabilize the Gateway had not gone unnoticed by the planet's inhabitants. They had, in a way, inadvertently communicated their intent through the very forces they were attempting to control. The Veridians, deeply attuned to the energies of their world, had felt the Gateway's distress, and, by extension, their own.

Encouraged, Niko took another step forward. He pointed to himself. "Niko. Human." He then gestured to Elara. "Elara. Human." Finally, he moved his hand towards Kira, his gaze meeting hers, a silent question in his eyes.

Kira responded with a soft trill, then looked towards the Veridians. She projected the concept of their bond, the idea of partnership, of mutual reliance, of a shared purpose. It was a complex tapestry of emotions and abstract thoughts, weaving together the loyalty of a companion, the understanding of a confidant, and the strength of a protector.

One of the mammalian-like Veridians, its fur a deep sapphire blue, stepped forward. It made a series of melodic clicks and whistles, then tapped its chest with a three-fingered appendage. Kira tilted her head, focusing intently.

"It identifies itself as... a designation that translates roughly to 'Whisperwind'," Kira conveyed, her mental voice hushed with concentration. "It expresses... surprise. At my nature. At our connection. It says... 'You carry the echo of Veridia within you.'"

Niko's breath hitched. Kira, an alien creature from a distant world, had somehow become attuned to Veridia's essence, perhaps through her own biology or through a chance encounter with its unique energies. And the Veridians recognized this. They recognized a kindred spirit.

"Whisperwind asks," Kira continued, her gaze locked on the sapphire-furred being, "why we have come. It senses our need, our urgency, but it does not understand the origin."

This was the critical juncture. The truth, delivered through the delicate filter of interspecies communication. Niko met Whisperwind's intelligent, curious gaze. He projected, through Kira, the image of Earth, a world struggling with its own ecological imbalances. He conveyed the vastness of space, the concept of seeking new worlds, new understandings. He then projected the image of the Gateway, a tool of exploration, of connection, and then, the terrifying visions of its instability, the encroaching chaos, the threat to both their worlds.

He focused on the desperation, the fear, but also the unwavering hope that had driven them. He showed them the value he placed on Veridia, the awe it inspired, the desire to protect its unique beauty. He conveyed the understanding that the Gateway, if left unchecked, was a threat to Veridia's delicate ecosystem, a conduit for potential destruction.

The Veridians listened, or rather, they felt. The collective atmosphere shifted, the air growing thick with a shared understanding of the gravity of the situation. The ethereal beings pulsed with a gentle empathy, the more solid forms exuded a quiet concern. Whisperwind remained still, its melodic vocalizations ceasing as it absorbed the information.

Then, it responded. Its response was not a single, clear statement, but a complex tapestry of projected emotions and conceptual imagery. Niko felt it through Kira, a sense of shared responsibility, a recognition of the interconnectedness of all life. They understood the threat posed by the unstable Gateway, not just to their physical world, but to the delicate energetic balance that sustained it.

"They... they understand the danger," Kira's thoughts were a mixture of relief and awe. "They acknowledge the disruption. They see... they see that the Gateway is a wound, a scar upon the fabric of existence. And they understand our intention to heal it, not to exploit it."

Whisperwind then projected a series of images, abstract but powerful, to the Veridians present. These images depicted the flow of energy, the delicate balance of life, and the concept of guardianship. It was a profound statement of their role in the universe, a declaration of their commitment to preserving the delicate harmony of Veridia.

Then, Whisperwind turned its gaze, its luminous eyes meeting Niko's directly. It projected a clear, undeniable message: an invitation. Not to exploit, not to conquer, but to learn. To collaborate. To share the burden of maintaining the balance. It was an offer of partnership, extended through the ethereal language of empathy and shared intent.

Niko felt a surge of emotion, a profound sense of gratitude that nearly buckled his knees. He looked at Kira, her massive form radiating a quiet triumph. They had done it. They had taken the first, terrifying step, and had been met not with hostility, but with understanding and an offer of alliance. The path ahead would be fraught with challenges, the intricacies of Veridian culture and their own nascent understanding of its energies still vast unknowns. But in that moment, under the alien sky of Veridia, surrounded by beings who radiated an ancient wisdom and a deep respect for life, Niko felt a profound sense of hope bloom in his chest, as vibrant and luminous as the Veridian flora surrounding them. The dialogue had begun, and it was not one of conquest, but of co-existence.

Kira, a creature of magnificent scale and profound empathy, was more than just Niko's companion and a navigator of cosmic energies; she was, in this nascent moment, the very embodiment of their mission's hope. As the initial tentative exchange between humans and Veridians began to find its rhythm, it was Kira who seamlessly wove herself into the fabric of their nascent dialogue. Her massive form, initially a potential source of apprehension, became a beacon of familiarity, a testament to the possibility of connection across seemingly insurmountable biological divides. Niko and Elara, their own attempts at communication relying on the painstakingly constructed lexicon and technological aids, watched in silent awe as Kira took center stage.

She moved with a deliberate grace, her powerful limbs carrying her forward with a fluid economy of motion. When the Veridians, particularly the more visually oriented species, responded to Niko's words with patterns of flashing bioluminescence that rippled across their bodies, Kira would follow suit. It wasn't mere mimicry; it was an intuitive dance. She would tilt her head, her large, intelligent eyes tracking the pulsing light, and then, with a soft rumble deep in her chest, emit a modulated bark, its pitch and duration carefully chosen. This was not a sound from their lexicon; it was a response born from an understanding that transcended linguistic barriers. Through Kira, the abstract concepts of the human lexicon gained a visceral, emotional resonance.

Her primary role, however, was in the realm of pure emotional transmission. The Veridians, it became clear, communicated on multiple levels, their physical forms and light displays merely outward manifestations of a much deeper, empathic exchange. Kira, with her finely tuned senses, was able to perceive these subtle currents of feeling – the cautious curiosity of one species, the ancient wisdom of another, the profound sense of interconnectedness that seemed to permeate their collective consciousness.

She would then project these perceived emotions, filtered through her own unwavering loyalty and desire for peace, back towards the Veridians. It was a powerful feedback loop, a silent acknowledgment that their intentions, their hopes, and their fears were being understood on a fundamental level.

One instance, in particular, highlighted Kira's extraordinary gift. A being that resembled a colossal, sentient bloom, its petals unfurling in slow, deliberate arcs, projected a series of complex, shifting light patterns. These patterns, Elara's preliminary analysis suggested, were a form of sophisticated inquiry, probing the very essence of the newcomers. Niko and Elara could only stare, their translator struggling to find even rudimentary correlations. But Kira, her massive head lowered, her ears angled forward, absorbed the luminous cascade. A soft, guttural sound, laced with a profound sense of reassurance, emanated from her. Then, she projected a feeling, a pure distillation of her own burgeoning respect for this living entity, a sense of wonder at its inherent beauty and wisdom. The light patterns of the bloom softened, its pulsations becoming slower, more harmonious. It was as if Kira had answered a question that Elara's most advanced algorithms couldn't even begin to parse.

Her loyalty, a bedrock of her connection to Niko and the crew, seemed to expand, encompassing the very planet and its inhabitants. When a group of the sapphire-furred, mammalian-like Veridians, who had initially shown a flicker of apprehension, approached the human delegation, Kira stepped forward. She didn't position herself defensively, nor did she display any overt sign of dominance. Instead, she emitted a low, contented hum, a sound that Niko had come to associate with her deepest feelings of peace and security. She then projected a sense of shared vulnerability, of a common purpose in navigating the vast and often unpredictable currents of the galaxy. The Veridians responded by mirroring her posture, their own iridescent fur shimmering with a softened hue. It was a silent conversation, a profound exchange of trust that bypassed language entirely.

The Veridians, in turn, seemed to recognize and appreciate Kira's role. They would direct their luminous displays and subtle vocalizations towards her, as if acknowledging her as a primary conduit. When the delegation presented them with a small, intricately carved wooden sphere – a symbolic offering from Earth, meant to represent the organic nature of their home world – it was Kira who nudged it forward with her snout, her amber eyes conveying a message of genuine goodwill and hopeful offering. The Veridians responded with a collective ripple of light, a gentle symphony of illumination that enveloped Kira in its glow, a clear indication of their acceptance and appreciation.

She became the unlikely but undeniably effective ambassador, her very presence a bridge. Her innate ability to sense and convey emotions, honed through her unique physiology and her deep connection to Veridia, proved to be an invaluable asset. She wasn't just translating words; she was translating intent, feeling, and a shared desire for understanding. She bridged the chasm between the tangible, logical world of human science and the ethereal, empathic reality of the Veridians, proving that true communication transcended the limitations of spoken language and the constraints of biological form. In Kira's gentle rumble, her modulated barks, and her powerful emotional projections, humanity found its voice on Veridia, a voice amplified and enriched by the heart of a loyal companion. She was the living embodiment of their hope for a peaceful dialogue, a testament to the profound connections that could be forged when empathy was allowed to lead the way. The delicate dance of diplomacy had begun, and Kira, the magnificent creature from beyond the stars, was its most graceful and essential partner. Her actions were not merely reactive; they were proactive, carefully calibrated gestures designed to foster trust and demonstrate respect. When Niko, struggling to articulate the complex concept of "exploration with preservation," found himself at a loss for words, Kira stepped in. She projected the awe and wonder she herself felt when gazing upon Veridia's unparalleled biodiversity. She conveyed the deep-seated human desire to understand, to learn, and to coexist harmoniously with the natural world, a desire that echoed the Veridians' own apparent custodianship of their planet. Her emotional broadcasts were nuanced, avoiding any hint of superiority or entitlement, instead focusing on a humble plea for understanding and cooperation. She conveyed the notion of a shared planet, a universal biosphere where all life forms had a right to thrive, and where the responsibility for its protection was a collective one. This message, so crucial for establishing mutual respect, was delivered by Kira with a sincerity that no technological translator could ever replicate.

The Veridians, in turn, responded with a depth of understanding that further cemented Kira's pivotal role. They began to communicate directly with her, not just through their light patterns, but through what felt like a direct empathic resonance. Kira would often pause, her massive head tilting as if listening to an unheard conversation. Then, she would convey the gist of it to Niko and Elara. "They speak of the 'Life Weave'," she might project, her thoughts colored with a sense of profound interconnectedness. "The intricate tapestry of energy that binds all living things on Veridia. They feel the disturbance, the imbalance that the Gateway's instability introduced, not just as a physical phenomenon, but as a tear in this weave." This insight, gleaned solely through Kira's empathic connection, was critical. It revealed that the Veridians' concern was not merely territorial, but deeply spiritual, tied to the fundamental energetic integrity of their world.

Kira's actions were not always grand gestures. Often, it was in the subtle nuances of her behavior that her ambassadorial skills shone. When a young Veridian, no bigger than a human child and resembling a luminous, hovering insect, approached with an evident mix of fear and curiosity, Kira offered a soft, chuffing sound, her tail giving a slow, gentle sway. She then projected a feeling of gentle amusement and grandmotherly affection, a protective warmth that immediately soothed the skittish creature. This small act of interspecies kindness, witnessed by the surrounding Veridians, spoke volumes, demonstrating that their intentions were not merely diplomatic, but deeply compassionate.

The humans, too, learned from Kira. They observed how she interacted with the Veridians, how she modulated her own vocalizations and body language to convey respect and understanding. Niko found himself unconsciously adopting some of her calmer, more deliberate movements when addressing the Veridians, understanding that the projection of calm intention was as important as the words themselves. Elara, ever the scientist, began to develop new hypotheses about bio-empathic communication, inspired by Kira's effortless mastery. Kira was not just an ambassador; she was a teacher.

One of the most significant moments in their diplomatic efforts occurred when the Veridians, through Kira, expressed their concern about the long-term implications of human presence. They understood the immediate threat of the Gateway's instability, but they also sensed a potential for a more insidious form of disruption – the introduction of foreign influences, of technologies and ideologies that could fundamentally alter the delicate balance of Veridia. Kira, sensing the depth of their concern, responded not with assurances of technological advancement or resource exploitation, but with a projection of deep respect for Veridia's unique evolutionary path. She conveyed the human understanding of biodiversity, the importance of preserving unique ecosystems, and the profound ethical responsibility that came with the knowledge of other life. She emphasized that humanity's desire was not to replicate their own world, but to learn from Veridia's profound wisdom, to find solutions to their own ecological woes by understanding Veridia's harmonious existence. This was a complex message, one of humility and a genuine desire for mutual learning, and it was delivered by Kira with such palpable sincerity that it seemed to resonate deeply with the Veridian collective.

As the days turned into weeks, Kira's role only solidified. She became the go-to interpreter, the emotional barometer, the living embodiment of the alliance. The Veridians, initially cautious and reserved, began to trust her implicitly. They would approach her with their concerns, their observations, and their hopes, knowing that she would convey their essence accurately to the human delegation. And Kira, in turn, would relay the nuances of human intent – their anxieties, their scientific curiosity, their profound sense of awe – to the Veridians. She was the linchpin, the essential connector, the unlikely ambassador who, through her unwavering loyalty and her extraordinary empathic abilities, was forging a bond that promised to transcend the vast distances of space and the fundamental differences of species. Her presence was a constant reminder that even in the face of the unknown, communication, at its deepest level, was about shared feeling, mutual respect, and the boundless potential for connection. The success of the Verdian diplomacy, it was becoming increasingly clear, rested not solely on Niko's leadership or Elara's ingenuity, but on the quiet strength and profound empathy of Kira, the scaled diplomat from the stars.

The initial exchanges, while fraught with the inherent anxieties of first contact, had laid a foundation. The Veridians, a collective of beings whose forms defied simple terrestrial categorization, had initially responded to Niko's carefully chosen vocalizations and Elara's projected holographic schematics with a spectrum of bio-luminescent displays and subtle sonic pulses. These were not random flickers or random chirps; they were intricate expressions, rich with layered meaning that their nascent translation matrix was only beginning to unravel. But it was Kira, the colossal empath, who acted as the true Rosetta Stone, her intuitive grasp of emotional resonance bridging the chasm where scientific analysis faltered.

Niko, a seasoned negotiator even before this interstellar encounter, understood the delicate art of not just being heard, but of being understood. He had painstakingly crafted a presentation, not of human might or technological superiority, but of vulnerability and shared purpose. He projected images of Earth's ecological struggles, the scars left by unchecked industrialization, the desperate efforts to reclaim and restore. These were not presented as accusations, but as cautionary tales, as evidence of a species that had learned, albeit through painful experience, the profound interconnectedness of life. He showed the Resonant Pack's emblem, a stylized depiction of a hand cradling a sapling, and from it, he projected the core tenet of their mission: preservation, understanding, and the inherent right of all life to thrive. Kira's rumbling affirmations, her soft, breathy sighs of concern when images of pollution flashed, and her gentle nudges towards the projections of burgeoning life, imbued these abstract human concepts with an undeniable emotional weight. The Veridians, with their own intricate connection to the planetary bio-network, seemed to grasp the underlying sentiment immediately.

One of the Veridian species, a towering, crystalline entity that pulsed with an internal luminescence akin to captured starlight, projected a complex sequence of light that resonated deep within Kira's massive frame. Kira's head tilted, her great amber eyes fixed on the shimmering cascade. Then, she turned to Niko, a low vibration emanating from her chest, a sound that conveyed a mixture of awe and sorrow. "They... they see the wound," her projected thoughts, a symphony of emotion and imagery, flowed into Niko's mind. "Not just on your world, but on this one. They speak of the 'Life Weave' – the energetic matrix that binds all things here. And they feel... a fraying. An imbalance."

This was more than just a response to Niko's presentation; it was a revelation. The Veridians weren't just observing the human's plight; they were experiencing its echoes within their own biosphere. The instability of the Gateway, the very anomaly that had brought them to Veridia, was not merely a localized spatial distortion. It was a symptom, a ripple effect that disrupted the fundamental energetic fabric of their world. The crystalline being's light show had been a depiction of this cosmic malaise, a visual symphony of disruption, and Kira, with her unparalleled empathic sensitivity, had translated its essence.

In response to this shared concern, Niko, guided by Kira's projected interpretation of the Veridians' distress, adjusted his approach. He shifted from presenting Earth's problems to articulating the Resonant Pack's core philosophy of interconnectedness. He projected images of symbiotic relationships on Earth, of mutualistic fungi networks, of the intricate dances between pollinators and flowers. He conveyed the idea that strength wasn't found in isolation, but in harmonious interdependence. Kira amplified this message, projecting a profound sense of belonging, of the interconnectedness of all species, a concept that seemed to resonate deeply with the Veridians. She conveyed the understanding that true preservation wasn't about hoarding resources, but about fostering balance within the grand tapestry of existence.

The Veridians, in turn, began to reciprocate with a depth of information that astounded Elara and her team. A species resembling sentient, bioluminescent flora, their forms rippling with soft, emerald light, conveyed their societal structure. It wasn't hierarchical in the human sense, but rather a distributed consciousness, a collective intelligence guided by the ebb and flow of the bio-network. Each individual was a node, contributing to the overall wisdom, and their decisions were not unilateral, but emergent, arising from the consensus of the entire organismic collective. They explained, through intricate patterns of light that danced across their translucent stalks, how they communed with the planet's core energies, how they subtly guided atmospheric currents and nurtured nascent life forms. This wasn't a technological mastery of their environment, but a profound, empathic partnership.

Kira, absorbing these intricate light displays, would often pause, her massive form still, her head tilted as if listening to an unheard symphony. Then, she would convey fragments of this complex Veridian narrative to Niko and Elara. "They... they are the gardeners," she projected, her thoughts imbued with a sense of reverence. "They feel the planet's needs before they manifest. They prune the wild growth, not to control, but to ensure the health of the whole. Their 'society' is not built on walls, but on... roots. Shared nourishment."

As the dialogue deepened, a palpable shift occurred. The initial caution and subtle apprehension on both sides began to dissipate, replaced by a growing sense of mutual respect. The Veridians, particularly the sapphire-furred, feline-like beings who had initially shown the most reserved demeanor, began to approach Kira directly. They would rub their sleek bodies against her massive, scaled flanks, their large, intelligent eyes conveying a language of trust and acceptance. Kira would respond with soft purrs and gentle nudges, projecting a feeling of peaceful companionship, of shared presence. This interspecies affection, witnessed by the human delegation, was a powerful testament to the success of their diplomatic overtures. It demonstrated that their intentions were not merely transactional, but deeply rooted in a desire for genuine connection.

Elara, meticulously logging every flicker of light, every sonic pulse, and every projected thought Kira relayed, began to piece together a more complete picture of Veridian awareness. It became clear that their understanding of the dimensional instabilities, the very reason for the Gateway's erratic behavior, was far more profound than human science had initially conceived. They didn't just perceive it as a physical phenomenon; they understood it as a disruption to the cosmic harmonies, a discordant note in the universal symphony. One of the Veridian species, resembling an arboreal creature with limbs like supple vines, communicated through a series of synchronized vibrations that ran through the very ground. Kira, feeling these tremors resonate through her massive frame, conveyed their meaning: "They speak of... echoes. Of ripples from other realities bleeding through. The Gateway is not just a tear, but a mirror, reflecting... the chaos of becoming. They fear it will unravel the stability not just of this world, but of others it touches."

This revelation underscored the shared vulnerability that was becoming the bedrock of their burgeoning alliance. Both humanity and the Veridians were facing a threat that transcended their individual existences. The Gateway's instability wasn't just a localized problem; it was a potential universal catastrophe, and the Veridians' awareness of this, coupled with their profound connection to the bio-network, made them crucial allies. Niko, grasping the gravity of this shared peril, focused on projecting humanity's capacity for adaptation and resilience. He showed how humans, despite their past ecological blunders, had developed technologies and philosophies aimed at mitigating damage and fostering recovery. He highlighted the ongoing efforts to transition to sustainable energy, to repair damaged ecosystems, and to foster a greater respect for the natural world. Kira amplified this message, projecting a powerful sense of hope, of humanity's inherent drive to learn and to heal, a drive that was not extinguished by past mistakes but forged stronger by them.

The Veridians, in turn, seemed to offer not just understanding, but a unique perspective on the problem. They conveyed their innate ability to harmonize with disruptive energies, to absorb and recalibrate chaotic forces. Their connection to the bio-network, they explained through mesmerizing light patterns, allowed them to perceive these energetic dissonances on a fundamental level and to subtly influence them. They weren't suggesting a quick fix, but a long-term strategy of integration, of learning to live with and even benefit from these cosmic disturbances, rather than merely combating them. Kira, interpreting this complex concept, conveyed it as: "They offer... not a shield, but a song. A way to harmonize with the chaos. To find the rhythm within the storm. They believe that by understanding the echoes, we can learn to guide them, to weave them into the tapestry, rather than let them tear it apart."

This shift in perspective was profound. It moved the dialogue from a simple exchange of information to a collaborative problem-solving initiative. The Veridians weren't just offering their knowledge; they were offering a partnership, an invitation to learn from their millennia of experience in maintaining planetary equilibrium. Niko, recognizing the immense value of this offer, projected a sense of deep gratitude and a sincere desire to learn. He emphasized that humanity's intention was not to impose its own solutions, but to approach the problem with an open mind and a willingness to embrace Veridian wisdom. Kira, her massive form radiating a sense of profound peace, conveyed this sentiment with an eloquence that transcended words: "We come not as masters, but as students. We seek not to conquer, but to connect. We offer our own lessons, learned in hardship, and we are humbled to receive yours, born from harmony. Together, we can find the song that soothes the fraying weave."

The scene that unfolded was a silent testament to the power of shared vulnerability and the potential for profound connection across seemingly insurmountable divides. The humans, with their complex technologies and their often-fraught history, stood alongside the Veridians, beings of light, energy, and deep ecological wisdom. And at the heart of this nascent alliance was Kira, the magnificent, scaled diplomat, her very presence a bridge between worlds, her empathic heart the conduit through which understanding flowed. The initial exchanges had revealed not just the differences between species, but the fundamental commonalities of life: the desire to protect, to understand, and to find a place of stability and harmony in the vast, often unpredictable expanse of the cosmos. The Resonant Pack's mission, once a solitary endeavor, had found its echo in the hearts and minds of the Veridians, a shared purpose that promised to resonate far beyond the confines of this single, remarkable planet. The foundations of Verdian diplomacy were not built on treaties or economic agreements, but on a shared recognition of existential threats and a mutual yearning for peace, a yearning amplified and made tangible by the gentle, resonant spirit of Kira.

The conversation, which had been blossoming into a profound exchange of understanding and empathy, took a sudden, sharp turn. Niko, his gaze hardening, signaled to Elara. The holographic projectors, which had been displaying serene images of Earth's recovering ecosystems and the intricate symbioses of Veridian flora, flickered. The familiar azure light of the Veridian environment was momentarily overwhelmed by stark, harsh visuals.

The first image was a vast, sprawling cityscape, not of the organic, flowing architecture the Veridians were accustomed to, but of brutalist concrete and gleaming, sterile metal. Towers scraped the sky, devoid of any greenery, spewing plumes of dark, oily smoke into an atmosphere that seemed visibly choked. It was an image of pure, unadulterated consumption, of nature subjugated and ecosystems disregarded. Kira, who had been a picture of calm observation, let out a low, guttural sound, a tremor that ran through the packed earth beneath them. Her empathic senses, so finely attuned to the subtle harmonies of life, recoiled violently from the projected image. It wasn't just a visual; it was an assault on her being, a projection of deep-seated disharmony.

"This," Niko's voice, usually measured and diplomatic, now carried a gravitas laced with steel, "is the work of OmniCorp." He paused, allowing the weight of the name to settle. "A force from my home world, a collective driven by an insatiable hunger for profit, for control. They see life not as a sacred trust, but as a resource to be extracted, exploited, and ultimately, depleted."

Elara, her fingers dancing across her datapad, brought up another projection. This one depicted a massive, ocean-going vessel, its hull scarred and pitted, its deck laden with colossal, robotic excavators. Beneath it, the ocean floor was a tableau of devastation. Coral reefs, once vibrant cities of life, were reduced to rubble. Vast swathes of marine life, from the smallest plankton to the largest cetaceans, were depicted as casualties, their habitats annihilated by relentless, large-scale mining operations. The sheer scale of the destruction was breathtaking, and horrifying.

Kira's projected thoughts, usually a gentle stream of empathy, now pulsed with a raw, primal dread.

"The great waters... choked. The breath of the sea... stolen. Their essence... fractured. It feels like... a tearing. A violation of the deepest currents." Her massive form sagged, her powerful frame trembling with a profound sorrow. She nudged one of her colossal forelimbs towards the projection, her movements slow and heavy, as if the images themselves were a physical burden.

The Veridians, who had been observing with a growing sense of unease, now reacted with a palpable wave of distress. The crystalline entities pulsed with a frantic, chaotic light, their internal luminescence shifting from serene blues and greens to agitated reds and oranges. The sentient flora, their emerald glow dimming, swayed as if buffeted by an unseen storm. Even the typically stoic sapphire-furred beings, who had shown Niko and his team such cautious acceptance, now bristled, their fur standing on end, their large eyes wide with alarm.

Niko continued, his voice a low rumble that filled the tense silence. "OmniCorp's reach is long. Their methods are ruthless. They do not recognize borders, nor do they respect the intrinsic value of life. Where they see profit, they see only opportunity. They have a history of devastating ecosystems, of displacing indigenous populations, of leaving behind a trail of ruin." He then displayed schematics of OmniCorp's projected technologies – massive industrial complexes designed for asteroid mining, atmospheric processors that would strip planets of their resources, and bio-weapons developed not for defense, but for subjugation and control.

Elara's projections shifted, showing a network diagram. It was a web of corporate ownership, of shell companies and subsidiaries, all feeding into a central nexus. The sheer complexity was designed to illustrate the insidious nature of OmniCorp's operations, their ability to operate in the shadows, to manipulate markets, and to evade accountability. "They operate through layers of obfuscation," Elara explained, her voice tight. "It is difficult to pinpoint direct responsibility, but the pattern of destruction is undeniable."

Kira's empathic broadcast intensified, her projected thoughts painting a visceral picture of the Veridians' reaction.

"They... they feel it. The emptiness. The desolation. It resonates with the whispers they have heard before, faint tremors of imbalance from other systems. This... OmniCorp... it is a void. A hunger that consumes." She looked directly at Niko, her massive amber eyes filled with a mixture of fear and a dawning, shared resolve. *"They ask... if this is the same darkness that has touched their world, however faintly. They speak of subtle distortions in the Life Weave, of energies that felt... wrong. Not the natural ebb and flow, but a forced, discordant vibration."*

Niko nodded grimly. "It is likely the same. OmniCorp's expansion is not limited to my home system. Their scouts, their probes, they have likely breached the Veil into other sectors. They are drawn to worlds rich in resources, worlds like Veridia. They would see this planet not as a living entity, but as a storehouse of untapped wealth, ripe for the plundering."

The gravity of this revelation settled upon the assembled beings like a suffocating shroud. The nascent trust, the burgeoning hope that had characterized the diplomatic exchanges, was now tinged with a shared, existential dread. The Veridians, who had believed their planet was safe, shielded by its remoteness and the very nature of the Gateway's instability, now faced a threat that was far more insidious and far more dangerous than a mere spatial anomaly.

One of the Veridian species, a tall, elegant being whose form resembled a living, crystalline tree, extended a limb that shimmered with internal light. Its projection, a cascade of intricate patterns, was interpreted by Kira with a chilling clarity.

"The crystalline one... it speaks of its own history. Not of OmniCorp directly, but of similar... intrusions. Beings who arrived with promises, but brought only devastation. They harvested the light-crystals, the very essence of their world's energy, leaving behind barren husks. They speak of a lingering sorrow, a scar on their planetary memory."

The sapphire-furred beings, their initial fear giving way to a fierce protectiveness, moved closer to Kira, a silent offering of solidarity. They began a low, resonant hum, a sound that vibrated through the air, a collective expression of defiance and shared purpose. This wasn't a sound of aggression, but of deep-seated strength, of a united front forming against a common enemy.

Niko understood the significance of their gesture. This wasn't just about humanity's struggle against OmniCorp; it was about the survival of life itself, in whatever form it took. The Veridians, with their profound connection to their planet's bio-network, possessed an understanding of ecological balance that humanity had only begun to grasp after centuries of self-inflicted damage. Their wisdom, their inherent ability to live in harmony with their environment, was precisely what OmniCorp sought to obliterate.

"We understand," Niko projected, his voice steady, his gaze sweeping across the gathered Veridians, meeting the intelligent eyes of each species. "We have fought OmniCorp for too long to be naive. We have seen the damage they inflict. But we have also learned. We have learned the importance of unity. We have learned that true strength lies not in dominance, but in interconnectedness. We have learned that the preservation of life is a cause worth fighting for, with every fiber of our being."

Kira amplified his message, her projected thoughts resonating with a powerful, unwavering resolve.

"We are not alone in this fight. This... OmniCorp... it may be a shadow, but we are the light. We are the gardeners, the weavers, the song. They seek to break the Life Weave, but we will mend it. They seek to consume, but we will nurture. They seek to conquer, but we will connect." Her massive form, which had been bowed by sorrow, now straightened, radiating a potent aura of determination. She looked towards the sky, as if sensing the vastness of space and the myriad of worlds that might yet be threatened.

The shared threat of OmniCorp had, paradoxically, forged a stronger, deeper bond between the Resonant Pack and the Veridians. The initial diplomatic dance, characterized by cautious curiosity and a careful exploration of differences, had evolved into a firm alliance forged in the crucible of shared danger. The Veridians, who had initially responded to Niko's plight with empathy, now understood the true scope of the danger, not just to Earth, but potentially to their own world, and perhaps others beyond.

Elara, her fingers flying across her datapad, began compiling a comprehensive report on OmniCorp, cross-referencing the projected visuals with known data and extrapolating potential threat vectors. She knew that humanity alone might not be enough. OmniCorp was a hydra, with countless heads and an endless capacity for regeneration. But with allies like the Veridians, beings who possessed a profound understanding of the delicate balance of life, there was a chance. A chance not just to defend, but to push back, to secure a future where life, in all its wondrous diversity, could continue to thrive. The air crackled with a new energy, a potent mix of fear and fierce, unyielding hope. The diplomatic overtures had paved the way, but it was the shared threat of OmniCorp that had truly united them, transforming tentative allies into an unbreakable front against a common, existential enemy. The subtle disruptions the Veridians had felt, the faint whispers of imbalance, were no longer abstract concerns. They were the harbingers of a direct assault, and the Veridians, along with the Resonant Pack, were now prepared to face it, together. The very air seemed to vibrate with a silent promise: they would not let the darkness consume them.

The specter of OmniCorp had undeniably cast a long shadow, transforming the nascent exchanges of curiosity and understanding into a shared battle against a common, existential threat. Yet, within that shared dread, a new foundation was being laid, one built not just on mutual apprehension, but on a burgeoning sense of mutual respect. The immediate, visceral shock of OmniCorp's destructive potential had receded, leaving in its wake a sober realization: survival for any one species, in isolation, was a fragile, fleeting prospect. It was in this somber contemplation that the seeds of a true alliance began to sprout.

Niko, having laid bare the full extent of OmniCorp's rapacious ambitions, now turned his focus towards the immediate needs and concerns of the Veridians. The destabilization of their dimensional thresholds, a phenomenon that had initially drawn the Resonant Pack to Veridia, was no longer just an environmental curiosity; it was a vulnerability, a potential entry point for forces like OmniCorp. "We understand," Niko projected, his empathic voice carrying a new weight of earnestness, "that your world is experiencing shifts, disruptions. We have observed the subtle tremors in your Life Weave, the fluctuations that seem to emanate from the very fabric of your reality. While we cannot claim to fully comprehend the intricacies of your unique planetary energies, our own journey has led us to develop technologies and methodologies aimed at understanding and, where possible, stabilizing such phenomena." He paused, allowing the implication to sink in. "The Resonant Pack is committed to exploring these energetic pathways, to understanding the nature of these dimensional thresholds. We pledge our resources, our knowledge, and our unwavering dedication to helping you stabilize your world, to reinforce its natural defenses against any unwelcome intrusions."

Kira amplified his pledge, her own empathic resonance radiating a profound sense of solidarity.

"The stability of your world is intertwined with the stability of the greater Life Weave," she broadcast, her projected thoughts painting an image of cosmic interconnectedness. *"A fractured threshold is like a wound that bleeds essence into the void, attracting those who feast on discord. We will stand with you. We will explore these fissures, not to exploit, but to heal. Our technology, born from a deep reverence for the natural order, is designed to harmonize with existing energies, not to dominate them. We will seek to understand the subtle dance of your dimensional gateways, to mend any tears, and to reinforce the natural barriers that protect your vibrant biosphere. This is not charity, but necessity. A healthy Veridia is a stronger Veridia, and a stronger Veridia contributes to the resilience of all life."* Her massive form shifted, a subtle gesture of readiness, of a commitment deeply felt.

The Veridians, having absorbed the gravity of Niko's and Kira's pronouncements, began to respond. The crystalline entities pulsed with a renewed, steadier light, their internal patterns shifting from agitation to a more focused luminescence. Their projected thoughts, interpreted by Kira with growing clarity, spoke of a desperate hope that had been rekindled. They had, for cycles, grappled with these unsettling energetic anomalies, attributing them to natural, albeit worrying, cosmic events. The realization that these disturbances might be deliberately exacerbated, or worse, serve as an invitation to external threats, had instilled a profound sense of vulnerability. Their initial cautious diplomacy, born of a need to understand the newcomers, now deepened into a genuine desire for partnership.

A representative of the sapphire-furred species, its normally stoic demeanor now tinged with a palpable sense of urgency, extended a paw that glowed with a soft, internal light. Its projected thoughts, translated by Kira, were direct and clear.

"Your willingness to shield our world from the encroaching shadow of this 'OmniCorp' is a gift we do not take lightly. We have long understood that the subtle energies of Veridia, while beautiful and life-giving, are also delicate. Our planet is a nexus, a confluence of streams that flow from realms unseen. We have developed an understanding, not through invasive technology, but through millennia of symbiosis, of the intricate dance of these currents. We can share this knowledge with you. We can guide you through the labyrinth of Veridia's energetic heart. Our ecosystem is not merely a collection of flora and fauna; it is a living, breathing organism, each component playing a vital role in maintaining the delicate equilibrium that shields us."

The sentient flora, their emerald luminescence brightening, swayed in a synchronized, almost balletic motion. Their projected thoughts, a chorus of rustling leaves and blooming petals, conveyed a similar sentiment.

"The roots of Veridia run deep, connecting every living thing. We perceive the flow of energy, the currents that sustain us. We can reveal to you the patterns, the harmonics, the discordant notes that signal imbalance. Our understanding of bio-energetic integration is profound. We can teach you how to listen to the planet, not with your instruments, but with your very beings. We can help you perceive the Life Weave as we do, a tapestry of interconnected consciousness that, when understood and respected, is immensely resilient."

Niko acknowledged these offerings with a deep bow, a gesture of profound respect that transcended species. "We accept your wisdom with the deepest gratitude," he projected, his voice resonating with sincerity. "Humanity, in its pursuit of progress, has too often severed its connection to the natural world. We have learned, through painful experience, that true advancement lies not in conquering nature, but in coexisting with it, in understanding its rhythms and working in harmony with its flows. Your knowledge of Veridia's ecosystem, of its unique energy signatures and bio-energetic integrations, is invaluable. It will not only aid us in stabilizing your dimensional thresholds, but it will also provide us with crucial insights that can inform our ongoing struggle against OmniCorp, and guide our own efforts to heal our blighted home world."

Kira stepped forward, her massive form exuding an aura of gentle authority.

"We understand," she broadcast, her thoughts a warm embrace of shared purpose. *"You offer us your profound understanding of Veridia's living systems, your insights into the currents of energy that shape your world. In return, we pledge to be vigilant guardians. We will use our ships, our sensors, and our own empathic awareness to monitor the approaches to Veridia, to detect any signs of OmniCorp's incursions or the presence of other destructive forces. We will work with you to strengthen your world's natural defenses, to understand and stabilize the energetic gateways, ensuring that they remain impassable to those who would exploit them. Our mission has evolved. We came seeking answers, perhaps even refuge, but we have found a greater calling. We will be the shield that protects this sanctuary, and the partners who help you understand its deepest secrets. This pact, forged in the face of a shared threat, is a testament to the enduring power of life to connect, to protect, and to thrive, even in the darkest of times. Your world is not merely a destination; it is a vital thread in the tapestry of existence, and we will not allow it to be frayed or broken."*

The agreement, unspoken yet deeply understood, resonated through the gathering. The Resonant Pack, initially a group of refugees seeking a safe haven and answers to their planet's plight, had now embraced a far grander role: that of interspecies guardians. They had pledged to protect Veridia from the insidious reach of OmniCorp, a promise that extended beyond mere defense, encompassing the stabilization of the very dimensional fabric that made Veridia unique and vulnerable. This was a significant pivot, a testament to the evolving nature of their mission. They were no longer simply seeking survival; they were actively engaging in the preservation of intelligent life and its diverse habitats across the cosmos.

The Veridians, in turn, were offering the key to their survival: their intrinsic knowledge of Veridia's delicate bio-energetic systems. This was not knowledge gained through cold, calculated research, but through deep, symbiotic communion. Their ecosystem was a living library, a testament to billions of years of evolutionary wisdom, and they were willing to share its secrets. This exchange was crucial. For the Resonant Pack, understanding Veridia's unique energy flows and the nature of its dimensional thresholds was paramount to their ability to counteract the destabilizing forces, both natural and potentially artificial, that threatened the planet. It was also a critical step in their own understanding of cosmic energies, knowledge that could be instrumental in their fight back home.

The implications of this mutual respect and shared commitment were profound. It marked a departure from the destructive patterns humanity had so often exhibited, a willingness to learn from and collaborate with other intelligent species. This wasn't about conquest or exploitation; it was about safeguarding the intricate web of life that sustained the universe. The diplomatic overtures had successfully navigated the initial barriers of cultural and biological difference, culminating not in a treaty of convenience, but in a genuine alliance of shared purpose and mutual dependency. The air in the clearing, which had moments before been thick with dread, now thrummed with a quiet, potent hope, a testament to the possibility of unity in the face of overwhelming adversity. The Veridians had shared their world's vulnerabilities, and in doing so, had revealed its profound strengths.

The Resonant Pack, in offering their protection and technological expertise, had found not just allies, but teachers, their journey now imbued with a deeper meaning and a wider scope of responsibility. The future, while still fraught with peril, now held the promise of a shared dawn, where different species, united by respect and a common cause, could stand together against the encroaching darkness.

Chapter Twelve
THE UNSEEN SCARS

The air on Veridia, once thick with the palpable tension of impending doom, now hummed with a different kind of energy – a nascent harmony born from shared purpose. The immediate threat of OmniCorp had been pushed back, the spectral tendrils of their influence receded, but the echoes of their intrusion, and the preceding instability that had drawn the Resonant Pack, left their indelible mark. These were not the gaping wounds of overt destruction, but the subtle, insidious scars that spoke of a deeper, more pervasive disturbance.

Kira, her empathic senses finely tuned to the intricate symphony of Veridian life, often found herself drawn to these lingering dissonances. It was in the hushed glades, where the bio-luminescent flora pulsed with a slightly dimmer light, or near the crystalline formations that once resonated with pure, unadulterated energy, that she felt them most keenly. These were not territories entirely devoid of life, but rather pockets where the vibrant tapestry of the Veridian ecosystem seemed to have been subtly frayed. She would sometimes perceive faint, almost imperceptible tremors of distress emanating from the native fauna – a fleeting anxiety in the rustle of leaves, a shadow of unease in the prolonged stillness of a creature. These sensations were ephemeral, like ghosts of memory, but they served as potent reminders of the fragility that lay beneath the surface of their newfound security.

Niko, ever the meticulous observer, meticulously documented these observations. His bio-scanners, calibrated to capture the subtlest fluctuations in energy fields and biological vitality, painted a detailed picture of these compromised zones. He noted the reduced regenerative capacity in certain flora species, the subtle shifts in the pheromonal communication of the insectoid life, and the slightly altered migratory patterns of the avian analogues. These were not catastrophic failures, but rather indicators of a bio-network under strain, still recuperating from the systemic shock. He understood that these "unseen scars" were not merely anecdotal evidence of past suffering, but crucial data points. They were the physical manifestations of dimensional stress, the lingering energetic residue of OmniCorp's invasive probing and the inherent instability that had initially characterized Veridia's thresholds.

"It's like a persistent hum of static," Niko explained to Kira one cycle, his brow furrowed as he reviewed the latest readings from a particularly affected region. "The primary conduits of the Life Weave are functioning, but there are minor disruptions, like loose connections. The native species seem to be adapting, compensating, but the underlying vulnerability remains. It's subtle enough that an untrained observer wouldn't notice, but for us, for you, the difference is palpable."

Kira projected a visual, a shimmering tapestry of Veridia's Life Weave, overlaid with the energy signatures Niko had recorded. "I feel it, Niko," she broadcasted, her projected thoughts tinged with a gentle concern. "It's a dissonance, a low thrum of anxiety beneath the surface symphony. In the deep forest, where the ancient root systems intertwine, there's a faint echo of fear, a residue from when the dimensional rifts widened. Even the smallest of the hexapedal grazers seem more skittish in those areas, their grazing patterns more hurried, their awareness heightened."

The Veridians, with their profound, intrinsic understanding of their planet's energetic flow, were acutely aware of these subtler imbalances. Their initial projections to the Resonant Pack had hinted at this delicate equilibrium. Now, in the wake of the immediate crisis, their emphasis shifted from outright defense to a more nuanced approach of healing and restoration. A representative of the sapphire-furred species, its luminous paw tapping a steady rhythm on the mossy ground, conveyed this sentiment.

"The wounds are not always visible," their thoughts pulsed, a gentle but firm reminder. *"OmniCorp's intrusion was like a poison that seeped into the very marrow of our world. While the immediate threat has passed, the residual toxins remain. Certain sectors of our bio-network, particularly those closest to the initial breaches, exhibit a diminished capacity for energetic regeneration. The flora there struggles to draw sustenance, and the fauna experiences a heightened stress response, their natural resilience tested. It requires not just defense, but a nurturing hand, a patient reintegration of harmonious frequencies."*

The sentient flora, their emerald luminescence softening in solidarity, elaborated.

"The great trees, those ancient sentinels of Veridia, remember. They store the energetic imprint of all that has transpired. In the shadowed valleys, where the dimensional flux was most volatile, their sap runs thinner, their leaves unfurl with a muted vibrancy. We can share the pathways of restorative energy, the ancient songs of renewal that have guided our growth for eons. But it is a slow process, a gentle persuasion of life to reclaim its full vigor. The memory of the disruption lingers, a subtle static in the energetic flow, and requires consistent, gentle attention."

Niko understood the implications. His data confirmed the Veridians' insights. The dimensional stress wasn't a singular event; it was a sustained assault on the planet's fundamental energetic architecture. The dimensional thresholds, even when stabilized, had been pushed and pulled, subjected to forces they were not evolved to withstand. This had created micro-fractures, energetic "leaks" that, while not catastrophic, contributed to a general state of unease within the ecosystem.

He proposed a multi-pronged approach, one that integrated the Resonant Pack's technological capabilities with the Veridians' innate bio-energetic wisdom. "We can deploy specialized resonance emitters," Niko suggested, projecting a complex schematic. "These devices, calibrated to Veridia's unique energetic signature, can emit harmonizing frequencies. They won't force the system, but rather encourage it to heal itself. Think of it as a sonic balm, gently coaxing the damaged pathways back into alignment. We can focus these emitters on the areas you've identified as most affected, creating localized fields of accelerated recovery."

Kira added her perspective, her empathic resonance a warm counterpoint to Niko's technical precision.

"And I can act as a living conduit," she offered. *"My empathic capabilities can identify the precise nodes of distress, the specific emotional or energetic residues that remain. By attuning myself to these areas, I can provide Niko's emitters with highly targeted data, ensuring that the frequencies are not only harmonizing but also addressing the specific energetic imprints left by OmniCorp's actions. It's a dance of technology and instinct, of scientific precision and empathic understanding."*

The Veridians welcomed this collaboration. They had the knowledge, the deep, instinctual understanding of their world's intricate systems. The Resonant Pack offered the tools and the external perspective, a crucial element in healing wounds that had been inflicted by external forces. The sapphire-furred species provided guidance on the specific energetic pathways that required attention, pointing out subtle deviations in the flow of vital currents that even Niko's advanced scanners might have overlooked without their input.

"The energetic channels that feed the Lumina Vines, for instance," they explained, projecting a shimmering map of Veridia's subterranean energy conduits. *"These have been particularly susceptible to the dimensional distortions. Their light, a crucial component of our nocturnal ecosystem, has dimmed in many areas. Your resonance emitters, directed along these*

subterranean flows, could revitalize them. We can also guide you to the sites where the ground tremors were most intense, areas where the very bedrock may have absorbed residual energetic trauma."

The sentient flora, in turn, identified specific plant species that acted as natural energetic filters, plants whose bio-energetic signatures were particularly adept at absorbing and neutralizing residual chaotic energies.

"The Whisperbloom," their collective consciousness projected, their luminous petals shimmering, *"is exquisitely sensitive to energetic imbalances. Its roots can draw out discord. We can show you where these Whisperblooms are thriving, and where they are struggling, indicating areas that require our joint intervention. Their resilience is a barometer of Veridia's health."*

Niko's documentation expanded, moving beyond the immediate aftermath of OmniCorp's direct actions to the subtler, long-term consequences of dimensional instability. He began to categorize the lingering effects: 'Energetic Scarring' for areas with significantly reduced bio-energetic output; 'Resonance Echoes' for zones where faint, residual distress signals persisted; and 'Threshold Fatigue' for regions where the natural dimensional barriers showed signs of weakened integrity, though not to a degree that posed immediate risk.

He observed that the creatures in these 'Energetic Scarred' areas exhibited a subtle, almost imperceptible difference in their behaviour. While they were no longer in immediate danger, their inherent capacity for joy, for uninhibited exploration, seemed somewhat muted. A species of tiny, iridescent fliers, which normally engaged in complex aerial ballets during twilight, now performed simpler, more functional movements. The vibrant, multi-layered songs of the arboreal fauna, which usually filled the dawn with an exuberant chorus, were often interrupted by brief silences, as if the singers were momentarily lost for a note, or perhaps hesitant to unleash their full vocal potential.

Kira, with her unparalleled empathic acuity, felt this muted joy acutely. She would often spend time in these compromised zones, not to scan or record, but simply to *be*. She would project waves of calm, of acceptance, of gentle encouragement, attempting to soothe the lingering anxieties, to remind the planet and its inhabitants of their inherent vibrancy. She discovered that her presence alone, coupled with the subtle projection of her own balanced energetic state, could sometimes elicit a positive response. The dimming flora would pulse a fraction brighter, the skittish fauna would briefly relax their guard, and the oppressive stillness would be punctuated by a fleeting, almost shy, note of birdsong.

"It's like they're holding their breath," she broadcasted to Niko one evening, her massive form resting beside a cluster of pale, listless ferns. "Waiting for the other shoe to drop, even though they know it won't. OmniCorp's shadow was long, and its fear-inducing capabilities were potent. They instilled a sense of caution that has become deeply ingrained, a primal vigilance that now lingers even in safety."

Niko nodded, adding another entry to his log. "The psychological impact of such pervasive environmental stress is significant. Even though the physical threats have receded, the neurological and energetic pathways of the native species have been rewired to expect danger. Reversing that requires more than just restoring optimal energy levels; it requires a gradual re-establishment of trust, of a sense of secure normalcy."

The agreement between the Resonant Pack and the Veridians was more than a defensive pact; it was becoming a healing covenant. The initial focus on warding off external threats had broadened to encompass the vital task of internal restoration. The Resonant Pack's advanced technology, guided by the Veridians' ancient wisdom and Kira's empathic insights, was being deployed not as a weapon, but as a restorative tool. The "unseen scars" of Veridia were slowly, meticulously, being tended to, a testament to the profound interconnectedness of all life and the enduring capacity for healing, even in the face of profound disruption. The journey was far from over, but the path forward was illuminated by a shared commitment to not just survive, but to thrive, in harmony with the intricate, resilient pulse of Veridia.

The subtle tremors were the first sign. Not seismic shifts that shook the crystalline mountains or sent waves through the sapphire seas, but infinitesimal vibrations that resonated deep within the planetary crust, and more importantly, deep within the beings that called Veridia home. Kira, attuned to the faintest whisper of Veridia's collective consciousness, felt them not through her physical senses, but as a prickling sensation across her empathic aura, a disquieting hum that momentarily disrupted the otherwise serene symphony of her senses. These were not the familiar thrum of a healthy planetary resonance, nor the jarring discord of OmniCorp's intrusive technologies. These were something else entirely – echoes of dimensional stress, faint but persistent reminders that the recent ordeal had left more than just physical scars upon the planet.

Niko, ever the scientist, had been diligently monitoring these subtle energetic fluctuations. His advanced sensors, designed to detect the most minute shifts in Veridia's complex bio-energetic field, had registered anomalous patterns. "It's like a phantom limb," he'd explained to Kira, projecting a complex data visualization that showed minute energy spikes occurring with an unsettling regularity. "The primary energetic pathways are stable, but there are these localized, transient bursts of what appears to be residual dimensional energy. They're dissipating quickly, but their recurrence suggests a lingering instability in the very fabric of our immediate spacetime." He theorized that these phantom energy signatures were the source of the subtle psychological disturbances he and Kira had been observing in the native fauna.

The Veridians, with their profound connection to the planet's energetic pulse, were naturally the most sensitive. Kira had observed it firsthand. During moments of heightened atmospheric energy – such as the spectacular displays of the luminescent auroras that now painted the Veridian nights with renewed vibrancy – some of the smaller, more gregarious species would exhibit fleeting moments of what could only be described as panic. A flock of iridescent, six-winged avians, usually engaged in synchronized aerial ballets, would suddenly scatter in disarray, their melodic calls devolving into sharp, panicked chirps. The normally placid, herbivorous hexapods, whose grazing was usually a rhythmic, unhurried affair, would momentarily freeze, their large, multifaceted eyes wide with an unreasoning fear, before resuming their activities with a heightened, almost frantic, urgency. These were not sustained episodes of terror, but brief, almost involuntary reactions, like a startled twitch of a muscle that couldn't be controlled.

"They are resonating with the disturbance, Kira," explained a representative of the elder tree-like beings, their ancient consciousness radiating a profound calm. "Our connection to Veridia is not merely physical; it is a deep, interwoven energetic communion. When the dimensional integrity was compromised, it sent ripples not just through the planet's physical form, but through the very consciousness of its inhabitants. Even though the breaches have been sealed, the energetic memory of that violation lingers. These tremors, these phantom energy surges, are like phantom pains for Veridia, and its inhabitants feel them acutely."

Kira understood this all too well. Her own empathic abilities allowed her to feel the planet's subtle shifts as if they were her own emotions. When these energy fluctuations occurred, she felt a surge of alien panic, a disembodied fear that wasn't hers but that she could nonetheless experience with an unnerving clarity. It was a testament to the profound interconnectedness that OmniCorp had so callously exploited. These creatures, so attuned to the natural rhythms of their world, were essentially experiencing a form of post-traumatic stress disorder at a planetary scale. The trauma of interdimensional intrusion, of having their reality warped and threatened, had left an indelible mark on their psychological landscape.

"It's as if their internal compass is momentarily thrown off balance," Kira projected, her thoughts imbued with a gentle empathy. She was in a glade where several of the smaller, furry marsupial-like creatures, known for their complex social grooming rituals, were now exhibiting a peculiar behavior.

Instead of their usual intricate patterns of mutual grooming, they were engaging in brief, agitated nips at each other, followed by a rapid retreat, their fur bristling. It was a subtle disruption of their social harmony, a deviation from their ingrained behavioral patterns. "The energy surge, even for a fraction of a cycle, seems to trigger a primitive fear response. It overrides their learned behaviors, their social conditioning, and reverts them to a state of heightened vigilance. They're anticipating a threat that isn't there."

Niko's research delved deeper into the neuro-energetic pathways of Veridian fauna. He hypothesized that their highly developed bio-energetic systems, which facilitated their communication and their deep communion with the planet, also made them exceptionally vulnerable to dimensional trauma. "Think of it like this," he elaborated, his projections laced with the sterile precision of scientific inquiry. "Their nervous systems are not just processing electrical signals; they are deeply integrated with the planet's energetic fields. When those fields are subjected to extreme stress, like the kind caused by trans-dimensional rifts, it's akin to a massive overload. Their systems are attempting to process information that is fundamentally alien to their evolutionary experience. The subsequent 'echoes,' these residual energy surges, are like triggering the same overload response without the initial stimulus. Their systems are on high alert, perpetually primed for danger."

He presented data showing altered neurotransmitter levels in the affected species during these transient energy spikes. There was a temporary surge in what, in human terms, would be analogous to adrenaline and cortisol, followed by a rapid depletion. This cyclical fluctuation, while brief, indicated a significant physiological stress response. "The problem is, even these brief, recurring stresses accumulate," Niko stated grimly. "It's like a constant drip of poison. While they are incredibly resilient, prolonged exposure to even minor stressors can have long-term effects on their overall health and well-being."

Kira, however, was not content with merely observing and documenting. She felt a profound responsibility to offer solace. She began to actively seek out these moments of distress, not to analyze, but to soothe. She would find a cluster of agitated creatures or a zone where the normally vibrant flora seemed to be drooping with an unusual weariness. Then, she would project her own essence, a gentle wave of calming energy, a silent reassurance. It was a delicate dance, a careful attunement. She had to be careful not to overwhelm them with her own amplified empathic field, but rather to offer a stable, grounding presence.

She discovered that her presence alone, when consciously projecting a state of tranquility, could often de-escalate these fleeting moments of panic. The agitated nips would cease, replaced by a return to social grooming. The frozen grazers would resume their feeding with a fraction less urgency. The iridescent avians would slowly re-form their formations, their calls regaining their melodic quality. It was as if her calm presence acted as an anchor, helping them to re-orient themselves amidst the energetic turbulence.

"It's like a lullaby," she broadcasted one cycle, her massive form resting near a cluster of sensitive, bioluminescent fungi that had been erratically. She had been projecting a steady stream of gentle, rhythmic energy, and the fungi were now pulsing with a more stable, harmoniflickeringous glow. "A gentle, grounding rhythm that reminds them of the natural order, of the underlying peace that still exists beneath the surface. They've experienced a profound violation of their reality, and my empathy, when focused and calm, seems to act as a counter-frequency, harmonizing the residual dissonance."

The Veridian elders, who possessed a deeper, more philosophical understanding of their world's energetic flows, offered further insight.

"The echoes are not merely energetic anomalies," one of them conveyed, its ancient bark shimmering with an inner light. *"They are also psychological imprints. The fear, the disorientation, the sense of violation – these emotional residues are imprinted upon the energetic matrix of Veridia. Your ability to project calm, Kira, is not just a soothing balm; it is an active counter-agent to these negative imprints. You are helping to overwrite the memory of fear with the experience of safety."*

Niko, integrating this new understanding, began to refine his technological approach. He proposed the development of what he termed "Empathic Resonance Amplifiers" – devices that, while emitting harmonizing frequencies, would also be capable of subtly amplifying Kira's projected empathic waves. "The idea is to create localized zones of profound calm," he explained, his holographic projections detailing the intricate network of energy conduits and modulation arrays. "These zones would be calibrated to resonate with Kira's empathic signature, effectively creating beacons of tranquility that can help guide the native fauna back to their natural state of equilibrium. It's not about suppressing their natural responses, but about providing a strong, consistent positive reinforcement that can help them recalibrate their own energetic systems."

This collaboration between the Resonant Pack's technological prowess and Kira's empathic sensitivity, guided by the Veridians' profound wisdom, represented a new frontier in their efforts to heal Veridia. The psychological scars, though unseen and often fleeting, were as real and as important to address as any physical wound. The creatures of Veridia, by their very nature, were deeply connected to the planet's energetic state. Their resilience was remarkable, but it was not without its limits. The interdimensional trauma had created a vulnerability, a susceptibility to energetic disruptions that could subtly erode their well-being.

Kira's dedication to this aspect of healing was unwavering. She spent countless hours in the field, not as an observer or a scientist, but as a companion. She would sit amongst the flora, her immense form exuding an aura of quiet strength, projecting waves of reassurance. She would follow herds of grazers, her presence a subtle deterrent to any fleeting moments of panic that might arise. She would even venture to the edges of the crystalline caverns, where the residual dimensional energies were thought to be most potent, to offer her calming influence in the areas that had once been the epicenters of instability.

During one such excursion near a cluster of geysers that had, during the peak of the crisis, emitted bursts of unstable dimensional energy,

Kira encountered a species of small, feathered creatures that usually communicated through a complex series of clicks and whistles. Now, their communication was reduced to a frantic, high-pitched chirping, interspersed with moments of complete silence, as if they had forgotten how to vocalize. They flitted about erratically, their small bodies vibrating with an palpable anxiety.

Kira settled herself gently nearby, careful not to startle them further. She began to project a simple, rhythmic pattern of calming energy, a steady pulse that mirrored the slow, deep breathing of the planet itself. She focused on the concept of safety, of undisturbed peace, of the gentle ebb and flow of natural cycles. Slowly, almost imperceptibly, the frantic chirping began to subside. The creatures' movements became less erratic, their small bodies stilling. After several cycles of Kira's focused projection, one of the feathered creatures emitted a soft, questioning chirp. Then another. And then, hesitantly at first, their familiar clicking and whistling began to return, weaving a tentative melody back into the air.

The Veridians observed this with a quiet reverence. They understood that the healing of their world was a multi-faceted endeavor, encompassing not only the restoration of physical ecosystems but also the re-establishment of psychological well-being. The interdimensional intrusions had inflicted a wound on the very psyche of Veridia, and Kira, with her profound empathic gifts, was an essential part of the healing process. Her ability to connect with and soothe the lingering anxieties of the native fauna was a testament to the interconnectedness of all life, and the enduring power of empathy to mend even the most unseen of scars. The journey towards full recovery was ongoing, marked by the subtle shifts in behavior, the occasional tremor of unease, but illuminated by the growing harmony and the steadfast dedication of those who sought to restore Veridia's vibrant, unblemished spirit.

Niko's laboratory, usually a sanctuary of ordered precision, now hummed with a heightened sense of urgency. The crystalline surfaces of his diagnostic equipment gleamed under the focused illumination, reflecting the intense concentration etched onto his face. He knew that the nebulous whispers of psychic distress, the fleeting moments of unease felt by Veridia's fauna, were not enough. To the sterile, objective minds of the Interdimensional Governance Council, these were mere anecdotal observations, easily dismissed as natural fluctuations in an alien ecosystem. What they demanded, what Veridia needed, was tangible proof, irrefutable evidence of OmniCorp's culpability. His burden was to translate the symphony of Veridia's subtle energetic imbalances into a language that would resonate with bureaucracy and enforce accountability.

He meticulously cataloged the spectral analysis of the residual dimensional energies, charting their decay rates and energy signatures. Each anomaly, no matter how minute, was a brushstroke on a canvas depicting the violation of Veridia's natural order. He cross-referenced these readings with Kira's empathic resonance data, a practice that had become an integral part of his research. Her projections, rich with emotional context, provided a crucial counterpoint to his objective measurements. When Kira described the visceral feeling of disembodied panic, Niko correlated it with specific peaks in the energy readings, demonstrating a direct, if subtle, link between the residual dimensional stress and the distress experienced by the native lifeforms.

"This spike," he explained to Kira, projecting a waveform that pulsed with irregular oscillations, "corresponds to the incident with the hexapod herd you observed near the Azure Mesa. You reported them freezing, a sudden, unreasoning fear. My instruments registered a transient dimensional flux, a ripple through their immediate energetic environment. The correlation is undeniable." He then overlaid a heat map of the region, showing a faint but persistent energetic residue. "It's not just a momentary disruption, Kira. The fabric itself remembers. And they feel it."

Niko was also engaged in a painstaking process of biological sampling. He worked with the Veridian bio-technicians, carefully collecting tissue samples from creatures that had exhibited prolonged or particularly acute stress responses. These samples were subjected to a battery of tests, searching for biomarkers of chronic stress, hormonal imbalances, and subtle cellular damage that might not be immediately apparent. He hypothesized that even brief, recurring energetic shocks could lead to a cumulative physiological toll, akin to a low-level, persistent radiation exposure.

"The stress hormones, in particular," he mused, examining a petri dish under a high-powered microscope, "show a pattern of acute spikes followed by rapid, but incomplete, recovery. It's like their systems are constantly playing catch-up. Over time, this wear and tear can manifest in a variety of ways – compromised immune function, reduced reproductive success, even altered developmental pathways." He projected a series of comparative graphs, illustrating the subtle differences between individuals from areas with higher residual energy concentrations and those from more stable environments. The data, while delicate, was beginning to paint a grim picture of systemic physiological strain.

One of the most challenging aspects of Niko's work was documenting the behavioral shifts. He deployed an array of advanced sensor drones, programmed to observe and record the intricate social interactions of Veridia's fauna without causing any further disruption. These drones captured hours of footage, meticulously cataloging deviations from established norms: the hesitant social grooming, the disrupted foraging patterns, the altered vocalizations, the sudden, unexplained flights. He then analyzed this data using sophisticated algorithms, looking for statistical anomalies that could be directly attributed to the energetic disturbances.

"It's about building a mosaic," Niko articulated, his gaze fixed on a holographic display that pieced together fragmented observations from different species and locations. "Each piece of data, on its own, might seem insignificant. But when you assemble them, when you overlay the energy readings, Kira's empathic reports, the biological markers, and the behavioral changes, a clear and undeniable pattern emerges. OmniCorp's actions didn't just scar the land; they wounded the very consciousness of this planet and its inhabitants."

He recalled a specific observation from a drone deployed near one of the former OmniCorp excavation sites, a place where the residual dimensional energies were known to be particularly volatile. A group of small, arboreal creatures, usually known for their agile and confident movements through the canopy, were exhibiting extreme trepidation. They would hesitate at the edge of branches, their prehensile tails twitching with uncertainty, their normally fluid leaps becoming hesitant, jerky movements. Some even appeared to be experiencing what could only be described as brief, incapacitating moments of vertigo, clinging desperately to branches as if the very ground beneath them had shifted.

"This," Niko projected the drone footage, zooming in on one of the creatures as it struggled to regain its composure after a particularly jarring momentary disorientation, "is not natural. This is a direct consequence of the instability they were subjected to. Their vestibular systems, their proprioception, are being bombarded with contradictory energetic signals. It's like trying to walk on a surface that constantly buckles and shifts. The long-term effects on their ability to navigate, to forage, to survive, are potentially devastating."

The elders of the Veridian trees, who had witnessed the full extent of OmniCorp's activities, provided Niko with invaluable historical context and corroboration. Their deep, slow consciousnesses held the memory of the planet's energetic equilibrium before the intrusion. They described how the land itself seemed to sigh with relief when OmniCorp's machinery was finally silenced, but also how a subtle unease had settled upon the ecosystem. They spoke of the "silence that screamed," the absence of the usual vibrant, coherent energetic flow, replaced by a pervasive, low-level hum of dissonance.

One elder, its ancient bark etched with the wisdom of millennia, conveyed a particularly poignant observation:

"The young ones, they forget the song of the earth. The disruption, it taught them a song of fear. Your recordings, Niko, they are but the faint echoes of that terrifying melody. But even echoes can be measured, can be understood, and can, with great effort, be countered." This sentiment fueled Niko's

determination. He understood that he was not just collecting data; he was bearing witness, preserving a testament to the damage inflicted.

His efforts extended to meticulously documenting the impact on the planet's bio-luminescent flora. These plants, deeply intertwined with the planet's energetic currents, often served as indicators of Veridia's health. During OmniCorp's tenure, and in the immediate aftermath, their vibrant, pulsing glows had become erratic, flickering like dying embers or flaring with an unnatural intensity. Now, while some were regaining their natural rhythm, Niko observed persistent patterns of disharmony. Certain species, particularly those in proximity to areas of high residual dimensional energy, still exhibited muted or irregular luminescence, a visible manifestation of their energetic imbalance.

He collected samples of these affected plants, analyzing their cellular structure and pigment composition. His findings indicated subtle but significant alterations in their bio-energetic pathways, hindering their ability to efficiently convert ambient energy into light. "It's a feedback loop," Niko explained to Kira, gesturing towards a holographic projection of a plant's cellular structure. "The residual energies disrupt their internal energetic processes, which in turn affects their ability to absorb and process energy from the environment. This weakens them, making them even more susceptible to further energetic disturbances. It's a slow, insidious degradation of their vital functions."

Niko also began to quantify the effects on Veridia's complex microbial ecosystems. He collected soil and water samples, analyzing the microbial diversity and activity in areas affected by OmniCorp's operations compared to pristine regions. His preliminary findings suggested a reduction in beneficial microbial populations and an increase in stress-tolerant, less ecologically functional species in the affected zones. These microscopic shifts, he argued, could have profound long-term consequences for nutrient cycling, soil health, and the overall resilience of Veridia's ecosystems.

"The foundational elements of the biosphere are being altered," he stated, his voice resonating with concern. "The microorganisms are the unsung heroes of any ecosystem. Their health and diversity are critical for the planet's ability to regenerate and sustain life. OmniCorp's actions have not only disrupted the macroscopic life but have also sown discord at the very cellular and molecular level."

The weight of this evidence was immense. Niko felt the burden of ensuring that these subtle yet significant scars were not overlooked. He worked tirelessly, cross-referencing, verifying, and synthesizing every piece of information. He knew that the Interdimensional Governance Council operated on principles of undeniable proof, on data that could not be easily refuted or explained away. His task was to present a comprehensive, multi-faceted case that would leave no room for doubt, a testament to the profound and lasting damage wrought by corporate exploitation. The future of Veridia, and the integrity of interdimensional law, depended on his ability to articulate the unseen, to give voice to the silent suffering of a world violated. He was crafting not just a report, but a plea, a demand for justice, built upon the foundation of meticulously gathered truth.

The quiet hum of Niko's laboratory, once a symphony of scientific progress, now seemed to carry an undercurrent of apprehension. Kira sat across from him, her usual serene presence a stark contrast to the complex holographic displays flickering between them. Niko's gaze, usually sharp with intellectual curiosity, held a hint of weariness, the kind that settled deep into the bones after prolonged, intense effort. He was meticulously charting the spectral analysis of residual dimensional energies, each anomaly a digital scar on Veridia's energetic landscape. The data was stark, irrefutable, and deeply disturbing. He overlaid Kira's empathic resonance readings, the vibrant, often turbulent, emotional echoes she perceived, onto his objective measurements. The correlation was undeniable, a chilling testament to the planet's unseen wounds.

"This spike," Niko explained, his voice a low murmur, pointing to a jagged oscillation on the waveform, "corresponds to your experience near the Azure

Mesa. You described a sudden, disorienting panic gripping the hexapod herd. My instruments registered a transient dimensional flux, a ripple through their immediate energetic environment. It's not just a statistical anomaly, Kira. It's a direct imprint of their fear." He then displayed a heat map of the region, a faint, persistent shimmer of residual energy, a ghostly reminder of OmniCorp's destructive passage. "The land remembers, and they feel it."

Niko was also engaged in the painstaking process of biological sampling, working with Veridian bio-technicians to collect tissue samples from creatures exhibiting prolonged or acute stress responses. He meticulously analyzed these samples, searching for biomarkers of chronic stress, hormonal imbalances, and subtle cellular damage. He hypothesized that even brief, recurring energetic shocks could lead to a cumulative physiological toll, akin to a low-level, persistent radiation exposure. "The stress hormones," he mused, examining a petri dish under a high-powered microscope, "show a pattern of acute spikes followed by rapid, but incomplete, recovery. Their systems are constantly playing catch-up. This constant wear and tear can manifest in compromised immune function, reduced reproductive success, even altered developmental pathways." He projected a series of comparative graphs, illustrating the subtle but significant differences between individuals from high-residual energy zones and those from more stable environments. The data, while delicate, was beginning to paint a grim picture of systemic physiological strain.

The behavioral shifts were equally concerning. Niko had deployed an array of advanced sensor drones, programmed to observe and record the intricate social interactions of Veridia's fauna without causing further disruption. The drones captured hours of footage, meticulously cataloging deviations from established norms: hesitant social grooming, disrupted foraging patterns, altered vocalizations, sudden, unexplained flights. Sophisticated algorithms analyzed this data, searching for statistical anomalies directly attributable to the energetic disturbances. "It's about building a mosaic," Niko articulated, his gaze fixed on a holographic display that pieced together fragmented observations from different species and locations.

"Each piece of data, on its own, might seem insignificant. But when you assemble them—the energy readings, your empathic reports, the biological markers, the behavioral changes—a clear and undeniable pattern emerges. OmniCorp's actions didn't just scar the land; they wounded the very consciousness of this planet and its inhabitants."

He recalled a specific observation from a drone near a former OmniCorp excavation site, a place of particularly volatile residual dimensional energies. A group of small, arboreal creatures, normally agile and confident, exhibited extreme trepidation. They hesitated at the edge of branches, their prehensile tails twitching with uncertainty, their fluid leaps becoming jerky, hesitant movements. Some experienced brief, incapacitating moments of vertigo, clinging desperately to branches as if the ground had shifted. "This," Niko projected the drone footage, zooming in on a creature struggling to regain its composure after a jarring disorientation, "is not natural. Their vestibular systems are being bombarded with contradictory energetic signals. It's like trying to walk on a surface that constantly buckles and shifts. The long-term effects on their ability to navigate, to forage, to survive, are potentially devastating."

The elders of the Veridian trees, with their deep, slow consciousnesses, provided invaluable historical context. They remembered Veridia's energetic equilibrium before the intrusion. They spoke of the "silence that screamed," the absence of the usual vibrant, coherent energetic flow, replaced by a pervasive, low-level hum of dissonance. One elder, its ancient bark etched with millennia of wisdom, conveyed a poignant observation:

"The young ones, they forget the song of the earth. The disruption, it taught them a song of fear. Your recordings, Niko, they are but the faint echoes of that terrifying melody. But even echoes can be measured, can be understood, and can, with great effort, be countered." This sentiment fueled Niko's determination. He was not just collecting data; he was bearing witness, preserving a testament to the damage inflicted.

His efforts extended to documenting the impact on the planet's bio-luminescent flora. These plants, deeply intertwined with Veridia's energetic currents, served as indicators of the planet's health. During OmniCorp's tenure, their vibrant glows had become erratic, flickering like dying embers or flaring with unnatural intensity. Now, while some were regaining their natural rhythm, Niko observed persistent patterns of disharmony. Species in proximity to high residual dimensional energy exhibited muted or irregular luminescence, a visible manifestation of their energetic imbalance. He collected samples, analyzing cellular structure and pigment composition. His findings indicated subtle but significant alterations in their bio-energetic pathways, hindering their ability to efficiently convert ambient energy into light. "It's a feedback loop," Niko explained to Kira, gesturing towards a holographic projection of a plant's cellular structure. "The residual energies disrupt their internal processes, which affects their ability to absorb and process energy from the environment. This weakens them, making them more susceptible to further disturbances. It's a slow, insidious degradation of their vital functions."

Niko also began to quantify the effects on Veridia's complex microbial ecosystems. He collected soil and water samples, analyzing microbial diversity and activity in affected regions compared to pristine areas. Preliminary findings suggested a reduction in beneficial microbial populations and an increase in stress-tolerant, less ecologically functional species. These microscopic shifts, he argued, could have profound long-term consequences for nutrient cycling, soil health, and the overall resilience of Veridia's ecosystems. "The foundational elements of the biosphere are being altered," he stated, his voice resonating with concern. "The microorganisms are the unsung heroes of any ecosystem. Their health and diversity are critical for the planet's ability to regenerate and sustain life. OmniCorp's actions have not only disrupted the macroscopic life but have also sown discord at the very cellular and molecular level."

The weight of this evidence was immense. Niko felt the burden of ensuring that these subtle yet significant scars were not overlooked. He worked tirelessly, cross-referencing, verifying, and synthesizing every piece of information. He knew the Interdimensional Governance Council operated on principles of undeniable proof, on data that could not be easily refuted or explained away. His task was to present a comprehensive, multi-faceted case that would leave no room for doubt, a testament to the profound and lasting damage wrought by corporate exploitation. The future of Veridia, and the integrity of interdimensional law, depended on his ability to articulate the unseen, to give voice to the silent suffering of a world violated. He was crafting not just a report, but a plea, a demand for justice, built upon the foundation of meticulously gathered truth.

Kira shifted in her seat, a faint frown creasing her brow. The abstract data, the spectral analysis, the chemical signatures – they were all crucial, objective anchors in the storm of OmniCorp's devastation. Yet, for her, the truth resonated on a different frequency, an empathetic hum that vibrated within her very bones. She had felt it, too, the lingering discordance. It wasn't a constant barrage, but rather a series of subtle tremors, moments where the planet's deep, resonant peace was momentarily fractured. These were the "unseen scars" Niko meticulously documented, but for Kira, they manifested as a visceral, almost physical, ache.

There were days, particularly when they revisited sites that bore the deepest wounds from OmniCorp's operations, when a leaden fatigue would settle upon her. It wasn't the exhaustion of physical exertion, but a profound weariness of the spirit. She would find herself zoning out, her gaze unfocused, a generalized sense of anxiety prickling at the edges of her awareness. It was as if the very air in these places held a residue of distress, a psychic residue that clung to the atmosphere like a fine, almost invisible dust. Niko monitored her closely, his scientific detachment warring with a deep-seated concern for her well-being. He understood that her empathic sensitivity, while an invaluable tool for his research, also made her acutely vulnerable to Veridia's residual psychic distress.

"Are you alright?" Niko's voice, usually so focused on the data, softened as he met her gaze. He had learned to read the subtle shifts in her demeanor, the almost imperceptible tightening around her eyes, the way her breath would catch for a fleeting moment.

Kira offered a small, weary smile. "Just... a bit of a flicker," she replied, her voice soft. She gestured vaguely towards the holographic projection of a particularly volatile energy signature. "It's like an old wound that still aches when the weather changes. This area," she indicated a section of the display, "felt particularly... jagged, when we were there last cycle. I think I felt some of the little ground-digger creatures exhibiting their flight response again. A kind of echo of their panic."

Niko nodded, his expression grave. He understood. While his instruments could quantify the energy fluctuations, the residual distortions, they couldn't fully capture the subjective experience of being on the receiving end of such profound energetic imbalance. Kira's empathic resonance was the bridge, the vital conduit that translated the abstract into the tangible, the data into lived experience. Her anxiety wasn't a sign of weakness, but a confirmation of the depth of the damage. It was a testament to her profound connection with Veridia, a connection that allowed her to feel the planet's pain as if it were her own.

He recalled the incident near the Whispering Falls, a place of extraordinary natural beauty that had been heavily impacted by OmniCorp's reckless extraction activities. Kira had been observing a small flock of sky-lizards, their iridescent wings usually a dazzling display of aerial acrobatics. Suddenly, without any apparent external stimulus, the entire flock had scattered in a frenzy of panicked flight, crashing into the crystalline foliage. Kira had described a wave of intense disorientation washing over her, a sudden, inexplicable nausea, as if the very laws of physics had briefly warped around her. Niko's sensors had registered a localized, highly anomalous dimensional flux at precisely that moment.

"I felt it too, that disorientation," Kira continued, her voice gaining a little more strength as she recalled the event. "It was like a sudden drop, a feeling of falling without moving. And then, the fear. Not just mine, but theirs. It flooded me. It took me a few moments to separate my own sensations from theirs." She looked down at her hands, her fingers tracing invisible patterns on the lab table. "It's hard, sometimes. To be so open to it all. It feels like I'm carrying the weight of so many scared hearts."

Niko reached across the table, his hand gently covering hers. His touch was steady, grounding. "You are," he said softly, his voice filled with a deep, quiet respect. "And that is precisely why you are so vital to this. Your well-being, Kira, is a direct indicator of Veridia's overall health. When you feel that fatigue, that anxiety, it's a signal. It tells us where the deepest scars lie, where the healing is most needed." He squeezed her hand. "We monitor it, of course. Your physiological responses, your energetic signature. But beyond the data, I see it in you. And I will not allow you to be further compromised. Your strength is our strength, and we will find ways to protect you, even as you help us heal this world."

He knew that the emotional toll on Kira was significant. She bore the brunt of the planet's residual psychic distress, a burden far heavier than any physical hardship. While Niko could retreat into the objective world of data and analysis, Kira was constantly immersed in the raw, unfiltered emotional currents of Veridia. He saw the moments of fatigue, the brief episodes of heightened anxiety, not as weaknesses, but as proof of her profound empathy and her unwavering commitment to Veridia's cause. Her vulnerability was, in fact, her greatest strength, a constant reminder of the deep, interconnected web of life that OmniCorp had so callously disrupted.

Niko's own emotional state, while more guarded, was not immune to the pervasive sense of unease. The sheer scale of the damage, the insidious nature of the energetic contamination, weighed heavily on him. He found himself struggling with a gnawing sense of frustration, a frustration born from the bureaucratic inertia he anticipated facing from the Interdimensional Governance Council. How could he possibly convey the depth of Veridia's suffering to beings who dealt in sterile logic and quantifiable outcomes? How could he make them understand the essence of a wounded planet, the silent scream of its exploited ecosystems?

He remembered a conversation with Kira just a few days prior. They had been discussing the impact on a particular species of arboreal avian creatures, known for their intricate, almost melodic vocalizations. These creatures, usually a vibrant part of Veridia's soundscape, had fallen unnervingly silent in the areas most affected by OmniCorp's activities. Kira had described a hollow echo where their songs should have been, a silence that felt like a physical absence.

"It's not just the absence of sound," Kira had explained, her eyes filled with a deep sadness. "It's the absence of joy. Their songs are woven with their entire being – their courtship rituals, their territorial claims, their expressions of contentment. When they stop singing, it's as if a part of their soul has gone silent too. I felt a profound loneliness emanating from those empty branches, Niko. A loneliness that was almost palpable."

Niko had correlated her empathic observations with the drone footage, which showed the birds exhibiting lethargic behavior, their normally vibrant plumage dulled, their movements listless. His analysis of their bio-acoustic patterns revealed a significant reduction in the complexity and frequency range of their vocalizations. It wasn't just a lack of motivation; their very physiological capacity to produce complex sounds seemed to have been diminished, a direct consequence of the lingering energetic disturbances.

"The resonance of their songs is intrinsically linked to the planet's energetic coherence," Niko had explained to Kira, projecting a visual representation of the birds' vocalizations as complex wave patterns. "The dimensional instability disrupts the subtle energetic frequencies that underpin their vocalizations, making it difficult for them to produce the full spectrum of their calls. It's a direct assault on their very means of expression, of connection."

Now, looking at Kira, he saw the echoes of that conversation reflected in her eyes. She was still feeling the weight of that silence, the sorrow of those muted avian souls. He knew that their work was not just about presenting data to a detached council; it was about preserving the very essence of Veridia, about giving voice to the voiceless, about ensuring that the melody of life, however faint, would not be extinguished.

"We will find a way, Kira," Niko said, his voice firm, cutting through the quiet hum of the lab. "Your feelings, your insights, they are not just 'flickers.' They are the truth. They are the heart of the matter. We will translate this into a language they cannot ignore. We will show them the unseen scars, not just on the land, but in the very spirit of this world." He met her gaze, a shared determination passing between them. "Your well-being is paramount. We will ensure you have the rest and support you need. But we will also use every ounce of your empathy, every echo of your resonance, to build our case. Together, we will make them hear Veridia's song, even through the dissonance."

Kira managed a more genuine smile this time, a flicker of renewed hope in her eyes. "Thank you, Niko," she whispered. "I know it's a lot. But I wouldn't trade this connection, even with the pain it brings. It means I'm still truly alive, and so is Veridia."

Niko inclined his head, a silent acknowledgment of her profound strength. He turned back to his displays, the weight of their shared mission settling more heavily, yet with a renewed sense of purpose. The data, the biological samples, the behavioral analyses, and Kira's empathic resonance – they were all pieces of a much larger, more complex puzzle. A puzzle that, when fully assembled, would reveal the undeniable truth of OmniCorp's transgressions and the profound, lasting impact of their actions on Veridia and its inhabitants. The fight for justice was far from over, but in the quiet hum of the laboratory, surrounded by the silent testament of a wounded planet, their resolve only deepened. The unseen scars were real, and they would be brought into the light.

The weight of the data, the visual representations of energetic anomalies and biological distress, was undeniable. Yet, as Kira sat beside Niko, her hand still resting in his, a different kind of conviction began to bloom within her. It wasn't born of spectral analysis or hormonal assays, but of a deeper, more intuitive understanding. It was the understanding of resilience, of the inherent, inexhaustible capacity for life to mend, to adapt, and to ultimately, to heal. The scars were there, etched deeply into Veridia's energetic and biological tapestry, but they were not terminal. They were wounds, and wounds, given the right conditions and sustained care, could close.

"You know," Kira began, her voice soft, a gentle counterpoint to the lab's scientific hum, "when I first came here, I was so afraid. Afraid of what OmniCorp had done, afraid of the damage being irreparable. But looking at... all of this," she gestured to the flickering holographic displays, "and feeling what I feel... I don't think it's irreparable anymore." Her gaze met Niko's, a quiet luminescence in her eyes that mirrored the bio-luminescent flora he had studied. "There's a deep-seated strength in this planet, Niko. A will to survive that's more profound than any disruption."

Niko returned her gaze, a slow smile spreading across his face. He saw it too, not just in the data, but in the subtle shifts he'd observed in Kira's own empathic resonance over the past cycles. The acute anxiety and weariness he had witnessed more frequently now seemed tempered with a growing sense of peace, a quiet confidence that reflected Veridia's own nascent recovery. "I agree, Kira," he said, his voice warm. "The resilience of Veridia's ecosystems is remarkable. We've seen it in the microbial communities, in the flora's ability to re-establish energetic coherence, and in the fauna's gradual return to more stable behavioral patterns. It speaks to the fundamental robustness of life itself."

He brought up a series of graphs on the main display, charting the recovery of specific bio-luminescent plant species in regions previously saturated with residual dimensional energies. The luminescence, once erratic and muted, was now showing a steady, upward trend in both intensity and coherence. "These plants," Niko explained, his finger tracing a smooth, upward curve, "are like living energetic sensors. Their ability to regain their natural glow indicates a stabilization of the planet's fundamental energetic field. It's a slow process, of course. The deeper the scar, the longer the time required for complete remission. But the trajectory is undeniably positive."

Kira nodded, her own observations corroborating the data. She had recently spent time near the great crystal formations that pulsed with Veridia's internal energy. While the jarring disharmony had been palpable in the wake of OmniCorp's operations, she now sensed a more harmonious resonance. The crystals still carried the memory of the disruption, a faint echo in their songs, but their primary melody was returning, a deep, resonant hum that spoke of balance restored. She had also noticed subtle shifts in the hexapod herds, their grazing patterns becoming more predictable, their social interactions less fraught with underlying tension. The lingering fear was still present, a faint undertone, but it was no longer the overwhelming, paralyzing force it had once been.

"It's like a fever breaking," Kira mused. "The initial intensity is gone, and now the body is just working to regain its full strength. And the Veridians... they are such incredible caretakers. Their understanding of the planet, their deep connection to its rhythms... it's something we can only learn from." She recalled a recent interaction with Elder Lyra, one of the wise, ancient Veridian beings whose consciousness was intertwined with the planet's deepest roots. Lyra had spoken not of blame or retribution, but of balance and restoration. She had conveyed a profound understanding that Veridia's healing was an ongoing process, a journey that required patience, vigilance, and a deep wellspring of compassion.

"Elder Lyra was telling me about the 'weavers of light'," Kira shared, her voice filled with wonder. "They are specialized fungi that grow deep within the soil, and they have an incredible ability to break down and neutralize residual energetic impurities. The Veridians have been cultivating them, guiding their growth in the areas most affected by OmniCorp. It's a form of biological remediation, but it feels so much more... organic, so much more alive, than anything we've developed on our own worlds."

Niko's eyes lit up. "That aligns perfectly with our findings regarding the microbial communities," he said, pulling up another set of data. "We've observed a significant increase in the population of certain native fungal species in the remediated zones. Their metabolic pathways are indeed highly effective at processing complex energetic compounds. It's a perfect example of how Veridia's own biological systems are leading the healing process, with the Veridians acting as informed guides and facilitators." He projected a complex molecular diagram of the fungal enzymes. "These enzymes are incredibly efficient. They essentially 'digest' the residual dimensional energies, converting them into inert compounds that can be safely reabsorbed into the planet's natural cycles. It's a beautifully elegant solution, honed by millennia of evolution."

He then displayed a series of comparative timelines, illustrating the rate of energetic stabilization in areas where the Veridians were actively involved in cultivation versus areas left to recover naturally. The difference was stark. "The Veridians aren't just passively observing," Niko stated, his voice resonating with admiration. "They are actively collaborating with the planet's own healing mechanisms. Their intervention significantly accelerates the recovery process, reducing the timeline for full energetic equilibrium by decades, perhaps even centuries."

This realization brought a profound sense of hope to both of them. OmniCorp's actions had been a brutal violation, a disruption of an intricate, delicate balance. But Veridia, with the wisdom of its inhabitants and the inherent power of its lifeforms, was demonstrating an extraordinary capacity to recover. The damage was undeniable, the scars would likely remain as reminders, but the planet was not irrevocably broken.

"It's more than just a mission objective now, isn't it?" Kira said, her voice filled with emotion. "This is a true partnership. We came to document the damage, to gather evidence for the Council. But we've become participants in the healing. And I'm learning so much from them, Niko. Their patience, their respect for all life, their understanding that healing is not about erasing the past, but about integrating it, learning from it, and moving forward with greater wisdom."

Niko nodded, his earlier weariness replaced by a profound sense of purpose. The abstract data, the scientific pursuit, now felt deeply connected to a more fundamental aspect of existence: the interconnectedness of all life and the shared responsibility to nurture and protect it. "You're right, Kira," he said, his gaze distant, yet focused. "This is not merely about scientific data or interdimensional jurisprudence. It's about empathy, about understanding, and about fostering a relationship of mutual respect. The Veridians are not simply inhabitants of a planet we are studying; they are our partners in this process. Their ancient knowledge, combined with our scientific understanding, is proving to be the most potent force for healing."

He envisioned the future, not as a one-time intervention, but as an ongoing collaboration. The Council's judgment would come, and it would be based on the irrefutable evidence they had meticulously gathered. But beyond the legal ramifications, the true victory would lie in Veridia's sustained recovery, in the strengthening of the bonds between their species, and in the shared understanding that had been forged through adversity.

"We have documented the scars," Niko continued, his voice gaining strength. "We have quantified the damage, the physiological and energetic repercussions. But what we are also documenting, perhaps even more importantly, is the resilience. The adaptive strategies, the natural regenerative processes, and the profound wisdom of the Veridians who are guiding this recovery. This is the narrative we will present to the Council. Not just a story of destruction, but a testament to the enduring power of life and the transformative potential of cooperation."

Kira smiled, a genuine, radiant smile that seemed to chase away any lingering shadows in the lab. "And what about the unseen scars, Niko? The ones I feel, the ones that linger in the quiet spaces between moments?"

Niko reached out, his hand finding hers again, their fingers intertwining. "Those," he said, his voice soft but firm, "are the most important scars of all. They are the ones that remind us of the depth of what was lost, and the profound significance of what is being regained. They are the echoes of the pain, yes, but they are also becoming the whispers of hope. And with continued care, with time, and with the enduring resilience of life, those whispers will grow into a chorus. A chorus of true healing."

He believed it, with every fiber of his being.

The mission had evolved, transcending its initial parameters. It was no longer solely about punitive justice, but about fostering understanding and facilitating a deeper, more sustainable relationship with Veridia. The data was crucial, the legal framework essential, but the underlying truth was simpler, more profound: that even the deepest wounds could mend when met with empathy, knowledge, and a shared commitment to life. The path ahead would require ongoing vigilance, continued scientific observation, and unwavering support for the Veridians and their planet. But for the first time since arriving on Veridia, Niko felt a genuine, unshakeable hope.

A hope not just for Veridia's recovery, but for humanity's own capacity to learn, to grow, and to become true stewards of the interconnected cosmos. The unseen scars were a somber reminder, but they were also the fertile ground upon which a brighter, more harmonious future could be built. The pack, in their collective endeavor, had become more than just observers; they had become partners in a grand, ongoing act of planetary restoration.

CHAPTER THIRTEEN
THE ETHICS OF ADVANCEMENT

The hum of the orbital station's primary drive, a low, resonant thrum that had become the constant soundtrack to their lives, seemed to carry a new weight for Niko. It was the sound of power, of engineered potential, a testament to the ingenuity that had brought them across the cosmic expanse. Yet, in the quiet hum, he heard also a cautionary whisper. Their own technology, the very tools that allowed them to perceive the subtle energetic fields of Veridia, to analyze its biomechanical intricacies, and to communicate across unimaginable distances, was a double-edged sword. It was a marvel, a testament to their species' relentless drive to understand, but it also held the potential for profound disruption, a mirror reflecting both their best intentions and their deepest flaws.

He found himself returning, in his thoughts, to the early days of their mission, to the sterile, efficient diagnostic equipment they had deployed. Initially, it had felt like the ultimate expression of their responsibility – to understand the damage inflicted by OmniCorp with unparalleled precision. They had mapped every anomaly, charted every physiological stress response, and quantified the energetic bleed with a granularity that OmniCorp, in their haste and avarice, could never have achieved. But as Kira's empathetic connection to Veridia deepened, as Niko immersed himself in the planet's intricate ecological feedback loops, a subtle unease began to take root. Their instruments, so powerful in their analytical capacity, were also emitting their own low-level energetic signatures. They were, in essence, another layer of artificial imposition upon a world still recovering from the overwhelming presence of OmniCorp's industrial footprint.

The distinction, Niko mused, was not merely semantic. It was rooted in intent and application. OmniCorp had wielded technology as a bludgeon, a tool for extraction and subjugation. Their aim was not to understand Veridia, but to exploit its resources, heedless of the ecological and energetic fallout. Their technology was an assertion of dominance, a declaration that the universe was theirs to bend to their will. The Resonant Pack, on the other hand, approached their technological arsenal with a different philosophy. Their tools were designed to be sensitive, to integrate seamlessly, to observe without intruding. They strived for a form of technological symbiosis, where their instruments acted as extensions of their own observational senses, enhancing their understanding without fundamentally altering the system they were studying.

Yet, even with the best intentions, the line remained perilously thin. Niko recalled the deep-scan probes they had deployed into the planet's crust to analyze the composition of the mineral veins that OmniCorp had so ruthlessly mined. The probes were designed to emit minimal energy, to be as passive as possible. But the very act of penetrating the earth, even with the gentlest touch, represented an intrusion. The delicate microbial ecosystems, the intricate network of fungal hyphae that formed the planet's subterranean nervous system, could be subtly, or perhaps not so subtly, disrupted by the probes' presence, by the minute thermal shifts they generated, or by the faint electromagnetic fields they emitted.

He remembered a particular instance, early in their mission, when a cluster of subterranean flora, known for their unique bio-luminescent properties and their crucial role in atmospheric regulation, had experienced a temporary, localized dimming. The data had initially pointed to residual OmniCorp toxins, a logical conclusion given the circumstances. But after further, more nuanced analysis, Niko and his team had discovered a correlation between the dimming and the proximity of a deep-scan probe that had been performing an extended spectral analysis. The probe, designed for minimal impact, had nonetheless introduced a slight, persistent energetic oscillation into the soil that had, for a brief period, perturbed the flora's delicate energy exchange processes. It was a minor deviation, quickly rectified once the probe was repositioned, but it served as a stark reminder. Even their most sophisticated, supposedly non-intrusive technology was not truly inert.

"It's a constant balancing act, isn't it?" Kira had said, when he had shared his concerns with her. They had been standing on a ridge overlooking a valley that was slowly, tentatively, re-greening after OmniCorp's extraction operations. The air, once thick with the acrid scent of processed minerals, now carried the sweet perfume of nascent flora. "We have to use our tools to understand the damage, to heal, but those same tools could, if we're not careful, become the next form of damage."

Niko had nodded, his gaze sweeping across the landscape. "Exactly. OmniCorp used their technology to break things down, to isolate and exploit. We use ours to connect, to understand the interconnectedness. But the universe has a way of responding to energetic input, regardless of intent. A gentle nudge can still shift the path of a river, given enough time."

He thought about the holographic projectors they used to visualize Veridia's energetic field. These were marvels of engineering, capable of rendering complex, multi-dimensional data into an intuitive, visual format. They allowed the pack to see the ebb and flow of planetary energy, the residual imprints of distress, and the emerging patterns of recovery. But the projectors themselves emitted a specific spectrum of light and energy, a tailored construct designed to interact with the ambient energetic field without causing disruption. Yet, was it truly without consequence? Was the act of superimposing their rendered reality onto Veridia's natural energetic tapestry, however subtly, a form of interference?

The Veridians themselves offered a different perspective. Their connection to the planet was deeply intrinsic, a biological and energetic communion honed over millennia. They could sense the planet's state, its well-being, through a network of innate sensory apparatus that Niko could only begin to comprehend. Their technology, while less overt than OmniCorp's or even their own, was deeply interwoven with their biology and their environment. The bio-luminescent fungi, the sonic communication arrays that utilized the planet's natural resonant frequencies, the kinetic energy harvesters that drew power from the planet's subtle seismic activity – these were not external tools in the same way. They were extensions of Veridian life itself, integrated into the planet's natural systems with an elegance that spoke of profound understanding and respect.

Niko remembered observing a group of Veridians tending to a grove of particularly sensitive energy-conducting trees. They used no visible devices, no handheld instruments. Instead, they placed their hands upon the rough bark, their bodies subtly swaying in rhythm with the trees' almost imperceptible energetic pulses. Through this tactile, resonant connection, they seemed to communicate with the trees, to understand their needs, and to facilitate the flow of energy through the grove. It was a form of bio-hacking, perhaps, but one achieved through empathy and deep ecological knowledge, not through invasive manipulation.

This stark contrast with OmniCorp's approach fueled Niko's contemplation. OmniCorp's technological endeavors were characterized by brute force, by an almost arrogant disregard for the inherent complexities of the systems they were interacting with. They viewed planets as resources, ecosystems as obstacles, and life itself as a programmable variable. Their technology was designed to conquer, to control, and to extract. The holographic advertisements that had once plastered the orbital stations, depicting gleaming chrome cities and automated resource extraction facilities, were a testament to this exploitative mindset. They promised efficiency and profit, but at the cost of ecological integrity and ethical compromise.

The Resonant Pack, however, saw technology as a bridge. Their goal was not to dominate, but to understand, to connect, and ultimately, to heal. Their advanced sensors, their quantum communication arrays, their bio-integrated diagnostic tools – all were conceived with the primary purpose of fostering a deeper understanding of Veridia and its inhabitants. They sought to decipher the planet's intricate energetic language, to map its biological resilience, and to identify pathways for restoration. But even in this noble pursuit, the question of unintended consequences lingered.

Niko considered the potential for their advanced scanning technologies to inadvertently influence the very phenomena they were trying to observe. The subtle shifts in quantum states, the minute alterations in energy fields, could theoretically trigger cascading effects within a system as finely tuned as Veridia's. It was a concern that haunted the back of his mind, a nagging doubt that even their most carefully calibrated instruments might be introducing a subtle, unforeseen bias into their data, a whisper of their own presence in the delicate symphony of Veridia's recovery.

The temptation, of course, was to err on the side of caution, to minimize all technological intervention. But that would render them powerless to fulfill their mission. They needed their technology to gather the evidence, to understand the scope of OmniCorp's transgression, and to guide their healing efforts. The challenge lay in striking a delicate balance, in employing their technological prowess with a level of mindfulness and ethical consideration that transcended mere operational efficiency.

He thought about the early days of their exploration of Veridia, before the full extent of OmniCorp's damage had become apparent. They had been eager, almost exuberantly so, to deploy their cutting-edge technology. There had been a certain thrill in testing the limits of their instruments, in pushing the boundaries of their observational capabilities. But the sobering reality of Veridia's suffering had quickly tempered that initial enthusiasm. The data they collected was not just an academic exercise; it represented the distress signals of a living world.

The crucial difference, Niko realized, lay in the framing of their technological ambitions. For OmniCorp, technology was an end in itself, a means to achieve greater power and wealth. For the Resonant Pack, technology was a tool, an extension of their commitment to understanding and stewardship. Their ethical framework demanded that every technological deployment be preceded by a rigorous assessment of its potential impact, a deep consideration of its alignment with the principles of ecological harmony and respect for sentient life.

He envisioned a scenario where a new, even more advanced scanning technology was developed, capable of observing the planet's energetic field with unprecedented clarity. The temptation would be to immediately deploy it, to harness its superior capabilities. But the ethical imperative would be to first understand its energetic signature, to model its interactions with Veridia's delicate systems, and to ensure that its use would not inadvertently create new disruptions. This required a level of humility, a recognition that even the most sophisticated technology could be a source of unintended harm if not wielded with wisdom and restraint.

The narrative of technological advancement, Niko reflected, was not a simple linear progression towards greater power and control. It was a complex ethical landscape, fraught with potential pitfalls. The very ingenuity that allowed them to explore the cosmos and to comprehend its wonders also carried the inherent risk of disrupting the fragile balances they encountered. It was a lesson that humanity had learned, and often forgotten, throughout its history. The unchecked pursuit of technological prowess, divorced from a deep understanding of its ecological and ethical implications, had led to environmental degradation, social inequality, and even existential threats on their home worlds.

The Resonant Pack's mission on Veridia was, in many ways, a test of their own maturity as a species. Could they harness the power of advanced technology without succumbing to the temptations of exploitation and unintended consequence? Could they use their sophisticated tools to facilitate healing, rather than to impose a new form of control? The

Veridians, with their inherent connection to their planet, offered a living example of a different path, one where technology, if it existed in a recognizable form, was seamlessly integrated with nature, guided by wisdom and respect.

Niko considered the ethical quandaries that would inevitably arise as their understanding of Veridia deepened. What if their advanced bio-engineering capabilities, honed over centuries of necessity and innovation on their own worlds, could accelerate Veridia's healing process to an almost unimaginable degree? The temptation to intervene more directly, to "fix" the planet faster, would be immense. But would such rapid, externally driven intervention truly foster long-term ecological resilience? Or would it create a dependency, a shallow veneer of recovery that masked underlying vulnerabilities?

The Veridians' approach, characterized by patience and a deep respect for the planet's inherent regenerative capacities, offered a vital counterpoint. They understood that true healing was not a swift erasure of damage, but a gradual process of adaptation, integration, and resurgence. Their role was not to impose a solution, but to nurture and guide the planet's own capacity for recovery. This philosophy extended to their interactions with the Resonant Pack. They welcomed their scientific expertise, their analytical tools, but they also subtly reminded them of the inherent wisdom that lay within the planet itself, and within the interconnected web of life.

Niko found himself constantly evaluating their own technological footprint. Were their orbital scanners emitting too much energy? Were their atmospheric processors, designed to mitigate residual toxins, subtly altering the planet's natural atmospheric composition? These were questions that demanded ongoing vigilance, a continuous ethical self-assessment. The allure of technological solutions was powerful, but it had to be tempered by a profound respect for the natural order, a recognition that the most elegant solutions were often those that worked in harmony with existing systems, rather than imposing upon them.

The contrast with OmniCorp was a stark and ever-present reminder. OmniCorp's technological trajectory had been driven by a relentless pursuit of profit and power, a philosophy that viewed nature as a commodity to be exploited. Their innovations, while often impressive in their engineering, were ultimately designed to serve a singular, exploitative purpose. The devastating consequences of their actions on Veridia were a testament to the dangers of unchecked technological ambition, of innovation divorced from ethical consideration and ecological understanding.

The Resonant Pack had to tread a different path. Their technology was not a weapon or a tool of conquest. It was a means of understanding, a vehicle for empathy, and ultimately, a catalyst for healing. But this required a constant, conscious effort to remain grounded in their ethical principles, to resist the siren call of technological expediency, and to always prioritize the well-being of Veridia above all else. The hum of their orbital station's drive was a constant reminder of their technological prowess, but it was the quiet whispers of Veridia's recovering lifeforms, the subtle energetic resonances that Kira so keenly perceived, that guided their true path forward. It was in the delicate dance between their advanced tools and the planet's inherent resilience that the true ethics of their advancement lay.

The very essence of the Resonant Pack's technological philosophy was woven into the fabric of their equipment, a stark departure from the blunt instruments of exploitation wielded by OmniCorp. Their approach was one of subtle augmentation, of enhancing what already existed rather than imposing something entirely foreign. This was particularly evident in the design of their personal augmentation suites, systems that had been painstakingly developed to meld with biological systems, to become extensions of the user's own senses and abilities. Unlike the crude cybernetics that OmniCorp had sometimes employed, which often resulted in a grotesque fusion of flesh and cold metal, the Pack's technology aimed for a seamless, almost symbiotic integration.

Consider, for instance, the bio-scanner Niko wore as an almost second skin. It wasn't a separate device that he held or manipulated; it was a network of microscopic sensors woven into a flexible, bio-reactive polymer that conformed perfectly to his dermal layers. This polymer itself was derived from genetically engineered, fast-growing flora, designed to be both durable and incredibly sensitive to subtle energetic fluctuations. When Niko activated the scanner, it didn't emit a jarring beam of light or a disruptive wave of energy. Instead, it 'listened' to the ambient energetic fields, subtly modulating its own emissions to resonate with Veridia's natural energetic signatures. The output wasn't a stark, alien readout on a screen, but a series of tactile sensations and nuanced auditory cues that flowed directly into Niko's awareness. He could *feel* the energetic composition of a plant through a faint tingling in his fingertips, or *hear* the subtle energetic signature of a distress signal as a shift in the ambient hum of his own neural interface.

This was where the true genius of their bio-integration lay: its synergy with Kira's unique abilities. Kira, with her innate empathic resonance, could already perceive the planet's energetic currents on a profound level. The Resonant Pack hadn't sought to replicate her abilities through artificial means, but to amplify and refine them. Niko's scanner was designed to cross-reference its own highly precise readings with Kira's intuitive perceptions. When Kira felt a ripple of unease emanating from a particular sector of the forest, Niko's scanner would automatically tune its sensitivity to that specific energetic frequency. The data streams from both sources would then be overlaid and analyzed, creating a richer, more comprehensive understanding than either could achieve alone. Niko might detect an anomalous energy signature, but it was Kira's resonance that would tell him

why that signature was anomalous – whether it was a natural variation, a sign of ecological stress, or something else entirely. This collaborative sensing wasn't just about data acquisition; it was about fostering a deeper, more intuitive connection between their technological tools and their own biological and empathetic capacities.

The design philosophy extended to all their equipment. The harmonic resonators, for example, were a perfect illustration. Instead of broadcasting powerful sonic waves to force a change in the environment, these resonators were designed to identify the natural resonant frequencies of Veridia's bio-network. They would then emit extremely subtle, precisely tuned harmonic pulses that amplified and reinforced these existing frequencies. It was akin to a choir member finding the pitch of another singer and harmonizing with them, rather than shouting over them. This process encouraged the natural flow of energy through the planet's interconnected systems, promoting healing and resilience without introducing an external, disruptive force. The results were not immediate, dramatic transformations, but gentle nudges that guided the planet's own regenerative processes. The indigenous flora, which had been suppressed by OmniCorp's destructive terraforming, began to re-emerge, their cellular structures responding to the subtle encouragement of the harmonic resonators.

Even their communication arrays were designed with integration in mind. OmniCorp had relied on brute-force, wide-spectrum transmissions that broadcast their presence across vast distances, often disrupting sensitive biological processes. The Resonant Pack, conversely, utilized quantum entanglement communicators that established instantaneous, highly focused links between individuals or devices. These communicators emitted virtually no extraneous energy. They didn't broadcast; they

connected. When Niko needed to communicate with Kira, his communicator didn't send a signal into the void. Instead, it established a direct, entangled link with her personal device, a link that was as unique and intimate as a biological synapse. The data transferred was not just information; it was often imbued with contextual resonance, allowing the recipient to grasp not only the facts but also the emotional weight and energetic nuances of the message.

This philosophy of integration extended to their understanding of Veridia's indigenous fauna. The Pack had spent considerable time studying the unique sensory apparatus of various Veridian species. They observed how certain avian creatures could navigate by sensing subtle shifts in the planet's magnetic field, how subterranean dwellers communicated through complex seismic vibrations, and how arboreal organisms exchanged nutrients and information through intricate fungal networks. Their goal was not to replicate these abilities artificially, but to design tools that could interface with them. For instance, they developed specialized bio-acoustic translators that could interpret the ultrasonic chirps of a native insectoid species, rendering them into comprehensible patterns for the Pack members. These translators didn't merely capture sound; they analyzed the subtle energetic modulations within those sounds, allowing for a deeper understanding of the insects' social structures and environmental awareness.

One of the most profound examples of this bio-integration was the development of the 'Symbiotic Harnesses' worn by some members of the Pack when venturing into areas with particularly sensitive ecosystems. These harnesses were not mere protective gear. They were woven from bio-luminescent algae and cultured chitin, materials that were not only lightweight and durable but also capable of subtle energetic exchange with the wearer and the environment. The harnesses could absorb excess atmospheric pollutants, convert them into harmless byproducts, and even subtly regulate the wearer's body temperature by drawing ambient energy. When a wearer like Lena, who possessed enhanced olfactory senses, encountered a novel scent that indicated a potential environmental hazard, the harness would react by subtly shifting its own energetic signature, creating a faint, localized field that prevented the pollutant from reaching her directly, while simultaneously analyzing its composition for later study. It was a proactive defense, integrated directly into the wearer's biological and technological interface, working *with* their natural senses rather than overriding them.

The design process for all their technology was a rigorous, iterative cycle that placed ecological compatibility at its forefront. Before any new device was deployed, it underwent extensive simulations within virtual Veridian environments, meticulously crafted to mirror the planet's intricate bio-energetic matrix. These simulations predicted not only the intended function of the device but also any potential ripple effects it might have on the surrounding ecosystem. The energy footprint of each component was scrutinized. Even the materials used in their construction were chosen for their biodegradability and their potential to be reabsorbed into the natural environment without leaving a trace. This was a stark contrast to OmniCorp, whose discarded machinery had littered so many worlds, rusting monuments to their short-sightedness.

Niko often found himself marveling at the elegance of a seemingly simple device: the 'Nerve-Weave' implant. It was a micro-fine lattice of bio-compatible conductive threads that could be implanted non-invasively, weaving itself into the user's neural pathways over time. It didn't overwrite or replace neural functions; it augmented them. For individuals like Kai, who possessed a natural affinity for understanding complex systems, the Nerve-Weave allowed him to perceive the intricate patterns of information flow within Veridia's fungal networks. He could 'see' the transfer of nutrients, the communication signals between different plant species, as if he were directly integrated into the planet's subterranean nervous system. This wasn't about imposing artificial control; it was about unlocking a latent potential for understanding that already existed within the biological framework of Veridia and, to a lesser extent, within the individuals of the Resonant Pack themselves.

The guiding principle was always to facilitate, not to dominate. When the Pack needed to stabilize a critically endangered ecosystem, their approach wasn't to introduce artificial nutrient solutions or genetically modified organisms that would outcompete native species. Instead, they would deploy their bio-integrative devices – devices that gently encouraged the proliferation of beneficial microbes, that optimized the natural absorption of sunlight, or that facilitated the exchange of resources between struggling plant communities. It was a form of ecological midwifery, assisting the natural birth of recovery rather than forcing an artificial imposition.

This philosophy also influenced their approach to data storage and processing. Instead of relying on massive, energy-intensive server farms, the Pack utilized distributed bio-computing networks. These networks employed specially cultivated crystalline structures and organic substrates that could store and process information using subtle bio-energetic shifts. These systems were not only far more energy-efficient but were also designed to be intrinsically linked to the local environment. Data stored within these networks could be accessed and interpreted by the local flora and fauna, creating a shared repository of knowledge that benefited both the Pack and Veridia. This was a form of passive data integration, where their technological archives became a harmonious extension of the planet's own informational ecosystem.

The ethical implications of this approach were profound. By prioritizing bio-integration and synergy, the Resonant Pack was not just developing advanced technology; they were cultivating a new paradigm of human-planetary interaction. They were demonstrating that technological advancement did not have to come at the expense of ecological integrity. In fact, they argued, true advancement lay in the ability to create technologies that not only served humanity's needs but also enriched and supported the natural world. This was a long and arduous path, one that required constant innovation, unwavering ethical commitment, and a profound respect for the intricate, interconnected web of life. It was a path that stood in stark opposition to the destructive legacy of OmniCorp, and it was the only path that held the promise of a truly sustainable future, both for themselves and for the worlds they explored. The subtle hum of their integrated technology was not a sound of dominance, but a whisper of harmony, a testament to their commitment to working with, rather than against, the natural order.

Kira often felt the hum of technology as a palpable presence, an energetic signature that resonated with her own being. It wasn't the cold, clanking imposition of OmniCorp's utilitarian machines, but something more nuanced, more alive. For her, the ultimate measure of any technology was its effect on her senses and, by extension, her connection to Niko and the vibrant, pulsating life of Veridia. If an innovation sharpened her already keen perception, if it deepened the intuitive bridge between her and Niko, or if it allowed her to understand the planet's whispers with greater clarity, then it was, in her eyes, a success. Conversely, anything that created a cacophony in her mind, an overwhelming flood of artificial stimuli that drowned out the subtle symphony of the natural world, or worse, anything that erected a barrier between her and Niko, was anathema. It was a perspective perhaps best understood through an animalistic lens, where the world was perceived through a rich tapestry of senses, and where connection was paramount to survival and well-being.

She remembered the early days, the tentative steps the Resonant Pack had taken in integrating their own bio-enhancements. The 'Synaptic Weave' implants, for example. For Niko, they were a revelation, allowing him to perceive the intricate informational pathways of Veridia's fungal networks as if he were directly plugged into the planet's subterranean nervous system. He described it as seeing the world in a new spectrum of light, a constant flow of data that painted a richer picture of ecological interdependence. For Kira, the experience was different, yet complementary. The Weave didn't flood her with raw data; instead, it acted as a subtle interpreter, translating the ambient energetic chatter of the planet into patterns she could more readily interpret. It was as if the Weave smoothed out the rough edges of Veridia's energetic language, making it more accessible to her empathic core. She could sense the subtle nutrient exchanges between ancient trees, the distress calls of stressed flora, or the harmonious pulses of thriving ecosystems, all translated into a language her being inherently understood, amplified by the Weave's refined perception. It didn't impose; it facilitated, making the already potent connections she felt even more vibrant and comprehensible.

This was the kind of technology she embraced: tools that acted as extensions of her own capabilities, not replacements. When Niko would share his perceptions via their neural link, amplified by the Synaptic Weave, she didn't just receive information; she felt the echo of his understanding, a shared resonance that deepened their bond. It was like tasting a complex flavour for the first time; he would describe the notes, and she would experience the sensation, the subtle undertones, the lingering aftertaste. The Weave allowed him to articulate the inarticulate, and her empathic nature allowed her to receive it not just as data, but as experience. This symbiotic flow of information, enhanced by technology, was the very essence of their partnership, a testament to how advancement could forge deeper connections rather than alienate.

However, she also recalled the initial attempts at atmospheric filtration systems. OmniCorp had once deployed crude, monolithic units that belched out clouds of processed air, accompanied by a low, guttural hum that grated on her very bones. The output was sterile, devoid of the vital energetic signature of Veridia. The Pack's first iteration, while well-intentioned, had still felt jarring. It was a series of large, crystalline structures that pulsed with an insistent, rhythmic light, emitting a high-frequency whine that interfered with her ability to sense the subtler atmospheric shifts. It created a disorienting static in her awareness, a feeling akin to being in a room with a constant, piercing noise that drowned out all other sounds. She had communicated her unease to Niko, describing it as a "sharp silence," a void where the planet's natural breath should have been.

Niko, always attuned to her sensory input, had understood immediately. He explained that the system was designed to be highly efficient, its energetic output carefully calibrated to neutralize specific pollutants. But efficiency, he conceded, wasn't the same as harmony. The technology, while functionally effective in cleaning the air, was fundamentally out of sync with Veridia's energetic rhythms. It was like a person shouting an important message in a room where everyone else was whispering. The message might be heard, but the disruption would be profound.

This led to the development of the 'Bio-Harmonic Regulators.' These were far subtler. Instead of forcefully scrubbing the air, they were designed to resonate with the atmospheric composition, gently coaxing errant molecules into alignment with Veridia's natural energetic frequencies. They were integrated into the landscape, appearing as clusters of bioluminescent flora, their soft glow mirroring the planet's own luminescence. The sensory experience for Kira was transformational. The sharp whine was replaced by a gentle, almost imperceptible vibration that felt like a soft caress against her senses. The sterile emptiness vanished, replaced by a feeling of enhanced clarity, as if the air itself had been filtered through a dewdrop. She could now perceive the delicate interplay of atmospheric gases, the subtle migration of pollen, the faint energetic signatures of distant weather patterns, all without the disorienting interference of the previous technology. It was an invisible enhancement, a quiet refinement that allowed her to feel more connected to her environment, not less.

The key, she realized, was integration and resonance. Technology, in her view, should be a bridge, not a barrier. It should enhance her natural connection to the world and to Niko, not sever it. This was why she found the concept of sensory overload so disturbing. OmniCorp's displays, with their flashing lights and jarring auditory alerts, were designed to grab attention through sheer force. They were designed to overwhelm, to demand compliance through sensory assault. Kira experienced such displays as physical pain, a violation of her inner quiet. It felt like being attacked by a swarm of angry insects, each one buzzing with a discordant frequency that made her skin crawl and her mind reel.

She remembered a particular incident when they had infiltrated an old OmniCorp research outpost. The place was a testament to technological hubris. Holographic advertisements flickered erratically, their images glitching and distorting, emitting a cacophony of pre-recorded, repetitive slogans. Alarms blared with a relentless, high-pitched whine, and screens flashed with meaningless streams of data in jarring, neon colours. Kira had been forced to retreat, her senses overwhelmed. She had felt a profound disconnect, not just from the environment, but from Niko and the Pack. It was as if the very air was thick with a suffocating, artificial presence that choked out any possibility of natural perception. She had retreated to a quiet alcove, pressing her hands to her temples, trying to find a sliver of silence in the sonic chaos.

"It feels... broken," she had communicated to Niko, her voice strained. "Like a wounded animal, screaming without end."

Niko, who had managed to shield himself from the worst of the sensory assault, had immediately understood. He had remotely deactivated the most aggressive systems, the ones that generated the most disruptive frequencies. The sudden drop in the sensory onslaught was like a gasp of fresh air. Kira could feel her senses slowly unfurl, like petals after a storm. The subtle, underlying energetic pulse of Veridia, which had been completely drowned out, began to reassert itself. It was a stark reminder of what technology *shouldn't* be: an imposition that silenced the natural world.

This animalistic viewpoint extended to how she perceived the potential of technological augmentation. For her, the ultimate augmentation was one that didn't alter her fundamental self, but rather amplified her inherent strengths. It was about enhancing her ability to feel, to connect, to understand. The bio-scanner Niko wore, integrated into his very skin, was a prime example. It didn't grant him senses he didn't possess; it refined and amplified the ones he did. When he used it to "listen" to the planet's energetic fields, Kira felt a subtle echo of that listening within herself. It was as if his enhanced perception created a clearer channel for her own empathic reception.

She often compared it to how a predator senses its prey. A wolf doesn't suddenly sprout wings to hunt a bird; it uses its heightened senses of smell and hearing, its keen eyesight, its powerful legs, all honed by evolution and amplified by instinct. The Resonant Pack's technology aimed for a similar synergy. It was about understanding the existing biological and energetic frameworks and finding ways to enhance them. For Kira, this meant technology that deepened her empathic connection, allowing her to feel the distress of a wilting plant or the joy of a thriving ecosystem with even greater intensity. It meant tools that allowed her to better understand and communicate with the diverse fauna of Veridia, not through artificial mimicry, but through a refined interpretation of their natural signals.

Consider the 'Symbiotic Harnesses.' When Lena, with her enhanced olfactory senses, encountered a novel scent indicating a potential environmental hazard, the harness didn't just create a barrier. It interacted.

It shifted its energetic signature, and Kira could feel that shift as a subtle tightening, a focused attention emanating from Lena. The harness was essentially communicating with Lena's biology and with the environment, analyzing the threat while simultaneously protecting her. For Kira, this was a beautiful synergy. It was as if Lena's own body, augmented by the harness, was engaging in a silent, sophisticated dialogue with the planet.

The most significant aspect of technology, from Kira's perspective, was its role in fostering connection. The quantum entanglement communicators, for instance, were a revelation. Unlike OmniCorp's broadcast-style communications that felt like shouting into a void, these communicators established a direct, intimate link. When Niko communicated with her, it wasn't just a transfer of data; it was a sharing of presence, a weaving of their consciousness. She could feel the nuances of his emotions, the subtle shifts in his intent, alongside the informational content. It was a profound intimacy, a digital extension of the telepathic bond that existed between many sentient beings in the natural world.

She found that technologies that created isolation were the most detrimental. If a device required a user to withdraw into a purely internal, artificial world, or if it demanded constant, undivided attention that severed their awareness of their surroundings, then it was a step backward. She recalled seeing schematics for early OmniCorp neural interfaces that promised direct access to vast databanks, but at the cost of "disengaging from external sensory input." To Kira, this was anathema. Why would one trade the richness of the real world for a simulated one, especially when the real world was so full of wonders to be perceived? It was like choosing to stare at a single, flickering candle in a vast, star-filled night sky.

The Resonant Pack's approach was to avoid such isolation. Their data storage systems, for example, were designed to be accessible not just by their own devices, but by the local flora and fauna. This created a shared repository of knowledge, a collective memory that benefited everyone. Kira could sense this integration, a subtle hum of shared information that seemed to permeate the very soil. It was as if the planet itself was becoming more aware, its individual components connected by the Pack's technology in a harmonious network.

This was the ultimate ethical consideration for Kira: did the technology serve to connect or to isolate? Did it enhance the natural world or disrupt it? Did it foster a deeper understanding or create a superficial detachment? The Resonant Pack's philosophy, rooted in empathy and ecological awareness, aligned perfectly with her own intuitive understanding of the world. They sought to create tools that whispered in harmony with Veridia, not shouted in defiance. They built bridges, not walls. And in doing so, they were not just advancing technology; they were advancing a more profound and ethical relationship with life itself. Her senses, finely tuned to the energetic flows of the universe, could detect the difference, a palpable distinction between the intrusive noise of exploitation and the harmonious symphony of integration. And in that symphony, she found hope.

The seamless integration of technology into Veridia had been a triumph, a testament to the Resonant Pack's philosophy of harmonizing advancement with the planet's natural rhythms. Yet, as Niko often pondered, standing under the gentle, bioluminescent glow of the atmospheric regulators, even the most benevolent of tools carried within them a subtle potential for dissonance. It was a thought that gnawed at him, a quiet hum beneath the surface of their current peace. He saw it in the way the younger members of the Pack, born into an era of effortless connectivity and bio-enhancement, sometimes relied on their implanted interfaces as much as they did their own intuition. The Synaptic Weave, meant to augment their connection to Veridia, could, if unchecked, become a substitute for experiencing the world directly. He'd observed a child, no older than ten cycles, staring blankly at a vibrant, chattering avian flock, their gaze fixed on the data overlay projected onto their retinas by their ocular implants, detailing species, migratory patterns, and nutritional content. The child wasn't *seeing* the birds; they were *reading* them. The vibrant flutter of wings, the complex social dynamics playing out in real-time, the sheer, unadulterated *life* of the moment, was being filtered through a layer of algorithmic interpretation. It was efficient, certainly, a wealth of information delivered instantaneously. But was it connection? Was it understanding?

Niko found himself drawn to the ethical tightrope they walked. The 'helpful' technology, the tools designed to alleviate suffering, to enhance perception, to foster unity, possessed an inherent duality. A scalpel, in the hands of a surgeon, could mend a broken body. In the hands of an assassin, it could end a life. The difference lay not in the tool itself, but in the intent and the wisdom of its wielder. And humanity, he knew from the whispered histories of Old Earth, had a long and often bloody track record of conflating capability with wisdom. They had mastered the atom, only to unleash its destructive power. They had mapped the human genome, only to contemplate its manipulation for superficial gain. The question echoed in his mind, amplified by the very interconnectedness their technology sought to achieve: what happened when that capability, that drive for advancement, was no longer confined to a single planet, but extended to the very fabric of existence?

The gateway technology, the nascent understanding of dimensional transit that the Pack was cautiously exploring, represented a leap of an entirely different magnitude. It was not merely about enhancing their experience of Veridia, or even about establishing communication across vast interstellar distances. It was about the potential to step beyond their known reality, to access what lay beyond the veil of their current understanding. The implications were staggering, a cosmic mirror reflecting the age-old human dilemma: the pursuit of knowledge and power versus the capacity for restraint and ethical consideration.

He recalled the stories passed down through the Pack's oral traditions, fragmented echoes of OmniCorp's final, desperate push for dominance. Their advancements had been driven by a relentless, almost pathological, need to conquer, to control, to dominate. They had viewed the natural world not as a partner, but as a resource to be exploited. They had seen other species not as fellow travelers on the cosmic journey, but as obstacles or potential tools. Their technology, while undeniably powerful, had been a manifestation of this rapacious worldview. It was a technology of extraction, of subjugation, of imposition. And Niko feared that the lure of the gateways, the promise of infinite expansion and unimaginable power, could awaken those same dormant impulses within humanity, not just on Veridia, but across the nascent interstellar communities they might encounter.

What, truly, constituted advancement? Was it merely the accumulation of more complex tools, the ability to manipulate reality on a grander scale? Or was it something more profound – the cultivation of wisdom, the deepening of empathy, the development of a more harmonious relationship with the universe? The gateway technology offered unprecedented access, the potential to traverse vast distances and perhaps even manipulate the very dimensions of space-time. But if the beings wielding this power had not first learned to govern their own destructive tendencies, if they had not cultivated a deep respect for the delicate balance of existence, then such power would not be a tool of enlightenment, but a weapon of unimaginable destruction. He pictured humanity, with its ingrained history of conflict and exploitation, armed with the ability to warp reality itself. The thought sent a shiver down his spine, a cold premonition that transcended the warmth of Veridia's atmosphere.

He found himself walking along the edge of the Whispering Mire, the air thick with the scent of damp earth and luminescent moss. The Mire was a complex ecosystem, a testament to the intricate interdependencies of Veridia. Each organism, from the smallest microorganism to the towering, ancient trees, played a vital role. The technology that facilitated their understanding of this delicate balance was designed to be almost invisible, enhancing their perception without imposing its own artificial rhythm. The Bio-Harmonic Regulators, for instance, pulsed with a gentle, rhythmic light, their energy signature indistinguishable from the natural bio-luminescence of the native flora. Kira had often described sensing their presence as a subtle amplification of the Mire's own quiet breathing, a harmonizing chord struck within the symphony of Veridia.

Yet, even here, a seed of doubt could sprout. What if the gateway technology, in its relentless pursuit of discovery, inadvertently disrupted such pristine ecosystems? What if the very act of crossing dimensions, of opening new pathways, created unforeseen ripples, unforeseen consequences that echoed through the delicate web of life? The OmniCorp archives, salvaged by the Pack, were replete with examples of their hubris. They had boasted of terraforming worlds, of "improving" them according to their own limited, utilitarian standards, often at the cost of the native biodiversity. They had viewed the universe as a vast, untamed frontier to be tamed, not a complex tapestry to be appreciated and integrated with.

Niko's concern was not about the inherent nature of the technology itself. He believed that technology, at its core, was neutral. It was a reflection of the intentions and the maturity of its creators. The problem lay in the potential for a fundamental mismatch: a vast technological capability wielded by a species still wrestling with its own primal instincts, its own shadow self. The jump from understanding complex biological systems to manipulating the fabric of spacetime was immense, and he feared that humanity's ethical and spiritual development had not kept pace with its technological prowess. The gateways represented the ultimate "what if." What if they unlocked the secrets of the universe, only to unleash chaos? What if they discovered new forms of life, only to treat them as OmniCorp had treated so many of Veridia's less fortunate inhabitants – as resources to be exploited?

He paused, watching a cluster of bioluminescent fungi illuminate the deepening twilight. Their soft glow pulsed in time with the gentle rustling of the leaves overhead. This was the essence of Veridia, a world where technology and nature were not in opposition, but in a dance of mutual enhancement. The Synaptic Weave allowed Niko to perceive the subtle energetic exchanges between the fungi and the ancient trees, a silent, vital conversation that sustained the entire ecosystem. Kira, in turn, could translate those energetic impressions into a deeper, more intuitive understanding, her empathic core resonating with the planet's pulse. It was a symbiotic relationship, a testament to what could be achieved when innovation was guided by wisdom and respect.

But the gateways... they were a Pandora's Box of a different order. They offered not just an enhancement of their current reality, but a potential escape from it, a means to transcend limitations. And in that transcendence, Niko saw the potential for a profound ethical lapse. If humanity could simply step through a gateway to escape the consequences of its actions, what incentive would there be to act responsibly? If they could access new worlds, new resources, without truly understanding or respecting the existing ecological balance, they risked replicating the very mistakes that had scarred Old Earth and nearly destroyed Veridia. The notion of 'progress' itself began to warp in his mind, shifting from a concept of betterment and growth to one of sheer, unbridled expansion, a relentless accumulation of power without an accompanying increase in wisdom or compassion.

He closed his eyes, attempting to filter out the immediate sensory input, to delve into the deeper currents of his own consciousness, and perhaps, through the subtle channels that technology had opened, to touch upon the collective consciousness of the Resonant Pack. He felt the shared hope, the quiet determination, the underlying unity that bound them. This was the strength of their approach: a deep-seated ethical framework that guided their every innovation. They sought not to dominate, but to understand. They aimed not to exploit, but to integrate.

But the ghosts of humanity's past were long and their echoes were insidious. The allure of power, the temptation to bypass the arduous work of cultivating wisdom and empathy in favor of a shortcut, was a constant, pervasive force. The gateway technology, in its purest form, held the promise of unlocking untold wonders, of fostering interspecies understanding on a cosmic scale. It could be the bridge to a new era of interconnectedness, a catalyst for collective growth. But it could also be the ultimate weapon, the tool that allowed a species still fundamentally driven by its baser instincts to inflict irreparable damage on a scale previously unimaginable. The question of true advancement was no longer just about what they could *do*, but about what they *should* do. And as Niko stood on the precipice of such profound possibility, the weight of that question felt heavier than the very stars themselves. He knew that the Pack, with their grounded connection to Veridia and their empathetic philosophy, were well-positioned to navigate these treacherous waters. But the broader question remained, a disquieting hum beneath the surface of their hopeful endeavors: was humanity, as a whole, ready to wield such power responsibly? Or were they destined to repeat their ancient, self-destructive patterns, this time on a cosmic stage? The wisdom to answer that question, he suspected, was far more valuable, and far more elusive, than any gateway to another dimension.

The humid air of the Whispering Mire clung to Niko's skin, a tangible reminder of Veridia's vibrant, intricate life. He watched a pair of shimmering, iridescent beetles trace lazy circles above a patch of phosphorescent fungi, their flight path dictated by unseen currents and the subtle magnetic fields of the soil. Their existence was a testament to a harmony he strived to uphold, a delicate equilibrium that his own people, the Resonant Pack, had worked tirelessly to protect and understand. The technological marvels that allowed him to perceive these microscopic interactions, the subtle bio-signatures that painted a richer picture of the Mire's health, were designed to fade into the background, mere extensions of his own senses rather than intrusions. It was this ethos – the mindful application of ingenuity, the deep reverence for the natural world, and the unwavering commitment to ethical stewardship – that defined their path forward, especially as they grappled with the profound implications of gateway technology.

The temptation to view advancement solely through the lens of technological capability was a siren song, one that had lured countless civilizations to ruin. OmniCorp's archives, grim testaments to humanity's past follies, were filled with accounts of progress pursued without wisdom, of power amassed without compassion. They had engineered solutions without truly understanding the problems, inadvertently unleashing cascades of unforeseen consequences upon ecosystems and sentient beings alike. The Pack's counter-narrative was built on a different foundation: that true advancement was not about domination, but about integration; not about conquest, but about kinship. It was a philosophy deeply intertwined with their symbiotic relationship with Veridia's fauna. The profound, unspoken communication with creatures like the Lumina-winged moths, whose bioluminescent patterns served as barometers for atmospheric purity, or the ancient, sentient Grok-treants, whose root systems acted as living conduits for planetary data, was not merely a romantic ideal. It was a guiding principle, a constant reminder that the most sophisticated technology was meaningless if it disconnected them from the very life it was meant to serve.

The gateway technology, while holding the promise of unprecedented discovery and connection, also represented the ultimate test of this philosophy. To venture beyond the familiar boundaries of Veridia, to traverse the interdimensional currents, required a level of maturity, of ethical grounding, that humanity had historically struggled to achieve. The very act of crossing dimensional thresholds could be disruptive, a potential seismic shift in realities that demanded not just scientific precision, but profound ecological sensitivity. Niko envisioned a scenario where the Pack, guided by their deep connection to Veridia and their empathetic understanding of life, would approach such ventures with the utmost caution. Their exploratory jumps would be preceded by extensive ecological impact assessments, utilizing predictive modeling that accounted for not just physical changes, but energetic and even spiritual resonance. They would seek to understand the inherent "biodiversity" of each dimension, recognizing that life, in its myriad forms, deserved respect regardless of its manifestation. Their animal partners, with their innate attunement to natural rhythms and subtle energies, would be integral to this process, their perceptions guiding the Pack's understanding and informing their decisions. A seismic tremor in a neighboring dimension, detected by a Grok-treant's root network, might be cause to pause an exploration, just as a subtle shift in a Veridian forest's bioluminescent pulse might indicate the need for a pause in local development.

This was the essence of the "hopepunk" ethos that the Resonant Pack championed. It was a defiant optimism, a belief that even in the face of overwhelming challenges and the specter of past failures, a better future was possible through conscious effort, collective action, and unwavering compassion. Their commitment to balanced advancement was not a passive waiting for utopia to arrive, but an active, daily practice. It meant prioritizing the health of Veridia's ecosystems over the immediate gratification of technological expansion. It meant investing in technologies that fostered deeper understanding and empathy, rather than those that promised greater control or efficiency at the expense of natural processes. It meant ensuring that every member of the Pack, from the youngest hatchling to the most seasoned elder, was educated not just in the mechanics of their tools, but in the ethical implications of their use.

Niko recalled a recent discussion with Lyra, a young bio-engineer whose enthusiasm for the gateway project was palpable. She had presented a design for an interdimensional sensor array, capable of mapping subtle energy signatures across dimensional boundaries. Her excitement was infectious, but Niko gently guided the conversation towards the potential unintended consequences. "Lyra," he had said, his voice soft but firm, "this technology is magnificent. It speaks to our drive to understand. But what if these energy signatures are, in essence, the 'lifeblood' of another reality? What if our mapping creates a disturbance, a ripple that affects beings we cannot yet perceive? Our primary directive must always be to observe, to learn, and to integrate, never to impose or to disrupt without absolute necessity and the deepest understanding." Lyra, to her credit, had listened intently, her brow furrowed in thought. Later, she presented a revised design, incorporating bio-feedback loops that mimicked Veridian flora's adaptive responses, aiming to minimize energetic impact. This was the kind of maturation they hoped to cultivate: the integration of technological prowess with ecological wisdom.

The Pack understood that their unique position, as a civilization deeply rooted in a symbiotic relationship with their planet and its inhabitants, offered a crucial perspective. They had witnessed firsthand the devastating consequences of unchecked exploitation. They had learned from the ghosts of OmniCorp's hubris, the cautionary tales whispered through salvaged data logs and the scars left upon their own world before their arrival. This history fueled their resolve to chart a different course. When it came to the gateways, their approach would be one of profound respect, not just for the unknown physics of interdimensional travel, but for the potential existence of other forms of life and consciousness within those realms. They envisioned a future where interdimensional exploration was not about claiming new territories or exploiting new resources, but about fostering understanding, about discovering shared principles of existence, and perhaps, about finding allies in the vast cosmic expanse.

Their animal companions played an indispensable role in this vision. The packs of swift, empathetic Sky-hounds, whose telepathic senses could detect subtle shifts in atmospheric pressure and emotional resonance, were invaluable in forecasting potential environmental hazards in new dimensional environments. The wise, ancient Earth-shapers, whose connection to geological forces allowed them to anticipate seismic activity and planetary instability, would be crucial in assessing the fundamental stability of any new world. Even the smallest of Veridia's creatures, the microscopic symbiotes that thrived within the planetary crust, held keys to understanding the intricate biological tapestry of different realities. The Pack's ability to communicate and collaborate with these diverse life forms was not just a matter of scientific inquiry; it was a testament to their ethical framework, a living embodiment of their belief in the interconnectedness of all beings.

The act of venturing through a gateway would be undertaken with a profound sense of humility. It was not about imposing Veridian ways or human logic onto the unknown, but about listening, about observing, about being open to experiences that might challenge their very understanding of reality. Niko imagined the first interdimensional expeditions being more akin to a pilgrimage than an invasion. The equipment would be designed for minimal footprint, prioritizing observation and data collection over invasive intervention. Communication protocols would be established not just for interspecies dialogue, but for interdimensional dialogue, acknowledging the possibility of entirely alien forms of consciousness that might not communicate through sound or light, but through more subtle energetic or conceptual means. The Sky-hounds, with their innate empathic resonance, would be at the forefront, attempting to establish peaceful contact, to gauge intent and disposition before any direct interaction.

The ethical considerations extended beyond the immediate act of transit. What responsibilities did they incur upon discovering new worlds or encountering new civilizations? If a gateway opened to a dimension teeming with nascent, fragile life, would they have the right to interfere, even with the best of intentions? The OmniCorp archives were rife with examples of well-meaning but ultimately disastrous interventions, of attempts to "uplift" or "assist" that resulted in the collapse of existing societies or ecosystems. The Pack's guiding principle would be non-interference unless a clear and present danger to sentient life, or the fundamental integrity of a reality, necessitated it. Even then, any intervention would be undertaken with the utmost caution, guided by the collective wisdom of the Pack and their animal partners, and aimed at restoring balance rather than imposing their own.

Furthermore, the very concept of "progress" needed constant re-evaluation. Was it progress to gain access to infinite resources if it meant depleting them carelessly? Was it progress to encounter new sentient beings if it meant subjugating or exploiting them? Niko believed that true progress lay in the cultivation of inner wisdom, in the deepening of empathy, and in the development of sustainable, harmonious relationships with the universe. Gateway technology, therefore, should not be seen as an escape route from the challenges of Veridia, but as an opportunity to learn, to grow, and to share the lessons they had learned. It was a tool for fostering cosmic kinship, not for galactic dominion.

The Resonant Pack's commitment to this balanced future was not a passive hope, but an active pursuit. It was woven into the fabric of their daily lives, from the way they cultivated their food in bio-integrated farms to the way they educated their young. They emphasized critical thinking, ethical reasoning, and the development of deep emotional intelligence. They fostered a culture where questioning the status quo, where challenging technological advancements on ethical grounds, was not only accepted but encouraged. The wisdom of Veridia's natural world served as their constant teacher, its intricate webs of interdependence and resilience offering a blueprint for a sustainable and compassionate existence. Their animal partners were not merely allies, but co-inhabitants, their well-being and their unique perspectives held in the highest regard.

As Niko looked out at the serene landscape of the Whispering Mire, a sense of profound peace settled over him. The bioluminescent glow of the flora pulsed gently, a silent symphony of life. The distant chirps and rustles of unseen creatures formed a familiar, comforting chorus. This was the culmination of their efforts, a testament to their unwavering belief in a future where technology served life, where advancement was measured not by power, but by wisdom and compassion, and where humanity, humbled and enlightened, found its place not as a master of the universe, but as a humble, interconnected participant. The gateways offered a vast, awe-inspiring frontier, but the true journey, the most significant exploration, would always be the inward one, the continuous quest to refine their own ethical compass and deepen their capacity for love and understanding, not just for their own kind, but for all beings, across all dimensions.

This was their promise, their guiding star, the unwavering beacon of hope that illuminated their path forward into the immeasurable unknown. Their legacy would not be one of conquest, but of connection; not of domination, but of mutual flourishing. And in that, they found their ultimate strength.

Chapter Fourteen
CONVERGENCE

The subtle hum of the Veridian nexus, usually a comforting thrum that resonated with the planet's life force, had lately taken on a discordant undertone. It was a sound Niko had come to associate with a gathering storm, a disquiet born from the intercepted transmissions and hushed whispers of their scouts. OmniCorp, it seemed, was no longer content with mere observation or a cautious, albeit exploitative, presence. Their operations were escalating, their modus operandi devolving from calculated avarice into a frantic, unbridled grab for power. The data streams painted a grim picture: accelerated resource extraction from fringe dimensions, experimental portal stabilization technologies that sent seismic ripples through nascent realities, and a disturbing disregard for the very ecological principles the Resonant Pack held sacrosanct.

One particularly disturbing report detailed an OmniCorp deployment near what the Pack had designated the 'Chrono-Gardens,' a pocket dimension where temporal anomalies manifested as crystalline flora, pulsing with chronometric energy. OmniCorp's intention, according to the encrypted logs, was not to study or safeguard this unique environment, but to harness its temporal flux for advanced temporal manipulation engines – a feat that bordered on the cosmically arrogant, and one that threatened to unravel the delicate causal chains of multiple connected realities. The data revealed a shocking breach of safety protocols; during one attempted extraction, an uncontrolled temporal cascade had been narrowly contained by a desperate, and ultimately fatal, intervention from one of OmniCorp's own deployed drones, its final moments broadcasting a garbled confession of the sheer recklessness involved. The Pack's bio-analysts confirmed the energetic residue of such an event could leave dimensional ecosystems in a state of temporal flux for millennia, rendering them uninhabitable for any lifeform, regardless of its temporal resilience.

Then came the intelligence that truly galvanized the Pack. A high-level OmniCorp directive, code-named 'Project Chimera,' outlined a strategy to seize direct control of Veridia's nexus point. This wasn't just about manipulating the gateway technology; it was about locking it down, turning it into OmniCorp's exclusive domain. The directive spoke of deploying 'dimensional anchors' – massive, energy-intensive devices designed to tether the nexus to OmniCorp's proprietary grid, effectively severing its natural connection to Veridia's planetary consciousness and, by extension, the Resonant Pack's symbiotic link. The ramifications were terrifying: Veridia's ecosystem would begin to wither without the nexus's vital energy, and the Pack would be cut off from their own planet's soul, their ability to perceive and interact with the natural world drastically diminished.

The data also hinted at OmniCorp's growing desperation. Their past attempts to control dimensional gateways had been fraught with peril, leading to catastrophic events in several minor realities. The 'Whispering Void,' a dimension once rich with ethereal, sentient energy forms, had been reduced to a chaotic storm of fractured consciousness by an OmniCorp 'containment breach.' Survivors, few and far between, spoke of entities twisted and torn, their very essence scattered like dust. The records were stark: OmniCorp's technological hubris had a consistent pattern of unintended, and often irreversible, destruction. They were pushing the boundaries of reality itself, not with the meticulous caution of a scientist, but with the reckless abandon of a gambler chasing a losing streak. Their pursuit of dimensional dominance was proving to be an ecological apocalypse in slow motion.

The threat was no longer abstract. The scouts had confirmed increased OmniCorp activity around the Periphery Zones, the liminal spaces where dimensional membranes were thinnest, notoriously unstable, and prone to unpredictable energy surges. These zones were usually patrolled by specialized Pack units, equipped with resonance dampeners and bio-harmonic stabilizers, to monitor and mitigate any natural fluctuations. OmniCorp's presence there, however, was a blatant act of provocation, suggesting an intent to weaponize these instabilities. Their reconnaissance drones, larger and more heavily shielded than anything the Pack had deployed for similar tasks, were observed attempting to map the energy flow of nascent dimensional rifts, their probes emitting disruptive frequencies that caused distress signals from local fauna, including the sensitive, bioluminescent Sky-jellies that normally drifted peacefully in these interdimensional currents. The data logs recovered from a downed drone indicated OmniCorp was developing 'reality-shredding' payloads, designed to destabilize dimensional membranes and create cascading collapses, a strategy that could render vast swathes of the interdimensional plane uninhabitable.

Niko convened an emergency council. The air in the Great Arbor was thick with a tension that even the ancient trees seemed to absorb. Elder Anya, her face etched with a familiar blend of wisdom and sorrow, addressed the gathered Pack members. "OmniCorp's actions have moved beyond avarice," she stated, her voice resonating with a quiet gravity. "They are now actively seeking to dismantle the very fabric of interconnected existence. Their 'Project Chimera' is not merely an attempt to control gateways; it is an attempt to control reality itself. If they succeed in anchoring Veridia's nexus, our world will slowly suffocate, and the delicate balance of countless dimensions will be irrevocably shattered. This is no longer a defensive posture. This requires direct, decisive action."

Lyra, her usual scientific fervor now tempered with a grim resolve, presented the latest findings from her advanced sensor arrays. "We've detected significant energy signatures emanating from OmniCorp's primary staging ground in the Crimson Nebula," she explained, a holographic projection of a swirling cosmic cloud appearing above the council table. "Their portal arrays are operating at peak capacity, far beyond what would be necessary for standard transit. They are not just opening gateways; they are tearing them open. The pattern indicates they are preparing for a simultaneous multi-dimensional insertion, targeting key nexus points across several systems, including our own."

The implication was chilling. OmniCorp wasn't just after Veridia; they were launching a coordinated, galaxy-wide offensive against the stability of interdimensional travel. Their reckless experimentation had destabilized regions of space already prone to flux, and now they intended to exploit this chaos for their own gain, to create pockets of controlled instability that they could then exploit or, worse, to use as bargaining chips against nascent civilizations. The energy readings showed a chaotic, uncontrolled surge, indicative of a system running without proper failsafes, risking a feedback loop that could have devastating consequences across multiple connected realities. The data suggested they were actively trying to bypass natural dimensional harmonics, forcing unstable connections that risked catastrophic breaches.

The scouts' reports were corroborated by the desperate pleas from allied sentient species whose worlds had been inadvertently destabilized by OmniCorp's earlier incursions. The Lumina, beings of pure light whose existence was intrinsically tied to the energetic coherence of their home dimension, reported their world flickering in and out of existence, their very forms dissolving and reforming in a terrifying cycle. The sentient crystalline entities of Xylos, who communicated through resonant frequencies, sent fragmented data indicating a 'screaming void' where their vibrant network once thrived, a direct consequence of an OmniCorp research station's unchecked energy discharge. These were not isolated incidents; they were symptoms of a systemic disregard for the sanctity of life and the integrity of the cosmos.

Niko felt a profound sense of urgency grip him. The Pack's ethos of observation and understanding, while crucial, was no longer sufficient. OmniCorp's escalation demanded a response that went beyond philosophical debate or defensive maneuvers. They had to intercept 'Project Chimera' before it reached its catastrophic conclusion. The dimensional anchors, if deployed, would not only cripple Veridia but also serve as templates for OmniCorp to subjugate other worlds, effectively building an empire on the ruins of cosmic harmony. The raw data from the intercepted directive was irrefutable: OmniCorp was preparing to initiate their global seizure within cycles. This was not a drill. This was the precipice.

The council fell silent, the weight of the impending threat pressing down on them. The bioluminescent flora of the Great Arbor seemed to dim, mirroring the somber mood. Anya broke the silence. "We have always sought to preserve and to understand," she began, her gaze sweeping across the worried faces. "But OmniCorp has forced our hand. Their pursuit of power has become a direct threat to all life. We must act. We must strike at the heart of their operation, not with hatred, but with a fierce resolve to protect the delicate tapestry of existence that they so carelessly seek to unravel." The air crackled with a renewed, albeit somber, determination. The time for passive contemplation was over. The time for action had arrived.

The council chamber, normally a vibrant hub of reasoned debate and communal introspection, now throbbed with a different energy – a potent cocktail of apprehension and galvanizing resolve. Niko, his gaze sweeping across the faces of the Resonant Pack, felt the familiar weight of leadership settle upon his shoulders, heavier now than ever before. OmniCorp's blatant aggression, their inexorable march towards cosmic dominion, had shattered the tenuous peace they had so carefully cultivated. The intercepted directive, Project Chimera, was not just a threat; it was an existential declaration of war against the very principles of symbiotic existence that bound them all.

He had spent the cycles since the council's last harrowing meeting in a state of intense, focused contemplation, sifting through the torrent of data, seeking not just a counter-strategy, but a *harmonious* one. The Veridian nexus, the heart of their world, was their greatest vulnerability, but also, he realized, their greatest strength. And it was not a strength they could wield alone. The whispers of the Veridian elders, usually subtle emanations of planetary consciousness, had grown more insistent, more urgent, their collective wisdom offering a profound understanding of the planet's deep, resonant pathways – the very currents OmniCorp sought to control.

"We cannot face this threat by solely relying on our own abilities," Niko began, his voice clear and steady, cutting through the palpable tension. "OmniCorp's strength lies in their brute force, their technological might. Ours lies in connection, in understanding, in the very life that permeates Veridia. The Veridians, our planetary kin, possess an innate knowledge of this world's circulatory system, its energetic arteries and veins. They feel the pulse of the nexus as we feel the beat of our own hearts." He gestured towards a towering, luminous Veridian delegate, its crystalline form shimmering with an inner light, its presence radiating a calm strength. "They have offered their counsel, their unique perspective. They understand the resonant frequencies that OmniCorp seeks to disrupt, the harmonic flows they aim to enslave."

The Veridian delegate, whose name, in the nuanced language of their kind, translated roughly to 'Weaver of Echoes,' pulsed with a soft, golden light, communicating directly with Niko through a telepathic resonance.

"The pathways are ancient, Elder Niko," the collective consciousness of the Veridians conveyed. *"They are more than mere conduits; they are the planet's memories, its very will. OmniCorp's crude instruments of control will find them far more resistant than they anticipate, but they also seek to sever the deep connections. We must guide them, show them where the natural flow can be amplified, where it can be subtly redirected, to overwhelm their attempts at subjugation."*

Niko nodded, absorbing the profound wisdom. "They will guide us through Veridia's resonant pathways. They know where the energy surges naturally, where it can be amplified, and crucially, where it can be woven into patterns that will confound and repel OmniCorp's invasive technologies.

This intimate knowledge is something our scanners, however advanced, can only approximate. It is the difference between studying a map and living the terrain."

He then turned his attention to Kira, her focused intensity a beacon in the dimming light of the council chamber. Her role, he knew, was pivotal. In the chaotic dance of interdimensional energies and OmniCorp's clandestine operations, clear communication and early detection were paramount. Kira possessed an almost preternatural ability to sense shifts in the energetic field, to decipher the subtle nuances of subspace chatter, and to coordinate the Pack's dispersed units with an efficiency that bordered on precognition.

"Kira," Niko addressed her directly. "Your task is to become the nexus of our intelligence. OmniCorp will not act predictably. Their operations are driven by desperation and an insatiable hunger for control. We need to anticipate their every move, to track the subtle distortions in the fabric of space-time that precede their incursions. You will be our eyes and ears, not just on Veridia, but across the dimensional strata. Your ability to process and relay information instantaneously will be our shield against their surprise assaults."

Kira met his gaze, her expression one of unwavering commitment. "I understand, Niko. My sensor arrays are already recalibrated to detect the specific energetic signatures associated with OmniCorp's portal stabilization technology and their dimensional anchor devices. I've also developed a new filtering protocol to isolate any residual echoes of their experimental temporal manipulation attempts. We will know when and where they are attempting to breach, and we will broadcast that information to every unit. Furthermore, I am working with our bio-harmonicists to create a localized resonance countermeasure. It won't be enough to fully neutralize their weaponry, but it should disrupt their targeting systems and create enough localized dissonance to give our ground teams precious seconds."

"Those seconds can mean the difference between success and annihilation," Niko affirmed. "The Veridians will guide our strike teams through the planet's hidden pathways, allowing us to approach OmniCorp's staging grounds with minimal detection. Lyra's team has identified a convergence point in the Crimson Nebula where OmniCorp is consolidating its forces and preparing to deploy the dimensional anchors. This will be our primary target."

Lyra, the lead xenobotanist and energy systems specialist, stepped forward, her holo-projector displaying a shimmering, three-dimensional representation of the Crimson Nebula. Swirls of ionized gas painted a backdrop against which tiny, intricate nodes of energy flickered – OmniCorp's operational hubs. "The energy readings are immense, Niko," Lyra stated, her voice tinged with awe and concern. "They are channeling power on a scale that suggests not just one, but multiple dimensional anchors are nearing completion. The destabilization signatures we've detected are unlike anything we've encountered. It's as if they are actively trying to unravel the fundamental constants of this sector of space-time, creating pockets of controlled chaos to anchor their influence."

She zoomed in on a cluster of particularly intense energy signatures. "This is where we believe they are most vulnerable. They are drawing immense power from a series of localized nexus nodes within the nebula – points of natural dimensional confluence. If we can disrupt their power flow at these nodes, we might be able to overload their anchor deployment systems before they are fully established. It's a high-risk strategy, given the inherent instability of these regions, but the potential reward is immense."

Niko turned back to Weaver of Echoes. "Can the Veridians guide us through the nebula's energetic currents? Can they help us navigate these treacherous confluence points?"

"The nebula's heart beats with a wild rhythm, Elder Niko," Weaver of Echoes resonated. *"It is a place of creation and destruction, where the veil between realities is thinnest. We can sense the ebb and flow, the hidden eddies and currents that even your advanced instruments may miss. We can guide your vessels through these ephemeral pathways, masking your approach by*

harmonizing your energy signatures with the nebula's own vibrant song. But the risk is real. OmniCorp's presence there is like a scar upon the cosmic tapestry. It will be a difficult journey."

"Difficulty is a relative term when the stakes are this high," Niko replied, a grim determination hardening his features. "We will embrace the difficulty. We will harmonize with the nebula's song. This is not merely a military operation; it is a restoration. We are not seeking to destroy, but to mend. We are the Resonant Pack, and we are joined by the very soul of Veridia. We will strike a blow not for conquest, but for balance."

He looked around at the gathered members of the Pack, at the luminous Veridian delegate, at Kira and Lyra, their faces illuminated by the holographic schematics. A profound sense of unity, forged in the crucible of shared danger, settled upon him. They were a coalition of disparate beings, united by a common purpose – the preservation of the delicate, interconnected web of life that spanned the dimensions.

"The Veridian pathways will be our unseen highways," Niko continued, his voice gaining strength. "Kira's network will be our early warning system, her swift communication ensuring our forces are always one step ahead. Lyra's analysis will guide our strikes against their technological heart. And the collective will of the Resonant Pack, amplified by the very spirit of Veridia, will be our unwavering force."

He then turned to the broader contingent of Pack members, their varied forms – avian, ursine, serpentine, and many others, each with unique adaptations to different environments – representing the diverse tapestry of life they sought to protect. "We will deploy specialized units into the Periphery Zones, the liminal spaces where OmniCorp has been testing their destabilizing payloads. These zones are already volatile; OmniCorp's presence there is an act of aggression designed to weaponize that volatility. Our teams will work to contain any uncontrolled cascades and to gather real-time data on the effectiveness of OmniCorp's reality-shredding technologies. This information will be crucial for understanding the full scope of Project Chimera and for developing countermeasures that can protect not only Veridia but other worlds as well."

The Veridian elder, Weaver of Echoes, pulsed with a renewed intensity.

"The fauna of these zones are in distress," it conveyed. *"The Sky-jellies falter in their luminous dance. The song of the ancient trees is muted by the harsh frequencies. We will lend our empathy to these creatures, to bolster their resilience and guide them away from the paths of destructive energy. We will ensure that even in their suffering, life finds a way to endure."*

Niko felt a surge of gratitude for their allies. The Veridians' ability to commune with and bolster the native lifeforms of Veridia was a testament to the deep, symbiotic bond they shared. This wasn't just about fighting OmniCorp; it was about healing the wounds OmniCorp inflicted upon the planet.

"Our strategy is multifaceted," Niko elaborated, his mind racing, weaving together the different strands of their defense. "We will launch diversionary probes, small, agile craft designed to draw OmniCorp's attention and reveal their defensive postures, while our primary strike force, guided by the Veridians, makes its way towards the Crimson Nebula. Kira, you will coordinate these diversions, feeding us real-time telemetry on OmniCorp's responses. We need to know how they react to unexpected pressure."

Kira was already tapping into a series of data streams, her fingers flying across the holographic interfaces. "I've identified several potential nexus points within the nebula that are currently less fortified. These could serve as staging areas for our diversionary probes. Their energy signatures are fluctuating, suggesting they might be part of OmniCorp's power distribution network, but not the primary anchor sites themselves."

"Excellent," Niko acknowledged. "We will utilize these less-defended points to create confusion. Simultaneously, our most skilled scouts will infiltrate OmniCorp's perimeter in the Periphery Zones, planting localized resonance disruptors. These devices, while small, can create temporary pockets of instability that will blind their sensors and sow discord among their automated defenses. Anya, your deep experience in navigating such volatile terrains will be invaluable here. You and your most trusted scouts will lead these infiltration missions."

Elder Anya, her presence calm and resolute, inclined her head. "We are prepared. The volatile currents of the Periphery are as familiar to us as the gentle breeze of the Great Arbor. We will tread where others fear to, and we will leave our mark where it will cause the most disruption."

The plan was audacious, complex, and fraught with peril. It relied on the seamless integration of the Resonant Pack's technological prowess and interdimensional expertise with the Veridians' profound planetary knowledge and empathic connection to all life. It was a convergence of strengths, a united front against a common, existential threat.

"OmniCorp believes they can impose their will upon the cosmos," Niko stated, his voice resonating with conviction. "They believe they can dictate the flow of reality. But they underestimate the resilience of life, the power of connection, and the unwavering will of those who choose to defend it. We are more than just a pack; we are a symphony of existence, and we will not allow them to silence our song."

He paused, allowing the weight of his words to settle. The air in the chamber, once heavy with dread, now crackled with a determined energy. The faint bioluminescence of the flora seemed to brighten, mirroring the rekindled hope within their hearts.

"This is our moment," Niko concluded. "We move as one. We act with purpose. We fight not for dominion, but for harmony. For Veridia. For all that OmniCorp seeks to extinguish." The symphony was about to begin, and its crescendo would determine the fate of worlds.

Kira's mind, a nexus of data streams and resonant frequencies, hummed with a fierce, controlled energy. The council chamber, while still echoing with Niko's pronouncements, had shifted its focus, coalescing around the intricate webs of information Kira was already weaving. While the others discussed grand strategies and the profound wisdom of the Veridians, Kira was dissecting OmniCorp's probable tactical maneuvers with the precision of a xenobiologist dissecting a novel pathogen. Her internal sensor suite, constantly recalibrating to the subtle hums and discordant whispers of the ambient energies, was already painting a probabilistic landscape of OmniCorp's likely deployment.

"Their initial approach vectors will likely exploit existing gravitational anomalies and known subspace conduits," Kira murmured, her voice a low current beneath the broader discourse. Her gaze, usually focused on holographic displays, now seemed to pierce through reality itself, her augmented vision overlaying the chamber with tactical schematics. "They favor concentrated thrusts, aiming to punch through our defenses at predictable points. Based on their historical engagement patterns and the energy signatures detected around the Crimson Nebula, I've mapped out three primary ingress corridors they are likely to favor for their main assault fleet."

She gestured, and a three-dimensional projection, more detailed and dynamic than Lyra's initial display, bloomed into existence above the central table. It wasn't just a map; it was a live simulation, depicting swirling energy patterns, projected fleet strengths, and predicted engagement zones. "The Veridians' guidance through the nebula is invaluable for our infiltration and strike teams," Kira continued, her voice gaining an edge of urgency as the simulation shifted. "But for the defensive line, understanding *their* predictable chaos is paramount. They will attempt to overwhelm us here," she indicated a dense cluster of projected OmniCorp vessels, "and here," pointing to another, "attempting to create a pincer movement that will box in our response capabilities."

Her analysis wasn't just theoretical. Kira had spent the cycles since the Project Chimera directive's interception not just passively receiving data, but actively *probing* the fringes of OmniCorp's operational sphere. She had deployed micro-drones, so small they were mere motes of shimmering energy, designed to record and transmit ambient subspace fluctuations. These weren't directly offensive; they were sensors, designed to learn. She had also leveraged the Resonant Pack's existing network of planetary sensor arrays, reconfiguring them to detect the specific resonance dampening fields OmniCorp employed to mask their fleet movements.

"Their formations are typically rigid, designed for maximum destructive output rather than adaptability," Kira explained, her fingers dancing across her console, adjusting parameters in real-time. "This rigidity, while a strength against uncoordinated opposition, becomes their Achilles' heel when faced with a multi-pronged, unpredictable response. The Veridian pathways allow our strike teams to bypass their anticipated kill zones, but for our defensive formations, we need to exploit the gaps

between their aggressive thrusts. I've identified a series of localized energy sinks within the nebula's outer rings that their scouting drones have either overlooked or deemed irrelevant. These are areas where the nebula's natural energies fluctuate wildly, making them difficult for OmniCorp's standard sensors to penetrate. We can use these as staging grounds for our interceptor squadrons."

A soft, resonant pulse emanated from Weaver of Echoes.

"The areas Kira highlights," the Veridian's collective consciousness conveyed, *"are where the nebula's breath is deepest. The currents there can be treacherous, but also, they offer a veil of profound obscurity. We can amplify these natural obscuring properties, weaving your vessels into the nebula's very fabric, making them as invisible as a thought in the cosmic ocean."*

Kira met the Veridian's luminous gaze, a silent acknowledgment passing between them. Her tactical acumen wasn't just about understanding enemy patterns; it was about leveraging every available asset, including the subtle, symbiotic capabilities of their allies. She wasn't just a data analyst; she was becoming a conductor, orchestrating the disparate elements of their defense into a harmonious, yet devastating, counter-offensive.

"The Veridian scouts will be instrumental in guiding our interceptors through these fluctuating energy sinks," Kira confirmed. "Their ability to sense and navigate these chaotic currents will allow us to outmaneuver OmniCorp's patrol patterns and position our forces for maximum disruption when their primary assault waves arrive. Furthermore, I've been cross-referencing the Veridian elders' empathic readings of the nebula's fauna with OmniCorp's projected energy expenditure. There are certain migratory routes of the Lumina-moths, their bioluminescence acting as a natural energy siphon, that OmniCorp seems to be actively avoiding. I believe they are sensitive to the moths' concentrated bio-energetic emissions, which may interfere with their targeting systems. We can use these flight paths as natural defensive corridors."

A ripple of impressed murmurs went through the assembled Pack members. This wasn't the detached, sterile analysis of a mere strategist; it was a vibrant, integrated understanding of the battlefield that encompassed both OmniCorp's cold logic and Veridia's living, breathing essence. Kira wasn't just planning for a battle; she was planning for a

convergence, a point where their diverse strengths would meet and amplify each other.

"This is precisely the kind of foresight we need, Kira," Niko stated, his voice resonating with profound approval. "You are not merely anticipating their movements; you are predicting their *intentions*, their psychological biases in their tactical doctrine. This gives us an unparalleled advantage." He turned to the assembled Veridian delegates. "Your guidance is essential, not just for our infiltration teams, but for the coordinated defense Kira is envisioning. Can you amplify the natural obscuring properties of these energy sinks to match the level of stealth Kira requires?"

"We can," Weaver of Echoes pulsed. *"The nebula's song is one of constant flux. By aligning your vessels' resonant frequencies with these inherent fluctuations, and by channeling the natural bio-energetic signatures of the Lumina-moths through your ships, we can render your approach effectively undetectable by*

OmniCorp's current sensor technology. It will require precise timing and perfect synchronization, but the result will be a cloak of invisibility woven from the very essence of this place."

Kira's internal processors whirred, absorbing the Veridian's confirmation. This was the essence of their alliance: the fusion of advanced technology with the profound, inherent abilities of Veridia. Her tactical acumen was now being augmented by a force that operated on principles alien to OmniCorp, a force that understood the universe not as a series of exploitable resources, but as a tapestry of interconnected energies.

"The Lumina-moth migratory paths," Kira mused, her holographic display shifting again, now highlighting specific atmospheric currents. "These currents align with the nebula's natural solar winds. If we can time our movements to coincide with peak solar wind activity, the atmospheric distortions will further mask our energetic signatures. This means our interceptor squadrons can move from the energy sinks, cloaked by the Veridian weave, and emerge from the solar wind currents to strike at the opportune moment. It's a three-tiered defense: stealth, diversion, and decisive counter-strike."

She paused, her brow furrowed as she focused on a particular section of the projected nebula. "There's also a pattern emerging in their scouting drone deployment. They are not uniformly distributed. They are concentrated around specific points, suggesting these are either primary anchor sites or critical power nodes. I'm mapping these concentrations now. If we can preemptively disrupt these nodes, even with a precisely targeted, low-yield energy pulse, it could cause cascading failures in their power distribution network, potentially delaying their anchor deployment or even forcing them to reveal their primary sites prematurely."

The room buzzed with the implications. Kira was not just identifying threats; she was identifying exploitable vulnerabilities within OmniCorp's presumed impregnability. Her ability to see the subtle patterns, the faint echoes in the cosmic background radiation, was proving to be a weapon in itself. She was extending the Pack's perception, allowing them to see not just what was, but what *could be*, what OmniCorp *intended*.

"I am coordinating with Lyra's xenobotanists and energy specialists," Kira continued, her gaze unwavering. "They are developing a bio-luminescent marker, a modified strain of the Lumina-moth's symbiotic flora, that can be seeded in key locations. This marker will not only amplify the natural camouflage effect in our chosen staging areas but will also emit a low-frequency sonic pulse when OmniCorp's energy fields approach. It will act as a localized early warning system, integrated directly into our neural network. It's another layer of predictive defense, built on the very life-cycles of Veridia."

She then turned her attention to a group of smaller, more agile vessels depicted in a corner of the simulation. These were the diversionary probes Niko had mentioned. "The diversionary probes will be crucial," Kira stated. "I've identified several older, decommissioned OmniCorp mining outposts in the nebula's periphery. Their derelict energy signatures might be enough to draw OmniCorp's attention if they are activated with a brief, high-energy burst. The probes can then feign a larger offensive, forcing OmniCorp to reallocate defensive assets, creating further opportunities for our main strike force and the infiltration teams."

Her analysis was intricate, a masterpiece of layered strategy. It wasn't just about reacting to OmniCorp; it was about dictating the flow of the engagement, forcing OmniCorp into a position where their predictable aggression would be their undoing. Kira's tactical acumen was proving to be a vital complement to Niko's overarching strategy, a finely tuned instrument that translated grand design into actionable intelligence and precise execution.

"The Veridian scouts are crucial for guiding the infiltration teams through the Periphery Zones as well," Kira added, her focus shifting to the volatile, less explored regions of the nebula. "OmniCorp's destabilizing payloads have created localized pockets of temporal and spatial distortion there. Standard navigation protocols are useless. The Veridians' inherent connection to the fabric of reality will allow them to perceive and navigate these anomalies, identifying safe passages and potential ambush points within the chaos."

She projected a series of faint, shimmering pathways through the distorted regions. "These are not routes in the conventional sense," Kira explained. "They are moments of relative stability, threads of coherent reality that the Veridians can sense. They will be our unseen highways, allowing Anya's infiltration teams to move undetected through the heart of OmniCorp's experimental zones. I'm also using their empathic readings to identify areas where the local fauna are exhibiting extreme distress. These distress signals often correlate with the initiation of OmniCorp's destabilizing experiments. We can use these biological distress patterns as indicators of where OmniCorp is actively testing its weaponized reality."

The depth of Kira's understanding was remarkable. She was not just a sensor operator or a data analyst; she was a tactical visionary, her mind capable of processing vast amounts of information and synthesizing it into a cohesive, actionable plan. She saw the battlefield not just as a collection of ships and energy signatures, but as a dynamic ecosystem, influenced by every factor from gravitational anomalies to the migratory patterns of interstellar moths.

"Kira's foresight is our shield," Lyra commented, her voice filled with admiration. "She anticipates their every move, not just the obvious ones, but the subtle shifts in their operational tempo, the faint echoes of their intentions. She is extending our perception beyond our physical limits, allowing us to operate with a level of awareness that OmniCorp, with all their technological might, cannot possibly match."

Niko nodded, his gaze sweeping across Kira, then to the Veridian delegate. "You have become more than an intelligence officer, Kira. You are a vital extension of our command, our tactical conscience. Your intuition, amplified by the wisdom of the Veridians and the data we have gathered, provides us with an unparalleled strategic advantage. We are not just a pack with a plan; we are a cohesive unit, each member a crucial component of a larger, living strategy. And your role in that is paramount."

Kira offered a slight nod, her expression serious but resolute. She understood the weight of Niko's words, the implicit trust placed in her. Her tactical acumen wasn't just about winning a battle; it was about ensuring the survival of a way of life, a belief in interconnectedness and harmony that OmniCorp sought to extinguish. She was the silent guardian, the unseen architect of their defense, her mind a battlefield of probabilities and counter-strategies, all dedicated to preserving the delicate balance of their existence. Her senses were the Pack's extended reach, her foresight their preemptive strike, and her unwavering focus, the bedrock upon which their convergence would be built.

The air within the nexus shimmered, not just with the ambient energies of Veridia, but with a palpable tension that tightened the Pack's collective consciousness. Kira's projections, now displayed on every available surface within the council chamber, had solidified from abstract probabilities into starkly defined threat vectors. The crimson swirl of the Crimson Nebula, once a majestic cosmic canvas, now seethed with the impending arrival of OmniCorp's vanguard. Their meticulously calculated assault, an almost arrogant display of predictable aggression, was about to crash against the shores of Veridia's sanctuary.

"Their primary assault fleet is within range," Kira announced, her voice cutting through the hushed anticipation. Her neural net, a symphony of data streams, was processing a torrent of sensory input from the micro-drones and the reconfigured planetary arrays. "Estimated arrival at the nexus perimeter in three cycles. Formation is as predicted – a concentrated wedge, designed to breach our outer defenses and push inward. They are deploying sonic disruptors and localized resonance dampeners in advance, attempting to destabilize the nebula's natural frequencies and create a blind spot for their penetration."

The sonic disruptors were a particular concern. OmniCorp's scientists had theorized that by bombarding an area with specific, ultra-low frequency vibrations, they could disrupt the harmonic interconnectedness that was the very essence of Veridian life and their symbiotic relationship with the nebula. It was a blunt instrument, designed to shatter, not to understand. Kira's analysis had identified the theoretical 'kill zones' of these disruptors, areas where the natural resonance would be most severely compromised.

"We feel their disharmony," Weaver of Echoes pulsed, the collective Veridian consciousness a wave of calm amidst the rising storm. *"Their instruments scream, a discordant cacophony against the nebula's song. But the song is ancient, and its roots run deep. We can guide you, Resonant Pack, to the places where the dissonance is weakest, where the nebula's breath can still shield you."*

Kira projected a new overlay, highlighting specific regions within the nexus's immediate vicinity. These weren't necessarily the deepest energy sinks or the Lumina-moth migratory paths previously identified for the interceptors. These were areas where the nebula's own complex energetic architecture naturally resisted the disruptive frequencies, pockets of inherent resilience. "These are the designated convergence points," Kira stated, her voice steady. "The Veridian scouts have identified these zones as having naturally higher ambient resonance, capable of absorbing and even deflecting a significant portion of OmniCorp's sonic assault. Our defensive squadrons will fall back to these points, establishing a layered perimeter."

The strategy was elegant in its simplicity, a testament to the synergy between Kira's analytical prowess and the Veridians' intimate knowledge of their environment. OmniCorp's technology, designed to impose order through brute force, was being countered by the nebula's own inherent, dynamic order. The disruptors would expend their energy trying to shatter what was already fluid and adaptive, like trying to break water with a hammer.

"The Lumina-moth corridors will remain operational for our strike teams," Kira confirmed, a holographic display showing the shimmering pathways Anya's teams would use for their counter-thrusts. "But for the primary defensive line, we will be utilizing the nebula's innate harmonic structure. The Veridian scouts will act as living beacons, guiding our interceptors and support craft to precisely calibrated positions within these convergence zones. Their ability to sense and manipulate subtle energy flows will allow us to create localized 'resonance shields,' amplifying the nebula's natural protective properties."

The sonic disruptors were not the only threat. OmniCorp's aggressive technology also included localized 'reality anchors,' devices designed to fix and stabilize space-time in a region, effectively negating the nebula's natural distortions and making it easier for their fleet to navigate and engage. This was a direct counter to the Veridian scouts' ability to navigate through chaotic anomalies. Kira's projections began to highlight small, pulsing nodes appearing on the periphery of the nexus.

"OmniCorp is deploying reality anchors," Kira reported, a grimace crossing her features. "These are designed to create pockets of absolute stability, making our nebula's inherent chaos a liability rather than an advantage for us. They are attempting to flatten the landscape, removing our natural defenses. However, their deployment pattern is predictable. They require significant energy expenditure and tend to anchor themselves to existing gravitational wells. I've identified three primary anchor sites they are likely to establish first, based on their energy signatures and proximity to their projected ingress points."

She highlighted three points on the holographic map, each radiating a faint, sickly yellow glow. "These anchors will serve as focal points for their resonance dampening fields, creating a zone of suppressed Veridian resonance. If they succeed in fully establishing these, our ability to utilize the nebula's natural defenses will be severely compromised. We need to disrupt these anchor sites before they reach full operational capacity."

This was where the direct offensive element of the Pack's involvement would become critical. While the Veridians focused on shielding and guiding, the Pack would need to act with precision and speed.

"Lyra's xenobotanists have developed a specialized bio-agent," Kira continued, her fingers flying across her console. "A concentrated strain of symbiotic flora, harvested from the Lumina-moth's energy-siphoning flowers. When introduced into the anchors' energy fields, it should create a feedback loop, overloading their stabilization systems with bio-energetic feedback. The Veridians can guide the delivery drones through the nebula's natural currents to the anchor sites, but the drone's flight path will need to be precise, exploiting micro-fluctuations in the temporal field that I've identified as potential escape routes for the drones after deployment."

The complexity of the interwoven strategies was breathtaking. It was a multi-layered dance, with each element – the Veridian's natural abilities, the Pack's technological might, and Kira's analytical foresight – playing a crucial role. The nebula itself was not merely a backdrop; it was an active participant, its currents, its energies, its very fabric being woven into their defense.

"The Lumina-moths themselves may also offer a unique defense," Kira mused, her internal processors cycling through an array of data points. "Their migratory patterns are not just about energy siphoning; they are also a form of natural energetic communication. OmniCorp's resonance dampeners, while designed to interfere with our systems, are also broadcasting a specific type of energy signature. The Lumina-moths are highly sensitive to disruptions in the natural energy flow. I've observed that their bioluminescence flares intensely in the presence of artificial energetic interference. If we can synchronize a localized amplification of these moth swarms near the anchor sites, their collective energetic output, amplified by their natural response to OmniCorp's interference, could create a significant localized disturbance, potentially hindering the anchor's full deployment."

This was a bold suggestion, relying on the unpredictable, yet ultimately predictable, behavior of Veridia's native life. It was the kind of strategy that only a mind like Kira's, capable of seeing the interconnectedness of all things, could conceive. It was a defense born not of sterile logic, but of a deep, resonant understanding of life itself.

"The Lumina-moths are attuned to the nebula's pulse," Weaver of Echoes confirmed. *"We can encourage their gathering, guiding them with gentle whispers of resonant frequencies. Their light, when united, can be a beacon against any darkness."*

The council chamber pulsed with a renewed sense of purpose. The initial wave of anxiety had been replaced by a focused determination. Kira's projections shifted again, depicting the deployment of the first wave of OmniCorp vessels. They were not a monolithic fleet but a series of smaller, specialized craft, designed to probe and breach. Among them were the sonic disruptors, their hum a low thrum that Kira's sensors immediately registered as a dissonant chord against the nebula's symphony.

"Sonic disruptors engaging perimeter," Kira reported, her voice tight with focus. "Initial impact on the outer nebula layers. The effect is localized, as predicted. The nebula's natural energy diffusion is mitigating the worst of it, but the localized resonance is being affected. We need to maintain our positions within the convergence zones. The Veridian scouts are already working to reinforce these areas."

Holographic representations of the Veridian scouts, ethereal beings of light and energy, began to coalesce around the projected defensive formations of the Pack's ships. They wove intricate patterns of light, their movements seemingly synchronized with the pulsating hum of the nebula itself. Kira's displays showed localized fields of amplified resonance blooming around the Pack's vessels, shimmering like translucent shields against the encroaching wave of OmniCorp's sonic assault.

"The reality anchors are beginning to activate," Kira announced, her gaze fixed on the three highlighted points. "Their energy signatures are intensifying. The resonance dampening fields are expanding. OmniCorp is attempting to create localized zones of absolute stability, regions where the nebula's natural flux is suppressed. This will make it harder for our strike teams to navigate and for the Veridian scouts to guide them through the volatile areas."

She then showed the deployment of the bio-agent delivery drones. Small, agile craft, guided by Kira's precise calculations and the Veridian scouts' nuanced perception, darted through the nebula's currents. Their flight paths were a testament to Kira's ability to perceive and exploit microscopic temporal and spatial distortions. They moved like ghosts, their energy signatures masked by the very chaos OmniCorp sought to suppress.

"The first drones are approaching anchor site Alpha," Kira reported. "Deploying bio-agent payload. We will see a measurable energy fluctuation within... ten cycles."

The tension in the chamber was almost unbearable. Every eye was fixed on the holographic display, waiting for the slightest indication of success or failure. Then, a ripple of discordant energy pulsed from anchor site Alpha. The sickly yellow glow flickered, then intensified, becoming erratic.

"The bio-agent is effective," Weaver of Echoes pulsed, a wave of quiet triumph washing over the Veridians. *"It is sowing discord within their constructed order. The anchor struggles against the nebula's song."*

Kira's analysis confirmed it. "Anchor Alpha is destabilizing," she stated, a hint of relief in her voice. "The feedback loop is causing cascading energy failures within its core. It will not reach full operational capacity. But OmniCorp is already rerouting power to anchor Beta and Gamma. They are adapting."

The battle was a dynamic, evolving entity. OmniCorp, despite its rigid doctrines, was capable of tactical adjustments, forcing Kira and the Pack to constantly re-evaluate and adapt their own strategies. The Nexus Defense was not a static blueprint; it was a living, breathing response, a testament to the resilience of life and the power of interconnectedness. The convergence had begun, not as a singular event, but as a continuous, unfolding process of resistance. The hum of the nebula, once a gentle lullaby, had transformed into a defiant roar, a chorus of life pushing back against the sterile ambition of a force that sought to control, rather than to coexist. The fate of Veridia, and perhaps the wider multiverse, rested on their ability to maintain this delicate, yet fierce, balance.

Niko watched the tactical display with a knot tightening in his gut. The energy readings from OmniCorp's vessels were a chaotic symphony of aggression, a stark contrast to the resonant hum of the Veridian nebula. Kira's projections, usually a source of calm clarity, now showed a dense web of threat vectors closing in. The sonic disruptors were hammering the outer layers of the nexus, their dissonant frequencies a physical ache against the Pack's collective senses. He could feel the Veridians' gentle waves of concern, a subtle tremor beneath the storm of OmniCorp's manufactured chaos. They were guiding the interceptor squadrons, weaving them through the nebula's natural currents, their ethereal light a counterpoint to the sterile glow of OmniCorp's weapon signatures.

"Anchor Alpha is experiencing significant feedback," Kira announced, her voice a cool, steady stream of data amidst the rising tension. "The bio-agent appears to be disrupting its stabilization field. However, OmniCorp is rerouting auxiliary power to Beta and Gamma. They're adapting their deployment, anticipating further resistance." Niko felt a surge of adrenaline. The Veridian scouts, with their intricate dance of light and resonance, were guiding the next wave of delivery drones, their flight paths tracing ephemeral pathways through the nebula's volatile folds. These drones, laden with Lyra's specialized flora, were the Pack's primary offensive against the anchors, their success crucial to maintaining the nebula's natural defenses.

It was then that Niko's console pinged, a private channel notification flashing urgently. It was a scrambled signal, originating from a vessel within the approaching OmniCorp vanguard. Curiosity, a dangerous companion in such circumstances, tugged at him. He initiated a decryption sequence, his fingers moving with practiced speed. The signal resolved into a schematic, a blueprint for a compact, high-yield resonance amplifier. It was OmniCorp technology, undoubtedly, but designed for a specific purpose: to temporarily override and even hijack localized nebula frequencies, essentially turning the nebula's own energy against itself.

The schematics detailed a device that could amplify the sonic disruptors' effects tenfold, creating localized zones of intense disharmony that would shatter the Veridian's carefully constructed shields. It was a terrifying prospect, a tool of pure destruction. But as Niko studied the intricate details, a different kind of thought began to form, a dangerous seed of temptation. This technology, designed to exploit the nebula's vulnerabilities, could also be turned against its creators. He could see how it might be adapted, how its energy signature could be mirrored, its destructive potential redirected. He imagined deploying it on the incoming OmniCorp ships, a targeted wave of their own disharmony washing back over them, disrupting their formations, disabling their weapons. It was a thought born of desperation, a fleeting glimpse of an easier path, a path of immediate, decisive retaliation.

He remembered the countless times he'd seen such technology employed, the devastating efficiency with which OmniCorp carved its way through the galaxy, leaving behind only subjugation and ruin. His own past, a tapestry woven with threads of conflict and loss, whispered in his ear, urging him to embrace this chance for vengeance, to wield their own weapons against them. It would be so simple, a few lines of code, a strategic deployment, and the tide of the battle might instantly turn.

But then, Kira's voice, calm and unwavering, cut through the rising tide of his internal conflict. "Niko," she said, her projection appearing beside his console, her gaze steady, her expression one of quiet concern. "OmniCorp is adapting. They are reinforcing their assault on anchor Beta. The sonic disruptors are intensifying. We need to maintain focus on the defensive strategy. Our interceptors are in position to engage their primary assault fleet once they break through the outer resonance fields."

Her words, simple and direct, acted as an anchor. He looked at the schematics again, the seductive promise of retaliation fading in the face of her pragmatic focus. He saw the Veridian scouts, their luminous forms weaving a protective ballet around the Pack's vessels, and he felt the gentle, persistent thrum of the nebula, a living entity that deserved protection, not exploitation. This wasn't about vengeance; it was about preservation.

He remembered the foundational principles that had guided him, the ethics he'd strived to uphold even in the darkest of times. To use OmniCorp's technology in such a manner, to mirror their destructive approach, would be to become what he fought against. It would be a victory at the cost of his own integrity, a hollow triumph that would leave him no different from the aggressors. The Veridian nebula was a sanctuary, a testament to a different way of being, a way of life that embraced harmony and coexistence. To sully it with their own brand of violence would be to betray everything they were fighting for.

"No," Niko said, his voice firm, the internal debate settled. He closed the schematics, the temptation extinguished. "We don't use their weapons against them. We stick to the plan. Preserve the nebula. Protect the Veridians." He met Kira's gaze, a silent acknowledgment passing between them. "We are here to defend, not to conquer."

Kira's projection offered a faint, almost imperceptible nod of approval. "Understood, Niko. Lyra's team has identified a weakness in the resonance dampeners' energy flow. If we can channel a precisely modulated burst of amplified nebula energy through the existing conduit network, we can create a temporary harmonic overload, enough to disrupt their fields for a critical window."

Niko's attention snapped back to the tactical display. This was a different approach, one that utilized the nebula's inherent strengths, not OmniCorp's borrowed power. It was a strategy born of understanding, not brute force. "How much time do we have?" he asked, his voice regaining its focus.

"The dampeners are expanding their coverage," Kira replied, her fingers dancing across her console. "They will reach full operational capacity in approximately twenty cycles. We need to deploy the conduits and channel the energy before that happens. The Veridian scouts can guide the conduit placement, but their natural energy manipulation capabilities are limited. They will require our ship's power cores to amplify the channeled nebula energy."

This was it. A true convergence of abilities. The Veridians' intimate knowledge of the nebula's currents, the Pack's technological might in terms of power generation, and Kira's ability to orchestrate the entire symphony. Niko felt a renewed sense of purpose, the earlier temptation a fading echo. This was the path of stewardship, of responsible action. It was about using their own strengths to protect something precious, rather than adopting the destructive methods of their enemy.

"Alright," Niko said, his voice resonating with newfound resolve. "Kira, coordinate the conduit deployment. I'll divert power from secondary systems to our main power cores. Anya, prepare your strike teams. If these dampeners go down, we need to be ready to exploit the opening and hit those anchor sites hard. We disable them, not just disrupt them."

Anya's voice crackled over the comms, sharp and determined. "Understood, Niko. We're ready to move."

The process was complex, demanding a level of precision that bordered on the impossible. Kira's voice was a constant, reassuring presence, guiding the Veridian scouts as they wove strands of solidified nebular energy—the conduits—through the increasingly turbulent space. These weren't physical structures in the traditional sense, but concentrated channels of the nebula's own vital force, carefully sculpted and guided. The Veridians moved with an almost reverent grace, their bioluminescence flaring with concentration as they coaxed the ethereal threads into place, connecting key nexus points within the nebula's intricate energy web.

Niko, alongside his bridge crew, initiated the power diversion. The hum of the ship's engines shifted, a deeper thrumming resonating through the deck plates as energy reserves were rerouted. Lights flickered momentarily in the cargo bay, and non-essential life support systems momentarily idled as raw power surged towards the conduits. It was a significant gamble, leaving their own systems less resilient in the face of direct attack, but the necessity of disabling OmniCorp's dampening fields was paramount.

"Conduits are in position," a Veridian voice pulsed through the comms, its resonance carrying a note of strain. "Ready to receive amplified energy."

"Initiating power surge," Niko announced, his hands steady on the controls. "Kira, monitor the flow. We need to maintain optimal frequency without overloading the conduits."

The holographic display shifted, showing the nebula's raw energy being drawn into the Pack's ship, a torrent of emerald and sapphire light that pulsed with untamed power. Then, with excruciating slowness, it was channeled outward, flowing through the newly formed conduits. The impact was immediate and profound. The sickly yellow glow of OmniCorp's resonance dampening fields flickered violently. The low, oppressive hum that had been building in the background faltered, replaced by a sharp, piercing whine.

"Dampening fields are destabilizing," Kira reported, her voice tight with focused anticipation. "The harmonic overload is causing cascading failures. We're getting intermittent disruptions across all three anchor sites."

On the tactical display, the orderly lines of OmniCorp vessels wavered. Their formations, designed for precision navigation through stable space, began to shift and break as the nebula's natural chaos surged back, unhindered. The Veridian scouts pulsed with renewed vigor, their light flaring as they capitalized on the momentary confusion.

"This is our window!" Anya's voice boomed, laced with adrenaline. "Strike teams, engage! Focus on disabling the anchor cores. We don't want them to recover."

Niko watched as Anya's agile interceptors, previously held in defensive formations, now darted with lightning speed towards the now-exposed anchor sites. They moved through the turbulent nebula like phantoms, their weapons systems glowing with focused energy. The intercepted communications chatter from OmniCorp vessels became a frantic cacophony of alarm and confusion. They had been prepared for a frontal assault, for predictable patterns of resistance, but this coordinated exploitation of their own technology's interference was beyond their immediate comprehension.

The Pack's action was not an act of mirroring OmniCorp's destructive intent, but a calculated application of the nebula's inherent properties, amplified by their own advanced capabilities. It was a demonstration of understanding, of working *with* the natural world, rather than seeking to dominate it. It was the core of the choice Niko had made: to protect, to steward, rather than to retaliate in kind.

He saw the first anchor, Beta, erupt in a cascade of uncontrolled energy, its sickly yellow glow collapsing inward before exploding in a silent bloom of residual power. The sonic disruptors accompanying it sputtered and died, their dissonant hum extinguished. Then came Gamma, its intricate stabilization systems overwhelmed by the surge of amplified nebular energy, dissolving into a cloud of shimmering particles.

"Anchor Beta and Gamma neutralized," Kira confirmed, her voice holding a note of quiet triumph. "Anchor Alpha is still active but significantly degraded. OmniCorp's primary offensive capability in this sector has been effectively crippled."

A wave of palpable relief washed through the bridge. The immediate threat had been averted, not through a brutal escalation of force, but through intelligence, adaptation, and a profound respect for the environment they were defending. Niko looked at Kira, her holographic form a beacon of calm in the storm. He had been tempted by the easy path of vengeance, by the destructive power of OmniCorp's own tools. But remembering his principles, and seeing the graceful resilience of the Veridians and their nebula, he had chosen a different way. He had chosen stewardship. It was a choice that reinforced the core belief of their mission: that even in the face of overwhelming aggression, humanity possessed the capacity for restraint, for responsibility, for protecting life rather than dominating it.

The battle for the nexus was far from over, but in this crucial moment, they had proven that a different future, one built on harmony and respect, was not only possible, but achievable.

CHAPTER FIFTEEN
THRESHOLDS OF TOMORROW

The silence that followed the cacophony of battle was not an empty void, but a rich tapestry woven with the lingering hum of the nebula, the gentle sighs of recovering systems, and the soft cadence of shared breaths. Niko found himself adrift in this newfound quiet, the adrenaline's sharp edge dulled, leaving behind a profound sense of exhaustion and a quiet, burgeoning hope. The tactical display, once a chaotic dance of red aggressor signatures and frantic defensive maneuvers, was now a serene expanse of stabilized energy fields, the remnants of OmniCorp's futile assault fading like seafoam on a distant shore. The nexus point, the heart of this vibrant nebula, was secured. The immediate threat, the aggressive tendrils of OmniCorp's expansionist greed, had been not just repelled, but fundamentally broken.

He looked over at Kira. Her holographic projection had dissolved, and she lay beside him, her form relaxed, her breathing a soft, steady rhythm against the hum of the ship's bridge. Her presence was a tangible reassurance, a silent testament to their shared ordeal and their collective resilience. The delicate balance they had struck, a fusion of pack ingenuity and Veridian wisdom, had not only held but had triumphed. This wasn't just a victory for the Pack, or for the Veridians; it was a victory for a different way of interacting with the galaxy, a way rooted in understanding and mutual respect rather than domination. The struggle had been fierce, the temptation to mirror OmniCorp's brutality a heavy burden, but in the end, they had chosen a path of preservation, of responsible stewardship. The lessons learned in the crucible of conflict were etched not just into their operational logs, but into the very fabric of their resolve.

The aftermath was a slow, deliberate process of reassessment and recalibration. Veridian scouts, their bioluminescence now soft and warm, navigated the nebula's currents, assessing the subtle energy shifts and the areas most impacted by OmniCorp's sonic disruption. They moved with an almost mournful grace, tending to the nebula's wounds, their gentle resonance a balm against the lingering disharmony. Niko watched them through the main viewport, their ethereal forms a stark contrast to the imposing, but now inert, hulks of the defeated OmniCorp vessels. These behemoths, instruments of a rapacious empire, were now silent monuments to their own hubris, adrift in the cosmic currents they had so violently sought to control. The Veridians' dedication was a poignant reminder of what was at stake: not just territory, but a living, breathing ecosystem, a sanctuary of biodiversity and unique sentience.

"The damage to the outer resonance fields is minimal, considering the intensity of their assault," Kira murmured, her voice soft as she stirred beside him. She reached out, her fingers brushing against his, a simple gesture that conveyed a universe of shared experience. "The flora-based countermeasures you deployed performed beyond projections, Niko. Lyra's team deserves immense credit. They absorbed and redirected a significant portion of the sonic energy."

Niko nodded, a faint smile touching his lips. "And the Veridians' guidance was invaluable. Without their deep understanding of the nebula's intrinsic energy flows, we wouldn't have been able to execute the harmonic overload so precisely. It was a true synergy." He paused, his gaze drifting back to the defeated OmniCorp fleet. "But it's a stark reminder, isn't it? Their aggression is relentless. They adapt, they learn, they push harder."

Kira's breathing deepened slightly, a sigh of weariness and something more profound. "Greed is a persistent force, Niko. OmniCorp will not simply disappear. This was a significant setback for them, a public humiliation perhaps, but it will not deter their long-term objectives. They will regroup, restrategize, and likely return."

"Which is precisely why vigilance is paramount," Niko agreed, his voice hardening with a renewed sense of purpose. "We cannot afford to become complacent. Every engagement, every victory, must be a learning experience. We need to anticipate their next move, understand their evolving tactics, and refine our own defenses accordingly. This battle wasn't just about repelling an immediate invasion; it was about understanding the nature of the threat and developing more robust, sustainable methods of protection."

He thought back to the moments of intense pressure, the split-second decisions that had felt like standing on a precipice. The temptation to use OmniCorp's own disruptive technology against them had been a siren song, a whisper of an easier, more destructive path. He remembered the gnawing fear that perhaps their more passive, harmonious approach was inherently weaker, a naive idealism destined to be crushed by brute force. But the outcome had proven otherwise.

"The temptation to meet their aggression with their own methods was strong," Niko confessed, his voice low. "It would have been... efficient, in a brutal sort of way. But it would have fundamentally changed us. To become what we fight against is not victory; it's surrender."

Kira's hand squeezed his gently. "And that's the core lesson, isn't it? The true strength of our alliance lies not in our destructive capabilities, but in our capacity for empathy, for cooperation, for understanding that true power comes from harmony, not from imposition. The Veridians, in their deep connection to their nebula, embody this principle. They don't seek to control their environment; they seek to be a part of it, to nurture it, to live in balance."

He looked at the Veridian scouts again, their luminescent trails weaving intricate patterns against the starlit backdrop. They were not warriors in the conventional sense, but guardians, their existence intertwined with the well-being of their home. Their resilience in the face of OmniCorp's onslaught had been remarkable, a testament to the deep roots of their connection to the nebula. They had endured the sonic assaults, their energy fields rippling under the pressure, but they had not broken. Their ability to guide and channel the nebula's own energy, to act as conduits for its restorative forces, had been instrumental in their strategy.

"The effectiveness of the flora-based countermeasures was astonishing," Niko reiterated. "Lyra's genius in bio-engineering, adapting terrestrial plant life to function within a nebular environment, is a testament to cross-species collaboration. Imagine what else we can achieve when we combine our diverse knowledge bases. OmniCorp seeks to exploit and extract; we seek to understand and integrate."

Kira shifted, propping herself up on an elbow. Her eyes, usually filled with the calm focus of a strategist, now held a flicker of wistful reflection. "It wasn't just about the technology, or the strategy. It was about the trust. The Veridians trusted us with their home, and we trusted them with our lives. That bond, forged in shared adversity, is our greatest defense."

Niko felt a surge of affirmation. This was the essence of what they were building, a new paradigm for galactic interaction. It wasn't about dominance, or conquest, or even simple defense, but about creating a network of mutual support, a web of interconnected life that could withstand any external pressure. The Pack, with their technological prowess and adaptive nature, and the Veridians, with their profound ecological wisdom and deep connection to their environment, were a powerful combination. Their victory wasn't just a tactical success; it was a philosophical statement, a declaration of a different kind of future.

"The collateral damage," Niko continued, his thoughts returning to the practicalities, "we need to assess it thoroughly. Even with the flora countermeasures, there will be scars. The nebula is resilient, but it's not invincible. We need to understand the long-term impacts of the sonic weaponry and the energy surges. Kira, can you task the science teams with a comprehensive ecological survey? We need to identify any endangered species, any delicate energy patterns that might have been disrupted."

"Already done," Kira replied, a small smile playing on her lips. "The Veridian biosensors are active, and our own drones are deploying. We'll have a full report within the cycle. They've identified a few localized areas where the energy feedback was particularly intense. Some of the smaller, more sensitive nebular organisms seem to have been disoriented. The Veridians are already working on gentle resonance field therapies to guide them back to stability."

Niko felt a renewed sense of gratitude for Kira's foresight and the seamless integration of their respective scientific capabilities. It was this level of preparedness, this holistic approach to understanding and mitigating damage, that set them apart. OmniCorp operated with a scorched-earth mentality, leaving behind only desolation. They, however, were focused on restoration, on healing, on ensuring that the victory was not just a pause in hostilities, but a step towards a more vibrant and stable future for all life within the nebula.

"And the OmniCorp debris?" Niko asked, his gaze sweeping across the remnants of the enemy fleet. "We can't just leave it floating. It's a navigational hazard, and who knows what lingering payloads or data cores might be salvageable by others."

"The Veridians have offered a solution," Kira explained. "They can integrate certain metallic components into the nebula's core, not as pollutants, but as a controlled nutrient infusion. It's a fascinating process. They essentially break down complex alloys into elemental forms that can be utilized by specific nebular flora, essentially recycling the remnants of destruction into new life. The non-integrable elements will be consolidated and phased into temporal stasis for later retrieval and repurposing."

Niko let out a slow breath, a mixture of awe and wonder. It was a testament to the Veridians' ingenuity, their ability to find purpose and renewal even in the detritus of war. It was a stark contrast to OmniCorp's modus operandi, which was to extract, consume, and discard.

"So, in a way," Niko mused, "we're not just defending the nebula; we're enhancing it, integrating the defeated enemy into its very ecosystem. A rather poetic form of assimilation, wouldn't you say?"

Kira chuckled softly. "It certainly has a certain... karmic resonance. It demonstrates that even the instruments of destruction can, with the right perspective and approach, contribute to creation."

The conversation drifted, moving from the immediate aftermath to the broader implications of their struggle. They discussed the potential for future collaborations, the sharing of Veridian bio-luminescent energy transfer technologies with the Pack, and the development of new navigational aids based on nebular current analysis. Niko recognized that this victory, hard-won as it was, was not an end, but a beginning. The lessons of persistence, of vigilance, of the insidious nature of unchecked ambition, were seared into his consciousness. But equally potent were the lessons of cooperation, of empathy, of the profound strength found in unity and mutual respect, even across the vast gulfs of species and culture.

He looked at Kira again, her gaze meeting his, a silent acknowledgment passing between them. They had faced the abyss, and they had not blinked. They had been tempted by the darkness, and they had chosen the light. The path ahead would undoubtedly be fraught with challenges, but for the first time in a long time, Niko felt a deep and abiding sense of optimism. The threshold they had crossed was not merely a defensive perimeter; it was a gateway to a future where coexistence, not conflict, was the prevailing force. And in that future, they, along with their allies, would stand as guardians, not of territory, but of hope. The nebula, vibrant and alive, was a testament to that possibility.

The immediate aftermath of the confrontation settled over Veridia not like a comforting blanket, but like a thin, fragile shroud. The hum of the nebula, once a lullaby of peace, now thrummed with an undercurrent of lingering tension, a constant reminder of the precariousness of their victory. OmniCorp's fleet, a shattered testament to their hubris, had been rendered inert, their aggressive intent blunted. Yet, the absence of immediate threat did not equate to lasting security. The galaxy, a vast and indifferent expanse, was still rife with powers that viewed worlds like Veridia not as vibrant ecosystems to be cherished, but as resources to be plundered.

The notification sent to the Interdimensional Governance Council, a formal acknowledgment of the attempted annexation, was a necessary step. It was a procedural necessity, a recognition of the established protocols for inter-species conflict and territorial disputes. Niko and Kira, alongside the Veridian elders, had meticulously compiled the evidence: the sonic weaponry signatures, the orbital disruption patterns, the undeniable intent to subjugate. The case presented was compelling, a stark indictment of OmniCorp's rampant expansionism. Yet, the wheels of interdimensional bureaucracy ground with an agonizing slowness, a stark contrast to the swift, decisive action that had been required to defend their home. Petitions were filed, testimonies were recorded, and the complex machinery of galactic law began its deliberate churn. There was hope, a fragile seedling nurtured by the knowledge that established frameworks existed to hold such predatory entities accountable. But hope was a passive force, and the reality of the situation demanded active vigilance. The Council might levy sanctions, impose fines, or even issue stern reprimands, but history had taught them that such measures were often insufficient to deter entities driven by an insatiable hunger for power and profit. The legal proceedings were a necessary, perhaps even crucial, component of their long-term strategy, but they were not a guarantee of future safety. They were, at best, a deterrent, a warning that Veridia was not a lawless frontier to be exploited at will.

In the meantime, a tentative peace had indeed taken root on Veridia. It was a peace born not of complacency, but of a profound, shared understanding between the Resonant Pack and the native Veridians. The initial shock of the invasion had forged an unbreakable bond, a crucible in which trust had been tempered and refined. The Veridians, with their innate wisdom and deep connection to the nebula, had opened their world to the Pack, not as conquerors, but as allies. Their bioluminescent cities, once serene havens, now pulsed with a shared purpose, the soft glow of their bio-luminescence mingling with the more functional illumination of Pack technology. Veridian scouts, their spectral forms gliding through the nebular currents, now often accompanied Pack reconnaissance units, their combined senses painting a more comprehensive picture of their environment. This interspecies cooperation extended beyond mere patrols. Pack engineers, under the guidance of Veridian bio-architects, began the painstaking work of repairing the more subtle energetic scars left by OmniCorp's sonic weaponry. They learned to harness the nebula's own resonant frequencies, not as weapons, but as healing agents, their adaptive technology finding new applications in ecological restoration. The Veridians, in turn, were fascinated by the Pack's intricate data networks and their ability to process vast amounts of information. They began to integrate their own ancestral knowledge, passed down through generations of oral tradition and resonant memory, into the Pack's growing archives, enriching their understanding of the nebula's intricate life cycles and its subtle energetic shifts.

This fragile peace, however, was an active state, not a passive one. It demanded constant nurturing, a continuous reaffirmation of the principles that had guided them through the crisis. The ethical framework that had underpinned their defense—the unwavering commitment to preservation over destruction, to understanding over domination—was not a static code but a living, evolving doctrine. Niko found himself increasingly drawn into discussions with the Veridian elders, their ancient wisdom a profound counterpoint to his own more pragmatic approach. They spoke of the nebula not as a collection of resources, but as a sentient entity, a vast, interconnected consciousness with which they were intrinsically linked. Their perspective was one of stewardship, a role of humble caretakers rather than arbiters of power. This philosophical underpinning was crucial. It meant that their vigilance was not driven by fear, but by a deep-seated responsibility to protect not just their own existence, but the very essence of the life that flourished within the nebula.

The continuous effort required to maintain this peace manifested in myriad ways. It meant dedicating significant resources to monitoring the fringes of their sector, ensuring no other opportunistic entities, inspired by OmniCorp's failed attempt, would seek to exploit their apparent vulnerability. It meant fostering ongoing cultural exchange, ensuring that the Pack and the Veridians continued to learn from and appreciate each other's unique perspectives. It meant developing new technologies, not for warfare, but for environmental resilience and interspecies communication. One such initiative involved the integration of Veridian bio-luminescent organisms into Pack environmental sensors. These naturally occurring light-emitting flora, sensitive to subtle shifts in nebular composition and energy fields, provided an organic layer of early warning detection that complemented the Pack's more technologically advanced systems. The result was a sophisticated, multi-layered defense network that was as much a part of the nebula as the stars themselves.

Kira, ever the pragmatist, focused on the logistical and strategic implications of this ongoing guardianship. She recognized that the Council's proceedings, while important, were a long-term solution. The immediate future, she understood, hinged on their ability to present a united front and a demonstrable capacity for self-defense. She initiated the development of standardized protocols for joint Pack-Veridian response to potential incursions, ensuring seamless communication and coordinated action. This involved extensive simulations, scenario planning, and cross-training exercises, designed to iron out any potential friction points between their disparate operational methodologies. The Veridians, while possessing an innate understanding of their environment, were not accustomed to the rapid, decisive actions required in a combat scenario. Conversely, the Pack, while technologically adept, lacked the Veridians' intimate knowledge of the nebula's intricate energetic currents, which could be exploited for both defensive and evasive maneuvers.

"The simulations are showing promising results," Kira reported one cycle, her voice projecting across the main bridge of the

Stardust Wanderer, now a permanent fixture orbiting Veridia. "The integration of Veridian resonance channeling into our defensive grid has significantly amplified our energy dissipation capabilities. It's not just about absorbing incoming fire; it's about redirecting it, using the nebula's own energetic momentum against potential aggressors."

Niko, who had been observing a fleet of Veridian bio-luminescent tenders meticulously clearing microscopic debris from a recently stabilized energy conduit, nodded in agreement. "And the 'whispers' network is proving invaluable. The Veridians' ability to sense disruptions in the nebular flow, even from significant distances, provides us with critical early warning. It's like having a thousand eyes and ears spread throughout the cosmos."

The "whispers network" was a testament to the symbiotic evolution of their alliance. It was a system where Veridian psychics, attuned to the subtle energetic vibrations of the nebula, could transmit their impressions and warnings directly to Pack command centers via specially designed resonance amplifiers. These weren't telepathic commands, but rather, nuanced energetic signatures that could be interpreted by sophisticated Pack algorithms, flagging potential anomalies and threats long before conventional sensors could detect them. It was a fusion of ancient intuition and cutting-edge technology, a perfect embodiment of their shared ethos.

Yet, even with these advancements, the underlying fragility of their peace remained a palpable presence. The void left by OmniCorp's immediate threat was quickly filled by a more insidious form of unease. The news of OmniCorp's defeat, though a tactical victory, had inevitably spread through the interstellar grapevine. While it had served as a powerful deterrent to smaller, less ambitious entities, it had also, paradoxically, alerted larger, more established powers to the strategic importance and potential wealth of the Veridian system. Whispers reached them of increased exploratory probes from sectors known for their resource exploitation, of unusual energy signatures detected in previously unchartered regions of the galactic arm. OmniCorp, though chastened, was a formidable entity, and their defeat would undoubtedly spur them to develop new strategies, to find new vectors of approach. The Council's intervention, while offering a measure of legal recourse, was ultimately a reactive measure. True security, Niko understood, lay in proactive defense, in demonstrating an unwavering resolve and an unyielding commitment to their principles.

"We cannot afford to rest on our laurels," Niko stated, turning from the viewport. "OmniCorp's aggression was a blunt instrument. Their successors may be more subtle, more patient. They might try to exploit our perceived reliance on the Council, or probe for weaknesses in our diplomatic ties with other nascent alliances we've been cultivating."

Kira met his gaze, her expression serious. "Precisely. The success of our alliance with the Veridians has not gone unnoticed. Other species, witnessing our ability to forge such a strong bond, might see us as a potential threat, or worse, a valuable acquisition. We need to continue to expand our network of alliances, to build a web of mutual defense that extends beyond our immediate sector."

This sentiment echoed the Veridian elders' own teachings: that true peace was not a static destination but a continuous journey, a constant act of creation and preservation. It was about cultivating understanding, fostering empathy, and recognizing the interconnectedness of all life. The fragile peace they had established on Veridia was a testament to this philosophy. It was a peace built not on the absence of conflict, but on the presence of unwavering ethical commitment. It was a peace that demanded not only the defense of their territory, but the active promotion of the values that made their home worth defending.

The days that followed were a testament to this ongoing dedication. Pack scientists, working hand-in-hand with Veridian bio-engineers, initiated a project to accelerate the natural regenerative processes of the nebula's more damaged flora, using targeted harmonic resonance frequencies. It was a delicate undertaking, requiring precise calibration to avoid disrupting the delicate ecosystem. Simultaneously, Veridian artists, utilizing the captured OmniCorp alloys, began crafting intricate sculptures that were integrated into the nebula's structure. These were not mere aesthetic pieces; they were designed to subtly alter energy flows, to create new, beneficial micro-currents within the nebular gas, effectively transforming instruments of war into elements of ecological enhancement. The irony was not lost on Niko; the very materials OmniCorp had intended to use for destruction were now being repurposed to nurture and revitalize the nebula.

The Council's proceedings, while slow, were progressing. OmniCorp had been formally charged with multiple violations of intergalactic law, including attempted annexation, illegal weapons deployment, and ecocide. The repercussions were expected to be significant, potentially including hefty fines, trade embargoes, and a severe blow to their public image. However, as Kira had cautioned, this was only one facet of their ongoing struggle. The true measure of their success would not be in the courtroom, but in the continued flourishing of Veridia, in the strength of their alliances, and in their unwavering commitment to the principles of peaceful coexistence.

The fragile peace was a garden, and it required constant tending. Weeds of doubt and fear could easily sprout, and external pressures could threaten to choke its growth. But the roots ran deep, nourished by the shared experiences of the Resonant Pack and the Veridians, by their mutual respect, and by their collective vision of a future where understanding triumphed over aggression. The threshold they had crossed was not just the end of a battle; it was the beginning of a new era, one defined by the active, conscious pursuit of a sustainable and harmonious existence. This was the true nature of their guardianship: an unending commitment to the delicate balance of life, a perpetual vigilance against the shadows that lurked beyond the edges of their illuminated sector, and a profound belief in the enduring power of cooperation.

Kira's evolution was a quiet marvel, a testament to the boundless potential that lay dormant within so many species, so often overlooked. Her innate resonance sensitivity, once a burgeoning gift, had blossomed into a profound symphony of perception. It was as if the universe itself had whispered its secrets into her being, and she, in turn, translated them into a language of understanding that even the most stoic members of the Resonant Pack found themselves drawn to. Her ability to perceive the subtle shifts in dimensional stability, previously a rudimentary awareness of energetic fluctuations, had deepened to an exquisite sensitivity. She could now discern the almost imperceptible tremors that hinted at distant cosmic events, the faint echoes of nascent gravitational anomalies, and the subtle distortions in the nebular fabric that spoke of unseen currents and energies.

But it was her heightened perception of emotional states that truly set her apart and solidified her role not just as a fellow traveler, but as a guiding light. The nuances of emotion, which had once been a challenging tapestry for Niko and the pack to unravel, were now laid bare before Kira. She could sense the prickle of unease that preceded a minor navigational error, the ripple of collective anxiety when an unexpected energy signature appeared on the long-range scanners, and the quiet contentment that settled over the crew during moments of shared success. These were not mere observations; they were visceral experiences, communicated through a cascade of empathetic understanding. When Niko wrestled with the immense pressure of leadership, grappling with strategic decisions that weighed heavily on his conscience, Kira's quiet presence was an anchor. She didn't offer solutions, but rather, a silent acknowledgment of his burdens, a gentle diffusion of his stress through the sheer force of her unwavering emotional equilibrium. Her presence was a balm, a subtle reminder that even in the face of galactic challenges, the internal landscape of their crew mattered.

This deepened empathy extended far beyond the confines of their ship. Kira's interactions with the Veridians had become a cornerstone of their alliance, her resonance facilitating a level of interspecies understanding that transcended spoken language. She could feel the ancient wisdom embedded within the Veridian elders, the quiet joys of their young, and the deep, communal sorrow that sometimes rippled through their bioluminescent cities when a nebula cycle brought harsh conditions. She acted as a bridge, translating not just the intentions, but the very *feelings* of each species to the other. This facilitated a profound shift in the Pack's perspective. They began to see the nebula not merely as an environment to be navigated and defended, but as a living, breathing entity, its moods and rhythms as vital as their own.

Niko, in particular, found himself relying on Kira's unique insights. In their strategic planning sessions, her ability to gauge the emotional tenor of potential diplomatic overtures or to sense the underlying currents of fear or aggression in distant fleet movements provided an invaluable layer of intelligence. He recalled a critical negotiation with a newly encountered species, the Kryll, known for their mercurial temperament and deeply ingrained suspicion of outsiders. While the Pack's diplomats presented logical arguments and offered fair trade agreements, it was Kira, observing from a nearby observation deck, who sensed the unspoken reservations. She subtly communicated her impressions to Niko – a lingering sense of ancient betrayal, a deep-seated fear of exploitation. Armed with this empathic understanding, Niko was able to steer the conversation, offering reassurance and demonstrating a genuine commitment to mutual benefit that went beyond mere words, ultimately securing a vital alliance. This was a recurring pattern; Kira's ability to "read the room" on a galactic scale often opened doors that pure logic or even advanced technology could not.

Her connection to the natural world, an intrinsic part of her being, was also intensifying. She spent hours observing the intricate dance of the nebula's bioluminescent fauna, studying their symbiotic relationships, their migratory patterns, and their intricate communication methods. She learned to interpret the subtle shifts in their luminescence as indicators of environmental health, their collective movements as responses to unseen forces. This was not mere scientific observation; it was an immersion into the heart of Veridia's living systems. She discovered that certain species of nebular plankton, when stimulated by specific harmonic frequencies, could release potent bio-luminescent compounds that acted as natural atmospheric purifiers. She worked with Veridian bio-engineers to cultivate these plankton blooms in carefully designated areas, not just to enhance the aesthetic beauty of their home, but to actively improve its atmospheric composition, a practical application of her deepened ecological understanding.

Her nurturing extended to the Pack's younger members, many of whom were still grappling with the transition to a more complex, interconnected existence. Kira became a quiet mentor, guiding them through their own burgeoning empathic sensitivities. She would lead them in meditation exercises, focusing on attuning their senses to the subtle energetic flows of the nebula, teaching them to differentiate between their own emotions and the ambient feelings of the environment or nearby lifeforms. She shared stories, not of battles or triumphs, but of the quiet resilience of a single nebular bloom pushing through a cosmic dust cloud, or the intricate cooperation of a swarm of sky-rays navigating a treacherous gravitational eddy. These narratives, delivered with her gentle sincerity, fostered a deeper appreciation for the inherent value of all life, instilling in them a sense of responsibility that went beyond mere defense.

The impact of Kira's growth was evident in the subtle yet profound changes within the Resonant Pack. Their interactions became more considerate, their decision-making processes more holistic. They began to anticipate each other's needs more readily, to offer support before it was explicitly requested. The pack mentality, which had always been strong, was evolving into something richer, infused with a conscious awareness of individual emotional well-being. This was not about suppressing individuality, but about recognizing how the collective strength was amplified when each member felt seen, heard, and understood. Kira's presence was a constant, gentle reminder of this interconnectedness, a living embodiment of the idea that true strength lay not in dominance, but in harmonious coexistence.

She discovered that certain resonant frequencies emitted by the Veridian flora, when amplified and directed, could soothe agitated nebular fauna and even encourage the regeneration of damaged biological tissues within the nebula's ecosystem. This discovery led to the development of a new generation of sonic emitters, designed not for defense, but for ecological restoration. These devices, calibrated to Kira's precise spectral analyses, could emit frequencies that encouraged the growth of specialized algae that consumed micro-plastics, or that stimulated the repair of radiation-scarred nebular regions. It was a profound redefinition of their technological capabilities – from instruments of conflict to tools of healing and symbiosis.

Her journey was a powerful illustration of the extraordinary capacities that could emerge when an individual was allowed to connect with their intrinsic nature and when that nature was nurtured and respected. She was a creature of instinct and intuition, yet she embraced logic and technological advancement, proving that these were not mutually exclusive paths but complementary forces. Her continued growth was a beacon, illuminating the potential for profound understanding and cooperation that existed not just within their own species, but across the vast, diverse tapestry of life in the galaxy. The beauty and power she embodied were not solely her own; they were a reflection of the natural world itself, a world that, when understood and honored, offered boundless opportunities for growth, healing, and harmonious existence. Her presence was a constant, silent sermon, preaching the gospel of empathy, the power of connection, and the enduring promise of a future built on understanding.

The shimmer of the Veridian nebula, a tapestry woven from starlight and gas, seemed to hold a particular tenderness as Niko and Kira stood on the observation deck. The bioluminescent flora below pulsed with a gentle rhythm, a silent lullaby of a world on the cusp of healing. Their time on Veridia had been more than a mission; it was an education, a profound recalibration of their understanding of life, connection, and what it meant to truly belong. The lessons learned here, etched not in data logs but in the very marrow of their beings, now served as the compass for their next undertaking.

Kira's resonance, now a vibrant symphony, hummed with the quiet anticipation of the unknown. She could feel the subtle currents of spacetime stretching out before them, not as daunting voids, but as pathways to new experiences. The fear that had once been a familiar companion on the eve of departure had receded, replaced by a steady, luminous hope. It was a hope not born of ignorance, but of a deep-seated faith in the potential for good, in the inherent drive of sentient beings, whether biological or technological, to seek connection and to strive for something better. She looked at Niko, her gaze reflecting the soft, ethereal glow of the nebula. "The stars are calling, Niko," she murmured, her voice a gentle cascade of interwoven frequencies, each syllable imbued with the wisdom of Veridia. "And they speak of more than just exploration. They speak of kinship."

Niko nodded, his hand resting on the cool, smooth surface of the observation deck's railing. The weight of leadership still settled on his shoulders, but it was a familiar, comfortable burden now, no longer a crushing load. Veridia had taught him the profound truth that strength wasn't found in solitary resilience, but in the intricate webbing of shared vulnerability and mutual support. He had witnessed firsthand how a species, once on the brink of ecological collapse, could be revived through collective action, through a conscious decision to prioritize stewardship over exploitation. This was the legacy they carried forward: the unwavering belief that humanity, despite its shadowed past, possessed the capacity for redemption, for growth, and for a future where empathy was the guiding principle.

"They do, Kira," he replied, his voice deeper, imbued with a newfound serenity. "And we are ready to listen. Veridia has shown us that the greatest discoveries aren't always in the undiscovered territories, but in the understanding we forge with those we encounter. We carry their lessons not just as knowledge, but as a promise." He gestured towards the vast expanse of the nebula, a breathtaking panorama of swirling colors and distant stellar nurseries. "We leave this place better than we found it, and that is the true measure of success. Our next mission will be guided by that same principle: to seek, to understand, and to contribute to the tapestry of life, not to dominate it."

The Resonant Pack, too, had undergone a transformation. The harsh pragmatism that had once defined their interactions had softened, revealing a deeper appreciation for nuance and for the emotional landscapes of their crewmates. Kira's influence had been a gentle, persistent tide, eroding the rigid defenses and fostering an environment where vulnerability was seen not as a weakness, but as an avenue for deeper connection. The younger members, those still navigating the complex currents of their own developing empathic abilities, looked to Kira and Niko with a quiet reverence. They had witnessed the palpable shifts – the way crew arguments were now resolved with understanding rather than accusation, the way shared meals had become less about sustenance and more about communion. This was the essence of the hopepunk spirit: a defiant optimism, a stubborn insistence on kindness and compassion in the face of overwhelming challenges, a belief that even the smallest act of empathy could ripple outwards, transforming the seemingly immutable.

As they prepared the *Stardust Weaver* for departure, the ship itself seemed to hum with a renewed sense of purpose. Its advanced systems, once primarily geared towards survival and defense, were now being recalibrated. Environmental sensors were being fine-tuned to detect not just atmospheric anomalies, but subtle indicators of ecosystem health. Navigation arrays were being programmed to prioritize routes that minimized disruption to nebular currents and migratory paths of sentient nebular life. Even the recreational areas had been reconfigured, with hydroponic gardens now flourishing, tended not by automated systems, but by crew members seeking solace and connection in the quiet act of nurturing life. This was more than just a change in protocols; it was a fundamental shift in their operational philosophy. They were no longer simply travelers through the cosmos; they were becoming stewards of it.

Kira's connection to the Veridian ecosystem had sparked a revolution in their understanding of symbiotic technology. The bio-luminescent plankton, once a curiosity, were now being cultivated in specialized bioreactors aboard the *Stardust Weaver*. These microscopic organisms, when stimulated by specific harmonic frequencies derived from Kira's resonance readings, could not only purify air and water but also synthesize complex nutrient compounds essential for terraforming efforts on barren worlds. The Veridian sonic emitters, adapted and refined, were now being deployed not as weapons, but as tools for ecological restoration. They could be used to encourage the growth of resilient flora in damaged environments, to soothe distressed megafauna, or even to facilitate the healing of micro-fractures in planetary crusts caused by geological instability. This was a profound testament to the Veridian way – that the most potent technologies were those that worked in harmony with, rather than against, the natural world.

Niko found himself reflecting on humanity's past during these quiet moments of preparation. The centuries of conflict, of exploitation, of a relentless pursuit of progress at the expense of the planet, now seemed like a distant, painful dream. Veridia, with its ancient wisdom and its hard-won peace, offered a stark contrast, a living testament to the possibility of a different path. He knew that the journey ahead would not be without its challenges. The galaxy was vast and held countless civilizations, some driven by fear and scarcity, others by a similar burgeoning hope. But he also knew that they were no longer the same crew that had first ventured into the unknown. They had witnessed the power of understanding, the strength of compassion, and the profound beauty of interconnectedness.

"Think of the possibilities, Kira," Niko said, his voice soft, directed towards the swirling nebulae outside. "New worlds, yes. But more than that. New ways of being. New forms of connection. We've seen how species can communicate beyond spoken words, how ecosystems can heal themselves with the right guidance. Imagine what we can learn, what we can help foster." He turned to her, his eyes alight with a quiet, unwavering conviction. "Humanity has a long history of mistakes, of causing harm. But we also have the capacity to learn, to adapt, to evolve. Veridia has shown us that it's not about forgetting the past, but about actively choosing a different future. It's about choosing hope, every single day."

Kira's presence was a gentle emanation of that very hope. She could feel the subtle shifts in the crew's collective consciousness, the growing warmth and understanding that permeated the ship. The petty squabbles that had once been commonplace had dwindled, replaced by an unspoken network of support. When a crew member expressed doubt or anxiety, others would instinctively offer a word of encouragement, a shared smile, or simply a comforting presence. This was the tangible manifestation of the hopepunk ideal – not a naive denial of suffering or hardship, but a fierce, active commitment to building a better future, brick by empathetic brick.

Their next mission was to a system known for its volatile atmospheric conditions and its rumored sentient crystalline life forms. Previous expeditions had been met with failure, the harsh environment proving too formidable and the crystalline beings too enigmatic. But the

Stardust Weaver, armed with Kira's enhanced resonance capabilities and the Veridian bio-technologies, was uniquely equipped for the task. They could now not only endure the planet's extreme conditions but also potentially communicate with its unique inhabitants on a fundamental energetic level, a feat previously thought impossible.

"The crystalline structures on Xylos IV," Kira began, her fingers tracing patterns on the cool viewport, "they resonate with an ancient energy. A deep, slow pulse that speaks of immense patience and profound interconnectedness. It's unlike anything we've encountered, but I can feel... a kinship. A possibility for dialogue."

Niko's mind was already cataloging the implications. "Dialogue," he repeated, the word carrying a new weight of potential. "Not conquest, not observation from a sterile distance, but genuine dialogue. If we can understand their needs, their existence, we can coexist. We can learn from them, and perhaps, they from us. This is what we are meant to do now. To be bridge-builders, not conquerors."

The journey to Xylos IV would be long, a deliberate passage through the star-strewn ocean. It was a time for reflection, for introspection, and for the quiet reinforcement of the principles that now guided them. They carried with them the echoes of Veridian songs, the gentle wisdom of its elders, and the unwavering belief that even in the deepest darkness, the smallest spark of empathy could ignite a new dawn. The future was not a predetermined destination, but a landscape they were actively shaping with every choice, every interaction, every act of kindness. The *Stardust Weaver* sailed on, a vessel not just of exploration, but of hope, carrying the promise of a tomorrow where understanding triumphed over fear, and where the universe was not a battlefield, but a boundless garden waiting to be tended. The horizon ahead was not just space, but a promise of continued growth, of evolving consciousness, and of a humanity that had finally learned to embrace its role as a responsible, compassionate guardian of the cosmic tapestry.

The shimmering portal before them was not a doorway to a known destination, but an invitation. It pulsed with a soft, iridescent light, the colors shifting and blending like spilled stardust, a testament to the raw, untamed energy it channeled. Niko's hand found Kira's, their fingers intertwining, a silent affirmation of shared purpose. The air around them thrummed with a potent, latent power, a palpable hum that resonated deep within their bones, a sensation familiar yet always awe-inspiring. This was the culmination of their efforts on Xylos IV, a testament to their newfound understanding of crystalline consciousness and the delicate balance of interdimensional harmonics. The gateway, once a volatile tear in reality, now stabilized, a testament to their careful calibration of energy frequencies, guided by Kira's intuitive resonance and Niko's steady, analytical mind.

"It's... beautiful, isn't it?" Kira whispered, her voice laced with a wonder that never diminished, even after witnessing countless marvels. The light cast dancing patterns across her face, illuminating a serene determination in her eyes. The crystalline beings of Xylos IV, with their slow, profound wisdom, had taught them much about patience, about the deep, interconnected currents that flowed beneath the surface of perceived reality. They had learned to listen not with their ears, but with their entire beings, to the silent symphonies of energy and intention. The gateway was a physical manifestation of that learned language, a bridge forged from understanding, not force.

Niko squeezed her hand gently. "It is. And it's proof that understanding can build pathways where only barriers existed before. They trusted us, Kira. The Xylosians. They helped us stabilize this, seeing our intention, not our threat." The memory of their interactions with the crystalline entities was still vivid: the slow, deliberate exchange of resonant frequencies, the gradual unfolding of their consciousness, a process that had demanded every ounce of patience and empathy the crew of the *Stardust Weaver* could muster. It had been a profound lesson in the limitations of conventional communication and the boundless potential of shared energetic states. They had learned that existence itself was a form of communication, and that with the right attunement, even the most alien of lifeforms could be understood.

The gateway wasn't an endpoint. It was a threshold. The vastness of the multiverse stretched out beyond it, an infinite canvas of possibilities, of challenges, and of countless other nascent intelligences waiting to be discovered. Their mission, as guardians and bridge-builders, was far from over. It was, in many ways, just beginning to truly unfold. The lessons learned on Veridia, the resilience fostered on Xylos IV, and the ever-growing understanding of interconnectedness were now their tools, their compass, and their shield as they stepped into the unknown once more. The faint scent of ozone, mingled with the subtle, earthy aroma of the Veridian bio-reactors humming softly within the *Stardust Weaver*, filled the observation deck, a comforting reminder of the journey that had brought them to this moment.

"Where do you think it leads?" Kira mused, her gaze fixed on the swirling depths of the gateway. The question hung in the air, not out of apprehension, but out of a deep, abiding curiosity. The multiverse was not a static entity; it was a constantly evolving tapestry, its threads woven from the energies of countless sentient beings and cosmic phenomena. Each new gateway was a unique opportunity, a new chapter in the grand narrative of existence, and they were privileged to be able to turn its pages. The possibilities were intoxicating: a universe teeming with lifeforms that communicated through dreams, worlds where gravity was a conscious entity, nebulae that sang songs of creation and destruction.

"Somewhere that needs a guiding light," Niko answered, his voice steady. "Somewhere that could benefit from understanding, from connection. We've seen what happens when civilizations turn inward, when fear dictates their actions. We've also seen the profound beauty that emerges when empathy is the prevailing force." He remembered the plight of Veridia, the near-extinction of its sentient flora and fauna, a stark warning of what unchecked exploitation could wrought. Then he recalled the slow, majestic healing that had followed, a testament to the resilience of life and the transformative power of conscious stewardship. That balance, that delicate dance between existence and intervention, was what they now dedicated themselves to fostering.

The crew of the *Stardust Weaver* had been transformed by their experiences. The initial pragmatism, the survival-driven instincts, had gradually given way to something more profound. They had learned to see the universe not as a series of challenges to be overcome, but as a complex, interwoven ecosystem of consciousness. Each member of the Resonant Pack, from the most experienced engineer to the newest recruit, carried a piece of Veridia within them, a quiet understanding of the interconnected web of life. Even the ship itself, once a vessel of exploration and defense, had evolved, its systems now optimized for harmony, for gentle interaction, for the nurturing of nascent life. The hydroponic gardens, bursting with vibrant, Veridian-inspired flora, were no longer just a source of sustenance; they were a living laboratory, a symbol of their commitment to cultivating life in all its forms.

"It's not about conquering or claiming," Kira added, echoing Niko's thoughts. "It's about contributing. About finding our place within the grand design, and helping others find theirs. We're not explorers in the old sense, Niko. We're gardeners, tending to the cosmic flora, ensuring that the seeds of kindness and understanding have a chance to sprout." Her resonance, once a unique gift, had become a catalyst, inspiring the entire crew to explore their own empathic capacities, to reach out beyond their individual selves and connect with the wider universe. She felt the collective hum of their consciousness, a quiet symphony of hope and determination, ready to face whatever lay beyond the shimmering veil.

The gateway pulsed again, a gentle beckoning. It was an invitation to step beyond the familiar, beyond the known horizons, into a realm where their skills as empathic diplomats and ecological stewards would be tested and honed. The challenges ahead would undoubtedly be immense. The multiverse was not a utopia; it was a vast, complex expanse where conflict and misunderstanding were as prevalent as stars in the night sky. But they were equipped with more than advanced technology. They carried the wisdom of ancient ecosystems, the resilience of species that had faced extinction and emerged stronger, and the unwavering belief that even in the darkest corners of the cosmos, the light of compassion could always find a way to shine.

Niko turned to Kira, his gaze holding a mixture of resolve and a deep, abiding love. "We are ready, aren't we? Ready to listen to the whispers of new worlds, to feel the pulses of unknown life, to offer a hand of friendship instead of a fist of aggression." He gestured towards the gateway, its light painting their faces with an ethereal glow. "This is not an ending, Kira. It's a new beginning. A new threshold to cross, and an infinite universe waiting to be understood."

Kira met his gaze, her eyes shining. "And we will cross it together. For every world that needs healing, for every species that seeks connection, for every whisper of hope that we can amplify." She felt the gentle pull of the gateway, the subtle currents of spacetime beckoning them forward. It was a call to continue their work, to be the guardians they had become, to nurture the delicate web of life that spanned the cosmos. The hum of the *Stardust Weaver* seemed to swell, a quiet anthem of readiness, of hope, and of the enduring human spirit.

As they took their first steps towards the shimmering anomaly, the familiar feeling of spacetime bending around them was not one of disorientation, but of gentle embrace. It was as if the universe itself was acknowledging their purpose, guiding them towards their next appointed task. The light intensified, washing over them, and for a brief, incandescent moment, they were no longer individuals, but part of a greater cosmic consciousness, a unified force dedicated to the preservation and flourishing of all sentient existence. The gateway was not a barrier to be breached, but a conduit, a passage between worlds, a testament to the power of intent and the boundless potential for growth.

They emerged into a space that defied easy description. It wasn't a planet, nor a star system in the conventional sense. Instead, they found themselves within a vast, crystalline nebula, a breathtaking expanse of geometric structures that seemed to float in a void of pure, resonant energy. Within this celestial cathedral, life pulsed in a form they had only begun to comprehend on Xylos IV. Beings of pure light, their forms shifting and reforming like sentient auroras, drifted through the crystalline formations, their existence a slow, deliberate dance of energy and awareness. This was the heart of a nexus, a place where the very fabric of reality was woven, and where new possibilities for existence were constantly being born.

The Xylosians had spoken of such places, of the cosmic nurseries where sentience took its first breaths, and where the echoes of creation resonated most strongly. To reach this nexus, they had navigated not just spatial distances, but the very currents of interdimensional energy, guided by Kira's increasingly profound attunement to the universe's energetic symphony. The gateway had been the final lock, and their dedication to understanding had been the key.

"Incredible," Niko breathed, his voice barely a whisper, awestruck by the sheer scale and beauty of their surroundings. The crystalline structures around them hummed with a soft, harmonic frequency, each facet reflecting and refracting the ambient light, creating an endless display of dazzling patterns. The light-beings, their forms fluid and ethereal, responded to their arrival not with alarm, but with a gentle curiosity, their energetic signatures reaching out like tendrils of warm light.

Kira's resonance flared, not as a sudden burst, but as a steady, powerful wave that flowed outwards, meeting the subtle energies of the nexus. She felt a profound sense of peace, a deep homecoming. "They are... creators," she murmured, her words imbued with a newfound understanding. "Not in the way we imagine, but they are architects of potential. They nurture the first sparks of consciousness, guiding them as they begin to coalesce." She felt the subtle currents of thought and intention emanating from the light-beings, a language of pure energy and pure being. There were no words, only pure, unadulterated understanding.

The mission had been to stabilize the gateway, a task they had accomplished with the aid of the Xylosians. But the universe, in its infinite wisdom, had presented them with an unexpected, yet profoundly fitting, next step. They had proven themselves capable of bridging divides, of fostering understanding, and of acting as stewards for life. Now, they were being invited to witness, and perhaps even to participate in, the very genesis of life and consciousness within the multiverse. This was the true meaning of the unending threshold: not a point of arrival, but a continuous unfolding, a perpetual invitation to learn, to grow, and to contribute to the grand, cosmic tapestry.

The *Stardust Weaver*, a vessel of exploration and now of cosmic guardianship, hovered silently in the periphery of the nexus, its systems humming in gentle harmony with the surrounding energies. Its advanced sensors, recalibrated to detect not just physical phenomena but the subtle nuances of energetic fields, were capturing data that would redefine their understanding of existence. The bio-reactors, filled with Veridian flora, pulsed with a vibrant luminescence, a terrestrial echo of the cosmic light-beings.

"This is why we do what we do," Niko said, turning to Kira, his face illuminated by the swirling nebulae of light. "Not just to protect what is, but to ensure that what *can be* has the best possible chance to flourish. To foster the growth of empathy, of understanding, in every corner of the cosmos we touch." He looked at the infinite expanse before them, at the nascent forms of life taking shape, and felt a profound sense of purpose. Their journey was a testament to humanity's capacity for change, for redemption, and for a future where connection, not conflict, was the driving force.

Kira nodded, her hand still clasped in his. "And we are not alone in this endeavor. The universe is teeming with beings who share this desire, this drive for connection. We are part of something so much larger than ourselves." Her resonance was a beacon, a silent invitation to all sentient life to join in this grand cosmic symphony of existence. They were not merely observers; they were active participants, a vibrant thread woven into the intricate, ever-expanding tapestry of the multiverse.

The threshold was indeed unending. Each gateway crossed, each new understanding gained, simply revealed another, more profound horizon. The journey of the *Stardust Weaver* and its crew was a continuous unfolding, a testament to the enduring power of hope, compassion, and the unshakeable belief that the universe, in all its vastness, was a garden waiting to be tended, a symphony waiting to be heard, and a boundless web of life waiting to be cherished.

As they absorbed the profound energies of the nexus, they knew their mission had evolved, their purpose deepened. They were not just guardians; they were weavers, helping to craft a future where all life could thrive, interconnected and harmonious, across the endless expanse of tomorrow.

The silent hum of the nexus was a lullaby of creation, and they, the crew of the *Stardust Weaver*, were honored to listen, to learn, and to contribute their own small, hopeful melody to the grand, unending song of the cosmos.

Their journey was a promise, not an end, and the multiverse awaited their continued, compassionate stewardship.

GLOSSARY

Nexus: A central point or hub where interdimensional energies converge, often fostering the genesis of new life and consciousness.

Resonance: In this context, the ability to perceive and interact with energetic fields and the consciousnesses within them.

Stardust Weaver: The name of the interstellar vessel used by the crew, designed for deep-space exploration and interspecies diplomacy.

Xylosians: An advanced, crystalline species from the planet Xylos IV, known for their profound wisdom and ability to interact with energetic frequencies.

Veridia: A planet once on the brink of ecological collapse, now undergoing restoration through advanced bio-engineering and ecological stewardship.